ABOLITION OF EVIL

ISBN: 1512079847
ISBN 13: 9781512079845

ALSO BY TED RICHARDSON:

Imposters of Patriotism

To my family

Acknowledgments

To my wife, Beth, thank you for all of your support and patience. Once again, you were a tireless champion and I couldn't have done it without you. And to Dina Rubin, thank you for your editing expertise.

For his generous assistance, a special thanks to Don Peterson, an expert on Lewis and Clark, particularly related to their time spent traversing the beautiful territory within what is now the great state of Montana.

I would also like to express my gratitude to the readers of the early drafts of this book, Steve Skillman, Jennifer Hoyer, and Greg Lancour. Your support and enthusiasm was greatly appreciated.

Finally, I would like to acknowledge all the good people working for the National Park Service—in particular those associated with Glacier National Park. Your tireless efforts preserving and protecting this magnificent national treasure are truly inspiring.

ABOLITION OF EVIL

A Novel

Ted Richardson

"The abolition of the evil is not impossible; it ought never therefore to be despaired of. Every plan should be adopted, every experiment tried, which may do something towards the ultimate object." — *Thomas Jefferson*

Prologue

June 1973

Blackfeet Indian Reservation, Montana

The two Indian teens raced side by side, their dirt bikes kicking up rocks and leaving a swirl of dust in their wake. The bigger boy, Tommy, yelled in youthful exuberance as he accelerated past his best friend. His shoulder-length jet-black hair shimmered in the early summer sun. His bright white teeth stood out in stark contrast against his dark skin, made darker by a fresh smattering of mud.

Despite the fact he was a year older than Tommy, Leonard was half his size. The two boys made an odd pairing but they had been inseparable since elementary school. Leonard pushed the throttle on his secondhand 1964 Honda 90 Trail bike to its limit to catch up with his friend. The max speed on the speedometer was listed at 60 mph but Leonard had never been able to get the well-used 87cc pushrod engine much over forty-five. And even that required a stiff tailwind.

The trail bikes were favored by most hunters and fishermen on the res, because they could handle rough terrain and climb just about anything. More importantly, they were lightweight, so they wouldn't get stuck in the mud. They had reached the foothills on the western edge of the reservation. Tommy shifted his bike into low gear and began to *climb. It didn't take long, however, for the smaller Leonard to overtake his man-child best friend—one of the rare occasions when Tommy's size proved to be a disadvantage. Leonard grinned and thrust his fist into the air as he crested Ghost Ridge first.*

The two boys paused to take in the picturesque view. Behind them, to the east, they could see for miles as the sweetgrass of Montana's Great Plains went on seemingly forever. To the west, directly in front of them, the Rocky Mountain front rose up rapidly and majestically. Its many peaks were still blanketed in white from the record snows of the past winter. Just to the north, straddling the border of Glacier National Park and the Blackfeet Reservation, stood an isolated block of Proterozoic rock known as Chief Mountain. It was the tallest of all the peaks at an elevation of over 9,000 feet. It was also one of the most sacred sites to the Blackfeet. Spiritual ceremonies had been held at its base for generations.

The old-timers claimed the small ridge the boys had just ascended was haunted by the spirits of a mythical tribe; thus the name Ghost Ridge. Tommy used to be fascinated by the story as a little boy, but had come to believe it was just another bullshit Indian legend the tribe elders always seemed to be trying to pass along to his generation. He'd been out on that ridge plenty of times and never seen or felt anything.

Ghosts my ass. *He reached into his shirt pocket for his lighter. He sparked up a fat joint he had rolled earlier that morning and took a long hit before passing it over to Leonard.*

They sat straddling their idling bikes, silently taking in the scenery and getting slowly stoned. Getting high had become a daily ritual for the two boys. Life on the res was isolated and filled with hardship, and they had a difficult time envisioning a future with much promise. Tommy began to feel a familiar wave of depression creep in around the edges of his psyche.

Not today. *He breathed in deeply, revved his engine, and took off. He was alive again as he barreled down the western slope of Ghost*

Ridge, hollering at the top his lungs.

The heavy snows of winter had given way to an unseasonably warm spring, causing serious flooding the previous month. As the boys reached the base of the opposite side of the ridge, they could see the significant erosion the last round of flooding had caused. Tommy pointed to a few new caverns carved in the side of the hill by the powerful runoff. The gaping crevices hadn't been there the last time the two boys had traveled out this way.

The sun was getting lower on the horizon and a glimmer from something on the ground caught Tommy's eye. He steered his bike in that direction. As he got closer, he saw an odd-shaped piece of metal sticking out from between two rocks. He killed the engine, slammed the kickstand with the heel of his boot, and dismounted. Once he rolled away the few loose stones surrounding the object, it became apparent he had uncovered some kind of metal helmet.

"What the hell is that?" Leonard asked, as he rolled to a stop ten feet behind Tommy.

"Hell if I know, but it looks old," Tommy answered slowly.

The crown of the helmet was tall and oval-shaped. The sides swept down and then turned up at the ends, almost like the top half of a duck's bill. It had a number of dings and dents, but considering its age, it seemed to be pretty intact.

Leonard walked up from behind Tommy and grabbed the helmet out of his hands, "Where do you think it came from?" he asked, turning it over to peer inside.

Tommy pointed toward the mountains and said, "Looks like the runoff from the spring thaw must have carried it here. Hell if I know from where, though." He looked back at Leonard, who had the helmet perched on his head and a shit-eating grin plastered on his face.

"What do you think? Pretty badass, right?" His eyes were still slightly glazed over from the pot and the helmet was too big for his head. He looked ridiculous.

"*Yeah, a real warrior, bro,*" *Tommy deadpanned. They both burst out laughing.*

Tommy took a step forward to grab the helmet off his friend's head, but Leonard was too quick. He darted out of the way. "Give it back, Lenny," he shouted, and started to give chase.

Leonard looked back over his shoulder. He could feel Tommy bearing down on him. He knew it wouldn't be long before his more athletic sidekick caught up and tackled him, so he quickly tossed the helmet back over his shoulder. Tommy caught it in midair, but in the process, caught his toe on a large stone. He stumbled and fell. Leonard flopped to the ground nearby in a fit of uncontrollable, stoned laughter.

A few minutes later, Tommy got up. "Come on, Lenny, it's getting late. We better head back before the sun goes down."

He lashed the helmet to his rear cargo rack and turned his bike in a southeasterly direction toward home. The boys were especially quiet on the long ride out of the foothills. Their adventurous day was quickly fading into a memory, replaced by the depressing reality of their everyday lives that lay just a few miles ahead.

A month later, Tommy was home alone in the double-wide trailer he shared with his mother and two older sisters. His father had fled the scene shortly after Tommy was born. A shiny new Cadillac had just pulled into the driveway. Tommy watched as an older white guy with neatly trimmed gray hair got out of the car and made his way toward the front door.

"Yeah?" Tommy said, warily pushing the door halfway open.

The stranger told Tommy he had seen the boy's picture in the newspaper and was interested in purchasing the old helmet he had found. Tommy could tell by the man's accent he was from somewhere else.

A couple of weeks earlier, the local paper had run a story about

Tommy and Lenny's discovery. The story had been picked up by some of the larger circulation newspapers in the nearby towns of Missoula and Great Falls. Tommy didn't have much need for a funny-looking old helmet, and some quick cash sounded good. Weed and beer didn't come cheap.

The man made an offer but Tommy smelled a bigger payday. He thought he could squeeze more out of the rich-looking guy, so he looked him square in the eye and asked for double. The stranger hesitated just long enough for Tommy to fear he might have blown his opportunity. But then the man reached into his pocket and pulled out a wad of bills. The exchange was made quickly. Tommy stuffed the cash in his jeans pocket and watched from the doorway as the Cadillac disappeared from view.

That was the last he ever saw of the man or the funny-looking helmet again.

1

Present Day

Savannah, Georgia

The plump middle-aged woman kept stealing glances at Matt as she browsed through a table full of architectural fragments. Matt had purchased the pieces at a local auction a couple of months earlier. The restoration of old homes in Savannah was a never-ending endeavor, so period doorknobs, window frames, fireplace mantles, staircase finials, and the like were always in demand. Plus, he had a weakness for the beauty and craftsmanship that went into nineteenth-century homebuilding. That's why he never passed up the opportunity to salvage a piece of Savannah's glorious past.

Matt smiled at the woman as she stole yet another glance at him. Finally, she got up the nerve to approach and said, "Aren't you the guy who found Washington's surrender letter?"

He guessed she must have hailed from Chicago because the word *the* sounded more like "da" and the word *guy* sounded more like "gay." Matt was more than prepared for the question. He'd heard it a thousand times over the past eighteen months.

He had become quite famous ever since he had unearthed a surrender letter written by George Washington during the Revolu-

tionary War. For a time, he had enjoyed all the attention as he traveled the media circuit, appeared on talk shows, and gave countless
interviews. The American public was fascinated by the story, and
Matt's effortless charm and athletic good looks had earned him a
legion of fans. He patiently explained to the portly woman and her
equally round husband that he indeed was *"dat gay,"* but of course
that was something they already knew.

They hadn't ended up in his 6,800-square-foot shop by accident. The only reason they came to Hawkins Antiques, located
inside a circa-1860s converted mansion, was to meet the famous
Matt Hawkins. They hadn't a clue about antiques and couldn't tell
the difference between Regency and Victorian styles if their lives
depended on it. But Matt always made time to talk, so he did his
best to patiently answer their questions.

His cell phone began to chirp, which finally gave him an excuse
to extricate himself. His good friend, James Fox, the executive
director of the Society of the Cincinnati, was calling. Matt walked
outside to take the call.

The Society of the Cincinnati was the nation's oldest patriotic
organization, founded in 1783 by officers of the Continental Army.
The society's stated purpose was "to promote knowledge and appreciation of the achievement of American independence." For the
past year, Anderson House, the society's headquarters in Washington, D.C., had housed the now-famous George Washington surrender letter exhibit, which had been viewed by tens of thousands of
curious Americans.

After catching up for a few minutes, Fox came around to the
reason for his call. "Matt, something remarkable was donated to the
society a couple of weeks ago. One of our members bequeathed a
rolltop desk used by William Clark when he was the superintendent of Indian Affairs back in the 1830s," he explained.

"You mean William Clark, of Lewis and Clark fame?" Matt

replied. Matt was an amateur history buff and had always been fascinated by the 1804 expedition that was the brainchild of Thomas
Jefferson.

"One and the same," Fox said excitedly.

"Wow, James, nice score," Matt said enthusiastically. As he
talked, he walked across the street from his shop and into the
beautiful confines of Monterey Square. Monterey was just one of
twenty-two beautiful square-shaped parks scattered throughout the
historic section of Savannah. He found an unoccupied bench and
sat down.

"Thanks, but I haven't even told you the best part," Fox said.
"Inside the desk, we discovered something even more remarkable—a cache of field notes written by Meriwether Lewis during
the final months of the Lewis and Clark Expedition."

"What?" Matt nearly shouted. "How is that even possible? I
mean, how come nobody ever found them before?"

"Well, the gentleman who willed the rolltop desk to the society was ninety-seven years old when he died. The desk had been
left untouched in his attic for more than fifty years. Nobody even
knew it was up there except for the old man. And he suffered from
dementia for years. According to his will, it had been passed down
to him by his grandfather who had acquired it shortly after Captain
Clark's death in 1838."

"And Meriwether Lewis's notes were just sitting inside the desk
all these years?" Matt asked, still in disbelief.

"Well, they weren't exactly sitting out in the open. In fact, they
were pretty well hidden. When the society received the desk, it was
in rough shape. It was filthy and stuffed with all kinds of junk. As
our curator was cleaning and preparing it for display, he came across
a clump of wadded-up old newspapers in the back of a bottom
drawer. Out of curiosity he unraveled the bundle. You can imagine
his shock when he discovered handwritten field notes from one of

America's most famous explorers wrapped inside."

"And you're sure they're real?"

"One hundred percent," Fox replied without hesitation. "We hired a highly credible authenticator. He assured us they were written by Meriwether Lewis."

"They must be worth a fortune," Matt said excitedly. "So when are you going public with your find? Lewis and Clark buffs are going to go crazy over this."

Fox paused before continuing, "Actually, it's funny you mentioned the word crazy, Matt, because that's the reason I'm calling."

"Sorry, James, but you've lost me now."

"Well, here's the thing. The notes were written in a somewhat rambling nature. You might even say they were incoherent in parts," Fox explained, his tone turning more serious. "You see, Lewis tells an unbelievable story about being captured by a tribe of Indians. More remarkably, he describes them as looking a lot like York, Captain Clark's black slave who accompanied them on the expedition."

"Wait a minute, James," Matt interrupted. "I've read a lot about the Lewis and Clark Expedition and I don't remember reading anything in the history books about Lewis being captured, let alone by a tribe of black Indians."

"That's because there was never any mention of it in Lewis and Clark's official correspondence. Believe me, we made a trip to the American Philosophical Society in Philadelphia and read copies of the original journals cover to cover, just to make absolutely certain," Fox related. "Like I said, it's an unbelievable story, and by unbelievable I don't mean remarkable. I mean we're not sure if we believe it."

"I guess I see now why you haven't gone public with your find," Matt said.

"That's not all," Fox continued, "Lewis also claims that during his short captivity he saw what he describes as a 'religious shrine.' And sitting atop this stone shrine was a helmet. He even drew a picture of it."

"What kind of helmet?"

"It's a conquistador helmet," Fox said. "There's really no mistaking the distinctive shape. It's the same type worn by de Soto, Coronado, and all the other famous Spanish conquistadors in the 1500's."

"That's incredible," Matt said.

"Actually, more like *impossible*," Fox corrected. "Spanish conquistadors never made it farther north than Colorado, which is more than a thousand miles *south* of where Lewis claims he saw the helmet."

Matt's mind was spinning trying to reconcile all of the improbabilities in Lewis's story. "So what happened next? Were they friendly? How did Lewis escape?" he asked in rapid succession.

"Whoa, slow down, Matt. I know you've got questions and we've still got a lot more to tell you," he said, "but we'd rather discuss the next part of the story in person. Buzz and I want to fly down to Savannah in Buzz's plane tomorrow afternoon. Are you available?"

"Believe me, James, even if I had box seats at Fenway, I'd give them away for this."

2

Present Day

Savannah, Georgia

Matt sat at a back booth at the Crystal Beer Parlor waiting for Fox and Buzz to arrive. The Crystal was a favorite eatery and bar among local Savannahians, and had been for more than seventy-five years. Matt had discovered it shortly after arriving in Savannah from New York City. His ex-wife had never understood what Matt saw in the old tavern—just one of many incompatibilities that had resulted in their divorce a decade earlier.

At the moment, however, Matt's mind was on a more recent woman in his life, Sarah Gordon. He had met Sarah during their harried search for Washington's surrender letter. The two had begun a whirlwind romance, which Matt thought had the makings of something special. But then Sarah accepted an offer to be an adjunct professor at a prestigious university in England. She was only halfway through her one-year commitment, and the distance had already taken a toll on their nascent relationship.

Fox and Buzz's arrival snapped Matt out of his melancholy. After ordering a round of beers, Matt couldn't wait any longer. "All right, guys," he said. "I've been pacing around like a madman ever since you called. What's the rest of the story?"

"Sorry for all the intrigue, Matt," Buzz interjected, "we're just not sure what to make of all this."

Buzz Penberthy was president general of the Society of the Cincinnati and James Fox's boss. At sixty-eight years old, he was nearly twice Matt's age. Although by looking at him you'd never know it. Despite their age difference, the two had become close friends.

"As you may know," Buzz continued, "Meriwether Lewis was thought to have been saddled with both depression and alcoholism—and he was even rumored to have contracted a bad case of syphilis on the expedition. So before taking his field notes at face value, we need to make sure these aren't just the demented ramblings of a man with a sore pecker and a bad hangover."

"Like I said to you on the phone," Fox said, ignoring his boss's off-color comment, "Lewis makes some pretty incredible claims. And being captured by a tribe of black Indians is just the first one. Finding a shrine with a conquistador helmet on top of it is the second. But there's more."

"More?" Matt said, "Don't tease me, James. Spit it out."

"It's what he describes next that really makes us question the truth behind his story," Fox continued. "Lewis claims the black tribe's mannerisms, customs, and style of building were unlike any Indian tribe he had ever encountered. He even goes so far as to say that some of their words seemed more *European* in origin than Indian."

"Come on, guys, that's impossible," Matt said. "I mean, no Europeans had ever made it that far to the interior of America by that time, right? Let alone black-skinned ones."

"That's what the history books tell us," Fox agreed.

"You guys aren't screwing with me, right?" Matt looked across the table with raised eyebrows. The two men shook their heads from side to side.

"When exactly did Lewis say this mysterious capture happened anyway?" Matt asked.

"He claims it occurred toward the end of the expedition, in July 1806," Fox said. "That would have been shortly after he and Captain Clark split up so they could explore more territory. Clark went south and Lewis headed north. Along the way, Lewis explored the Marias River, not too far from the present day Blackfeet Indian Reservation near Glacier National Park in Montana. Evidently he was on one of his many famous solo walks when he was surprised and captured."

"So let me get this straight," Matt said with more than a touch of skepticism, "we've got authentic field notes written by Meriwether Lewis."

"That's right," Buzz confirmed.

"And these field notes describe his capture by a mysterious, European-sounding tribe of black Indians."

"Right again."

"And these black Indians apparently worshipped a Spanish conquistador helmet, even though the Spanish never made it anywhere close to Montana," he concluded.

"That about sums it up," Buzz said with an ironic smile.

"I'm beginning to think your theory about this being the ramblings of a sick man is probably true. Maybe the pressure of two years in the wilderness finally got to our fearless captain, or maybe he was tripping after eating a bad mushroom," Matt said, only half-joking.

"We thought so, too," Fox said, "until we found something that may actually lend credibility to Lewis's wild claims." He reached into a manila folder and pulled out a copy of an old newspaper clipping.

"We did a little research to see if there had ever been any findings

of Spanish conquistador antiquities that far north. The only reference we could find was this single newspaper article," Fox explained.
"It appeared in the *Great Falls Tribune* in 1973." He handed it over
to Matt.

The black-and-white photograph in the article was grainy, but
Matt could easily make out the grinning faces of two teenage Indian
boys. The next thing he noticed nearly took his breath away. The
larger of the two boys held a helmet in his hands; a helmet that
matched Meriwether Lewis's sketch to a tee.

"Holy shit," Matt said, amazed.

"I'll second that," Buzz replied dryly.

Matt quickly scanned the short article. "It says the boys found
the helmet out in the western hills of the Blackfeet Reservation.
I assume that puts it pretty close to where Lewis said he saw the
helmet?"

"It does," Fox said.

"But the article doesn't say much else. What happened to the
helmet the Indian boys found?"

"That's where the mystery deepens," Buzz's tone became serious.
"We looked but there are no other references to the boys' discovery—anywhere."

"There are lots of unanswered questions, Matt," Fox interjected, "which is why we came here today. Like you, we first believed
Lewis's claims too preposterous to be true, but when we found this
picture in the newspaper, it changed everything."

"I agree. So where do I come in?" Matt asked.

Buzz answered, "Before we go public with our discovery of
Lewis's field notes, we need to do our homework. That means
following up on this lead." He pointed an index finger at the article
on the table. "Since we came up empty searching the Internet for
additional information, I think it's time to do a little boots-on-the-
ground recon."

Buzz was an ex-navy fighter pilot, and even though he had long since retired, military jargon was still part of his lexicon. He continued, "We found out that one of the Indian boys in the photo has long since died. But the other one, Tommy Running Crane, is still alive. And he's still living on the Blackfeet Reservation in Browning, Montana." Buzz smiled, the familiar twinkle returning to his steel-blue eyes. "So, what do you say, Matt. You up for a trip to Montana?"

Buzz knew Matt couldn't resist a good historical mystery. So he wasn't surprised when his impulsive younger friend didn't hesitate for a second.

"I'm due for a vacation anyway, Buzz. Count me in."

3

Present Day
Blackfeet Indian Reservation
Browning, Montana

Getting from Savannah to Browning was no easy task. It had taken Matt and Buzz a full day of connecting flights through Atlanta and Salt Lake City just to reach the state of Montana. Great Falls International was the closest airport to Browning but it was still 125 miles southeast of where they needed to be. Since it was almost midnight when they arrived, they found a hotel close to the airport and went straight to bed. The next morning, with steaming cups of coffee in their hands, they climbed into their rental car and made the two-and-a-half-hour drive to their final destination.

Browning was the largest community on the Blackfeet Reservation. Although at less than a square mile and fewer than a thousand residents, it wasn't much of a town. It was, however, the seat of the Blackfeet Nation's tribal government. So that's where Buzz and Matt decided to begin their search for Tommy. Somebody in town surely could help them locate the boy from the newspaper article who had discovered the conquistador helmet more than forty years earlier.

The town of Browning had definitely seen better days, or at

least Matt hoped it had. Outside of the ubiquitous presence of fast-food chains and a handful of dated motels, there didn't seem to be a whole lot of commerce going on. The only local business Matt could see with at least a smattering of cars in the parking lot was a brightly painted Indian Trading Post. Matt assumed this catered mostly to tourists passing through Browning on their way to Glacier National Park, thirty miles to the northwest.

At more than three thousand square miles, the Blackfeet Indian Reservation was larger than the state of Delaware. But jobs were scarce in this remote section of northwest Montana, just south of the Canadian border. In fact, Matt had read somewhere that unemployment topped a staggering seventy percent on the res. Perhaps this explained the large number of young men milling about with seemingly nothing but time on their hands.

They hadn't received the friendliest of welcomes, especially when they had started to ask around about Tommy Running Crane. Stony faces and wary stares had netted them next to nothing regarding his whereabouts. Finally, toward the end of the day, they spotted an old man sitting on a bench outside a gas station. After a little coaxing and a pack of Marlboros, he told them they might be able to find Tommy at a popular local watering hole. It was just down the road.

The bar was named Stick's. He warned them it might not be the safest place for two white men asking a lot of questions. He also informed them that Tommy was known as Big Tom now. Since Tommy would now be in his mid-fifties, Matt asked if the old man could tell them what he looked like. He replied simply they'd know him when they saw him.

It was late afternoon by the time Matt and Buzz walked into Stick's. The sign out front said Restaurant & Lounge but Matt saw no sign of a kitchen. It was the kind of place that looked like a fight had just happened, or was about to. It was dimly lit and had sticky floors and mismatching tables and chairs. An old jukebox played Toby Keith through scratchy speakers. A couple of guys were shooting pool in the far corner. It was still early, but the bar was far from empty. Maybe seventy percent unemployment and the lack of anything better to do accounted for the turnout.

The two men didn't go unnoticed as they made their way to a couple of empty stools. "Looks like we just cast up on the wrong shore," Buzz said under his breath. Matt ignored the comment and tried to remain calm. But it was difficult to ignore the twenty sets of suspicious eyes that had followed them across the room.

Whiskey seemed to be the drink of choice—and a $2.50 Black Velvet special advertised on a grease board above the register explained why. Playing it safe, Matt ordered a couple of longneck Budweiser's. The bartender looked like he'd seen it all in his lifetime, twice.

As they scanned the bar, nobody stood out to them as a candidate for Tommy, a.k.a. Big Tom. Matt snuck a peak at his folded-up copy of the 1970s newspaper article. But he knew the boy's face in the picture probably bore little resemblance to the present-day version of the man. Buzz was doing a little recon of his own when he spotted the door to the men's bathroom open. He elbowed Matt in the ribs. When Matt turned his head in the direction of Buzz's wide-eyed stare, he took in the biggest man he'd ever seen in his life. They watched in silence as the behemoth strode across the room and sat down heavily at the other end of the bar.

"I think your date has arrived," Buzz commented, always the comedian, reaching for his beer.

"My date?" Matt said.

"Well, I'm sure as hell not going over there to talk to that brute," Buzz said with a smirk.

"I thought coming out here to find Tommy was your idea," Matt volleyed.

"Don't worry, I'll watch your blind side," Buzz said reassuringly. He nudged Matt. "Go on, now, time's a wasting."

Matt shook his head at his wiseass older friend. "Oh what the hell," he said. "Just be ready to run if this thing goes south." The truth was, there was no one else Matt would rather have covering his backside then Buzz Penberthy.

Matt was by no means small and he knew how to handle himself in a fight. But as he approached the other end of the bar, his six-foot-two-inch, two-hundred-pound frame suddenly felt woefully insufficient. Even sitting down, Matt could tell Big Tom had him by at least a half a foot and a hundred pounds. Matt approached cautiously. He sat down slowly, making sure to leave an empty bar stool as a buffer between himself and the man they had traveled close to twenty-five hundred miles to find. He took one last look across the bar at Buzz, who winked while taking an exaggerated pull on his long neck bottle of beer. Matt rolled his eyes and returned his attention to Tom.

"Excuse me," Matt began. "Are you the guy they call Big Tom?"

The Indian lifted his impossibly large head and looked hard at Matt. He grunted and returned to the newspaper spread out in front of him.

Close enough now to see the lines etched on Tommy's face, Matt thought he looked closer to seventy than a man in his mid-fifties. *He must have led a hell of a rough life.* He forged ahead, "I've come a long way to find you and..."

"Find me? You some kind of cop or something?" Big Tom's look went from disinterested to menacing in a flash.

"What? No, no...I'm not a cop," Matt responded hastily. "Far from it. I'm an antiques dealer and I came across a newspaper clipping from 1973." He fumbled for the article, unfolded it, and placed it flat on the bar.

Big Tom's face softened somewhat as he looked at a picture he hadn't seen in years. But he returned to his paper without a word.

"I was hoping you could tell me what happened to the helmet you were holding in that picture," Matt said.

Silence.

"It looked pretty old and I wondered if you could tell me anything about it," Matt pressed his luck.

Still nothing.

Matt took a twenty-dollar bill out of his wallet and placed it on the bar in front of Big Tom. He also motioned to the bartender, who had been eyeing him warily ever since he sat down. He ordered two beers. Then he waited. He had learned from his days as a bond trader on Wall Street that patience often paid the biggest dividends.

A few minutes later, Big Tom finally spoke, "What do you want to know?"

Matt didn't hesitate, "For starters, where did you find it?"

"Out near Ghost Ridge."

"Ghost Ridge? Where's that?"

"Western part of the res, near Glacier Park," he said slowly.

Big Tom was evidently a man of few words. *This may take a while.* He took a deep breath and continued, "Where do you think it came from?"

"Dunno," Big Tom said. He was losing interest and, once again, returned to his paper. Matt noticed he hadn't made a move for either the beer or the money.

He changed gears. "So what happened to it? Do you still have it?"

"Sold it," the Indian said, without looking up.

Sensing he was losing the big man, Matt took out another twenty and placed it on the bar. "Tom, it's kind of important that I find that helmet. Can you tell me who you sold it to?"

The second twenty seemed to do the trick. For the first time, Big Tom looked Matt in the eye. He sighed deeply and began to speak slowly, prying the memories loose from the gray matter of his brain like gum from the bottom of a shoe.

"A couple weeks after me and Lenny found it, some old white guy pulled up in front of my mom's house in a fancy Cadillac. He was real interested in that old helmet, just like you. Paid me a lot of money for it and left. I never saw him again and hardly ever talked about it—until you showed up."

Big Tom looked suddenly very tired. Was it the memory of his dead friend, Matt wondered, or did conversation simply disagree with him? Then, all at once, he swiped the two twenties off the bar and hoisted his large frame off the bar stool.

Without thinking, Matt stepped in front of the giant to prevent him from leaving. He instantly regretted his decision when he took in the full size of the man towering over him. It occurred to Matt that not too many people had probably ever put themselves in the direct path of Big Tom—and lived to tell about it. But surprisingly, Tom didn't seem upset, just mildly annoyed.

Matt spoke quickly, "I noticed you were looking at the Want Ads." He pointed at the discarded newspaper on the bar. How about I give you a hundred dollars to take me out to the place where you found the helmet."

Big Tom stared at Matt for what seemed like an eternity. Finally, he said, "Two hundred." Without waiting for an answer, he rattled off an address and told Matt to pick him up in the morning.

Buzz and Matt didn't linger too long after Big Tom departed. They couldn't be sure, but the looks they were getting from the locals seemed to be increasing in hostility. They chose not to wait around to find out if it was just their imagination. They quickly paid for their beers and headed for the door.

The moment the two men turned to leave, the bartender picked up the phone behind the bar and began to dial.

4

Present Day

Blackfeet Indian Reservation

Browning, Montana

They got lost twice on the way to Big Tom's house, located thirty miles north of Browning, near a place called Duck Lake. Most of the smaller roads weren't even mapped in these remote areas, so GPS wasn't worth a damn. Finally, they pulled into a long driveway—at the end of which sat a simple, prefab house. It was small but tidy looking.

As they pulled up to the home, Buzz spotted Big Tom emerging from a rusty storage shed adjacent to the house. He was dressed in jeans, work boots, and a black T-shirt. The words *Chief Mountain Hot Shots* were written across the front of his shirt.

Matt got out of the car. "Morning," he said, as Big Tom approached.

"Mm hmm," Tom muttered. He walked straight past Matt and back into his house.

"I think he's warming up to you," Buzz quipped with a grin.

Matt smiled. "Yeah, I can see that. My boyish charm is really winning him over."

A few minutes later, Big Tom slammed the front door shut

behind him and headed toward the car. He had a well-worn fatigue hunting jacket slung over his shoulder. Even though the calendar read June, the mornings were still pretty cool this far north. It was a fact that neither Matt nor Buzz had considered when they packed mostly short-sleeve shirts for their trip to Montana.

Matt was about to offer the front seat to Tom, but he had already heaved himself into the back without comment. Before ducking into the passenger seat, Matt looked across the roof of the car and saw the face of a grim-looking woman staring back at him from the kitchen window. A second later the face had disappeared behind a sun-faded curtain. *Real friendly folks.*

Outside of an occasional "take a left" and "go straight here" directional comment, Big Tom remained a man of few words. He opened up a little bit when Matt asked about the Chief Mountain Hot Shots. According to Tom, they were an elite firefighting crew based on the reservation. The crew had more than earned their elite status fighting forest fires for the past twenty years. The shirt was a gift from Tom's nephew, who was one of the most respected members of the crew.

They headed in a northwesterly direction toward the revered Chief Mountain, which they could see rising up impressively in the distance. Matt said, "If you don't mind my asking, what happened to the other boy in the picture with you—I think his name was Leonard?"

"Lenny was my best friend—knew him since we were little kids. But he got mixed up with the wrong people. Started drinking, but that wasn't the real problem—hell, everybody around here drinks. It was the drugs he couldn't handle." He paused as his mind sifted through distant memories. "Anyway, he got AIDS and died. Dirty needle they said. That was over twenty years ago." He stared out the window, as if in a trance.

"Sorry," Matt mustered, wishing he hadn't asked about Leonard.

Changing the subject, he said, "Are we getting close?"

"In about a mile, there'll be a dirt road on the left. I'll tell you where to pull off. There's a gate but the chain's busted, so we can get through."

Sure enough, when they pulled off, Tom hopped out and pulled the chain free with ease. He swung the gate open.

"Follow this road for about four miles until it ends," he said, climbing back in. "Then we'll have to hike in about a mile. Hope you guys brought hiking boots."

For the first time, Matt thought he saw a smile playing around the edges of the big man's mouth. Matt looked down at his feather-weight running shoes, smiled, and said, "We'll manage."

They bounced along on the severely rutted road going no more than thirty miles an hour. Any faster and their car might never be rentable again. Around a sharp bend, Matt had to slam on the brakes to avoid a truck parked in the middle of the road. Two official-looking men were leaning against the hood—thick arms folded challengingly across their chests. Buzz brought the car to a skidding stop.

"Son of a bitch," Big Tom muttered. "Res police."

The more senior looking of the two motioned for Buzz to roll down his window. "Where do you think you guys are going?" he said. "You know this is private land, right?"

Buzz lied, "We're just sightseeing. The gate back there was open, so we didn't see the harm."

It wasn't until he got closer to the vehicle that the officer spotted Big Tom sitting stoically in the backseat. "Tom, what the hell are you doing out here—you know these two?" he said, surprised.

"Tour guide," Tom deadpanned, sounding more like Tonto, the Lone Ranger's stereotyped Indian sidekick, than himself.

Matt could tell by his flip response and the look on his face that Tom didn't like these guys.

"Funny, big man," the officer responded tersely, clearly pissed off at Tom's lack of respect. "You know damn well this land is bought and paid for, so why don't you boys find somewhere else to play."

"There are a lot of things bought and paid for around here, eh, J. C.?" Tom replied evenly, but with a hard stare.

"Fuck you, Tom," the res police officer said, losing his cool for the first time. "Now, unless you want to spend the night in jail, I'd suggest you and your friends turn this piece of shit around and get the hell off this property. Besides," he said. He forced a smile, but it appeared more as a sneer, "your favorite bar in Browning should be opening up any minute now—and I know you don't want to miss that, do you, Tom."

Matt could see Tom's grip tighten around the armrest of the door. But to his credit, he didn't take the bait. Afraid that things might deteriorate if they stuck around any longer, Matt smacked Buzz's thigh with the back of his hand. It was time to leave.

"Our mistake, officer," Buzz said, rolling up his window. He put the car in reverse, did a three-point turn, and headed back in the direction they had just come.

As they turned around, a white Ford F-150 pickup truck passed them going the other way. The words *Spate Industries* were written in bold blue letters across the front door panel.

"Who is Spate Industries?" Matt asked.

"They're the ones who own all this land," Tom answered tersely, "or at least they own the lease rights to the land."

"Lease rights?" Buzz asked, confused.

"Spate Industries is a big-ass oil company. They bought the drilling rights to thousands of acres out here on the res—including the tract of land we're supposedly trespassing on."

Matt jumped in, "What did you mean back there, with that 'bought and paid for' comment?"

Tom shook his head slowly. "The res police are corrupt. Everybody knows it, but nobody can do anything about it. They're pretty

much on Spate's payroll, so they make it their business to protect the
company's interests." Big Tom returned to staring out the window,
but he hadn't lessened his grip on the armrest.

*Those guys had really gotten under his skin. Was it the comment
about the bar being open or something else,* Matt wondered. Either
way, he was beginning to believe there was more to Tom than met
the eye. And, in spite of Tom's stoic demeanor, Matt was beginning
to like the big Indian. Anybody who flipped the bird at authority
was OK by him.

They finally reached the paved road again, mercifully leaving
the heavily potholed Ho Chi Minh trail in their rearview mirror.
They turned south and drove on in silence. A few minutes later, a
big hand smacked down on the back of Matt's seat, palm up. "You
owe me two hundred bucks," Big Tom declared, dead serious.

Matt turned around. "What?" he said incredulously. Then the
realization hit him and he smiled, "You knew we were going to be
stopped today, didn't you? You knew those guys would be here
and that they'd turn us away." Matt shook his head with grudging
respect. "Easiest two hundred bucks you'd ever make, right Tom?"

"Deal's a deal," Big Tom replied simply. Then he winked.

Matt looked over at a smiling Buzz and then he burst out laughing. *Yup, I definitely misjudged Big Tom.* He reached into his wallet
and counted out five twenty-dollar bills. He placed them into the
oversized paw that remained palm-up on the back of his seat.

"Here's half. We're not quite done with you yet, big guy," Matt
said.

They continued down the road. Now it was Matt's turn to look
out the window, lost in thought. He was thinking through their
next move when another question popped into his head.

"Hey," he said, turning around again to face Tom, "how long has
Spate Industries been drilling out here anyway?"

"Years," was all Tom said.

5

Present Day

Oklahoma City, Oklahoma

The brothers sat in a plush private dining room atop the same corporate office building their family had owned for the past five decades. At only twenty-one stories high, it seemed relatively modest compared to the recently completed fifty-story office tower that now dominated the Oklahoma City skyline. That was fine by the brothers. Their family had always chosen to keep a low profile.

They sat in front of a fifteen-foot, floor-to-ceiling window. It gave them an unobstructed view of the Oklahoma River that ran right through the middle of the largest city in the state. The meal had been prepared by a private chef who had learned his craft at some of the finest restaurants in Paris and New York. The waitstaff was superbly trained and could anticipate the men's demands before being asked. Dinner had just been cleared.

A cloud of blue smoke encircled the two men as they puffed mightily on eight-inch Cuban cigars that cost more than eighty dollars apiece. The sommelier had just finished pouring two snifters of French cognac. Then he disappeared into the kitchen, leaving the men to talk in private.

The two siblings met like this at least once a month—alternating between Oklahoma City and Manhattan—to catch up on their family business dealings. At seventy, Oliver was the older of the two and still resided in the state in which the men had been reared. Landon, three years younger than his brother, lived in New York City, in strategic proximity to the Wall Street financial institutions that quietly managed the family's vast holdings. The two men had inherited their privately held company and the fortune that went with it from their father more than forty years earlier. Each owned a fifty percent stake in the company.

"Looks like that lawsuit in Texas is about to go away," Oliver said, referring to a wrongful death suit that had been brought against their company. "Our lawyers got most of the charges tossed out. So the families decided it would be in their best interest to settle out of court. Only cost us a couple of million."

"Not bad considering it probably would have cost us a hundred million if it had gone to trial," Landon noted.

"As usual, our guys kept a lid on the whole thing. And they made sure that the families agreed to keep their mouths shut as part of the deal. By the way, we need to be sure to take care of the mayor down there; he really came through for us," Oliver said.

"What about Tennessee?" Landon moved on to the next topic. "Can you believe the Feds filed a seventy-three-count indictment against us? Don't they have anything better to do with their fucking time? We employ two-thirds of the people in that backwater town and they want to shut us down—all over some bullshit EPA study that claims our emissions are causing cancer."

While Oliver was tall, with patrician good looks, there was nothing cultivated about Landon. His stocky build and foul mouth were more akin to a dockworker than a blue blood. And while his capricious personality had a certain bad-boy appeal to the opposite sex, he could just as quickly turn brutal when crossed. His foul mouth and temper had caused many over the years to underestimate his intelligence—a miscalculation he always used to his advantage. Because the truth was, beneath the crass exterior he was as brilliant as his brother was calculating. Together they made a formidable team, which is how they had avoided serious government interference for decades. In the past year, however, the current left-leaning presidential administration had become much more aggressive in pursuing corporate environmental violators.

"Our lawyers will handle it; they always do," Oliver said confidently. "By the time they're done with the Feds, we'll pay a slap-on-the-wrist fine and be back in business as if nothing ever happened." Then he leaned forward in his seat. "We can't take our eye off the big picture right now, little brother," he counseled. "We're so close to achieving our dream. And when we do, no government agency will be able to touch us."

"I know, I know. I'm just so damn tired of this administration's antibusiness policies," Landon grumbled.

"Don't worry about the current administration," Oliver countered, his eyes taking on an increased intensity. "The federal government and their socialist policies will soon be a thing of the past. Regulators, corporate taxes, unionized labor—all of it will be gone, replaced by a truly free market economy."

"You're right," Landon said. "We've been working our whole lives for this moment. I guess I can remain patient a little while longer."

They returned to their cigars and cognacs. A few moments later, Oliver broke their reverie and said, "There is one disturbing item that's come up."

"What's that?"

"I got a call from our contact in Montana. Evidently someone's been sniffing around the res asking a lot of questions." Uneasiness had crept into Oliver's voice.

"Who? What do they want?" Landon asked anxiously, taken off guard by this unforeseen development.

"Two men showed up out of nowhere and started poking around. That's all I know at this point," he replied tersely.

"We need to figure out what they're up to—and quickly, Oliver."

"Don't worry. I'll get the situation under control before it goes any further," Oliver responded.

But the concern etched on his face belied his confident demeanor.

6

Present Day
Blackfeet Indian Reservation
Browning, Montana

Stick's Restaurant & Lounge was even more crowded than the first time they had visited. After their run-in with res the police earlier that morning, Buzz and Matt had had an unproductive balance of the day. They had made their way around the town of Browning and talked to some of the older locals. Unfortunately, very few of them remembered the discovery of the helmet, and those who did had largely forgotten about it. Big Tom had agreed to meet up with them that evening at Stick's—which is the only reason they had returned to the less-than-welcoming, rundown bar.

They were on their second beer and there was still no sign of Tom. "You think he's coming?" Buzz asked.

"I don't know," Matt said, feeling a bit frustrated. "He's the only lead we've got, so I hope so. My gut tells me he's got more to share with us. I can tell you this, though, if he doesn't show, we're going back out to his house again tomorrow. And we're not leaving until Big Tom tells us every last detail about that helmet and the guy who bought it from him."

"You gonna beat it out of him, big boy?" Buzz joked.

"Me? You're the military man. Don't you know some torture techniques or something?" Matt volleyed back sarcastically.

"I must have missed that class," Buzz smiled.

As they ordered another round, an old man approached them from behind. The men hadn't noticed him until he spoke up, "Are you the two guys been asking around about Big Tom's helmet?" he said loudly.

"Jesus," Matt exclaimed, startled by the deep voice that came unexpectedly from over his shoulder. He spun around and saw an ancient-looking Indian man. His face was tanned and deeply lined and his nose was curved like a hawk's beak. The thought occurred to Matt that if Mount Rushmore had included a carving of an Indian chief, it would have been this guy's face.

"We're the guys," Buzz answered. He extended a friendly hand. "My name's Buzz and this is Matt."

The old Indian shook their hands with a surprisingly firm grip. He said, "I'm Charlie, though most people call me Crooked Nose."

The name was fitting, although he could also have been called Missing Teeth, since he had more gaps than enamel in his mouth. The old man stared at the men intently, his chin thrust forward. "Heard you were out in the foothills earlier today," he said.

"We were," Matt replied, wondering if anything they had done since they arrived in Browning had gone unnoticed. "But we didn't get very far. We were turned back by the reservation police."

The man's eyes darkened. "Stay away from Ghost Ridge," he warned firmly.

"Hey," Buzz said, holding up his hands defensively, "we don't want to cause anybody trouble. We just want to explore the area a little bit, that's all."

"Just stay away. It's for your own good."

"Look, no offense, but we've already been threatened once today," Matt said, starting to become irritated. "We know all about

Spate's land leases and..."

The old Indian cut him off, "Not a threat, a *warning*."

Buzz could see the genuine fear in the man's eyes. He'd seen it a thousand times in the eyes of young fighter pilots back in Vietnam. "What do you mean a warning?" he asked.

"Ghost Ridge is haunted."

The two men shared a skeptical look. But Crooked Nose persisted.

"You," the Indian said to Buzz, "you were a warrior once."

Buzz glanced at Matt with a raised eyebrow before replying, "Yes, a long time ago."

"Once a warrior, always a warrior," the Indian said dismissively. "Those hills were once filled with great warriors."

"What happened to them?" Matt asked, still wondering how the old man knew Buzz had been in the military.

"Old Crooked Nose will tell you. But first, whiskey," he said, looking Matt in the eye.

Matt got the not-so-subtle hint. A minute later, the bartender delivered a Black Velvet special. The old Indian took a loud, slurping sip. And then another. A slow song played on the jukebox. Matt noticed a drunken couple, half-stumbling, half-dancing on the sticky bar floor, making out clumsily.

He turned back to Charlie as the old man started to talk again. "An ancient tribe once lived in those foothills. The men were fierce warriors and the women were strong and proud," he said, looking at Buzz. "They were here long before my people, the Blackfeet, came to the area."

A ruckus broke out behind them. Evidently, the wife of the dirty-dancing man showed up and had immediately gotten into it with the other woman. She grabbed her by the hair and began repeatedly smashing her fist into the other woman's face. A couple of guys quickly separated them and escorted the aggressor out of the bar. Her sheepish-looking husband followed closely behind. Matt shivered at the thought of what was in store for that poor guy when he got home.

"That never used to happen here," the old man said sadly. "It seems that my people don't want to do anything anymore except drink and fight. It's shameful."

Matt gently prodded, saying, "So you were telling us about the ancient tribe."

"Yes. Like I said, they were proud and strong. And they couldn't be killed—arrows bounced off of their chests." He pounded his chest with his fist as he spoke. "Some believed they were evil spirits and that their jet-black skin was proof they came from the bad place."

Buzz and Matt reacted simultaneously at the mention of the color of their skin. Matt beat Buzz to the punch and said, "Did you say they had jet-black skin?"

"Yes, their skin was darker than a crow feather."

Matt and Buzz locked eyes and shared the same thought, *could this be the black tribe that Lewis had written about in his field notes?*

Buzz spoke up, "So if they couldn't be killed, then what happened to them."

"A great storm came through the mountains one day. Legend says booms of thunder rumbled all day long, and when the storm passed the dark tribe was gone, carried away by the Great Spirit," he said ominously. "Not a trace of their village was left. No bodies, no homes, nothing. They were never seen again." He paused before adding, "But their spirits live on to this day. And those spirits are very protective of their ancient home—in those hills you visited today."

"Guess that explains the name Ghost Ridge. So you really believe it's haunted by the dark tribe?" Matt asked.

"I know it is, because I've been out there myself..."

But before the old Indian could say another word, a heavyset man approached quickly. He was wearing a white cowboy hat. Two large eagle feathers protruded from a bandana wrapped around the brim.

"Crooked Nose," he said in forced joviality, "you telling your crazy stories again?" He put a beefy arm around the old man and began to usher him away firmly. "Don't pay attention to old Charlie here," he said over his shoulder to Matt and Buzz, "he's just a crazy old drunk."

"Hang on a minute," protested Matt, getting up. But two men stepped in and blocked his way.

Crooked Nose was ushered out a back door by the man in the white cowboy hat. Before the door closed behind them, the old Indian looked back toward the bar. And that's when Buzz saw it— fear had returned to his eyes.

At the hotel later that evening, Matt was propped up in bed working on his laptop computer. In the middle of answering an e-mail related to his antiques shop, a ping sounded. It alerted him a new e-mail had just arrived. Before he opened it, he noticed that the sender of the message was marked 'Unknown'. *That was a bit odd.* The message itself was more than just odd however, it was downright scary.

Be careful. You are dealing with very powerful men who will stop at nothing to protect their interests. This is bigger than you know. You are not safe here.

The message was signed, *A. Friend.*

"What the fuck," Matt said out loud. *Someone is clearly trying to scare us off. First the res police, then old Crooked Nose, now this.*

Matt didn't scare easily, however. In fact, threats usually had the opposite effect on him. They made him dig in his heels and increase his resolve. Even so, before switching off his bedside lamp for the evening, he got up and threw the dead bolt on his hotel room door.

Sleep didn't come easily that evening.

7

Present Day

Blackfeet Indian Reservation

Browning, Montana

The next morning, Matt and Buzz decided to pay a visit to the reservation police headquarters in downtown Browning. They hoped to obtain permission to access Spate Industries leased land in the foothills near Ghost Ridge. On the way over to the station, Matt filled Buzz in on the anonymous e-mail he had received late the prior evening.

"So what do you make of it?" he asked Buzz.

"Well, either someone is trying to scare us away or they are what they say they are—a 'friend' trying to warn us," Buzz replied. "Neither option makes me feel all warm and fuzzy, though, if you know what I mean."

"I know exactly what you mean. Which is why I slept like shit last night," Matt said. "This whole thing is just so bizarre. I mean, what's everybody so afraid of around here?"

"You got me, partner. Let's see what the local sheriff has to say for himself. Although if you believe what Big Tom said about the res police being on Spate's payroll, I'm not sure we're going to get very far."

The police station was a one-story cement-block building surrounded by a chain-link fence. They entered the dreary-looking structure and asked the gum-smacking woman sitting behind the front desk if they could see the police chief. After waiting more than twenty minutes, they were finally escorted in. His office looked like it hadn't been redecorated since the building had opened in the late 1970s. The decor consisted of cheap wood-paneled walls, an industrial-looking green metal desk, worn carpeting, and a series of vintage black-and-white aerial photographs of the town of Browning nailed unevenly to the paneling.

It wasn't the interior design that caught the attention of Matt and Buzz, however, it was the heavyset man sitting behind the desk—more specifically, the white cowboy hat with two familiar-looking eagle feathers. The nameplate on the desk read "Chief Hall." At least the man who had ushered Crooked Nose from the bar the night before now had a name.

"Welcome to Browning, gentlemen," the police chief said loudly. He stood up and came around to the front of his desk. His belly protruded prominently below his thick chest. His girth, however, had the effect of making him look powerful rather than fat. "Sorry we didn't get a chance to chat last night, but it was time for old Charlie to go home. He tends to get ornery when he gets drunk."

Introductions were dispensed with quickly and the chief cut to the chase. "Now what brings you two all the way out here to our little town?"

Matt chose to let the Crooked Nose incident go for now and answered the question. "We're amateur history buffs who came across a story of an interesting discovery that happened on the reservation back in the early '70s." He went on to recount their finding the newspaper clipping of Big Tom holding what appeared to be a conquistador helmet. He purposely left out the part about Meriwether Lewis's field notes, figuring the less he shared the better, at this point.

"Conquistador helmet?" the chief said with exaggerated skepticism. "I've never heard that one before."

Matt glanced over at Buzz with an annoyed look that said *bullshit*.

Before Matt could stir the pot, as he was prone to do, Buzz jumped in saying, "Either way, we were hoping to have the chance to look around the Ghost Ridge area. That's where we were with Big Tom yesterday. But a couple of your men turned us away."

The chief forced a belly laugh and said with a disingenuous smile, "Ahh, Ghost Ridge, I guess old Crooked Nose told you his favorite story. Look, fellas, there isn't anything out there in those hills except dirt and rocks. Old Charlie never does tire of that old tale, though." He laughed again—a forced, raspy cackle.

"Well, if that's the case, then you wouldn't mind if we go out there and see for ourselves," Matt challenged. "We promise not to get in anybody's way."

The chief's eyes narrowed. "I'm afraid that's not going to happen," he said. "That land is strictly off-limits. It's private property. That's why the signs say No Trespassing Allowed." He wasn't laughing anymore.

The tension in the room was interrupted by the entrance of a tall, strikingly beautiful woman who strolled through the open door of the chief's office. She had long, blond hair and even longer legs. She was busy putting her cell phone away, having just hung up from a call. When she looked up she was surprised to see the chief had guests. "Oh, I'm sorry, Chief," she said. "I didn't realize you were in the middle of a meeting." She turned to leave.

"No, it's OK, Ms. Christie, these boys were just leaving," he said, turning to Matt and Buzz. "Sorry you had to come all this way for nothing."

Matt ignored the chief's brush-off. He took a step forward and said, "Hi, my name's Matt Hawkins." He never missed an opportunity to meet a beautiful woman. And besides, he was very curious how someone who looked like her fit into the black-and-white picture that was Browning, Montana. Clearly, she was not from here—her expensive tailored suit told him that. In fact, she looked more out of place in this town then they did.

"Samantha Christie," she said. Her smile commanded all of Matt's attention. As she grasped his hand, she tilted her head slightly to the side and looked at him quizzically through ultramarine eyes. "Have we met before?"

Matt had gotten that a lot, ever since the numerous television appearances that followed his discovery of George Washington's surrender letter. He replied simply, "I must have one of those faces."

She held his grasp a little longer than appropriate and said, "Yes, you do." That smile again.

The chief cleared his throat and asserted himself once more. "These two were caught trespassing out by Ghost Ridge," he said. "They seem to think a—what'd you call it—oh yeah, a conquistador helmet was found out there forty years ago. I told them that land was privately held and off-limits to the general public. No wild goose chases allowed." He smirked.

"Oh, I see," Samantha said.

Matt ignored the chief once again. "What brings you to Browning?" he asked Samantha. "If you don't mind my asking, you don't look like you belong here."

"Alright, guys, let's go," the chief said and began ushering them out of his office.

"No, it's OK, Chief," Samantha said. "I work for Spate Industries. We're a large oil company based in Oklahoma. But we have drilling rights on thousands of acres of land here on the Blackfeet Reservation—including the area out by Ghost Ridge." Her tone had turned suddenly professional.

Matt couldn't hide his disappointment when she said she worked for Spate. But it certainly explained what she was doing in a remote outpost like Browning.

"Well, it sounds like you're the real authority around here. Maybe we should have been talking to you in the first place," Matt said, enjoying taking a dig at the chief. "How about it, would you be willing to let us take a look around Ghost Ridge?"

She replied, "No, I'm afraid the chief's right, that area is off-limits. It's really a safety concern, with all the heavy machinery and trucks moving back and forth on those roads. You can appreciate the liability involved if someone were to get hurt." Her response sounded like a well-rehearsed script.

Not willing to give up the fight that easily, Matt tried a different approach. "Why don't you come with us? That way you can ensure we don't get into any trouble." He smiled mischievously, turning on the charm.

The chief had reached his limit. He said firmly, "The answer is *no*, and this meeting is over. We've both got more important things to do today then play tour guide to you two." He herded them out of his office and closed the door.

As they walked out the front door of the building and into the parking lot, Buzz noted dejectedly, "Looks like another dead end."

"Yeah, and it's beginning to piss me off. I see what Big Tom meant. The police around here are definitely dirty. It oozed out of the chief's pores," Matt said angrily.

A voice called out from behind them. It was Samantha Christie. She hurried over just before they got into their car.

"I'm glad I caught you," she said. "Sorry about the chief; he takes his job very seriously. Sometimes he can come on a little strong."

"Really, we hadn't noticed," Buzz replied dryly.

"Listen, I'll see what I can do about getting you access to Ghost

Ridge. I can't promise anything, but I'm willing to make a couple of phone calls," she said amiably.

She reached into her bag and wrote her cell phone number on the back of her business card. She handed it to Matt. "In the meantime, if you have any questions, I can be reached on my cell," she smiled again, showing off her perfectly aligned, bright-white teeth.

The sun's rays reflected off her eyes and they shined like gemstones. Matt was mesmerized by their luster for a half beat. Finally, he said, "Yeah, well, thanks." He tucked the card into his shirt pocket. Samantha tilted her head sideways again as if she wanted to say more, but then she simply nodded and walked away.

As they were driving out of the parking lot, Buzz cracked, "Easy on the eyes, eh, big fella?"

"Who? Oh, you mean the leggy blond back there, with the perfect face and a body that won't quit?" Matt said sarcastically, "She's alright, I guess."

"Mm hmm," Buzz grunted. Then he asked, "So where to next, Romeo?"

Turning more serious, Matt answered, "I think it's time we paid Big Tom a visit to find out why he stood us up last night."

It was quiet when they pulled up to Tom's house, save for the two feral cats that scampered behind the storage shed at the sound of the approaching car. There was another car in the driveway that hadn't been there the day before. The shades were drawn on all the windows.

Matt had an uneasy feeling as he approached the front door.

There was no doorbell so he rapped his knuckles lightly against the wood frame. When there was no answer, he knocked a little more firmly. Thirty seconds later the door opened with a loud squeak. A well-built man who looked to be about Matt's age stood in the open doorway. He eyed the two men warily but didn't speak.

"Sorry to bother you," said Matt, taking the lead, "but we're looking for Tom. Is he home?"

The man's eyes were red. He looked like he had been crying; or maybe he was stoned. Matt couldn't be sure.

"Who are you?"

Matt explained who they were and about their excursion with Tom the day before. A look of understanding passed over the man's face and his body relaxed visibly. "He told me about you guys," he said. "I'm Bobby, his nephew."

"The Chief Mountain Hot Shot?" Matt said with a smile, remembering the T-shirt Tom had worn the day before.

The man nodded sadly. Something wasn't right.

Matt looked at Buzz and then said, "Look if we came at a bad time, we apologize. We just wanted to ask your uncle a couple of questions."

Bobby stepped out of the front door and pulled it halfway shut behind him. He paused, as if trying to collect himself.

Then he blurted out, "Uncle Tommy is dead."

"What?" The two men reacted in shocked unison.

Bobby glanced back into the house and continued in a hushed voice, "They found him off of Route 89 late last night. The police told us that a semi ran him down. It was a hit and run. Nobody saw it and the son-of-a-bitch driver never stopped. The truck hit Tommy so hard, they said pieces of him were scattered all over the road. It took them more than two hours to find all the body parts."

The grisly description was given matter-of-factly by Big Tom's nephew. Matt guessed he was still in shock—or maybe his firefighting experience had made him numb to violent death.

Matt's head was spinning. A host of images of Big Tom flashed through his mind in rapid succession. The cocky wink he had given him from the backseat of the car the day before; his enormous hand resting on the back of Matt's seat after asking for his "fee." But just as quickly those recollections were replaced with gruesome images of bloody body parts strewn across the highway.

Matt felt sick to his stomach.

"We're very sorry, son," Buzz said, placing a hand on Bobby's shoulder. A tear ran slowly down Bobby's face. He quickly brushed it aside.

The men stood there unmoving. A hawk screeched above them and the wind kicked up a small dust cyclone in the driveway. The awkward silence was finally broken.

"He was supposed to meet us last night," Matt said gently, "but he never showed. That's why we came out here today."

Bobby looked up. "What time?" he asked intently.

"Around seven," Matt replied. "We stayed until ten but then we gave up and left."

Bobby had a concerned look on his face. He looked off into the distance before he spoke again. "The time fits. My aunt said he left the house a little before seven last night. But that's the last she heard from him—until the res police showed up at the house at five this morning."

"Jesus," Matt muttered.

"Why was he walking on the highway so late at night anyway?" Buzz asked, trying to make sense of the events that led to Big Tom's death.

"Res police claim he was drunk and wandered out into the road," Bobby explained.

"That's a goddamned lie," a voice shrieked from behind the half-open front door. As the door opened wider, Matt noticed it was the same woman he had seen the day before peering warily at him from behind the kitchen curtain. Her eyes were unfocused and her face was red and blotchy. She'd been crying.

"Aunt Sheila, you should be resting," Bobby said gently.

"Tom hadn't had a drink in over three months," she shrieked through heavy sobs. She made her way outside unsteadily. "This was no accident. They killed him."

Bobby took a step toward his aunt, "Come on now, Auntie, calm down."

"He was murdered," she screamed. She lunged at Matt. "And it's your fault." Her hands clawed at the air in front of Matt's face. He took a reflexive step back. Her eyes were full of hate and anger. Bobby reacted quickly and grabbed hold of his aunt before she could do any damage.

"We were doing fine until you came along. And now my Tommy is *dead*." Spittle flew from her mouth and snot bubbled out of her nostrils. She was hysterical and inconsolable.

Matt and Buzz stood there frozen in place, not knowing what to do.

"His blood is on your hands," she yelled out, struggling to free herself from her nephew's embrace.

"It's OK, Auntie, I'm here," Bobby said soothingly. He maneuvered her back toward the house.

"You stay away from me," she shouted, pointing at Matt. "Stay away from me," she shouted one last time, before her legs gave out. She collapsed heavily into her nephew's arms. He half-walked and half-dragged her back through the front door of the house.

Bobby looked over his shoulder with a pleading look. The men got the message. They hurried to their car and left.

They drove down Big Tom's long driveway and turned onto the main road. They spotted a Spate Industries pickup truck parked in a pull-off not more than a hundred yards ahead. As Buzz drove by, Matt twisted around to try to get a look inside the heavily tinted windows of the front cab. But all he could make out was the outlines of two men sitting inside.

"What the fuck is going on in this town, Buzz?" Matt blurted out in exasperation, turning back around. He was feeling angry, scared, and guilty all at once. He couldn't shake the look of utter despair on Sheila's face—or the accusation that Big Tom was murdered because of them.

"Hell if I know, but I can tell you one thing," Buzz replied, "I don't believe in coincidences—I think somebody didn't want Tom talking to us."

"You think they killed him?"

"Just a gut feeling—but yes I do. I just don't know who 'they' are."

Matt stared out the window in silence. Buzz knew the wheels were turning in his younger friend's mind. He'd seen that determined look before on Matt's face. Finally, Matt reached into his pocket and pulled out his phone.

"Who are you calling?" Buzz asked.

Matt held up his hand. "David," Matt said, speaking into his phone, "it's Matt Hawkins, and I could use your help."

David Becker was an investigative journalist for the *New York Times*. He had broken the Washington surrender letter story and had been a friend to Matt ever since. Matt filled Becker in on the events of the past couple days. Then he explained what he needed from him.

When Matt was done with the call, Buzz, who had overheard the brief conversation, said, "You think *they're* the ones involved in Big Tom's death?"

"I don't believe in coincidences either," Matt replied through gritted teeth, "and that Spate truck on the side of the road back there is no coincidence. They're watching us, Buzz." He paused before adding, "So I think it's time we found out a little bit more about Spate Industries."

8

June 1963

Oklahoma City, Oklahoma

The two boys wanted desperately to be playing baseball with their friends. Their father would hear none of it. Today they were welcoming a very important person into their home—the president of the John Birch Society. Not only were his two boys to be present, they would listen to every word that was spoken.

Even though they were only teenagers, Oliver and Landon Spate had been card-carrying members of the John Birch Society for more than three years already. Their father had insisted on it and so they had little choice. George Spate was the law in the Spate household as well as the company that bore his name—Spate Industries. And he ruled both with an iron fist. Employees who questioned his wishes were fired on the spot. His sons, on the other hand, did not get off so easy.

If they expressed a contrarian view or disobeyed their father in any way, they were beaten with their choice of a belt or switch. The last time this happened was when Oliver had dared to question his father after George had taken a black pen to his son's history textbook. He had determined that the public school system in Oklahoma was filling his son's mind with misinformation. So he sat down one day at the *kitchen table and crossed out any passage that, in his view, was deemed socialist or un-American. When he had finished, more than half the text had been blackened out.*

The reason for the VIP visitor this day was to discuss what to do about the "commie-traitor" that currently held the Office of the President of the United States—John F. Kennedy. In the eyes of George Spate and his comrades within the John Birch Society, Kennedy was the worst thing that could have happened to the country. For starters, he was a Democrat. Not only that, he was the worst kind of democrat—a liberal one. Very few men got under the skin of the "Birchers," as they had become known, quite like President Kennedy. They had labeled him a traitor for supporting what they believed to be the communist-controlled United Nations. And they accused him of being anti-Christian for lying to the people about an alleged previous marriage and subsequent divorce. Today they would be discussing a strategy to ensure he would not be reelected the following year.

The John Birch Society had been called a fringe element, even by mainstream conservatives like William F. Buckley. In the view of conservatives, the society members had gone too far with their extreme views on the supposed communist infiltration of American society, as well as their vociferous opposition to the civil rights movement. Not to mention their desire to see the federal government's powers severely curtailed. But there wasn't a more fervent believer in every one of these principles than George Spate.

So the boys grew up diligently reading copies of the John Birch Society monthly bulletin. They helped their parents stuff envelopes, write postcards, and hold recruitment meetings in their home. Eventually, after years of indoctrination, the beliefs of the father were embraced by the sons. The ideological torch, in addition to the enormous family fortune, was formally passed to Oliver and Landon when their father died in 1975.

9

Present Day
Oklahoma City, Oklahoma

Oliver Spate's home was impressive but not over-the-top exces-
sive. As with everything pertaining to the private lives of
the Spate brothers, understatement was always the goal. They had
grown up listening to the mainstream establishment label their
father a zealot—a part of a fringe element. They had learned the
hard way it was much easier to further their agenda if they shunned
the spotlight and operated behind the scenes.

Early on in their careers, both Landon and Oliver had taken
very active roles in the Libertarian movement—a political movement that believed in limiting the span of control of government
in favor of an unregulated free market economy. Oliver had even
run for the U.S. Senate, hoping to change the way American government operated from a position of power on the inside. He lost in a
landslide. In the end, the brothers felt that the very public fallout
from their extreme views on the role of government had damaged
the Spate family's carefully crafted reputation.

Instead of throwing in the towel, however, they quietly

retrenched. Their disastrous political experience had taught them the American public would not buy into their extreme views unless they could establish more legitimacy. So that's what they would do. This time, however, they would deliver their message under the radar. It had taken them forty years, but they were at last in a position to achieve their glorious endgame. Their stealth efforts had succeeded beyond their wildest dreams.

The brothers were playing a game of squash on Oliver Spate's custom-built home court. The two men had always been extremely competitive at anything they ever did. And squash was no exception. The match was even, at two games apiece, and Oliver was leading 11–10 in the final game. He only needed one more point to beat his younger brother. Something he never tired of doing.

Before he could serve for the final point, however, Landon's cell phone buzzed for the third time in less than five minutes. He had ignored it the first two times, but someone was clearly intent on reaching him. He held up his hands and called for a timeout, over the loud objections of his brother.

"What?" Landon barked into the phone. A vein in his thick neck was pulsating with every heartbeat. He was breathing heavily and grabbed a towel to wipe sweat from his brow. "Jesus Christ, hang on a minute." He called his brother over and put the caller on speaker so they could both listen. It was their contact in Browning calling to give them an update.

"Hawkins and his friend visited the police station this morning," the contact said. "They're not going away. In fact, they asked for special permission to gain access to the site."

"What's with these guys? Why are they so curious about a goddamned helmet that was found more than forty years ago?" Landon was speaking more to his older brother than the person on the other end of the line.

"That's not all," the contact said. "They also know about Big

Tom's death. They went out to his house and Tom's nephew told them the news. These guys are unpredictable so I can't guarantee what their next move will be. What do you want me to do?"

"What do we want you to do?" Landon asked irritably, his voice beginning to rise. But before he could continue, his less-volatile older brother cut him off.

"What we want you to do," Oliver Spate said in a calm but strained voice, "is to make them go away." He leaned his tall frame down so he was closer to the phone's speaker, and continued, "And if you're not up to the task, then we'll find someone who is. Do I make myself clear?"

"Yes, but..." the contact started to say.

"No *buts,*" Landon interjected forcefully. "We pay you a shit-load of money to protect our interests on that godforsaken reservation, so start protecting."

"Yes, sir, I'll take care of it."

After hanging up the phone, neither man felt much like finishing the squash match. The situation in Montana had escalated. And it had them extremely worried.

"Oliver, if this thing blows up, we're finished."

"I know little brother."

"We've always been able to buy our way out of trouble in the past, but we both know this is different," Landon persisted. "That won't work this time."

"I'm well aware of that," Oliver snapped back. "We can't afford to take any chances with this one, and we won't."

10

Present Day

Blackfeet Indian Reservation

Browning, Montana

Matt and Buzz were in a stunned funk as they drove from Big Tom's house back toward town. What had started out a couple of days earlier as a simple excursion to Montana may have cost a man his life. Matt was having trouble making sense of it all. His head was swimming with unanswered questions. *If Big Tom had been murdered—then why? Was a conquistador helmet worth a man's life? If not the helmet, then what else was out in those hills worth murdering for? And how the hell was Spate Industries involved in all of this?*

Matt wasn't prone to headaches, but when he got one, it was usually a doozy. He massaged his temples with his fingers to try to relieve the pressure that was building. He glanced out the side mirror again and saw the same vehicle he had spotted a few minutes earlier. It was behind them, just a few cars back. They had made a couple of turns along the way, but the beat-up old Volvo was still there. Matt knew he was probably being paranoid, but he kept watch anyway.

"What are you thinking about over there?" Buzz asked. It was the first time either man had spoken in the past fifteen minutes. They had already traveled most of the way back into town.

"I don't know what to think right now, Buzz. I'm feeling guilty as hell, for one thing. If it turns out that our meeting with Big Tom caused his death, I'm not sure I could live with that."

"Let's just take one thing at a time, Matt. Maybe Tom's death really was an accident," he said, although his words carried little conviction.

"It's possible, but neither of us believes that for a second. We both know it's too coincidental that he was on his way to talk to us when he disappeared," Matt said.

As they approached the first stoplight on the outskirts of town, Matt glanced in the side mirror again. The car was still following them. *Another coincidence?* The light turned red and they came to a stop.

"Fuck this," Matt said. Anger had replaced paranoia in his seesaw of emotions. He thrust open the passenger door and scrambled out.

"What are you doing?" Buzz called after him, startled by Matt's abrupt exit. But it was too late. His impulsive friend was already out the door and in a full sprint toward the car behind them.

As Matt approached the Volvo, he noticed the look of utter surprise on the face of the driver. He also noticed the driver was a *she*—and that she was alone. Her window was rolled down.

Matt slammed both hands down on the window frame and said angrily, "Why have you been following us?"

The woman jerked away from Matt and leaned toward the passenger side of the car. "What are you doing? Are you crazy?" she stammered.

"You've been following us for the last five miles," Matt insisted, convinced it had not been his imagination.

"What are you're talking about? I wasn't following you," she said defensively.

Not to be deterred, Matt thrust his arm into the car and switched the ignition off. He snatched the keys and said, "If you say so. But I'm taking these just to make sure." He turned and stalked away.

"Hey, you can't do that," the woman yelled. She opened her door and chased after him. The stoplight had switched to green. Someone leaned on a car horn behind them.

Matt ignored it. He pivoted back around to his pursuer and said, "Look, lady, I've had a really bad day. So either you tell me the truth or I'm going to get in my car," he pointed toward the rental car with a befuddled-looking Buzz inside, "and leave you here in the middle of the road."

The honking car gave up and maneuvered around them. "Get out of the road, assholes," the driver yelled as he accelerated past.

The woman realized Matt was serious so she held up both hands in resignation, "Alright, alright, you win. I *was* following you," she admitted. "But it's not what you think."

Matt jangled the keys in front of him, waiting for her to elaborate.

"I'm worried about my grandfather, OK? I think he might be in danger," she blurted out, looking suddenly embarrassed. "I thought you might be able to help. That's all, I swear." The concerned look on her face gave Matt pause.

"Who the hell is your grandfather?" Matt challenged, still not ready to buy her story.

"You spoke to him at Stick's last night," she said before adding, "he's known as Crooked Nose."

"Crooked Nose?" he said, perplexed. Then the pieces started to fall into place. "Oh God, did something happen to him, too?" he said with panicked concern. He couldn't bear being responsible for another person's death.

"No but, look, can we do this somewhere else?" she said, glancing around as if to remind Matt they were standing in the middle of the road. "I'll follow you into town," she suggested, holding out her hand for the keys to her car. "I know a diner where we can talk."

Matt considered the offer. "OK," he agreed, "but I'll drive." After filling Buzz in on the conversation, he walked back to the old Volvo and got into the driver's seat.

The woman reluctantly climbed into the passenger side of her own car. "Since you're driving my car," she said in exasperation, "do I at least get to know your name?"

"Matt," he said simply.

"I'm Ally," she replied, before adding dryly, "thanks for asking."

Matt suddenly felt foolish. "Sorry," he apologized, "it's been a long day."

"Yes, it has," she agreed.

They sat in a booth toward the back of the diner. Another establishment in Browning that looked like it had been frozen in time—circa 1975. Loud orange wallpaper and vinyl booths with so many holes in the seats Matt wondered what held them together. He introduced Buzz and they ordered some food. They weren't particularly hungry, but Buzz had insisted that they eat something. He had learned a long time ago, from his days in the military, that no matter how horrific the circumstances, they were always made worse by an empty stomach.

"Pretty name," Buzz said, attempting to break the ice with Ally. "My wife's name was Addy, short for Adeline. Is there more to the name Ally?"

"My real name is Alsoomse." She smiled. "It means 'independent.' My grandfather named me, but I've gone by Ally for as long as I can remember." At the mention of her grandfather, her smile disappeared, replaced again by a worried look.

For the first time, Matt took a good look at Ally. She was just as beautiful as Samantha Christie. Unlike Samantha, however, Ally looked like she belonged here. She had the smooth, brown skin and the jet-black hair of a Native American woman. Her eyes were almost as dark as her hair. And they emitted a fierceness that did her Indian name justice.

There is definitely an independent streak in this woman. "So what makes you so worried about Crooked Nose?" Matt asked. "You said he was in danger."

"Actually, I said he *might* be in danger," she corrected. "I became panicked after I heard what happened to Big Tom last night."

Matt gave her a quizzical look. "Word travels fast around here," he said.

"You have no idea. But I didn't find out through the gossip channel this time. I'm friends with Sheila, Big Tom's wife," she explained. "She and I go way back. Anyway, her nephew, Bobby, called me early this morning. He asked me to help him console his aunt. I had just left their house when I saw you two pull into his driveway. So I waited. And then I followed you into town."

"How did you even know who we were?" Buzz asked. It was his turn to be confused.

"It seems as though I'm the only one in town you two haven't talked to since you arrived," she said with a wry smile.

Buzz chuckled. "We did make the rounds yesterday, I'll give you that," he admitted.

"Actually, I went over to check on my grandfather late last night after work," she said. "I work nights," she added. "Anyway, he told me about talking to you guys at Stick's."

"Did he mention how your town's fine sheriff forcibly escorted him out the back door of the bar?" Matt asked.

"He did. And that's part of the reason I got worried."

"But you didn't panic until you talked to Big Tom's wife. Why?" Matt inquired.

"It was something Sheila said to me this morning. She said you two came to Browning to talk to Tom about a helmet he found back when he was a kid. And, she said it was because of you that..." she paused and looked down.

Matt finished her sentence for her, "It's because of us he was killed."

"Yes," she said softly, "she thinks that somehow his death is related to that helmet he found. She told me that Big Tom took you guys out to Ghost Ridge yesterday. And that's what got me nervous. Because nobody knows Ghost Ridge better than my grandfather."

"What is it about Ghost Ridge that makes everyone so nervous? Does it have anything to do with that legend your grandfather told us about—the one about the dark tribe that mysteriously disappeared?"

"I don't know," she said as she shook her head. "All I know is my grandfather used to hike in those hills back in the day, looking for gold. Then one day he just stopped. And he never went back."

Why?" Buzz asked.

"Something spooked him. He never talked about it, but he made it clear to me those hills were cursed. He forbade me from ever going out there. He gave me the same warning he said he gave you last night," she said ominously, "to stay away from Ghost Ridge."

"Look, Ally," Matt said, "I'm sorry, but I just don't believe in ghosts." Ally's eyes flared with anger, so he held his hands up and offered, "But I do believe your grandfather was genuinely afraid of something out there."

"You've got to understand that my people believe in spirits of all kinds. But I think there's more to it than that," she said, the intensity never leaving her dark eyes. "He was spooked by something real. And I think it has something to do with Spate Industries."

Her accusation took the men by surprise. Buzz was the first to respond, "Why do you think they're involved?"

"Because they guard Ghost Ridge like it's Fort Knox," she answered quickly.

"Well that's understandable, given the value of oil these days," Matt reasoned.

"But that's just it. In the thirty years they've been out there, they've never found any oil. In fact," she leaned in and in a hushed voice said, "they've never even dug a well."

"What?" Matt said in disbelief. "That can't be."

"It's no secret, Matt. In fact, it's pretty well known. Everyone just assumed they had their reasons," she said. "And those land leases bring so much money into the reservation that nobody ever wanted to upset the applecart."

"So why are you willing to question their motives now?" Buzz prodded.

"Because things have changed. Now, Big Tom is dead. And my grandfather is the logical choice to be next—especially since he talked to you two."

"And you think it has something to do with that helmet Big Tom found?" Buzz asked.

"I don't think it was a coincidence he was killed the day after you two arrived asking him to show you where he found it; no."

Buzz and Matt shared a knowing look. They had said almost the exact same thing in the car less than an hour earlier.

Ally continued, "Can I ask you guys why you came looking for that helmet anyway? And please don't tell me you were just curious. Nobody comes all the way out here to this forgotten part of the country on a whim. I think there's something you're not telling me."

Matt looked at Ally in a new light. She was clearly very perceptive and he couldn't help but be impressed with her courage. Following them as she had was exactly what he would have done if their roles had been reversed. He admired her gumption. So he made a split-second decision to trust her.

"There is another reason we came here," he began.

Matt figured they were running out of leads and that, at this point, they had nothing to lose. So he told her everything—from the discovery of William Clark's desk to Meriwether Lewis's lost field notes to his hard-to-believe story about being captured by a tribe of black Indians. And finally he told her about the shrine Lewis claimed he saw. The shrine adorned by a conquistador helmet that looked remarkably similar to the one Big Tom found out near Ghost Ridge.

"Wow, that's not the answer I expected," she said, shaking her head at the unbelievable events that had led them to her Blackfeet Nation home. "So what are you going to do now?" she asked, looking a little bewildered, still trying to process what Matt had just shared.

Buzz jumped in, "We have a lead we want to pursue down in Great Falls, but after that we're not sure what else we can do." The lead Buzz was referring to was a Lewis and Clark expert that Director Fox had found for them. The expert had agreed to meet with them the next day.

Ally brightened and said eagerly, "I'd like to come with you. I think I could help."

"I don't know," Matt said.

"I know this area better than you two. And besides, as you've already found out, two white guys asking lots of questions isn't exactly a formula for success around here," she reasoned. Then she smiled and said, "Please."

Buzz chuckled. "I think that's the best offer we've had all day. Don't you, Matt?"

"It's OK by me, as long as you're willing to put up with this pain in the ass," he said, jerking a thumb toward Buzz, sitting next to him in the booth grinning like a fool.

They agreed to meet the next morning to make the long drive back to Great Falls.

On the way out of the diner, Ally reminded Matt, "Unless you're planning on driving me home, I'm going to need my keys back."

Matt had forgotten he still had her car keys stuffed in his pants pocket. "Oh shit, sorry," he said, handing them over. But when he looked at Ally, her face was ashen. Her hand was over her mouth and her arm was outstretched. She was pointing in the direction of their rental car.

The car had been vandalized, badly. A crude stick figure of a man had been spray-painted upside down on the driver's side door. According to Ally, it represented the Blackfeet symbol for death. They could also see that the back window had been smashed in.

As they approached the car to assess the damage, they noticed something else—and it caused a shiver to crawl up Matt's spine. A dead crow had been eviscerated and tossed onto the front seat. Ally explained the crow was a spirit animal for the Blackfeet.

It was associated with a bad omen—sometimes, even death.

11

Present Day

Great Falls, Montana

The city of Great Falls sat on the northern Great Plains near the center of the state of Montana. The town had gotten its name from a series of five large waterfalls located in close proximity along the upper Missouri River. When Meriwether Lewis became the first white man to lay eyes on the falls in 1805, it was a spectacular sight to behold. As the river wound its way across the landscape, it dropped more than five hundred feet—creating a spray that could be seen from miles away. Over the years, however, a series of hydro-electric dams had been installed that tamed the flow of the mighty river. Nevertheless, as Matt steered the rental car along the road that hugged the river's winding eastern bank, it still remained a breathtaking view.

Matt marveled at how Lewis and Clark and their Corps of Discovery portaged their cottonwood dugout boats and tons of equipment and supplies up from the river's edge more than two hundred feet below. And then lugged the entire load across eighteen miles of prairie. It was a miraculous accomplishment, and one that had enabled them to continue on their incredible journey across the continent.

Matt kept stealing prolonged glances out the driver's side window. So much so that Ally had to remind him to keep his eyes on the road. They had a hard enough time explaining the vandalized vehicle to the rental agency when they had swapped it out for another model the day before. The last thing they needed was a second wrecked car on their hands.

They were headed toward the Lewis and Clark Interpretive Center where they were scheduled to meet up with Ron Patterson—one of the world's foremost experts on Lewis and Clark. Montana, and Great Falls in particular, had more than its share of Lewis and Clark aficionados. This was because the famous explorers spent more time and traveled more miles there than in any other state.

As they wandered through the lobby of the 25,000-square-foot building, Matt took in one of the center's signature features—a life-size replica of the type of cottonwood dugout boat used on the journey. The exhibit depicted the heavy boat being hauled up the sheer bank of the Missouri River. It spanned the entire eastern stairwell and ran at a forty-five-degree angle from the main level to the floor below. Its intended effect was to create an appreciation among visitors for the incredibly arduous nature of the almost two-and-a-half-year journey that opened up the American West. Matt shook his head in awe.

He turned around just in time to spot a large, jovial-looking fellow lumbering in their direction. The man had a round face and a shock of white hair with matching white beard and mustache. Matt took an instant liking to the man's warm smile and easy manner.

"Ron Patterson," he announced, slightly out of breath. "Sorry, I lost track of time. Today is envelope-stuffing day. We're sending out our monthly mailing asking donors for their support. It's the only way we stay in business," he explained. Then he patted his midsection and chuckled. "Plus, I don't move as fast as I used to—just can't seem to say no to my wife's pies."

After introductions were made, he led them back through a small maze of administrative offices and out through a glass door to a cement patio that overlooked the Missouri River. They sat down at a small café table.

"So how can I help you?" Ron said amiably. "Mr. Fox, I believe his name was, said you had some questions concerning a discovery of some kind up in Browning? But he didn't say how it's related to the Lewis and Clark Expedition."

Matt glanced over at Ally before speaking, unsure of exactly where to begin. He decided to start with a question. "Do you recall the discovery of a helmet on the Blackfeet Reservation back in the early seventies?" he said, cutting straight to the mysterious find.

"A helmet?" Ron replied, taken aback by the odd question.

"Yes, a conquistador helmet to be exact." Matt pulled out the newspaper clipping of a teenaged Big Tom holding the helmet. "This appeared in the *Great Falls Tribune* so I thought you might remember it, given your interest in history."

Ron removed a pair of small reading glasses from his shirt pocket. He scanned the article and accompanying picture. "Oh yes, I do remember this now. But as I recall, it was a hoax, wasn't it?" The glasses perched on the end of his nose looked tiny on his wide face.

"A hoax," Matt blurted out in surprise, "what do you mean?"

"Well, this was a long time ago. In fact, my wife and I—we've been married for forty years now—had just gotten engaged around that time. But I do remember hearing that the helmet disappeared before anybody had the chance to verify its authenticity. So people just assumed the two boys had made the whole thing up to get attention."

Matt looked crestfallen. *Is it possible this whole thing had been a hoax?*

Ron could see the disappointment on Matt's face so he said, "I'm sorry to be the bearer of bad news son. But I'm afraid if you came all this way to see me about that helmet, I'm not going to be of much help."

He smiled apologetically at Ally and then turned back to Matt. "I must say, I'm a little confused as to how Messrs. Lewis and Clark fit into all of this. Mr. Fox led me to believe you folks wanted to tap into the vast knowledge I've got squirreled away up here," he said, tapping playfully with his index finger on the side of his head. "But I'm not sure what a conquistador helmet has to do with the Lewis and Clark Expedition."

Matt took a deep breath and then said, "Mr. Patterson, what I'm about to tell you is not public knowledge. And when I'm finished you'll understand why." He paused before continuing, "The man who called you to arrange this meeting, James Fox, is the executive director of an organization called the Society of the Cincinnati."

"Yes, he explained that to me," Ron acknowledged, "and I did a little research on them after his call. They have a fascinating history."

"Yes, they've been around since the American Revolution. Anyway, one of their members donated a desk that was once owned by William Clark when he was superintendent of Indian Affairs back in the 1830s," Matt explained. He went on to recount the discovery of the lost field notes penned by Meriwether Lewis that were found inside, and Lewis's remarkable story of being captured by a tribe of black Indians. Matt also described the helmet Lewis sketched in his notes.

Matt watched the congenial expert's face as his mind worked through what he had just been told. Ron snapped his fingers loudly. "So you think the story of the boys' finding the helmet was real, don't you?" he said excitedly. "You think they found the same helmet Lewis wrote about."

"We do. At least, we did. But now we're not really sure," Matt fumbled for the right words. He tried a different tack, fishing for anything that might corroborate Lewis's claims. "Have you ever heard of a black tribe like the one Lewis described?"

Ron pondered the question for a moment before answering, "No, I'm afraid I haven't. And as you can imagine, I've read *all* the journals from the expedition. And not just Lewis and Clark's journals, mind you. Others on the expedition kept journals. All of the sergeants and a few of the privates as well, but unfortunately none of them mention the black tribe you described."

Ally spoke for the first time, "Many of my people believe a black tribe once lived in the foothills near where Lewis says he was captured."

"Ah, the legend," Ron said, nodding his head with a knowing smile.

Ally was caught off guard for a moment and her eyes flashed with anger. She wasn't sure if he was making fun of her, so she replied seriously, "Many of the elders believe it to be more than just a legend." Then she added suspiciously, "How is it that you know of it anyway?"

Matt took notice of her quick temper. He admired her fiery nature but hoped he was never on the receiving end of it.

"Oh, in my youth I did a summer of volunteer work on the reservation. That was a pretty popular thing to do back in the '60s," he explained. "Some of the old-timers shared their stories with me." Realizing he may have offended Ally, he added, "I'm sorry young lady, I just assumed it was a legend."

Ally softened. "No apology necessary. I'm just a little protective of my people and our traditions."

"As well you should be," Ron replied genuinely.

There was a pause in the conversation. The wind rustled the tall grasses that surrounded the center. Clouds began to accumulate. It looked like it could rain at any minute.

"Do you think we're crazy?" Matt asked, a little sheepishly.

Ron looked at him intently. He seemed to consider his response before answering. Finally, he said, "As a matter of fact, no, I don't think you're crazy. President Thomas Jefferson ordered Captain Lewis to keep diligent records of all of his observations. And I have no doubt Lewis took that order very seriously." He paused and scanned the darkening horizon as he spoke. "I also know what people say about him—that he was depressed and stricken with syphilis. Both of which are true, by the way. But if he put pen to paper and recorded it, then I believe it happened. Meriwether Lewis would not fabricate a story like that. It would be completely out of character for him."

"If that's true, then why didn't..." Matt started to say.

"Why didn't his accounting of the black tribe and the conquistador helmet appear in any of the official journals?" Ron finished Matt's question for him.

"Exactly," Matt replied.

"I'm afraid I don't have a ready answer for that one," he admitted.

They sat quietly for a minute before Ron spoke up again. "I suppose there is one possibility," he said.

He had Matt and Ally's full attention, so he continued, "I'm sure you've heard the conspiracy theories surrounding Lewis's death on the Natchez Trace in Tennessee?"

Matt and Ally both shook their heads no. Ron explained, "Captain Lewis was on his way back to Washington from St. Louis in 1809. He needed to resolve some financial issues with the War Department pertaining to the Missouri River Fur Company, of which he was part owner. He was also going to meet with President Jefferson regarding the long overdue publication of his official journals from the expedition. Naturally, Lewis had all the journals with him. They were stowed in trunks large enough to be carried by a pack horse."

Ron Patterson was in his element telling stories about Lewis and Clark, and it showed on his face. He had become quite a popular and sought-after tour guide for travelers who wanted to spend their vacations hiking the same trails that Lewis and Clark had traversed. He had also once led floats down the Missouri River for the more adventurous souls, though a recent heart scare and surgically implanted pacemaker had curtailed these more strenuous activities considerably.

"Now, this is where it gets interesting," he continued. "Along the way, Lewis stopped for the night at a place called Grinder's Inn located just south of Nashville. It was here that, according to official accounts, he put a gun to his head and took his own life. But many people believe he didn't commit suicide." He paused dramatically before concluding, "They believe Meriwether Lewis was *murdered.*"

"Murdered?" Ally gasped, "Why?"

"Good question," Patterson replied. "Some people think he was killed for his journals. They believe Lewis was murdered and that some of the journals were stolen—purportedly to keep the information they contained a secret. These conspiracy-theory believers claim the set of eighteen small notebooks filled with meticulous observations and artful sketches that have survived to this day are, in fact, incomplete. They insist at least one or maybe more of the books are missing."

"Are you implying that one of these missing journals could have contained the story about the black tribe and the conquistador helmet?" Ally asked. "But why would anyone want to keep that a secret?"

Ron chuckled. "I'm a historian, not a conspiracy theorist, Ally. But I must admit, given what you told me today, it's something to ponder," he said.

For every step forward, Matt felt they seemed to take another step back. "I plan to do more than just ponder," Matt said, feeling the familiar sense of frustration returning once again.

Matt was not the most patient of men. He liked to make fast decisions and he thrived on progressing toward an end goal. It was why he had been such a successful bond trader back in his Wall Street days. His trades weren't always winners, but his ability to synthesize information quickly and act with confidence had more often than not helped him come out on top. But now he was in a situation where he didn't have all the information he needed to draw an informed conclusion. And this put him at a severe disadvantage. He knew he needed to do something to tip the scales in his favor—and for Matt that usually meant taking action.

"What do you mean by that, Matt? Ally asked, confused.

"I mean we're going back to Ghost Ridge."

"But how, with Spate's men and the res police crawling all over the place?" she asked.

"I haven't gotten that far yet, Ally, but we've got to try," Matt answered, "because I think the answers to all our questions are somewhere out in those hills."

12

Present Day

Great Falls, Montana

The MacKenzie River Pizza Company was conveniently located right next door to the hotel where Matt had reserved two rooms for the night. They were sitting on the outside patio facing the Missouri River.

By the time the pizza arrived they each had already finished two local craft beers. Matt smiled as he watched Ally down her first slice in record time. She ripped a second one free and dropped it on her plate. She was tiny, at no more than five feet two inches tall, but she ate like a truck driver. He wondered how she maintained her petite figure. He found himself wanting to know more about her.

"Hey, I told you my story but I don't know anything about you," Matt prodded. He wiped red sauce from the corner of his mouth with a napkin.

On the ride down to Great Falls he had shared an abridged version of his background with her. That he was a transplanted Yankee living in Savannah, Georgia, and the proud owner of a fixer-upper mansion that doubled as an antiques shop. He also told her how he had achieved his quasi-famous status as an amateur historian.

"There's not much to tell, really," she answered evasively.

"Come on, Ally. Everyone's got a past. If you don't open up you're going to have to fight me for that last piece of pizza," he teased, just as she took a big bite out of another slice.

That brought a smile of embarrassment to her face. "Oh God," she said through a mouthful of food, "sorry." She swallowed hard. "My grandfather always told me I eat like a man. I just get so hungry, you know what I mean?"

Matt laughed. "It's fine, you don't have to apologize. I just wonder where you put it all," he said, eyeing her small physique.

"Fast metabolism, I guess." She smiled.

"So, anyway, tell me your story. We're not leaving here until you do," he said, while flashing his trademark crooked grin. Matt had a way of getting people to talk—especially if he was interested in them. He had a natural magnetism that people found difficult to say no to—especially people of the opposite sex.

"Alright, alright, but it's really not that exciting. I'm an only child, born and raised on the reservation. Unfortunately," her voice dropped, "my folks were killed in a car accident when I was in high school. After they died, I lived with my grandfather, Crooked Nose, until I went to college."

"I'm sorry. That must have been hard, especially as a high school kid."

"It was. It's been fifteen years and I still think about them every day. But I'm lucky to have Charlie in my life. I don't know what I'd do without him."

Matt now understood why she was so determined to keep her grandfather out of harm's way. "So where did you go to college?" he asked.

"I got a scholarship to the University of Montana in Missoula. I studied nursing and came back to the reservation. Got a job working at a 24-hour medical clinic in Browning. Remember I told you that I worked nights—that's why. Nights are the busiest. We get knife wounds from bar fights, domestic abuse cases, and lots of drunk-driving accidents. Never a dull moment," she sighed before adding, "I'm sure you've heard that alcoholism is a huge problem on the res."

Matt nodded. "So why did you come back?" he asked. "You could've gotten a job as a nurse anywhere."

"I thought about it, believe me. But the res is my home," she said, "and there was also this guy," she admitted.

"Ah, the high school sweetheart," Matt said.

"Something like that. We were young and stupid and got married way too soon. Thank God we never had any children. That would have made it tougher to end it."

"So it's over?"

"Way over."

"Do you mind if I ask what happened?"

"He was there when I needed a friend, right after my parents died. It was great for a while. We had our blow-ups, of course, especially when I was away at college. Roy was insanely jealous and put constant pressure on me to come home. He got a good job as a mechanic and had saved up enough money to buy us a little house. So after I graduated, I came home. But the honeymoon was short-lived," she said, shaking her head at the bad memories.

"Does he still live on the res?"

Ally's eyes hardened just for a moment. Matt took notice.

He held up his hands and said, "Hey, if this is too personal, I understand."

"No, it's OK." She shrugged. "You'll probably find out eventually."

"Find out what?"

"Well," she said quietly, "I kind of shot him."

"Oh," Matt said. Then he added sarcastically, "Ally, you *kind* of feel like eating pizza or you *kind of* feel like going to the movies—but you don't *kind of* shoot somebody."

He smiled empathetically. "So what happened?"

"He started drinking. Shocker, I know. Anyway, we fought about it a lot and then it started to get physical. Stupidly, I let the abuse go on for too long. Then one night he took it too far and I just snapped. I'd had enough." She was lost in her thoughts for a moment before continuing, "He passed out on the couch. I got his 20-gauge shotgun, loaded it, and pulled the trigger—shot him right there in our living room," she said somberly.

Most of the patrons had long since paid their bills and left, leaving Matt and Ally alone on the outdoor deck. He couldn't see the river because it was obscured by a stand of trees. But he could hear a faint whooshing sound as it rolled past where they sat. Finally, he asked tentatively, "Did you kill him?"

"Oh God, no," Ally said emphatically. "Evidently the cartridge was a lighter gauge—used for hunting birds, I guess," she explained. "Plus, I was aiming a little lower than his heart." A half-smile appeared around the edges of her mouth. "Let's just say he's playing with one less marble these days."

"Ouch." Matt winced, instinctively reaching for his groin. "I guess he had it coming, though."

"You have no idea," she said seriously. Then she added more lightheartedly, "Guess who had to stitch him up later that night at the clinic?"

"You did not," Matt said, smiling in disbelief.

"Oh yes I did. Not surprisingly, the divorce came quickly after that—at his request." She smiled and downed the last of her beer.

"I bet," Matt said, shaking his head in amazement. *There is no denying it, Alsoomse is one hell of an independent woman.*

Back at the hotel, Matt decided to have a nightcap at the hotel bar. Ally declined, saying she was exhausted. She took the elevator up to her room. After ordering a whiskey, Matt took out his phone and dialed David Becker's number. It was a little late back east, but he wanted to see if the *New York Times* investigative reporter had dug anything up on Spate Industries.

"Matt, I'm glad you called. I was going to call you in the morning," Becker said enthusiastically.

"Great, what'd you find out?" Matt replied eagerly.

"Landon and Oliver Spate, the two brothers who run Spate Industries, are not your average corporate titans, I can tell you that."

"How so?"

"Well, for starters, their old man was a dyed-in-the-wool anti-communist and an original member of the John Birch Society. He was a real piece of work. Radical right wing all the way—thought the government was run by a bunch of leftists, wanted the New Deal dismantled, fought against the civil rights movement, and felt most federal programs should be gutted. He believed in a Libertarian utopia, where businesses and individuals would be free to do just about anything without government interference."

"Sounds like a pretty convenient philosophy for the CEO of a multibillion-dollar oil company," Matt interjected.

"Without a doubt," Becker agreed. "In fact, he went out of his way to rail on government oversight agencies like the Environmental Protection Agency, the Securities and Exchange Commission, and even the Federal Bureau of Investigation. He claimed they infringed upon the free market economy that the country was founded on. In fact, he believed most all government agencies should be eliminated. As you said, these views were clearly self-serving to someone focused on the profitable bottom line. But make no mistake, he was fervent in his beliefs."

"I don't doubt it," Matt said. "So where is he now?"

"He's been dead for forty years," Becker replied. "His sons, Oliver and Landon, have run the company ever since. And believe it or not, they're even scarier than their father."

"Why's that?"

"Well, let's just say that *ideologically*, the apple didn't fall too far from the tree. But *practically*, the approach of the sons has been much more subtle. And, frankly, much more effective," Becker explained. "They realized early on one of their father's biggest mistakes was that he and his Bircher cronies didn't sow the seeds of a credible message at the local level. There were too many chiefs and not enough Indians. So they made sure not to repeat that same mistake."

He continued, "It's only recently been reported by the mainstream press that the Spates are the money behind a vast and sophisticated network of grassroots political organizations. Like the Birchers, these organizations manipulate facts and stretch the truth to further the Spates' radical personal agenda. But the difference is many Americans falsely believe these groups are independent and therefore credible. So their radical message has actually started to gain a following."

"Jesus, that's a little scary," Matt mumbled.

"It's more than a little scary, Matt, because it's working. They're starting to sway public opinion, and their candidates are winning at the polls. And *that* makes the Spate boys a hell of a lot more dangerous than their old man."

"Dangerous?" Matt asked, still trying to comprehend the bigger picture.

"Two spectacularly rich zealots with radical antigovernment views who are highly organized qualify as dangerous in my book. And I'm not the only one who thinks so. Now that the curtain has been pulled back a little bit on the Spates' grassroots machinery, the political mainstream is pulling their heads out of their asses and starting to take notice. And what they're seeing scares the hell out of them."

"With Spates' money and their extreme politics, I can see why. But why are they doing all of this? I mean, what's the Spates' endgame?" Matt asked.

"That's the sixty-four-thousand-dollar question, and one I don't have a ready answer for. Even with the revelations from the most recent publicity, still not much is known about Landon and Oliver Spate. They purposely keep a very low profile. But I'm telling you, they are not to be underestimated. They will absolutely play dirty if anyone gets in their way—just ask their younger brother."

"Wait, there's another brother?" Matt asked, confused.

"Yup—Harry, the self-proclaimed black sheep of the family. Evidently, younger brother Harry didn't share his brothers' increasingly radical views. So about twelve years ago, Oliver and Landon coerced the company's board of directors into buying him out. He lives on an island somewhere now, collecting art and staying as far away from his estranged siblings as possible."

"And I thought my family was dysfunctional," Matt said sarcastically.

"No kidding," Becker agreed. "But I haven't even told you the juiciest detail."

"Well, shit, David, don't hold out on me," Matt said, his interest piqued.

"I was curious to see where the Spate family money originally came from so I began to go further back in time," Becker began. "It wasn't easy because the family tree got a little convoluted in the late nineteenth century. But what I discovered was that the Spates' forefathers didn't make their original fortune in oil." He paused. "You're never going to guess what industry it came from."

"David," Matt shouted impatiently.

"Alright, are you ready for this?" Becker toyed with Matt one last time before finally revealing the answer. "The *fur* trade."

"The fur trade? Are you kidding me?"

"Believe it or not, the family patriarch, a character named Jedediah Spate, signed an exclusive agreement with President Thomas Jefferson in 1809. This agreement gave Jedediah Spate exclusive rights to open up the northwest fur trade all the way out to the Pacific Ocean."

"Holy shit," Matt blurted out.

"That simple but powerful agreement made Jedediah Spate millions of dollars—and set the Spate family up financially for generations." Becker continued, "Over the years, as the fur trade declined, the family diversified into real estate. Turns out they didn't get into the oil business until the early part of the twentieth century.

"But it gets even better," Becker said. Then he paused before dropping the final bombshell. "The fur trade route to the Pacific Ocean went right through the middle of Blackfeet country, in northwest Montana."

There was silence for a good thirty seconds—so long that Becker had to ask if Matt was still there.

"I'm here," Matt said. His mind was spinning with the new information. Finally, he said, "Son of a bitch, the Spate family connection to that land goes back more than two centuries, not just thirty or forty years."

"That's right. They were there long before the U.S. government ever created the Blackfeet Reservation," Becker said.

"Goddamn, David, this is the connection we've been looking for," he said excitedly. "I suspected they were hiding something out in those foothills, and now I'm sure of it."

"Yeah, but what?" Becker asked as if to remind his friend they

still had no clue what Spate Industries was so determined to keep
hidden from them.

"I have no idea, but I intend to find out," Matt replied with
renewed determination.

By the time he got up to his room, Matt was so pumped up that
sleep was out of the question. Instead, he surfed the Internet doing
his own research on the Spate family. That's when another anonymous e-mail appeared in his Inbox. He opened it apprehensively
and read the single line. It said:

Big Tom's death was no accident. A. Friend

13

January 1, 1807
Charlottesville, Virginia

The private library at Thomas Jefferson's Monticello home was the largest of its kind in the United States at that time. More than six thousand volumes lined the shelves that ran from floor to ceiling and covered every inch of wall space in his custom-built study. Even more impressive was that this was Jefferson's second library collection. His first had been lost in a fire when his family's home burned to the ground almost forty years earlier.

Monticello itself was a lifelong labor of love for Jefferson. The home was situated in the small town of Charlottesville on the summit of an 850-foot-high peak with extensive views of the Blue Ridge Mountains. He had begun building his plantation home in 1769 and was only now completing its interior. His responsibilities to his country as secretary of state, vice president, and finally as president had prohibited him from spending as much time as he would have liked on its completion. And continuous redesigns based on his ever-changing architectural tastes had also caused countless delays.

Meriwether Lewis had at long last returned to Monticello after almost four years away—and Jefferson was ecstatic. Lewis had once *served as Jefferson's personal secretary shortly after his inauguration in 1801. During this time, the two men spent a lot of time together. They ate together, spent the evenings together, and attended functions in each other's company. A special bond formed between the two men during this time, one that played a large part in Jefferson choosing Lewis to lead the expedition to explore the American West. Before embarking on his cross-continent journey, Lewis had spent months living in Jefferson's home, being personally tutored and mentored by the president. The two had spent countless hours poring over books on navigation, botany, and geography—in addition to reviewing an exhaustive set of instructions listing all the things the president wanted to know about the unexplored western territory.*

Finally back at Monticello, Lewis had spent the better part of the afternoon regaling the president with extraordinary tales from his adventurous trek in search of the Northwest Passage. Jefferson's disappointment with the news that no such water route existed was quickly replaced with fascination at the many discoveries Lewis shared with him. The wildlife the expedition encountered, the natural wonders they observed, and, of course, the diverse number of Indian tribes whom they had met along the way.

After an early dinner, the two men, glasses of wine in hand, returned to Jefferson's library suite to continue their discussion in private. Jefferson desperately wanted to see the map of the western two-thirds of the continent Captain Clark had rendered. He was more than curious to understand exactly what he had acquired from Napoleon when the United States purchased the Louisiana territory for $15 million in 1803. Equally important to him was to understand the geography of the extreme northwest that lay beyond the boundaries of the Louisiana Territory. Jefferson knew an accurate and detailed map would be critical if the United States were to capitalize on the profitable fur trade the West could provide. That's why he tasked the two leaders of the Corps of Discovery—Meriwether Lewis and William

Clark—to keep detailed journals, maps, and drawings of exactly what they saw and whom they encountered along their route.

When at last Lewis revealed Captain Clark's map of the western territories, Jefferson could no longer contain himself. The country's third president got down on his hands and knees so he could examine the meticulously rendered four-foot-wide map more closely. Lewis had no choice but to join his sixty-three-year-old mentor on the floor of the president's personal library.

"You must pass along my compliments to Captain Clark. This is an exquisitely drawn map," Jefferson said, as he studied the paper laid out in front of him.

The president continued to intently study Clark's graphic representation of the northwestern United States. As he did so, he conjured images in his own mind of the glorious country he so wished he could see for himself. He noted every last detail and asked dozens of clarifying questions of Lewis.

Finally, Lewis felt it time to discuss another matter of great import to both men—the fur trade. "Sir," he began, "I believe we have found a superior route for transporting furs from America to the Orient."

Up to that point, the British had controlled much of the North American fur trade. The Hudson's Bay Company and the Northwest Company gathered furs throughout the Canadian northwest and shipped them east to Montreal. Eventually, they were shipped across the Atlantic to London, before making their way to their final destination, the Orient. Lewis's proposal was intended to usurp Britain's control over the fur trade. It involved shipping furs from the interior of the United States westward over the mountains and down the Columbia River. They would then be shipped directly across the Pacific Ocean to the Canton market—effectively cutting the British out of the American commercial fur trade altogether. The furs would arrive in the Orient not only faster but also in better condition, ensuring the American's goods would command a premium price. Lewis shared all this with Jefferson and awaited his response.

Jefferson considered his young protégé's bold plan in silence for a few moments. Finally, a smile began to play at the corners of the president's mouth. He leaned over and clapped Lewis on the shoulders and said, "I think it's a brilliant plan, son."

Lewis smiled broadly, as he so yearned for the respect and admiration of Jefferson, who was like a father to him.

"This will take the sting out of not finding a Northwest Passage waterway," Jefferson noted. "You know my detractors in Congress are waiting to seize upon my every failure. But the profits that will surely come with cornering the fur trade market will silence their criticisms."

"There is one thing, sir," Lewis added hesitantly.

"What troubles you, my boy—your plan seems quite sound."

"The Indians, sir, they could present a problem," Lewis stated.

"But you said yourself most of the tribes and their chiefs are friendly and willing to trade with us," Jefferson replied.

"They are," he paused. "But there is one tribe I have not yet mentioned."

"Please continue, Meriwether," Jefferson said with a hint of concern, "you mustn't leave anything out."

"Very well, sir," Lewis said. He took a deep breath and began, "Towards the end of the expedition, I was on a solo hike when I was attacked by a tribe of Indians unlike any I had ever encountered."

Lewis went on to tell Jefferson about his capture by a tribe of black Indians. He told Jefferson of their aggressive nature, the color of their skin, and their European mannerisms. He spoke uninterrupted for twenty minutes, stopping only after telling Jefferson the story of how he had escaped by breaking free from the ties that bound his hands and feet. How he had slipped away unnoticed in the middle of the night and traversed rugged country for hours without stopping. Miraculously, he had somehow made it back to his men.

Jefferson's brow remained furrowed long after Lewis had finished talking. Lewis had seen this intense concentration on the face of the president before, and he knew better than to interrupt him.

Finally, Jefferson spoke up, "You say these men looked like Negroes?"

"Yes, sir, jet-black skin and kinky hair—very similar in appearance to the slaves you have here at Monticello."

The president seemed slightly rankled by the comment, but he recovered and said, "Could these be Maroons?" he asked.

Jefferson had grown up hearing stories of escaped slaves, or "Maroons," as they had been labeled. These slaves escaped from southern plantations and established "free colonies" in the Great Dismal Swamp in the southeastern portion of his home state of Virginia. Hundreds of runaway slaves had found their way to these colonies, choosing to live in the brutal conditions of the swamp rather than being forced to live a life of captivity on a plantation.

"I couldn't say, sir, but some of their words sounded familiar—not English mind you, but unlike any Indian dialect I've ever heard."

"This is unsettling, to say the least," Jefferson muttered, absently rubbing his chin with the fingers of his right hand.

As a southern plantation owner, the fear of slave uprisings was never too far removed from Jefferson's thoughts. During his first term as president he had supported Napoleon's efforts to quell a rebellion on the island of Saint-Domingue, a French colony. A part of him feared a successful rebellion on a nearby island would embolden slaves in the United States. On a personal level, Jefferson had accumulated much of his personal wealth by the use of slave labor. And emancipation of any kind would be disastrous to his financial well-being.

"Clearly, this Negro tribe must be dealt with," he stated ominously.

"I agree, sir. That's why I propose we send a party to negotiate an agreement to access their lands," Lewis replied.

"Negotiate? We do not negotiate with the Negro," he raised his voice in anger. Lewis was shocked into silence by Jefferson's outburst.

Seeing the look on Lewis's face, Jefferson softened his tone, "Nego-

tiating with the Indians is one thing. They are noble savages who I believe can be civilized—and in time, even become full citizens. But the Negro is a different beast altogether. They are incapable of higher learning. And besides, they're lazy and prone to thievery."

"So what do you propose we do, sir?"

"They are clearly a threat and must be dealt with as such. Let me think on it." Then he brightened and said, "But let this not dampen our mood. Please, show me the rest of this marvelous map."

But as Lewis returned to Clark's hand-drawn map, Jefferson's brilliant mind remained distracted by the troublesome Negro tribe.

14

Present Day

Montana

They were traveling close to one hundred twenty knots and Matt's stomach was flopping around like a fish on dry land. It wasn't so much the speed that was making him nauseous; it was the choppy air. They were being buffeted around inside the hot cabin like kernels in a popcorn maker. He swore to himself, as he listened to the never-ending *whoomp, whoomp, whoomp* of the rotor blades above his head, this was going to be both the first and last time he ever stepped foot inside a helicopter.

It had all started with a phone call from Ron Patterson, the Lewis and Clark expert they had met a few days earlier. He had come up with an idea. At Patterson's request, the two men had met for lunch at Bert and Ernie's, a throwback downtown Great Falls tavern. Over burgers and fries, the enthusiastic Lewis and Clark expert had shared his thoughts.

"I was reading a fascinating article yesterday on the ancient sites of Machu Picchu in Peru," Patterson chatted excitedly. "Archaeologists are trying to map some of the original trails used by the Incas more than a thousand years ago."

"Mm hmm," Matt said while taking a big bite out of his bacon cheeseburger.

"Evidently, this particular area was in a rugged mountainous zone, with deep valleys and steeply sloped peaks. Some of the ridges there can climb to an altitude of more than twenty thousand feet."

"Uh-huh," Matt nodded politely.

Patterson took a big swig of iced tea before continuing, "So, naturally, I thought of the foothills on the Blackfeet Reservation—Ghost Ridge, I think you called it—you were so interested in exploring."

"I'm sorry, Ron, but I'm not sure I'm following you," he replied, reaching for a French fry.

"You see," Ron continued, undeterred, "most of the Peruvian slopes and ridges are covered with dense clouds and thick forest vegetation all the way up to almost twelve thousand feet. As you can imagine, this makes it very difficult and time-consuming to perform archaeological digs. So before they commit to putting a team on the ground, they do aerial reconnaissance first."

"What kind of reconnaissance?" Matt perked up.

"This is where it gets interesting. They use remote sensing cameras that let you see ancient landmarks, like roads, causeways, settlement patterns, and other man-made structures that aren't visible from the ground. They allow you to pinpoint and study features that over the centuries have become hidden *beneath* the ground."

"Very cool," Matt admitted.

"I thought so, too. Then I remembered you and Ally telling me about how the res police wouldn't allow you to access the land where the helmet was found. It occurred to me an aerial reconnaissance of this type might be a way around that obstacle. You could do your snooping from a couple of thousand feet up in the air." He smiled conspiratorially.

Matt knew he had found a kindred spirit in the ebullient Lewis and Clark expert the minute he had met him. He laughed and said, "I like your way of thinking Ron. It's brilliant."

"I don't know about brilliant. But I was just so excited the other night after you told me the story about Meriwether Lewis and those field notes you found I couldn't sleep. So I picked up a magazine and came across this article on remote sensing cameras. It was almost as if the hand of fate was somehow involved. And naturally, I thought to call you," Patterson said.

"I'm glad you did. But there's one problem; actually a couple of problems. I don't have a remote sensing camera and I don't have a plane," he said dejectedly.

"Hope is not lost, my young friend," Patterson said brightly. "You think I'd bring you an idea without a plan to execute it?" his voice raised an octave. "Now that would be downright cruel, wouldn't it?" He smiled broadly.

Matt smiled back and said, "I'm all ears, Ron. What've you got?"

That was two days ago. And the way Matt felt now, bouncing around in the helicopter, he almost wished he had skipped that lunch with Ron Patterson.

"You don't look so good," Ally's voice came through the headset. She wore a concerned look.

"I'll be alright, but you better have a barf bag ready just in case." Matt tried to smile, but his attempt at humor did nothing to alleviate his misery.

"Never been up in one of these before?" she asked.

"No, it's my first time, and probably my last," he muttered. "How does all this bumping around not bother you?" Matt remarked, noticing how nonchalant Ally appeared to be. He couldn't be sure, but she looked like she was enjoying herself.

"Oh, it's not that bad, and the view is so beautiful," she said. "Oh look, there's Chief Mountain," she yelled like a little kid, pointing out of the cabin window. She had been shouting out landmarks nonstop as they began approaching the Blackfeet Reservation.

Despite feeling like shit, Matt had to smile at her enthusiasm.

"Almost there," came the voice of Stu Patterson, Ron's forty-two-year-old son, from the pilot's seat of the chopper.

"Thank God." Matt breathed.

Stu Patterson had recently retired from the air force after getting his twenty years in. He now worked for a local tour operator based in Great Falls. They specialized in outdoor adventures—everything from white-water rafting to mountain climbing to helicopter tours. That had taken care of problem number one for Matt—access to a helicopter.

Acquiring a thermal imaging camera had been the second obstacle, but Stu solved that one as well. Evidently, he had been stationed for a time at Malmstrom Air Force Base in Great Falls and still had a lot of friends there. A buddy let him borrow one of the military's state-of-the-art cameras used for remote sensing. That's how, less than forty-eight hours after meeting with Ron, Matt found himself flying a couple of thousand feet above the reservation.

Suddenly Ally shouted, "There's Ghost Ridge."

A shot of adrenaline surged through Matt's veins. He sat up straighter in his seat and peered intently out the window.

"I'll mark that ridge as ground zero. Reduce our speed and begin a search grid." Stu's voice sounded tinny through the headsets. "We'll be taking continuous video as well as snapshot photos every ten seconds," he explained. The sophisticated thermal imaging equipment was strapped to a steel framework suspended just below the nose of the helicopter. It could be controlled remotely.

"So how do these cameras work?" Ally asked the senior Patterson.

"Well, I'm no engineer, but from what I've read they are able to detect minute temperature changes related to the things we humans leave behind," Ron explained. "By using thermal imaging they can pinpoint where soils have been artificially disturbed by humans—because different layers of soil will hold water differently."

Stu chimed in, "My buddy on the base who lent us the camera said this particular device has an imager so sensitive it can detect a one-degree heat differential from as far as ten thousand feet away. Of course we'll be less than two thousand feet away, so that should increase its effectiveness."

"Wow, pretty impressive," Ally replied.

"So what will we see once the images get developed?" Matt asked.

"The way I understand it, traces of past activities, like an agriculture field or buried stone architecture, will appear as a different color on the pictures. Stu's friend will use a sophisticated computer program to create visualizations of the data. Any anomalies revealed will represent areas of interest."

"So we'll be looking for a particular color to appear on the images?" Matt replied.

"Exactly, the ground surrounding a target of interest will register slightly warmer on the sensing spectrum than the section of terrain that has not been disturbed by humans. Therefore, it will appear more red than blue."

"You've done your homework, Mr. Patterson," Ally exclaimed, impressed with his knowledge.

"I have read a lot over the past twenty-four hours, that's for sure."

"Thanks again for arranging all of this," Matt said.

"Not at all, Matt, I'm as excited to find something out here as you are. After all, if the history surrounding Lewis and Clark's expedition is going to be rewritten, then I want to be a part of it." Patterson breathed heavily into the headset.

The cabin went quiet for a time as the chopper crisscrossed the western foothills of the Blackfeet Reservation, continuing along its grid-like search pattern. Everyone was lost in thought. Matt had finally grown more accustomed to the back-and-forth movement of the helicopter and didn't feel nearly as sick. He was peering out the window when a thought suddenly occurred to him.

"Hey, Ally," he said into his headset.

"Yes," she replied.

"Do you notice anything unusual out your side?"

"Not really. There's nothing but rocky hills and valleys straight out to the eastern entrance of Glacier Park."

"Huh, I guess you were right then."

"Right about what?"

"About Spate Industries. I haven't seen a single oil derrick."

She nodded in understanding. "Like I said to you, Matt, that's the strangest part about all of this, they've never even *tried* to find oil out here."

"I understand that now. It's just that seeing it with my own eyes makes it very real. And it makes me very nervous. Because they've gone to a hell of a lot of trouble to keep something out here a secret," he said anxiously. "Whatever it is they're guarding has to be incredibly important to them."

They had no idea that at that exact moment in the hills two thousand feet below them there was someone watching. He had been tracking their helicopter through high-powered binoculars ever since it had first arrived.

15

Present Day

Great Falls, Montana

They gathered around a computer in Ron Patterson's office at the Lewis and Clark Interpretive Center. The first images began to scroll across the screen. At first, it was difficult to interpret the meaning of the thermal photographs because the colors appeared rather haphazard, as if they had been smeared on the page by a kindergartner playing with finger paints. They printed out dozens of photos and spread them on top of a large conference table. When they were finished, the table looked like a large abstract work of art splashed in hues of blue, green, yellow, and red.

It wasn't until they compared the color printouts to a set of topographical maps that the story began to unfold. After establishing exactly which part of Ghost Ridge each of the thermal photographs corresponded to, they began to focus their search.

"Remember, the areas of interest will appear more red, since thermally speaking, the color red signals a warmer underground area. These will be the areas that, at one point in history, have been disturbed or modified by humans," Patterson explained.

"There are a lot more red areas than I expected, Ron. Where do we begin?" Ally asked.

"Look for patterns," Matt answered, before the Lewis and Clark authority had a chance to respond.

Ally raised her eyebrows. She smiled and teased, "Since when did you become such an expert?"

Matt smiled back and said, "I did a little online research of my own last night after getting back from our 'hurlicopter' ride." Matt had created the nickname for the helicopter after unceremoniously vomiting into a paper bag on the return flight to Great Falls.

"I'm surprised you could see straight when you got back to the hotel. You didn't look so good, especially after your 'walk of shame.'" Ally stifled a chuckle.

When they had landed back in Great Falls the day before, Stu, the pilot had insisted it was a rite of passage for the offender to carry his own barf bag off the plane. The crew was in hysterics when Matt had crossed the very public tarmac and tossed the full bag into a large dumpster.

"Very funny, smart-ass," Matt cracked, still slightly embarrassed. "Anyway," he quickly changed the subject, "what I learned was it's not just the color red we should be looking for, but rather defined patterns of red, right Ron?" Matt looked over at Ron Patterson.

"That's exactly right. We humans tend to build things in a linear fashion—in straight lines and with defined edges," Patterson explained. "Like roads, villages, and dwellings. So we should be looking for red images with a defined shape or signature."

They laid more photos onto the table so they now had an even larger colorful thermal swath of Ghost Ridge spread out in front of them. They studied the images intently.

"Look over there," Ally suddenly spoke up. She was pointing toward the left corner of the conference table, to an area on the map that corresponded to the northwest section of Ghost Ridge, abutting Glacier National Park. "You see these straight lines," she said as she walked around the table and placed her index finger on one of the printed images, "these don't look like they were made by Mother Nature."

"I think you're right, Ally," Patterson exclaimed. "See how defined this edge is relative to this one." He pointed to a blotchy red image on a different printed image.

"And look here," Ally continued, "there's another red line running parallel to the first one, maybe sixty yards away."

The two men stared at the photos. "It's hard to make out, but I believe these are adjacent corners here and here," Patterson was talking more to himself now. Then all of a sudden he blurted out, "Well, I'll be damned."

"What do you see?" Matt and Ally asked in unison.

Patterson picked up a grease pen and ruler from the table and started to draw directly onto the printed color images. "If I connect these two parallel lines…" the pen squeaked loudly on the glossy paper, "and this edge to this edge…" he pulled his hands away, "we have a perfect rectangular shape." He was smiling broadly now.

"What does it mean?" Ally asked, confused.

"Son of a bitch," Matt exclaimed as the realization struck him. He looked across at Patterson, "There used to be a fort on that land, didn't there?"

"Apparently so," Patterson replied. "I can think of nothing else that would be this size and shape other than an enclosure. Or, as you say, a fort."

"But how is that possible?" Ally asked, "I know for a fact the Blackfeet never built any forts. And you guys told me there were no Americans or Europeans out this far west until Lewis and Clark got here in the early 1800s."

Nobody had an answer for the undeniable thermal facts that lay on the table in front of them.

"Maybe it was built sometime later in the 1800s," Matt posited.

"Well, I suppose there is that possibility," Patterson admitted. "But I know the history of this state better than most. And I can assure you there is no record of a fort ever being built close to that area."

Matt exhaled loudly and said, "So we've got a fort built in the middle of nowhere but we have no idea who built it?"

"I'm afraid so. And you can look at all the thermal images you want to, but the only way you're ever going to peel back the layers of this mystery is to do a little 'ground truthing.'"

"A little what?" Ally asked.

"Sorry, I'm just showing off," Patterson admitted with a sly grin. "It's a term I picked up from my research on remote sensing. It means the process of physically visiting the locality."

"Meaning what, exactly," she countered.

"Meaning you and I have to find a way to get on that land and do a little investigating up close and personal—on foot," Matt said.

Ally didn't hesitate for a second. "I'm game, Matt," she said, "but Spates' men may not be too thrilled with the idea."

They broke for lunch and came back ready to tackle a number of problems. First, they needed to find a way to gain access to Ghost Ridge. Then they would have to perform a hasty archaeological dig. And finally, they would have to leave. And all without being detected.

The group had shot down a number of ideas as either implausible or too dangerous. Matt was frustrated and running low on patience. Finally, Ally offered up another solution.

"Why not hike in from the Glacier National Park side?" she said.

"Hike in?" Matt asked with a quizzical look.

"Yeah, the site is located right on the border of the park. Spates' men have complete control over the eastern side, but the western approach is relatively unguarded, because that land is the property of the U.S. government."

"That's an interesting idea, Ally," Patterson offered.

"I agree, but that's a long hike in," Matt said, referring back to the topographical maps. "It looks like the road closest to the site ends here—at least ten miles to the west of the fort site." He pointed to the spot with his index finger.

"I never said it would be easy," Ally said with a smile. "We'll need a permit and it will definitely be a hike. But I've got a connection in the National Park Service. I can make a call and see what kind of help he can provide us. So what do you think?" she asked Matt, an eager intensity blazing in her eyes.

"I think it's the best idea I've heard yet," Matt had to agree.

"I concur. But with my ticker acting up, my wife has asked me to cut back on the long hikes. I'm going to have to sit this one out," Patterson said with a look of rejection. "But I'm willing to help out. Just let me know what I can do."

"You've done more than enough already, Ron. We can't thank you enough," Matt replied.

"It's decided then. Let me make a call to the park service office and see if I can reach my park ranger friend," Ally said excitedly. She pulled her cell phone out and started to dial.

Patterson turned to Matt and said, "I think you'll need a couple of backpacks just in case you find anything of interest. And you better bring sleeping bags and some provisions. Depending on your progress, you may have to camp for the night, and it can get pretty cool out there in the evenings." Then he added, "Don't worry, I can supply you with everything you'll need. I take small groups who want to retrace Lewis and Clark's steps out camping all the time. Let me see what I can muster."

Before Matt could reply, the enthusiastic expert was hurrying out the door to begin rounding up the necessary gear.

16

Present Day

Glacier National Park, Montana

The bill to establish Glacier National Park was signed into law on May 11, 1910, by President William Howard Taft. Before that date and even for years afterward, due to its remote location, very few Americans had ever set foot inside its sixteen-thousand-square-mile boundaries. Today, it was still one of the most pristine places in North America—primarily because no major areas of dense population existed anywhere near the park. The Crown of the Continent, as it had been dubbed, remained one of the largest and most intact ecosystems in North America. In fact, almost all of its original native plant and animal species could still be found within its one-million-plus acres.

Matt had read about the history of Glacier National Park in a handful of pamphlets he had picked up in St. Mary's, a town just outside the eastern entrance to the park. He and Ally had passed through there earlier that morning on their way to meet up with Ally's park ranger contact. He knew most of what he had read he could have picked up on the Internet, but it wouldn't have been the same. To Matt, there was nothing like flipping through local tourist literature to get a real feel for a place.

Matt had not been prepared for the beauty of Glacier Park. Around every bend in the road was another craggy peak that reached six or seven thousand feet in the air, or another icy lake, some with depths of more than four hundred feet. *How the hell did I find myself here?* But he knew full well he had been hooked the minute Buzz and Fox shared with him their discovery of Meriwether Lewis's lost field notes. His need to solve the puzzle and his impulsive nature had taken over from there.

He had always been that way, driven to find the answers to questions, to solve the unsolvable. His natural curiosity had helped him excel in school, earning him a scholarship to Brown University. It had also served him well on Wall Street where he had created algorithmic, high-frequency trading applications for bonds; an innovation that helped the firm capture millions of dollars in trading efficiencies. A by-product of his curiosity, however, was his impulsiveness, which had gotten him into trouble on more than one occasion. Evidence included a failed marriage, a dilapidated mansion in Savannah, and a '66 Chevy truck that spent more time in the shop than on the road. A more rational man would never have tolerated these imperfections in his life. *Screw it, where's the fun in that.*

He was having a hard time grasping the scale of this part of the country, which was dominated by mountains carved into their present gloriousness by glaciers from the last ice age. He had spent his entire life as an East Coast guy, born and raised in the quaintness of a New England shipping village just north of Boston. When he traveled, it was limited mostly to the confines of large cities. This was different. As Ally navigated their car through the park, Matt's nose remained glued to his window as the majestic scenery scrolled by.

Sensing his awe, Ally said, "Kind of takes your breath away, doesn't it?"

"It's amazing," he replied.

She had to smile at Matt. He was certainly a contrast in styles. He could be tough and stubborn, yet he had a sensitive side she found intriguing. She glanced over at him staring out the window like an adolescent boy, and said, "Growing up in this area, you forget how beautiful it is. I guess you take it for granted after a while."

"I know, when I lived in New York City, I used to laugh at the tourists gawking at the skyscrapers. Now look at me."

They rounded the next bend in the road and a magnificent historic hotel came into view. It looked like it had been plucked right out of the Swiss Alps and dropped down inside the park. The hotel had a chalet design and hugged the eastern shore of a sizable lake. The foundation was made of stone with a wood superstructure. And an expansive balcony ran the entire length of the building, so guests could enjoy the spectacular views of the pristine lake below them and the snow-capped mountains emanating out in every direction.

"Wow," Matt exclaimed.

"This is Many Glacier Hotel," Ally said. "It was built by the Great Northern Railway and was completed in 1915. Back then, only the wealthiest could afford to stay here."

"I'm beginning to think Glacier Park is America's best-kept secret," Matt said. "I wish we could look around some more." Then he turned to Ally, and in a serious tone added, "But unfortunately we don't have the time. So where are we meeting this guy—Bobby was it?"

"His friends call him Bear," Ally said. "He's the only Native American currently working here at Glacier Park. It was a real honor when the National Park Service hired a Blackfeet, and Bear works very hard to educate visitors on our people's history with this land."

She pulled to a stop in the outdoor parking lot situated on a rise above the hotel. "There he is," she said, before hopping out of the car and jogging toward Bear. They embraced like old friends. After introductions were made, they quickly moved on to reviewing the logistics of their western approach to Ghost Ridge.

"I'm going to drive you guys as far as I can in my Jeep," Bear said. "There's a small fire road that winds out about three miles from here. From there, I've plotted the best course for you to take. I chose the flattest route. One that utilizes game trails we've discovered over the years." He pulled out a map he had marked up with specific instructions. He handed it over to Ally along with a compass.

"Just like when we were kids, eh, Bear?" she said with a smile.

"Just be careful, Ally," Bear said with all seriousness. "This isn't like a vision quest. After I drop you off, you'll be on your own out there. And you know as well as I do there are lots of things that can kill you—like grizzlies, snakes, and mating moose, just to name a few."

Ally reached out and squeezed Bear's shoulder. "I'll be careful. And thanks for doing this," she said. "I know you could get in a lot of trouble if anyone found out you dropped us off in a restricted area of the park."

"This meeting never happened and we never had this conversation," he deadpanned in an affected secret agent voice. Then he laughed and said, "Let's go."

Ally and Matt had been hiking for close to two hours and had covered more than six miles. The terrain turned out to be more arduous than they had anticipated. *If this is the flat route, I'd hate to see the mountainous one.* The packs on their backs were made of lightweight material. But the sleeping bags, small shovels, specimen bags, and other provisions had begun to feel heavier as the miles came and went. They stopped and sat on a moss-covered fallen tree to rest. They drank water from a canteen and listened to a small waterfall as it cascaded lazily down an outcropping of rocks twenty yards behind them.

"So you and Bear grew up together?" Matt asked. He had been wondering if their outward affection toward one another was based in a past romantic relationship. It was really none of his business, but for some reason he found himself curious. It was then that it suddenly occurred to him how much Ally's easy-going personality and easy-on-the-eyes looks had grown on him.

"Bear was like a big brother to me. He's five years older, but his family was close to mine. He kind of looked out for me, especially after my parents died," she answered. She suddenly looked up at Matt and smiled devilishly. "You think Bear and me had a thing, don't you?" Then she laughed heartily and Matt looked away embarrassed. "Matt," she said, and looked at him with a sly grin, "I think you're jealous."

"Jealous? Me, no, I'm not the jealous type. Besides, he's too short," he joked as if to make light of the whole thing. But Ally's gaze didn't waver. It was as if she could read his thoughts. He couldn't look away if he wanted to—and he didn't.

Finally she broke the silence. "Matt, there hasn't been anybody serious in my life since my divorce." Now it was her turn to look away embarrassed. "I don't know why I told you that, I just thought you should know."

The midday sunlight sneaked through the trees and silhouetted Ally's face. She blinked slowly and her long eyelashes seemed to close and open in slow motion. Matt was transfixed. He made a move to reach out and touch her face. Her lips were moist in anticipation. But then something stopped him.

He looked away abruptly and said, "We better get going. We've still got a lot of ground to cover."

They were on their feet and moving once again. About an hour later they crested a hill, and a familiar-looking ridgeline appeared less than a mile in front of them. They had finally made it to Ghost Ridge.

They got down on their hands and knees and spread the thermal photos out on the ground. The breeze had suddenly freshened so they used small stones to keep the loose pages from blowing away. It took them a few minutes, but they eventually matched up the photographic images to the landscape that lay in front of them. After gaining their bearings, they gathered their things and covered the last part of the journey in less than thirty minutes.

As they approached the "area of interest" as designated on their thermal printouts, Matt glanced cautiously in all directions. Neither of them spoke and they tried to walk softly for fear of being discovered. After a time, however, it became apparent they were alone. There was no sign of anyone from Spate Industries—anyone at all, for that matter.

The area that had appeared most red on the thermal printouts was slightly northwest of Ghost Ridge. They could spot it less than a half mile in the distance. A small stream ran swiftly along the eastern edge of the area that, according to their hypothesis, had once been home to a tribe of people. Hopefully it was the same European-sounding black tribe Lewis had written about.

Matt spoke up first. "I've got to tell you, Ally, there's nothing very special-looking about this spot. I can't distinguish anything that would indicate a fort once stood here."

"I was thinking the same thing," she said, "but we've got to trust those images are telling us the truth. Something has to be buried beneath our feet."

"OK, I'm going to start exploring the northwest edge, over by that small hill. Why don't you start on the southeast end by the stream," he suggested. "We'll work our way toward each other.

Look out for anything in the topography that has a man-made shape. If either of us finds a high-potential area, then we'll focus our excavation efforts there."

They spent the next two hours crisscrossing the football field–size area, but to no avail. There were a couple of false alarms. But for the most part, all they found were rocks, shrub-like vegetation and other natural debris from the spring runoff down the mountains. Their feet hurt and they were tired and getting hungry. The sun was getting lower on the horizon.

Ally sat down on a large rock, exhaled deeply, and said, "I think we better make camp soon. We're clearly not hiking out of here today. Maybe a fresh start in the morning would do us some good."

Matt knew she was probably right. But he was frustrated and not quite ready to give up. "Tell you what, let's keep looking for another hour and then we'll find a spot to camp for the night."

17

Present Day

Glacier National Park, Montana

Montana lived up to its Big Sky moniker that evening. It was a crystal-clear night and there were more points of light overhead than Matt had ever seen in his life. They had already spotted two shooting stars streaking across the horizon. A crescent moon was inching silently toward the heavens. *Who needs television when Mother Nature provides this kind of entertainment.*

They had devoured sandwiches and a large bag of dried fruit packed by Ron Patterson. They had also found a pleasant surprise inside Ally's pack—a quart-size box of red wine. They toasted their considerate benefactor and sat next to a crackling campfire contentedly sipping their wine from paper cups.

"Nice job with the fire, Matt. And I thought you were a city boy," she teased.

"Not always. I grew up in New England, remember. We have cold winters there, too," he replied. "Our house was small but it did have a pretty good-size fireplace. My dad taught me how to build a fire when I was a boy, and it's something I've never forgotten."

The air was still. A great horned owl made a *who-hoo-o-o* sound in a far off tree. "What's a vision quest?" Matt asked abruptly.

"Excuse me?"

"Sorry, that came out of nowhere, didn't it. It's just that earlier today Bear mentioned this hike wasn't like a vision quest. I was just wondering what he meant by that," Matt said, stoking the fire with a stick. Sparks erupted from the embers and snaked their way skyward before burning out and melding into the surrounding darkness.

"Oh, that," Ally said, recalling her friend's remark.

"I mean, I've heard of them, but I'm not exactly sure what they are. I have this picture in my head of you running around in the woods somewhere, stoned on peyote," Matt said with a crooked grin.

"Well, you got the woods part right," Ally said smiling. "There was no peyote, however, at least not on my vision quest."

"I'd like to hear about it," Matt said genuinely.

Ally thought for a moment before speaking. "A vision quest is kind of like a rite of passage where you transition from childhood to adulthood. As a teenager, you're sent into the woods or backcountry where you spend three or four days alone. It's supposed to be a time of reflection and meditation. You're supposed to seek spiritual guidance to try to find your sense of purpose in life," she said.

"Wow, I'm not sure I'd send my daughter into the wild alone."

"Truth be told, I think my dad was nearby. He never admitted to it, but my mom let it slip one time." She smiled sadly at the memory of her parents whom she lost at way too young an age.

"So what did you discover about yourself?" Matt continued probing.

"Well, the first thing I learned was I stink at catching small game. So I was starving by the time it was over." She chuckled. "But it was a wonderful experience. To be truly alone in nature is a little scary for sure, but also magical. And it does give you the opportunity to be contemplative." She paused before continuing, "I guess I learned I could do anything I set my mind to—and that not relying on anyone can be liberating." Matt couldn't be sure if it was the reflection of the flickering flames in her dark eyes but they seemed to burn with added intensity.

"Sounds to me like you found your independence out in those woods," Matt said softly. Then his eyes met hers. "And it suits you well."

Ally slid closer to Matt, her eyes never leaving his. Her lips found his and she kissed him deeply. He kissed her back. She leaned into him.

Suddenly, the fire popped loudly as an air pocket inside a damp log exploded from the heat. Matt broke their embrace. "Sorry," he said quietly, looking down toward the fire.

Ally sat up straighter and brushed a strand of hair from her face. "You're thinking about someone else, aren't you?" she asked perceptively.

"It's complicated, Ally."

"Lucky girl," she added.

"We shared something pretty intense. But it all happened so fast and then she moved to England. I'm not sure what we have anymore. It's confusing, to say the least."

"It's alright, Matt. You don't owe me an explanation." She reached up and put her hand gently against his cheek. Then she stood up.

"It's late and we've got a big day tomorrow," she said as she unfurled her sleeping bag next to the fire.

To Matt's surprise, she proceeded to strip off all of her clothes until she stood in front of him completely naked. The nipples on her small, round breasts were made hard by the evening chill. Her brown skin reflected the fire's dying glow. But it was the tattoo that transfixed Matt. It was an exquisitely drawn design of a fierce-looking snake with venom dripping from two sharp fangs. It started at the top of her closely shaved pubic hairs and ended just below her breasts, almost as if it had just slithered out from inside her. The contrast between the savage imagery and the beautiful woman it adorned was stark—and strangely provocative.

She couldn't help but notice the surprise on Matt's face. "I sleep in the nude. I guess it's an Indian thing," she said, without mentioning the ink etched into her stomach. Then she climbed into her bag.

Just before rolling over and settling deeper into her bag, she smiled coyly back at Matt. "I'll leave it unzipped in case you get scared by a bear."

The fire had died an hour or so after Ally had gone to bed. Matt hadn't slept a wink. He was restless. He couldn't get the image of Ally out of his mind—standing naked in front of him without a shred of inhibition. She was unlike any woman he had ever met, that much was certain. Finally, he got up and walked quietly to where she lay. He stripped his clothes off and slipped inside her sleeping bag. And his reason for doing so had nothing to do with a fear of bears.

They arose early and were back at the fort site by nine. This time they decided to expand their search beyond the perimeter of where they thought the fort might be. Matt was across the stream that ran along the eastern edge of the site, a bit closer to Ghost Ridge.

He was digging at the bottom of a rise when his trowel suddenly hit upon something. It caught his attention because it didn't sound like metal clanking against a stone. It was more of a dull thud, which struck Matt as odd. He knelt down and pushed a few loose stones aside to take a closer look. He saw a smooth, rounded surface barely protruding out of the damp sand. He dug around the object with his hands until he could get hold of it. He tugged on it gently. A sucking sound could be heard as the wet sand reluctantly released the object from its grasp.

After freeing it from its earthen tomb, Matt watched in fascination as an earthworm slithered out of a perfectly round hole in the oddly shaped stone. His fascination turned to shock, however, when he realized he wasn't holding a stone at all.

It was a human skull.

Matt had the reflex to bolt when it hit him he was holding someone else's head in his hands. He stood up too quickly and the skull tumbled out of his hands. It fell to the wet ground with a thwack. He silently chided himself for being so skittish. It was clear the skull had been there a long time. This was not evidence of a recent crime scene.

He knelt down and picked it up again. He turned it over in his hands. It was covered in filth, so he carried it over to the nearby stream and let the current wash away the dirt and sand. The lower jaw was missing, but other than that, the skull was remarkably intact. He called out to Ally and she came running over.

"Oh my God, Matt," she said, raising her hand to her mouth in shock. "Where did you find it?"

"Over there," he replied, pointing about twenty yards to the east.

They returned to the spot and searched for more human remains. But they found nothing else.

Just then, Matt's phone buzzed. He had lost cell service back at the campsite, but being out in an open area must have helped with the reception. He looked down and was shocked by the text message he saw. It read:

They're coming. Leave now! A. Friend

"Ally, we gotta go," Matt exclaimed, his head suddenly on a swivel, scanning the ridgeline above them.

"What? Why?" she said, confused at his sudden paranoia. "We've got the rest of the afternoon and you just found a skull. We can't stop now."

"Look," he said, and held up his phone screen so she could read the message. "They know we're here. We need to leave, now." He grabbed her by the hand and started to run.

They quickly retrieved their backpacks and slung them over their shoulders, but not before Matt stuffed the skull securely inside his backpack. A boom sounded in the distance. Confused, he looked around just as he heard another boom. It occurred to him he had heard that sound before—when he had been shot at in Monterey Square in Savannah—and he knew exactly what made it.

"Gun," he shouted, and pulled Ally to the ground with him. A rock exploded where they had just been standing. They frantically got to their feet and ran for the tree line less than a hundred yards away. Matt had Ally by the hand and they ran serpentine-style in hopes of evading the shots that continued to ring out behind them.

"Jesus Christ," Matt shouted as a bullet ripped a hole in his pack, narrowly missing his right shoulder. "These guys aren't screwing around."

"We need to take cover," Ally yelled, pointing to a large boulder just ahead of them.

They scrambled behind a huge piece of granite that had been carved out of the surrounding mountains and deposited on the valley floor by the annual spring flooding. It was barely big enough to shield the both of them, but they were safe for the moment. Ally shimmied out of her pack and reached into a side pocket. To Matt's astonishment, she pulled out a Beretta handgun. She searched some more and pulled out a clip. In one smooth motion she slammed it into place with the palm of her hand.

Matt's mouth fell open. "Where the hell did you get that?" he said between heavy breaths.

"I always carry one since, you know, the wife-beating husband I was once married to," she answered quickly, while peering around the rock to see exactly where the shots had come from.

Matt shook off his surprise. "They're up on that ridge by that leaning pine tree. I saw a flash when I looked over my shoulder, right before the second shot," he said.

"Good eye, Matt," she said, impressed. "Got any ideas?"

"Well, that steep ridge is preventing them from getting any closer. So if we can reach that tree line behind us, I think we'll have a chance to get the hell out of here."

"I agree."

Matt's mind was racing. Then an idea occurred to him.

"They're out of range for that handgun. But when they hear return fire their natural inclination is going to be to take cover. At least until they figure out what you're shooting with," he said while calculating the space between them and the forest. They had cut the distance by more than half. It was only about forty yards away now. Matt figured it would take him no more than seven or eight seconds to make it there. "When I make a break for that tree line, I want you to send a few rounds their way. That should buy me enough time to get more than halfway home."

"Then what?" Ally asked.

"Then they'll start shooting at me. But I'm fast and they'll only have two or three seconds at most to line up a shot and squeeze it off before I reach safety."

"It's too risky, Matt," she said, shaking her head. "We don't know how good these guys are, and three seconds is plenty of time to line up a target."

"I won't be running in a straight line, Ally. Don't worry, I'll make it. The longer we sit behind this rock, the more time we give them to figure out a way down here."

He grabbed hold of her hand and said, "It's the only chance

we've got." He gave her a reassuring squeeze. "Right after you fire, I want you to take off in that direction toward the woods," he pointed in a different direction than the route he was going to take. "I'm taking my pack because it's got the skull inside, but I want you to leave yours behind. It'll just slow you down. My guess is they'll be focused on me, not you. But keep your head down just in case. And run in zigzags."

She leaned in, kissed him quickly on the lips, and said, "OK, let's do this. I'll see you in the woods."

Matt pivoted around, crouching on all fours. He took a deep breath and said, "One, two, three, go."

He exploded from behind the rock like a sprinter from the starting blocks. Ally popped up from behind the large rock with her arms extended out in front of her. In a well-practiced shooter's position, she fired off four rounds in quick succession. She glanced to her left and saw Matt running in serpentine fashion, his strong legs pumping up and down. So far no shots had been fired from the ridge. She turned and sprinted in the opposite direction from Matt. She had run about twenty yards when she heard the first shot and then the second. She didn't dare look in Matt's direction for fear of what she might see, and also because she might trip on a loose stone. And if that happened, she'd be dead.

Matt was only a few yards away from the woods when the first shot rang out. Out of instinct, he darted hard to the left. He stumbled and almost lost his footing. Then the second shot came. He dove right and tumbled into the woods. He'd made it.

Then he heard another shot. Why?

"Shit," he barked. Without hesitation, he ran parallel along the tree line until he came to the spot where Ally was supposed to be. She wasn't there. The he saw her. She was laid out flat, no more than five yards from the safety of the forest.

"Ally," he screamed, but she remained unmoving.

Matt burst out of the trees and ran frantically toward her. A shot from the ridgeline whistled past his ear. But his focus remained on Ally. He scooped her up in his arms and, in one motion, pivoted and scrambled back in the direction he had just come. He noticed blood oozing from the side of her head. *Oh, God no.* He stumbled forward, half-falling, half-running. Finally, he lunged for the cover of the dense woods. Splinters flew above his head as one last round smacked into a large pine.

Matt got to his knees and rolled Ally's limp body over. She was unconscious and blood had matted her hair. He ripped off a piece of his shirt and applied it to a spot just above her right temple. She moaned. Matt breathed a sigh of relief. She was alive.

As he cleaned her wound, he realized the bullet had only grazed her temple. It had knocked her out cold, but other than a nasty headache, she would be fine in a day or two. He wasn't a particularly religious man, but he looked toward the heavens anyway and mouthed a silent "thank you."

He carried her in his arms for the first mile or so. This was no easy task with the bulky pack on his back. But thankfully, she probably didn't weigh more than a hundred pounds. Only when he felt like they weren't being followed did he stop by a small stream to clean and dress Ally's head wound. She had regained semiconsciousness and was insistent she could walk. Leaning heavily on Matt for support, she was able to continue on.

It was dusk by the time they made it back to the trailhead just east of Many Glacier Hotel. They were battered, bruised, and exhausted, but they had made it out alive.

18

Present Day

Savannah, Georgia

Matt sat behind the wheel of his vintage 1966 Chevy C10 pickup truck. He was driving south on Whitaker Street toward Forsyth Park, in the historic district of Savannah. It felt great to be home again. He had arrived back in town two days earlier and had spent most of that time catching up on paperwork at his antiques shop. Before hopping on a plane in Great Falls, he had shipped the unearthed skull in a package to Hank Gordon. He was now on his way to Hank's circa-1870s Victorian home to see what he had been able to discover about its origins.

Hank was the father of Sarah Gordon, Matt's absentee girlfriend. Matt hadn't seen Sarah in over six months. And living four thousand miles apart had cooled their relationship considerably. She had moved to England to teach and also to work on a new book about George Washington. It was based on their discovery of the now infamous surrender letter the Founding Father had penned in 1778 during the Continental Army's winter encampment at Valley Forge.

Matt knew that long-term relationships had never been his

strong suit. He also knew he still had strong feelings for Sarah. But lately, their phone calls had become less frequent. And when they did speak, Sarah seemed distracted. He was confused, to say the least, and on top of that he felt guilty about the night he had spent with Ally. But he couldn't deny the attraction he felt for the fiercely independent Native American beauty. He ran his hand through his wavy, sandy-blond hair and exhaled deeply as if to assuage the troubling thoughts rattling around inside his head. He couldn't.

He pulled up in front of Hank's beautifully restored home and knocked on the front door. Hank greeted him warmly. The two men made their way into the living room. It was stuffed with antiques collected over the years at local auctions and on European travels, and as the result of an ongoing eBay addiction. Luckily, Matt's strained relationship with Sarah hadn't dampened the fatherly affection Hank felt toward him. Ever since their Washington surrender-letter adventure, the two men had met regularly for morning coffee at a nearby café or for an end-of-day beer at the Crystal.

Hank had called that morning to say he had some news on the skull. Matt hurried right over. After sitting down, Matt couldn't wait any longer. "Alright Hank," he said, "I'm dying to hear what you were able to find out."

"Well, I can tell you this—the plot, as they say, just thickened," he replied with a wink and a smile.

After receiving the skull in the mail, Hank had taken it to a forensic anthropologist friend who worked at the Georgia Bureau of Investigation's Division of Forensic Sciences. Their Coastal Lab was located on Mohawk Street in Savannah. There, the expert had performed a DNA analysis on the grisly artifact.

"Now don't go drawing this out, Hank, I know how you like to tell stories," Matt chided the former high school history teacher. Hank Gordon had been a beloved teacher in the Savannah public school system for close to thirty years. He had retired a decade or so earlier, shortly after his wife had passed away from cancer.

"Oh, you're no fun." Hank waved away Matt's objection as if shooing a fly. "But alright, I'll cut to the chase." He paused and stroked his white goatee before continuing, "The skull you found is apparently from an adult male. And it's also quite old. Over two hundred years old, give or take a few years."

"Wow," Matt replied. "How the hell did your guy determine that?"

"Carbon dating," Hank replied matter-of-factly. He searched among the loose papers and magazines scattered around the coffee table. "Evidently, carbon dating is a common method used by scientists to establish the age of bones or objects. I wrote it down here somewhere because I knew you'd ask. It's pretty technical." He finally found what he was looking for, a small pad with some handwritten notes. "Here it is. My friend at the lab said, and I quote, 'radioisotope carbon-14 is taken up by an organism in life. As the half-life of carbon-14 is known as being 5,700 years, the amount of the isotope remaining in the sample can be used to calculate its age.'"

"Sorry I asked," Matt grunted.

"Yes, well here's where it gets really interesting. One might even say unbelievable."

"There's more?"

"Oh yes," he paused dramatically, "You see, the adult male this skull once belonged to was of *African* descent—specifically West African."

"Holy shit," Matt said, exhaling loudly. He immediately stood up and began pacing back and forth across Hank's living room. The sky outside had darkened. Thunderstorms were forecast for later in the day.

Hank had seen this behavior in Matt before. It usually meant he was trying to piece together a puzzle in his mind. "Tell me what you're thinking, Matt."

"Remember I told you about the black tribe Lewis wrote about? Remember he described them as looking like York, Captain Clark's black slave?"

"Yes, I do."

"Don't you see, Hank? This could be proof there really was a black tribe. Proof that Lewis wasn't lying or stoned or even drunk when he wrote about being captured by a tribe of black Indians."

Matt shook his head in stunned amazement. Then he said with some frustration, "Of course, it still doesn't answer the question of how the hell a tribe of African black people ended up in northwest Montana in the early 1800s."

"And don't forget the question of what ultimately happened to them. It would appear as though they disappeared without a trace," Hank added.

Matt sat down heavily in the one-hundred-thirty-five-year-old Greek Revival side chair near the window. He had a lot to absorb.

After a few minutes of quiet contemplation, Hank smacked the coffee table with the palm of his hands and exclaimed, "Wait a minute, I've got an idea."

Matt snapped to attention. "What?" he said.

"I met a professor at a University of South Carolina alumni function a few years back. I believe he taught African American history. And if I remember correctly, the speech he gave at the alumni affair was on the subject of the slave trade. He might be able to answer the question of whether it's plausible a man of African descent made it that far into the interior of the country at that time."

"Will he remember you?" Matt asked.

"Heavens no, I barely met the man. But that won't stop me from picking up the phone," he pointed to a vintage rotary dial phone sitting on a hand-carved side table, "and dialing up my alma mater to track him down," he said with renewed vigor.

Matt had to smile at the seventy-something-year-old man who had the enthusiasm of a twenty-year-old. "Let's do it," he said.

Hank called the university and was able to secure the name and number of the man he had met a few years before. His name was Dr. Horace Lane, but when they called his office he didn't answer. They left a message asking him to call Matt's cell phone at his earliest convenience.

Matt thanked Hank for all his help, got in his truck, and headed back to his store.

Halfway back to Monterey Square, Matt's phone rang. When he answered, he was surprised to hear Dr. Lane introduce himself. Matt spent the better part of the ride back to his shop explaining who he was and what he was calling about.

At one point, as he spoke, Matt was afraid Dr. Lane was going to hang up on him. He had told him an admittedly unbelievable story. A story that included the details of Meriwether Lewis's claim of being captured by a tribe of black Indians, the mystery surrounding the conquistador helmet, and finally Matt's discovery of a centuries-old African male's skull just outside Glacier National Park in northwest Montana. Matt wouldn't have blamed the professor if he had written him off as a lunatic. Thankfully, he didn't.

"Hmm," Dr. Lane murmured, "there's something Meriwether Lewis said in those field notes that's very intriguing to me."

"Which part?" Matt said eagerly, glad the professor had decided to stick around.

"The part where Captain Lewis alleged to have spotted a shrine with a helmet on top," he replied. "Are you absolutely sure he was referring to a conquistador helmet?"

"We're as sure as we can be. I can fax you a copy of his drawing if you like."

"That would be helpful. But for the moment, let's allow that it was a conquistador helmet," the professor rationed. Then he asked another clarifying question, "And just to be clear, you said your forensic expert determined the skull you found was of West African descent?"

"That's right."

"Fascinating," he said before falling silent.

After a few moments, Matt heard Dr. Lane mumble, as if he were speaking more to himself than Matt, "Is it possible?"

"Is what possible, Doctor?" Matt perked up, albeit confused.

Silence.

"Doctor?"

"Yes, I'm still here. If everything you say is true, then the only plausible explanation is that a black conquistador somehow established a colony in northwest Montana."

"Black conquistador?" Matt blurted out, now completely confused. He had arrived in the driveway behind his antiques shop but remained seated in the front seat of his truck. The air was thick with humidity and it had started to drizzle.

"My apologies. If you will allow me," Dr. Lane said. "Do the names Ponce de León, de Soto, and Cortés sound familiar to you?"

"Of course, they were all Spanish conquistadors who explored North America back in the 1500s."

"Indeed. How about Juan Garrido—is that a familiar name to you?" the professor asked, knowing it wouldn't be. It was as if he were lecturing to a class of freshman.

"No, that one's not familiar. Who's he?"

"He's another Spanish conquistador who was exploring the interior of America back in the 1500s," the professor said.

"How come I've never heard of him?"

"Probably because Juan Garrido was black," he stated matter-of-factly.

"You're kidding me."

"Not at all. It's a known fact black slaves participated in every major Spanish expedition in the Americas. What's not as well known is that some black men were not slaves at all. They were considered armed auxiliary. They may have started out as slaves, but they earned their freedom by fighting alongside Spaniards. And the concept of a black conquistador did not end after these early campaigns either. It survived in various forms throughout the Spanish conquests in the Americas—right up until the early 1600s, with Juan de Oñate's failed attempt to establish a settlement in New Mexico."

"I had no idea, Professor." Matt sat stunned in the cab of his truck. His breath had started to fog up the windows. He decided to make a dash for the front door of his shop. "Hang on a sec," he said. He slammed the door of his truck shut and sprinted through the rain.

He burst through the door of Hawkins Antiques and quickly made his way to his office. But not before Christina, his smart-ass store manager, yelled out, "Nice of you to come to work today, boss."

Matt reached the relative solitude of his office. He immediately returned to the conversation with Dr. Lane. "So are you saying the tribe Lewis described was actually descended from a group of escaped slaves led by one of these black conquistadors?"

"I'm only raising the possibility. It's the only way I can reconcile your discovery of a skull of West African descent *and* the presence of a conquistador helmet in northwest Montana," Dr. Lane reasoned.

"Let's say you're right, Doctor, then how did they get there?" Matt challenged.

"We can't know for sure. If I had to guess, I'd say they escaped from the Spaniards during one of their last expeditions into America. Freedom is a strong motivator. But to make it that far north, they had to have been led by a soldier—someone who knew how to lead, organize, and fight. And a black conquistador would have been equipped with body armor and a helmet—which could explain the helmet Meriwether Lewis saw." He paused before continuing his hypothesis, "And if this black conquistador led these African slaves to their freedom, then he would have been revered in his lifetime, probably even worshipped long after his death. And *that* might explain the religious shrine that, according to Meriwether Lewis, the helmet sat atop."

"That's quite a theory, Professor. So when do you think this band of escaped slaves arrived in the foothills where I found the skull?" Matt asked.

"Well, we know conquistador expeditions ended in the early 1600s, so my guess would be sometime around then, but that's just speculation," Dr. Lane said.

"You realize what that would mean, right?" Matt asked, as a strange thought suddenly occurred to him. Without waiting for a reply, he answered his own question, "It would mean a group of escaped African slaves was establishing a colony in America around the same time as Plymouth Colony was being established by the Pilgrims in Massachusetts."

"That's true, but I can't help but be reminded of another East Coast colony, established slightly earlier in history. Around the 1580s," the professor offered.

"Which one is that?" Matt asked.

"The famous Lost Colony of Roanoke Island, off the coast of North Carolina. They disappeared, too, without a trace," he said ominously.

"Jesus, Professor, what the hell have I stepped into?"

"A conundrum, that's for certain," Dr. Lane replied. "But if you bear with me a few more minutes, I have one additional theory. It has to do with that legend you told me about—the one about the black tribe being invincible."

"What about it?"

"You told me arrows allegedly bounced off their chests, correct?" he asked.

"That's what the legend said," Matt answered with undisguised skepticism.

"Before you dismiss it out of hand, there may be a plausible answer for that story as well," Dr. Lane said. "I've studied American Indians extensively as well," he went on to elaborate, "and back in the 1850s there was a famous Comanche Indian chief named Iron Jacket. He, too, was thought to be invincible. There were stories of arrows bouncing off his chest as well. In fact, it was believed by many he had the power to blow bullets aside with his breath. Some Texas Rangers even claimed to have seen it with their own eyes."

"Seriously?" Matt said, astonished.

"Absolutely. But sadly, Iron Jacket was not invincible. And the explanation of his purported supernatural powers became clear after he finally was killed. Turns out he always wore a Spanish coat of mail into battle, which protected him from most light-weapons fire." He paused before explaining, "Evidently the Comanches found some armor the conquistadors had left behind more than a century before, during their forays into Arizona. Perhaps your black tribe had chain mail as well, which could explain the legend of their invincibility."

Matt shook his head in amazement at the vast knowledge of Professor Lane as well as the enigma that was Ghost Ridge. It was all getting stranger by the second. "You honestly think the black tribe was real and that their roots can be traced back to black conquistadors?"

"It's just a hypothesis, Matt. But it fits."

19

Early 1600s

The New World (American Northwest)

*H*e cut a very imposing figure. *Standing at more than six feet tall, he was powerfully built, with a thick neck and broad shoulders. His head was completely bald but his face was adorned with a thick black mustache and beard, trimmed to a point as was customary for the time. His white teeth stood out in stark contrast to his unusually, even for an African man, black skin. He had a stern disposition, but as he looked around at the little colony built by the sheer force of his will and determination, even he had to smile.*

It had been nine months since they had arrived in these foothills that leaned up against the largest mountains he had ever laid eyes upon. It had been an arduous journey of more than a thousand miles through some very rough country. But they had made it. And not a single person had perished along the way. From his vantage point high above the encampment, his large head pivoted left and right and he marveled at what he saw. He couldn't help but be filled with pride with all that he and his troop of former slaves had accomplished.

After arriving the prior fall, they quickly began building a fort to protect their nascent colony before the winter set in. A soldier and veteran of many expeditions, he knew it was imperative to build an enclosure to protect his people. He had personally designed the forty-meter square structure that contained a watchtower, a well, and a guardhouse. Trees were plentiful, so a source for building timber was not an issue. The perimeter walls were constructed quickly. Inside the four walls they built a series of oval-shaped huts they had spotted being used by some of the Indian tribes they had encountered along their journey. They would have to build enough to house forty-three residents—30 men, 11 women, and two children, both born during the preceding winter. They were all either descendants of African-born ancestors or mixed-race Iberian-born ancestors. And as former slaves, every one of them was technically the property of the kingdom of Spain. But all of that was in the past now, thanks to their revered leader, Juan Ruiz.

Juan Ruiz was born in West Africa, but had been captured and sold into slavery as a young boy twenty years earlier. Juan was not his birth name, but it was the most common male Christian name in the Spanish-speaking world in the sixteenth century, and so it became his. He had grown up in the Caribbean colonies and began fighting alongside Spaniards as a teenager. His size, intelligence, and fearlessness had served him well. Eventually, he became part of the armed black auxiliary and was well on his way to earning his own freedom. But that had been before the revolt.

Back on that fateful day, the leader of the expedition and a large contingent of his soldiers had departed camp for a weeklong scouting mission. The ill-fated expedition included close to a hundred white settlers, including women and children, who had volunteered to start a colony in the New World. And it also included approximately forty slaves and one black conquistador—Juan Ruiz.

Prior to this journey, Ruiz had never questioned his authorities. He had fought and killed for a country that was not his. And he had done so bravely without as much as a second thought. His sole focus was on achieving his freedom. If he had to kill a thousand men to do so, then so be it. He was the last person anyone would have suspected of leading a revolt. But this time was different.

The Spaniard in charge of the expedition was a ruthless man who drove his soldiers hard and his slaves harder. His stated mission was to establish a Spanish colony in the interior of the New World. And to mine for gold that had been rumored to be plentiful in the region. But to date, they had found no gold and he was beginning to become frustrated. He drove them so hard that three of his own soldiers deserted. But he had swiftly tracked them down and had them killed without mercy. And just to ensure none of the slaves got similar ideas of desertion in their heads, he decided to make an example out of one of them.

His men herded the slaves to the center of camp. The Spaniard strode purposely forward. He grabbed one confused African slave boy by the arm and forced him to his knees. His sword glistened in the sunlight. Then, one violent movement later, the sword flashed through the air and separated head from body.

Juan Ruiz had seen plenty of men killed in such fashion in his lifetime. He himself had inflicted such violence against his enemies. But this was an innocent boy. The sight of the boy's head landing with a bloody thud on the ground caused something inside Ruiz to snap. Even though he remained still, watching alongside his fellow soldiers, he made a silent vow that no more of his black brothers would die needlessly.

They had been camped along the wide river that bisected this vast new country when Ruiz seized his opportunity. He had been planning the uprising for weeks and was just waiting for the right moment. When the officers and most of the soldiers had left camp, Ruiz knew it was time. He covertly armed a dozen or so male slaves and they swiftly overpowered and killed the small contingent of soldiers remaining in camp. They spared the families of the white settlers, but left them to fend for themselves. They quickly gathered all the supplies they could carry, loaded two oxen wagons, and set out in a northwardly direction on foot. They would have at most a three-day head start.

They followed the wide river north until it merged with another large river. They prayed the heavy thunderstorms that came nightly would cover their tracks. They slept little and lived off fish from the river and game they hunted with a handful of crossbows they had stolen from the Spanish soldiers they had killed. They trekked tirelessly for many weeks until they were sure they were not being followed. Their relentless pace ceased only when the second river they had been following ended in the foothills they now called home. Taking no chances, Juan Ruiz had ordered the immediate construction of a fort just in case the Spaniards had decided to pursue. They hadn't.

Even so, now that the spring thaw had softened the ground, Ruiz continued to keep his guard up. He and the men had begun construction of a four-foot-deep moat to further protect their encampment. The moat that now ringed the outer walls was almost complete, and within a few days they would divert water from a nearby stream to fill it. They had accomplished a lot, but there was always more to do.

Ruiz made his way down from the watchtower. He was dressed in the quilted cotton jacket, long sleeveless shirt, and tall leather boots of a professional fighting man—a conquistador. Stored in his sleeping quarters were his chain mail vest and metal armor. He donned them only when he went to battle against some of the more aggressive Indian tribes in the area. The most crucial piece of armor to a Spanish soldier was his helmet. But curiously, Ruiz never wore his. Perhaps it was because it reminded him of his prior life of subservience and service to a country for which he had no allegiance.

So the distinctively shaped morion metal helmet, a symbol of the power and authority of the Spanish conquistador, remained stowed away, unused. Not that it mattered; Ruiz did not need symbols of authority and respect, for the people he had helped set free already worshipped him like a god.

20

Present Day

New York, NY

David Becker sat in his eleventh-floor office inside The New York Times Company's newly constructed skyscraper on Eighth Avenue. He looked like a reporter straight out of central casting, with black-rimmed glasses and long, unkempt brown hair that touched the tops of his shoulders. He wore faded jeans and an untucked white button-down oxford. He had just finished spreading cream cheese on an onion bagel. One would never guess he was the top investigative reporter at the renowned *Times* newspaper. Or that he had won two Pulitzer Prizes for Investigative Reporting in his career. He was handsome in a cerebral, hippy kind of way, but his tired blue eyes gave away a life that revolved around constant deadlines.

As he dialed Matt Hawkins's cell phone, he got up from his cluttered desk and walked over to the floor-to-ceiling windows that faced Eighth Avenue. He gazed down at the streets below and smiled to himself. He recalled a funny episode from a couple of years earlier when someone had decided to scale the outside of the New York Times building. More than a few had tried over the years.

One nut even made it all the way to the top, where he was promptly arrested by New York City's finest. Most simply gave up and turned back around. But this particular guy stopped right outside Becker's window and camped out for about four hours. He had a banner and was shouting in protest to something. But a gust of wind tore the banner from his hands and the traffic noise at street level drowned out his voice. Frustrated, the poor guy finally gave up and descended from his perch, his message undelivered.

"Well, if it isn't my favorite investigative reporter," Matt answered Becker's call with typical sarcasm.

"Hey, Matt," Becker said, scratching his scruffy, five-day-old beard.

As he spoke, Becker glanced at the notes he had taken in handwriting only he could decipher. He had scrawled them onto a yellow legal pad, using a No. 2 lead pencil. Becker was old school.

He said, "I'm calling because I want to share a theory I have about the identity of 'A. Friend.'"

While Becker was doing his digging on Spate Industries, Matt had shared with him the mysterious e-mails he had received from the anonymous sender. The most recent one, which had warned Matt and Ally they were in imminent danger near Ghost Ridge, had probably saved their lives.

"OK, shoot," Matt said.

"Remember I told you about the third brother, the black sheep who got excommunicated from the family?"

"Yeah."

"Well, the more I read about this guy, the more it makes sense to me that maybe he's your Deep Throat," Becker said. He was referring to the famous informant that helped *Washington Post* reporters Bob Woodward and Carl Bernstein expose President Richard Nixon's 1972 Watergate scandal.

"How so?"

"The falling out between the brothers got ugly. In fact, the case was tied up in courts for the better part of a decade. Even though Harry Spate, the black sheep brother, eventually settled for a buyout of close to a billion dollars, he was extremely bitter at how it all ended."

"But that was a long time ago, David. Do you really think he's still interested in bringing his brothers down? Especially since he's as rich as a king and living like one somewhere on an island in the Caribbean?" Matt asked skeptically.

"He's got the motive and the means, and in my business, that makes a suspect, Matt," Becker replied.

"I'll grant you that, but I'm not totally convinced."

"Tell you what. I'll scan all the material I've accumulated on the family, and on Harry Spate, in particular. I'll e-mail it to you so you can have a look for yourself and make up your own mind," Becker offered.

"That would be great, David. And thanks for your help."

One thing about owning a mid-nineteenth century, three-story mansion is something was always in need of repair. Today it was the first floor bathroom that Matt made available to customers of Hawkins Antiques.

His head was literally inside the toilet investigating the source of a leak when Christina, his store manager, peered into the closet-size room.

"Rough night last night, eh, boss?" she cracked.

"Funny, Christina, now hand me that wrench before I make you fix this thing," he replied testily. He was in no mood for her perpetual ribbing.

Christina and Matt had been carrying on their sibling-like

banter ever since she had first walked through the door of his shop three years earlier. Her spunk was one of the main reasons he had hired her. And over the years they had developed a special bond. But one would never know by their continual mutual harassment.

"Hey, this thing wouldn't be broken if you had listened to me," she scoffed. "I told you to put a padlock on the door a long time ago. Customers can hold their water until they get home as far as I'm concerned."

"Are you finished?" Matt asked, craning his neck so he could eye Christina while fiddling with a pipe fixture behind the toilet.

"Come on, Matt, they act like this is a gas station...it's gross. They wouldn't treat their own bathrooms like this," she argued.

"The wrench, Christina," Matt pleaded.

"Fine," she said. She slapped the wrench into Matt's outstretched palm and stormed off.

It was late in the day by the time Matt returned to his laptop to review the materials Becker had sent him. He was surprised to see so many files when he opened the electronic folder attached to the message.

"Whoa, Becker, you've done your homework," he said out loud, even though he was alone in his third-floor apartment.

He opened the first file and began to read. An hour later, he was still sitting at the circa-1920s mahogany Kittinger desk in his study. He clicked on an article about Harry Spate from the *Miami Herald* that had been published fifteen years earlier. Evidently, at the time, Harry had made a large donation to establish a contemporary art museum in the vicinity of Miami Beach. There was nothing of particular interest to Matt until he spotted a picture toward the end of the article. Standing next to Harry Spate at the ribbon-cutting ceremony was a teenage girl that looked very familiar. Matt looked closer. He knew he had seen this girl before, but he couldn't quite place her face.

Finally, it dawned on him the girl in the picture was the spitting image, albeit a younger version, of Samantha Christie, the spokesperson for Spate Industries. Matt looked down at the caption beneath the photo and was surprised to see Samantha Christie's name was nowhere to be found. His surprise turned to shock, however, when he read that the sixteen-year-old girl was identified as Harry Spate's daughter—*Samantha Spate.*

"What the hell?" Matt blurted out, sitting up ramrod-straight in his chair.

He sat staring at the fifteen-year-old photo, trying to convince himself the young girl in the picture was not the same woman he had met in the police chief's office out in Browning, Montana. But it was no use. Her model-like features gave her away. There was no mistaking it. Samantha Christie was actually Samantha Spate, the daughter of the renegade brother.

Matt's mind was racing with possible explanations, but he couldn't come up with anything. Finally, as was his nature, he had an impulsive idea. He began rummaging through the drawers of his desk. Not finding what he was looking for, he ran from his study to his bedroom. He frantically searched the top of his dresser. Finally, he spotted it. Samantha Christie's business card, the one she had given him in the parking lot outside the police station. He flipped it over and found the cell phone number she had handwritten on the back. He didn't hesitate for a second before dialing.

Matt was angry. Big Tom was dead, Ally had been shot, and Samantha Christie had lied to him. And all roads kept leading straight back to the Spate family. It was time to get some answers.

Samantha picked up on the third ring, "This is Samantha Christie," she said politely, clearly unfamiliar with the number of the caller.

"This is Matt Hawkins," Matt said abruptly.

"Matt, what a surprise, how are you?" she asked.

"Not good, Ms. Christie," Matt said coolly.

"I'm sorry to hear that, Matt. Did something happen?" she asked with genuine concern. Samantha Christie, a.k.a. Samantha Spate, was a cool customer. Angry callers are something she was clearly accustomed to as the company's spokesperson.

But Matt wasn't buying it, "Come on; don't play dumb with me."

"Matt, I really don't know what you're so upset about. But if there's something I can do to help, I'll be glad to try," she said calmly.

Her calmness only increased Matt's ire. "Are you serious?" he seethed. Then he took a deep breath to calm himself down. He realized he did not want to have this conversation over the phone. He needed to speak with her face-to-face.

He continued in a more steady voice, "Actually you can do something to help. You can fly down to Savannah tomorrow and meet with me in person, on my turf."

"I'm afraid that's impossible, I've got to..." she started to say.

"Samantha," he cut her off abruptly midsentence, "if you don't come to see me, then I'll be forced to go public with what I've found out about your employer *and* about you." He knew this would get her attention.

It did.

"Matt, I have no idea what you're talking about," she said. But there was an edge in her voice now. Was it fear? Matt wondered.

She continued, "Please tell me what you think you know and maybe I can explain."

"There's a bar called the Crystal Beer Parlor. Meet me there at two p.m.," he said.

He hung up without waiting for her response.

21

Present Day
Savannah, GA

The lunch crowd had thinned by the time Matt arrived. He grabbed a back booth facing the door. He wanted to see Samantha when she walked in. He was nervous because he was about to confront the enemy. But at least the meeting was going to happen in a place that was like a second home to him, the Crystal Beer Parlor. There was a lot to like about the Crystal—great food, nostalgic decor, and friendly people. But for Matt, his attachment to the place went deeper.

It reminded him of some of the classic old bars in his hometown, on the north shore of Massachusetts. In fact, the Crystal looked a lot like the first bar he had gone to with his dad, back when Matt was just a teenager. Inside his hometown bar you were just as likely to find a dockworker knocking back a cold one as you were the local banker. Matt hadn't quite reached the drinking age, but his father had insisted his first beer should be with him. He was going to teach his son how to drink. Matt didn't have the heart to tell him he had already snuck beers in the woods plenty of times with his friends.

Loud laughter snapped Matt out of his reminiscence. He smiled inwardly as he eavesdropped on a group of old-timers arguing over a bad call being replayed on the television behind the mahogany bar. He glanced to his left and saw the 1940s-style menu boards hanging on the walls and felt a pang of sadness. *This was Dad's kind of place.* His father had passed away years before, but Matt still missed him dearly.

The door opened and sunlight silhouetted the hourglass-shaped figure of Samantha Christie. Her long, blond hair hugged her shoulders luxuriously. She was dressed in a fitted, white jacket over a Tory Burch pink-and-black panel dress. It was the perfect combination of professional and sexy. Michael Kors black leather platforms extended her already long, toned legs, which drew considerable attention. Even the regulars at the bar stopped arguing and turned to gawk— self-consciously sucking in their guts—as Samantha sashayed past. She caught Matt's eye and angled his way.

"I had to rearrange my entire schedule to be here," she said in agitated tone. She slid gracefully into the booth, sitting directly across the table from him.

She absently tucked a loose strand of hair behind her ear as she spoke. "I'm not even sure why I came," she said with a huff, before adding, "especially after you hung up on me yesterday." Her full lips were pushed out in a slight pout that distracted Matt for half a beat.

"Sorry about that," he said, "but I'm not a big fan of your employers at the moment."

"I gathered that. You sounded very upset. In fact, if I remember correctly, you said if I didn't come here you were going to go public with something." She stared at him evenly and said flatly, "I don't usually answer to threats." The pouty runway model was gone. She was all business now.

Matt smiled wryly. "I bet you're very good at what you do."

"I like to think I am." She looked at her watch and exclaimed impatiently, "Look, I don't have a lot of time, so can you please tell me what this is all about?"

"I'd love to," he answered calmly. He took a long swig from his frosty mug of beer and began, "It all started with a discovery of some lost field notes written by Meriwether Lewis."

He went on to tell her everything—from his visit to Browning to Big Tom's disappearance. He recounted the black tribe described by Meriwether Lewis and the African skull he had unearthed. Samantha listened attentively but said nothing.

Matt continued to recount the past couple of weeks. He told her about the legend Crooked Nose had described; about the black tribe that allegedly lived in the foothills out near Ghost Ridge; and of their mysterious disappearance.

"This is all very fascinating, Matt, but I'm not sure how it applies to Spate Industries." she said in confusion.

"Ah, your *employer*," he said irritably. "I was just getting around to the infamous Spate clan." Samantha shifted uncomfortably in her seat. It was her first outward sign of anxiety.

"Evidently, Spate Industries has an *extra special* interest in the Blackfeet Reservation. We became aware of this special attachment after we were denied access to Ghost Ridge by the res police—who I'm told are on your employer's payroll, by the way."

Samantha's expression darkened but Matt forged ahead before she could voice any denials. "It got us to wondering: Why does your company guard Ghost Ridge like King Tut's tomb is buried out there?"

Samantha made a motion as if to speak, but Matt held up his hand and said, "And please don't feed me that bullshit line that you're keeping people out for safety reasons. Because we both know there isn't any heavy machinery out there. And there never has been. No trucks. No bulldozers. Not one fucking oil derrick." He did not try to hide his agitation.

"I can explain," Samantha began to say, but there was no stopping Matt. He was rolling now.

"And do you know why?" he pressed on. "Because your company is hiding something—something they don't want me or anyone else to find. I haven't figured out what it is," he continued, "but make no mistake, I will not go away until I do." He finished and leaned back in his seat. But his eyes never left hers.

Now that she finally had a chance to get a word in, Samantha said, "Matt, I think your imagination is running a little wild."

"My imagination," he spat out. "Did I imagine being shot at out in those foothills? Did I imagine the woman I was with getting knocked out by a bullet that grazed her temple?"

Samantha raised a hand to her mouth in apparent shock. She averted her eyes. When she looked back at him a moment later her demeanor had changed. She appeared truly stunned by Matt's revelation. "Someone shot at you?" she asked.

"Yes, Samantha, they did, and they were shooting to kill," he said.

"I...had no idea, Matt," she stammered.

Her dazed reaction caught him off guard but he wasn't about to let her off the hook that easily. He reached for a folder on the seat next to him. He pulled out a copy of the newspaper article from fifteen years earlier that Becker had found. It contained the irrefutable picture of Samantha as a teenager standing next to her father, Harry Spate.

"Yeah, well I'm having a hard time believing you," he said, "considering you're a member of the family." He slid the photo from the newspaper across the table, and added, "What I can't understand is why the daughter of the black sheep Spate brother is working for the enemy?"

Samantha didn't make a move to pick up the article. She didn't have to. She could see the picture clearly from where she sat. She recognized her slightly slouched shoulders, a by-product of the self-consciousness she had felt at the time about her height. At five feet eleven she was taller than most of the men standing beside her in the picture. She recalled how she felt that day, a combination of proud, shy, and awkward. It seemed like a lifetime ago.

She exhaled slowly. Without looking up, she said quietly, "Matt, you don't know what you're getting into."

He could see the defeat in her body language, and his tone softened, "You're right, which is exactly why I called you here today, Samantha. I wanted to give you the opportunity to be straight with me and tell me what the hell is going on out there," he said.

She stayed quiet for a few minutes. Matt waited patiently. When she finally looked up, she looked different somehow. He couldn't quite put his finger on it, but her face seemed to reflect a mixture of both resignation and relief. The facade was gone, almost like an actress who had left the stage and come out of character.

"It's true, Matt," she said, looking around anxiously to make sure nobody was listening, "except for one thing, I'm *not* working for the enemy."

Now it was Matt's turn to be confused.

She took another deep breath to compose herself and then continued, "My father and I have been working together for years trying to expose my uncles for who they are, corrupt bastards who will do anything for a profit."

Matt's mouth hung open. He was blindsided by this unexpected turn of events. He said, "So you're telling me you work for Spate Industries but you're really a mole for your father?"

"I guess that's one way to put it. It wasn't always like that, though."

"What do you mean?"

She fiddled nervously with a leftover cocktail napkin on the table. "My uncles aren't stupid men," she said quietly. "They only considered hiring me because my father and I had a terrible falling out after I graduated college. It was shortly after he was kicked out of the family business. I was young and naive," she explained, "and I didn't see the harm in continuing to visit my uncles in Oklahoma even though my father forbade it. I had always been their favorite niece and they had always been nice to me. So I didn't believe my father when he tried to convince me they were...evil." She chose her last word carefully.

"So what happened?" Matt asked.

"As you can imagine, when Dad found out about my visits to my uncles, it didn't sit very well with him. In fact, it caused a huge rift in our relationship. So much so that we stopped talking and didn't see each other for a number of years."

Matt shook his head in amazement. He motioned for the waitress to bring him another beer. He looked at Samantha to see if she wanted anything, but she shook her head no.

She went on, "Then one day, they offered me a job in the family company...and I accepted it. Looking back at it now, I'm sure they did it to spite my father, but I was too dumb to recognize it for what it was."

"So what happened then?"

"I changed my last name to Christie to avoid having to deal with the obvious questions. Nobody ever knew my true connection to the Spate family. And it turned out I was pretty good at handling the press. So, in time, they made me the company's chief spokesperson." She paused, and then added with a grim expression, "That's when the veil was lifted on the true character of my uncles and the true nature of the family business. That's when I understood what my father was trying to tell me. And that's when I made the decision to stop working *for* my uncles and to start working *against* them."

"What do you mean?"

"I mean I very quietly reconnected and reconciled with my

father. I told him everything, and we decided to work together. I began funneling him copies of internal documents, half of which I didn't even understand. But I knew they would make sense to my father. Slowly, over time—and I'm talking years Matt—we compiled an extensive file on their illicit activities. But we still hadn't found the one thing that could bring them down for good... until you showed up out of nowhere."

She went quiet and looked away.

"Go on," Matt implored.

Samantha looked up suddenly. She had a worried look on her face and seemed to be having second thoughts. "Matt this is bigger than you think. Are you sure you want to get involved?" she asked sincerely.

"I'm already involved, Samantha. I feel responsible for one death and nearly two," he said, referring to Big Tom's suspected murder and Ally's near miss. "I've been shot at, lied to, and stiff-armed at every turn. Believe me, I'm in up to my ass. So please," he prompted, "don't hold back."

Matt's stubbornness and pride had served him well over the years, but these same character traits had caused him some problems as well. It wasn't his nature to back down from a fight, even if the odds were stacked against him. His parents had instilled in him core values of integrity and accountability—plus he had always had a soft spot for an underdog. Maybe that was a by-product of being a long-suffering Red Sox fan. Either way, the fight with Spate was on and Matt was ready to scrap if necessary.

"OK," Samantha acquiesced, "the truth is my uncles aren't just corrupt, they're very dangerous men. I wouldn't put it past them to kill you or anyone else who got in their way." Then she quickly added, "But you've got to believe me, Matt, the first I heard about you being shot at was when you told me today." Matt believed her.

"And before you ask," she said, "I don't know anything about

Big Tom's death either. I don't want to believe they murdered him, but I can't deny the possibility."

"But why are they going to such extremes? What the hell is so important to them about Ghost Ridge?" Matt asked.

"I don't know that either. But I can tell you this, when you showed up and started asking questions about the conquistador helmet Big Tom found, they got very nervous. And these are men who don't get nervous about *anything*."

"Why is that?"

"Because they're used to getting away with everything," she replied. "They always have, and they believe they always will. They have a cadre of lawyers, three separate lobbying firms in Washington, and a host of politicians on the payroll. If they get in trouble for an oil spill or a benzene leak at one of their plants, they simply pay a fine and move on," she continued in disgust. "And if someone happens to get cancer or die because of their gross negligence, their team of slick lawyers descends on the victim's family and settles out of court before the lawsuits are ever filed."

"Jesus Christ," Matt said, "how can you continue working for these guys?"

"Don't you get it?" Samantha raised her voice in indignation. "You think I like going to work every day scared to death someone is going to find me photocopying sensitive files or taping a phone conversation?" Her eyes welled up, but she blinked back the tears. "I have no choice. The only way my uncles are ever going to be brought to justice is if someone *on the inside* can compile enough evidence against them."

"You're taking a hell of a risk, Samantha. Why?"

She thought for a minute and then gave a series of reasons. "Because of how they treated my father; because I feel guilty as hell for not believing my dad in the first place; because I've grown to hate my uncles for being the corrupt men that they are; because they've hurt and likely killed people in the name of profit; but most of all because they expect to get away with it," she finished, looking suddenly exhausted.

Matt had a lot to take in. But one thing he felt in his gut was Samantha was telling him the truth. Nobody could fake the passionate hatred etched in her face. He suddenly felt sorry for her—for the lie she had to live every day; for the stress she was clearly under; and for being born into such a fucked-up family.

"I believe you, Samantha," he said quietly.

She smiled weakly. "Thank you," she said, but this time she couldn't stop the tears from coming.

Matt reached across the table and covered her trembling hands with his. He gave them a reassuring squeeze. "You're not alone anymore. The posse has arrived," he said with a crooked smile.

She laughed and wiped the tears away with a damp cocktail napkin. "Sorry for crying, I'm usually pretty good at hiding my emotions."

"It's OK," he countered, "my mother used to tell me that a good cry always made you feel better."

"Somehow I don't see you as a crier," she replied, smiling through her sniffles.

"Are you kidding? You should see me after the Red Sox lose," he deadpanned.

They fell silent for a moment. The ball game on the television had ended and the men at the bar started weaving their way toward the exit.

Matt and Samantha were the only people left in the bar. She said, "I think I'll take that drink now." Matt laughed and motioned for the waitress. He hated to admit it, but Samantha Spate was starting to grow on him.

"Matt," Samantha said, her face turning serious once more, "I wasn't kidding when I said you scare them. I saw it in their faces when they heard about you snooping around the reservation."

"Yeah," he said, "but why?"

Samantha shook her head. "I don't know, maybe it has something to with that skull you found."

"Maybe, but that doesn't give us much to go on," Matt answered realistically.

"Maybe not, but when someone's afraid it means they've got something to hide. My uncles actually taught me that, and it usually turns out to be true."

"I don't know, Samantha," Matt said skeptically.

"Don't you see," Samantha cut him off with a renewed intensity, "you may be close to discovering their Achilles' heel, the one thing that if exposed to the world, would damage their reputation beyond repair." Then she added, "This just may be the chink in the armor my father and I have been looking for all these years."

Matt absently ran his finger around the rim of his beer mug. Samantha had shared more than he could have ever expected. And he was still trying to process everything he had heard. The rules of the game had definitely changed.

But one thing hadn't changed—the key to solving this riddle was still somewhere out on Ghost Ridge.

22

Present Day
Fredericksburg, Virginia

About halfway between Washington, D.C., and Richmond, Virginia, sat a lovingly restored 1817 colonial-style farmhouse. Buzz Penberthy and his wife had purchased the house and property with the hopes of spending their golden years there together. Sadly, Buzz's beloved Addy passed away from cancer not long after they had settled in. Buzz now lived alone on the sprawling thirty-five-acre piece of farmland that stood out like an emerald isle in a sea of encroaching subdivisions and strip malls.

Fredericksburg had at one time consisted mostly of farms, but the majority of them had long since succumbed to development. The only reason Bingo Field had been spared was because the large red dairy barn and accompanying soaring white silo on the property were considered iconic landmarks. The entire thirty-five-acres were now protected by a conservation easement, effectively preventing Buzz's home from ever being touched by a bulldozer. Even so, as Buzz steered the car toward the main entrance to the farm, Matt couldn't help but notice a brand new 7-Eleven and McDonald's around the corner. They hadn't been there the last time he had visit-

ed. *Yet another sign of the relentless advancement of so-called progress.*
Matt felt suddenly depressed.

Once they turned off the main road and passed through the
bricked entryway however, Bingo Field began to work its magic on
Matt. He recalled the calming effect it had on him the first time he
drove up the long, winding drive. Perhaps it was the quaint farmhouse with its expansive front porch and five charmingly misaligned
brick chimneys. Or maybe it was the natural aquifer on the property that pumped pure, cold water from somewhere deep below the
earth's surface through a rocky creek that bisected the farm. Whatever it was, the pieces and parts that made up the place worked in
perfect harmony to lift a man's spirits.

After they settled in, Buzz grabbed two shotguns from his gun
locker. "Let's go blow off some steam," he said.

The two men hopped on an old ATV and headed to an open
field toward the rear of the property. Buzz had a skeet range set up
and loved to shoot clay pigeons whenever he could. He loved the
sport because it both stirred his competitive juices and relaxed him
at the same time.

Along the way, Matt caught his friend up on what had happened
since he had returned from Montana. They had already spoken a
few times by phone, so Buzz knew about Matt and Ally's discovery
of the skull out near Ghost Ridge—and the astonishing revelation
the two-hundred-year-old skull was of African origin. So Matt
focused on his meeting earlier in the week with Samantha Spate,
a.k.a. Samantha Christie.

Buzz loaded his pump-action shotgun and yelled, "Pull." Even
though he also owned a semi-automatic shotgun, he preferred the
challenge of shooting his trusty old pump action. It required fast,
consistent precision and it was a hell of a lot of fun to shoot. Matt
sent the first two clay discs slinging into the air, down range above
an open grassy field. Buzz fired and the first pigeon exploded. In

a flash, he pulled the 12-gauge shotgun's sliding forearm back and pushed it forward before firing again. Two for two—as the second clay pigeon was obliterated.

When he finished shooting, Buzz shook his head in astonishment. "You mean to tell me that beautiful creature is a Spate? Well I'll be goddamned." He wiped his brow with the back of his hand and said with a wry grin, "Bet you didn't see that coming."

"Not in a million years. But she's not just any Spate, Buzz," Matt said. "She's the daughter of Harry, the renegade brother who got booted out of the family business."

"And she's been working undercover for her father all these years?" Buzz asked, still in disbelief.

"That's what she claims. Evidently, they've been working together trying to compile enough evidence on Spate Industries, and on Oliver and Landon specifically, to file criminal charges against them."

"Remarkable," Buzz acknowledged. He reloaded the shotgun and handed it over to Matt.

"Pretty brave, too," Matt said as he put his earplugs in. He assumed a shooter's position and yelled "pull." He hit the first clay target but missed the second one on the high side.

Returning to the conversation, he said, "These are some bad boys, Buzz. According to Becker, they've gone to extremes to promote their antigovernment agenda. Digging up dirt on politicians who don't align with their ideology, and funneling millions into nasty campaigns. You get the picture. And not just that, Samantha told me dozens of wrongful death lawsuits have been filed against the company for chemical leaks and oil spills. But somehow, none of them have ever stuck," Matt explained.

"Let me guess, lots of lawyers and lots of payoffs?" Buzz shook his head in disgust.

"Only for those who choose to go away quietly," Matt said.

"Samantha hinted that if you became a thorn in their side they wouldn't hesitate to harm you."

"Like Big Tom?" Buzz said.

"Yes, like Big Tom. And like me and Ally out on Ghost Ridge," Matt said angrily.

The two men took turns shooting for the better part of an hour. Matt wasn't bad, but Buzz was perfect. "I don't think you missed one." Matt marveled before joking, "Clearly you've got too much time on your hands, old man."

"Practice makes perfect, sonny." Buzz winked. Then he turned more serious. "Jesus, I'm sorry I got you into this mess," he said apologetically. "This whole thing was supposed to be nothing more than a fun trip to Montana to investigate a conquistador helmet, for Chrissakes."

Matt waved him off. "I'm a big boy, Buzz," he said, "and you're not the reason I'm upset. I'm just pissed off I haven't been able to figure out a way to get to these bastards."

The two men had returned to Buzz's front porch by then. They sat drinking their beers and staring out over the rolling hills of Bingo Field. Some chickens scratched in the dirt by the silo and a dog barked in the distance. A few horses Buzz allowed neighbors to board in his barn at no charge grazed lazily in a grassy field.

Buzz was troubled by a comment Matt had made earlier, so he asked, "You said something before. When referring to Samantha, you said she *claimed* she's been working on the inside against her uncles. Don't you believe her?"

"I don't know what to think, Buzz, because this whole thing is so unbelievable. I mean, come on, missing notes from the Lewis and Clark Expedition that led to a conquistador helmet that led to an African skull. And all these things are somehow tied back to one of the richest families in America. And to top it all off, the daughter of the excommunicated brother has been working undercover for years trying to build a case against her crooked uncles?" He was incredulous. "This is like a bad dream."

"But you're not going to wake up and have it all just disappear," Buzz said, and then added with a smile, "this ain't *The Wizard of Oz*, kid."

"No, unfortunately it's not."

"So what does your gut tell you?" Buzz continued with the metaphor, "Is Samantha more like Glenda the Good Witch or is she closer to the Wicked Witch of the West?"

Matt looked across at his friend and answered honestly, "She's a bit of a mystery."

Buzz laughed. "All women are a mystery," he said. He got up out of his weathered rattan armchair. "Come on, I'm getting hungry, let's fire up the grill and get some dinner going."

A full moon was on the rise.

It appeared enormous as it crested the horizon, dwarfing the four-story dairy silo in the foreground. There were no clouds that evening, so the craters on the moon's surface could be seen clearly without the aid of a telescope.

The two men watched in silence as Earth's natural satellite inched its way skyward. It slowly morphed in color from pumpkin orange to wheat yellow. It wouldn't be long before it would be high enough in the sky to shed the dusty pollution of Earth's atmosphere. Then it would assume it's more familiar translucent porcelain glow.

Buzz struck a match, illuminating his face. He expertly cupped the flame and let it barely lap at the end of his cigar. He gently rotated the cigar in his mouth while drawing in air, resulting in a nice even ember. The tip glowed bright orange a few seconds later.

"Looks like you've done that once or twice before," Matt kidded his friend.

"Someone once told me if you kiss a cigar, it will kiss you back," Buzz replied. "If you treat it like a dog, it will turn around and bite you." He winked.

"I'll have to remember that," Matt said. "By the way, I thought you quit smoking?"

"Haven't had a Marlboro in over ten years," boasted the former two-pack-a-day man, "but," he admitted, "I still enjoy an occasional stogie."

Matt plucked a cigar from Buzz's leather humidor and said, "Can't blame you for that."

"So what's next, Matt?" Buzz asked, switching the conversation back to the Spates and Ghost Ridge.

"Ideally, I'd like to get back on that property. But I'd also prefer not to be a human shooting target again," he said dryly.

"Oh, come on, they missed you the first time. They'll probably miss again," Buzz cracked.

"Probably, huh, are you volunteering to go in my place?" Matt shot back, good-naturedly.

"Hell no, the last time I volunteered for something it cost me the next thirty years of my life," said the ex-navy man who had seen combat in both Vietnam and Desert Storm. The real truth was Buzz dearly missed serving his country. And he'd gladly do it all over again. If the navy called and asked him to climb back into his old F-4 Phantom fighter plane, he wouldn't hesitate for a second.

"Seriously, Buzz, there's got to be another way to figure out what those guys are hiding out there."

"Yeah, like what?" Buzz asked skeptically, running a calloused hand across his crew cut scalp.

"That's why I came up here, *oh wise one,*" he said sarcastically. "I was hoping you could help me with some ideas."

"And I thought it was because you liked my cooking," Buzz

returned dryly.

"Shit, I can get charred steaks anywhere," Matt fired back at his friend.

"Alright, wiseass, so where do you want to start?" Buzz growled. He reached into a cooler that had been strategically placed between the two men and grabbed another cold one.

"Well, I've been thinking a lot about the contract Thomas Jefferson made with Jedediah Spate," Matt began.

"You mean the agreement that gave Spate exclusive rights to the fur trade out to the Pacific?" Buzz clarified.

"Exactly, that's what essentially started it all for the Spates. It's where their fortune originated, so I figured that might be as good a place as any to begin."

"OK. So what's your angle?"

"Well, something's been bothering me ever since Becker told me about it," Matt said. "Why didn't Jefferson give that contract to Meriwether Lewis instead of Spate? After all, it was Lewis's plan to begin with and, don't forget, Lewis also had his own fur trading company by then—the Missouri Fur Company."

Matt rose from his seat and began to pace, something he did often when he was trying to think through a problem. "Don't you think it's a little strange Jefferson opted to go with Spate's company and not Lewis's? I mean, Jefferson was like a father to Lewis, so it just doesn't make sense."

Buzz was used to his younger friend's intensity, so he wasn't surprised when Matt began stalking around his front porch. He had also learned to trust Matt's instincts. If something didn't add up for Matt, he was most likely on to something. Buzz knew his job in these situations was to prod Matt with questions and hypotheses until they were able to pick up a trail that hopefully led to some answers.

Buzz offered, "Could it have been because Jefferson didn't

believe Lewis to be capable? By all accounts, Lewis was a depressive alcoholic."

Matt quickly countered, "Lewis's history of depression was well known to Jefferson *before* the expedition, as were his drinking habits. Yet he still entrusted him with a mission as critical as the exploration of the western half of the country."

"Good point," Buzz had to agree. He thought for a few moments and then tried a different tack. "What about the black tribe?"

"What about them?" Matt asked.

"Let's say, for the moment, Lewis was telling the truth about his capture by the black tribe," Buzz posited. "And certainly the skull you discovered goes a long way toward corroborating his story," he added. "Maybe Jefferson's choice of Spate over Lewis had something to do with dealing with the tribe."

"But why choose Spate? Lewis had firsthand knowledge of the tribe and knew exactly where they were located. Wouldn't he have been the logical choice to negotiate trading rights with them?" Matt reasoned.

"I guess so," Buzz agreed.

The cicadas began their rhythmic clicking. They started out quietly and gradually built to a loud crescendo before repeating the senseless commotion all over again. When Buzz had first purchased the property, their monotonous singing kept him up all night. Now he hardly noticed.

The men sat quietly for a few minutes listening to the property come alive with a cacophony of noises. In addition to the cicadas, they could make out the sounds of bullfrogs, crickets, and the occasional eerie call of a lone barn owl hunting for his dinner.

Finally, Matt spoke up with anticipation, "Hey, Buzz, do you think it's possible that a copy of the original agreement between Jefferson and Spate still exists?"

"It's a long shot Matt," Buzz said pragmatically. "But," he brightened and said, "it's not a bad avenue to pursue."

"What do you mean?"

"I mean Thomas Jefferson was a prolific letter writer. I read somewhere once he wrote and received as many as fifty thousand letters in his lifetime."

"Fifty thousand?" Matt remarked in astonishment. He was thinking back to his college days and how hard it had been to find the time to write even a couple of letters a year to his mother.

"He couldn't give a speech worth a damn, but the man could write," Buzz interjected. "Anyway, his collection of letters isn't just limited to family matters either. They deal with his political and business dealings in Paris, Philadelphia, New York, and Washington."

"Wait a minute—are you saying his collection of letters still exists?"

"It's not all in one place, but yes, the majority of it still exists. The problem is that something like nine hundred different repositories have at least some part of the collection. His personal papers are literally scattered across the globe," Buzz noted somberly.

"Well, shit, where would we even begin?"

"Don't lose faith, my boy. The good news is one of the repositories is the American Philosophical Society in Philadelphia. Jefferson was president of the APS at one time, so they have the largest collection of his papers and correspondence. From before, during, and after his presidency," Buzz said.

"Why is that good news?" Matt asked.

"Because the Society of the Cincinnati just happens to have a very *collegial* relationship with the American Philosophical Society." Buzz smiled.

"And you just happen to have a connection there, don't you?" Matt smiled back at his friend.

"I have connections everywhere, Matt," Buzz boasted. "But

in this case," he added, "the connection predates me by a couple of hundred years. You see, many of the first members of the SOC were also the APS's first board members and contributors, including Washington, Lafayette, and a bunch of others."

"So you can get me in?" Matt asked, cutting to the chase.

"I might consider it," Buzz joked. "Depends on how much money you've got in your wallet."

23

July 22, 1806

Lewis and Clark Expedition

Marias River, Northwest Montana

Meriwether Lewis had said his good-byes to Captain William Clark more than three weeks earlier. For the first time in their more than two-year journey, the two men would be separated for an extensive period of time. Lewis had decided that by dividing his command, he and Captain Clark would be able to explore twice as much territory and bring back that much more information to President Thomas Jefferson. It was decided that Lewis would explore the Marias River to the north while Clark would descend the Yellowstone River to the south. They would reunite at the junction of the Missouri and Yellowstone Rivers in six weeks' time—assuming everything went according to plan.

So far, the highly ambitious and highly risky plan for separate explorations had proven successful. Lewis and his team of six men had no encounters with Indians of any kind and the hunting had been plentiful. In one day alone they felled five deer, three elk, and a bear. Two days later, having reached the plains of Montana, they happily munched on roasted buffalo hump after encountering a herd that numbered in the thousands. Their biggest threat thus far had been *from the swarms of mosquitoes, for which they had little defense. Then on the morning of July 12, disaster struck. Seven of their seventeen horses went missing. Lewis suspected an Indian hunting party had made off with them in the middle of the night. As a result of losing almost half his horses, he was forced to divide his party yet again. He made the decision that he and three other men would continue up the Marias River. Even though they were armed with rifles, he knew they were essentially defenseless if they encountered twenty or thirty mounted warriors. Still, he was not about to abandon his stated mission of exploring the entire length of the river.*

Ten days later, Lewis and his party of three men had made excellent progress, encountering relatively few difficulties. When they reached the northernmost point of Cut Bank Creek, a branch of the Marias, Lewis decided to make camp for a couple of days. They were only twenty miles east of the Rocky Mountains. They would rest the horses, make celestial observations, and explore the surrounding area by foot.

Throughout the expedition, Lewis had often taken solo hikes, sometimes covering more than twenty miles in a day. As the sun rose on the morning of their second day in camp, he set out once again on another such exploration. He was in good spirits as he headed in a northwesterly direction toward the majestic mountains that stood in such stark contrast to the grassy plains to the east. The country was magnificent, the temperatures were pleasant, and there was an abundance of food.

He estimated he had covered close to ten miles in the four hours he had been walking. The sun had reached its apex. After stopping to quench his thirst from an ice cold stream, he decided it was time to turn around and head back to camp. But as he lifted his head from the water and wiped his face dry with the back of his sleeve, he spotted three mounted Indians on the opposite bank.

He froze.

His rifle was on the ground next to him and he didn't dare make a sudden move for fear of alarming the fierce-looking warriors. At first glance, he thought it was the angle of the sun casting dark shadows on their faces. But when he looked again, he realized that wasn't the case at all. The Indians' faces were black as coal. As he slowly stood up, he nonchalantly reached out and picked up his rifle. Just as he did, five more warriors emerged from the trees behind the first two. Lewis called out a greeting and used his free hand to make a sign of friendship. But the warriors did not respond. A twig snapped behind him. Lewis pivoted around quickly, but it was too late. He was clubbed unconscious.

A short time later, Lewis awoke disoriented and with a throbbing headache. He guessed that it was late afternoon since the sun was much lower in the sky. He tried to move but couldn't. That's when he realized his hands were tied behind his back to a wooden post buried in the ground. He looked around and tried to get his bearings. They had evidently brought him back to their village, but he was having trouble making sense of the inhabitants. He shook his head and blinked a few times, not believing what he was seeing. These were like no Indians he had ever encountered before.

At first he thought they might have painted their skin black as some sort of ritual. But when a curious young Indian boy approached Lewis, he could see it was their natural color. As the boy ran away giggling, he also noticed that his hair was short and kinky. The thought occurred to him that these people looked more like York—Captain Clark's African slave who had accompanied them on the expedition—than any Indian.

As was his training, Lewis immediately began to make mental observations of his surroundings. He scanned the horizon and spotted an odd-looking mountain to the northwest that rose significantly above the rest. It was flattened on top. There was a stream on the eastern edge of the camp running north to south. He could see women filling large clay jugs at the water's edge. The village itself was located in a flat valley between two ridgelines that ran parallel to the camp. The living enclosures were oval in shape and approximately twelve feet in diameter. Lewis counted forty that he could see from his vantage point, but he assumed there were at least twice as many in total. The frames of the lodges were made out of timber and covered in buffalo skins staked into the ground with sharp stones.

He had seen similar-looking structures in other Indian villages. But there was more order and symmetry to the design of this one. The camp was laid out in a rectangular shape and it appeared to have been there a very long time. Lewis guessed these were not nomadic people; this was their permanent home. Remarkably, he spotted what appeared to be the ancient remains of a walled enclosure that had at one time surrounded the encampment. But he knew there had to be another explanation, for Indians did not build forts.

Four men approached. One strode forward and unsheathed a long knife. Lewis immediately began to thrash about thinking he was going to be run through. But instead, the warrior sidestepped him and expertly sliced the ties that bound his hands to the post. Two other well-formed men pulled him roughly to his feet and marched him in the direction of the rocky ridgeline just to the east of the village. They traversed up a steep embankment before disappearing inside a dark cave.

It took a moment for Lewis's eyes to adjust to the darkness. When he did, he realized that it wasn't completely dark inside. There were small fires burning every twenty yards or so to guide their way. The narrow hallway soon opened up into a large chamber. Men lined the walls of the chamber and a large fire burned in the center of the room. The smoke rose and disappeared into fissures in the ceiling that Lewis assumed must eventually lead back outside. The men appeared to be older in age, as their faces were weathered and their closely cropped hair had turned white. The men sat silently on the floor looking with curious interest at the stranger in their midst.

Lewis was nudged from behind. As he stumbled forward, he could see a large stone pedestal twenty paces in front of him. It had a strange-looking metal helmet sitting on top. As he got closer, he became even more perplexed. He had seen this type of helmet before—in Spanish paintings—but he could not fathom how it could have ended up in this place. Who are these people?

But the mystery only deepened when the chief sitting at the base of the stone pedestal opened his mouth to speak. He didn't speak to Lewis, but rather addressed the council of elders. It was a strange dialect that Lewis couldn't quite place. The accent sounded nothing like what he had heard in his dealings with the Mandan, Sioux, Nez Perce, Shoshone, or any other Indian tribe, for that matter. There were some words that sounded remotely familiar to him but he couldn't quite place. He tried to interject but was silenced by a punch to the ribs by a large warrior standing next to him. After a lengthy discussion, the council seemed to reach an agreement. Lewis was ushered back outside.

Day had turned to night and the temperature had dropped considerably. Lewis had no idea what the men inside the cave had determined to be his fate. And he didn't intend to stick around to find out. It was quite dark by the time the warriors retied his hands to the wooden stake in the center of the village. For good measure, this time they also bound his feet. "Damn," Lewis muttered as the men disappeared into the darkness.

He immediately began to struggle in an attempt to loosen his binds. He searched the grounds nearby for anything that might help him cut the ropes from his hands. But it was no use. Frustrated and exhausted, he dropped his head to his chest. As the cool evening air dried his perspiration, he began to shiver. Not long after, some adolescent boys approached the spot where Lewis sat spent. They fanned out in a circle around him. One at a time, in an apparent test of their manhood, they inched forward to see how close they could get to Lewis before losing their nerve.

One brave boy got close enough to poke Lewis's shoulder. Emboldened, the rest of the boys closed in. The next one grabbed his hair. A third kicked him in the shin. That was enough for hardened explorer. He roared and bared his teeth like a wounded grizzly. It seemed to do the trick, as the boys turned and ran. But before they disappeared around the closest lodge, one boy picked up a rock and hurled it in Lewis's direction. It skittered across the ground harmlessly, falling short of its intended target.

Lewis was despondent. He couldn't believe his journey would end here. He wasn't afraid of dying, but he was devastated at failing his mentor, President Jefferson. He lifted his head. His eyes went wide with hope as he got a closer look at the rock lying just beyond his outstretched legs. It appeared to have a sharp edge. If he could somehow get hold of it, he might just have a chance to escape. He arched his back and kicked his feet out in front of him as far as they would go. On the third attempt, his right heel landed on top of the stone. Using his foot, he carefully dragged the stone back toward his body.

He slid down as close to the ground as possible and assumed a fetal position. He shimmied his body back and forth until the stone inched closer and closer to the stake. Finally, he moved it close enough so he could just reach it with his fingertips. He had been at it for more than an hour and needed to pause to collect his strength. He knew he had to proceed carefully, because this would be his only chance at escape.

He grabbed the stone precariously in his right hand and positioned it so that the sharp edge was facing the leather binds. He leaned hard against the stake for leverage. The idea was to use his body to create an up and down sawing motion. It took a little practice, but he finally found his rhythm. Every time he felt like he was making headway however, the rock would slip from his hands and he'd have to start all over again.

Progress was painfully was slow. Every now and then, someone would check on him and he would freeze, afraid they had seen what he was doing. But fortunately they paid him little attention. His captors seemed more interested in the celebration happening in a communal lodge at the far end of the village. And by the increasingly staggering gait of the warriors who happened by, Lewis guessed why. There was apparently plenty of drinking going on.

At long last, the stone jerked in his hands as one of the leather straps gave way. Overjoyed, he quickly sliced through the other strap. Before cutting the ties from his feet, however, he paused to rub his wrists and flex his fingers. Once the blood was circulating again, he leaned down and cut the final straps. He was free. Now all he had to do was get out of the village undetected.

Just as he was formulating his escape route, he heard someone approaching. A young warrior stumbled out of the shadows. Thinking fast, Lewis had just enough time to throw the leather cording back around his feet and quickly place his unbound hands behind the stake. If the warrior were to get close enough, he would clearly see that the bindings around his feet were way too loose. It was a haphazard job, but Lewis prayed it would be enough.

It turned out to be the same warrior who had checked on him earlier. This time, however, he came even closer to where Lewis lay on the ground. He looked unsteady on his feet and Lewis hoped his drunken state would make him less observant. That's when Lewis looked down and noticed the rock lying by his side. He silently cursed himself for not tossing it out of the way. The Indian took another step forward before coming to an abrupt stop. Lewis was sure the warrior had spotted the rock and that his escape had been sniffed out. He readied to charge.

But for some reason, the Indian turned quickly and hurried back into the shadows. A moment later, Lewis understood why. He could hear him throwing up. Breathing a sigh of relief, he quickly reached down and tossed the stone behind him in case the warrior decided to return. After waiting ten minutes he decided the Indian must have returned to the celebration. It was time to make his break.

He quietly slipped out of camp. He remembered the position of the late day sun and headed in the opposite direction—east. After all the walking he had done over the past two years, he was in excellent physical condition. He alternated running and walking for miles. He sloshed through streams so as not to leave a trail and he didn't stop to rest until he saw the sun begin to rise in front of him.

It was nightfall by the time he reunited with his men back at Cut Bank Creek.

24

Present Day
Philadelphia, PA

Matt arrived in Philadelphia just before noon. He had made the two-hundred-mile drive from Fredericksburg in just over three hours. Buzz had arranged an access pass that would allow Matt entry into the APS's Library Hall.

He still had a little time to kill before his scheduled appointment, so he paid a visit to Independence National Historic Park—where the Declaration of Independence and the U.S. Constitution had been debated and adopted. It was just a stone's throw away from the APS's headquarters. As he took in Philadelphia's historic sites, he felt like a kid again.

Growing up in Massachusetts, one of the original thirteen colonies, Matt had been hooked on American history at an early age. His mom had once driven him to nearby Lexington. There, they had visited a Revolutionary War–era tavern that still had visible in its thick wooden front door a bullet hole from one of the very first skirmishes that had started it all. Young Matt had stuck his finger inside the hole and imagined himself standing up to the oppressive British Redcoats and fighting bravely for his country's independence.

As a teenager, Matt had even contemplated becoming a soldier. His dad had served two tours in Vietnam and been awarded a purple heart. Matt had always figured he would follow in his father's footsteps and enlist in the marine corps. But it didn't work out that way. Scholarship offers from a host of Ivy League schools had placed him on a different path.

His dad had never been big on sharing his emotions, so Matt had become adept at reading his face. He knew when he was disappointed or disapproved of something, even though he'd never say so. That's how Matt knew he'd let him down by not serving his country. The same way he knew he disapproved of Matt's choice of a Wall Street career. "Bean counters" is what his father had called people in the financial world—guys who didn't do anything worthwhile except make money from other people's money. Matt had eventually traded in the world of finance to focus on his love of antiques and American history. But his father had succumbed to a heart attack by then. Even after his father's death, Matt realized, he was still trying to please him.

These were the thoughts running through his mind as he made his way toward the impressive Georgian facade of the American Philosophical Society's Library Hall. On display in the front lobby was a handwritten draft of the Declaration of Independence authored by Thomas Jefferson. The crossed-out words, notes in the margins, and alterations to the text, were clearly visible, offering proof that drafting the pivotal document was a painstaking and collective effort. Something today's politicians had forgotten how to do. As he stood in front of the specially framed exhibit, he marveled at the extraordinary group of men that had come together during that time to give birth to the greatest democracy the world had ever known.

"Mr. Hawkins?" a voice called out from behind him.

A prim young man approached and introduced himself stiffly

as the associate librarian and curator of manuscripts for the library.

"Thanks for seeing me on such short notice," Matt offered.

"If you'll follow me, please," the man said in a clipped tone, bypassing any niceties. "I'll take you to the Jefferson manuscript collection."

The man appeared to be a bit put off by Matt's presence. Matt thought he could even detect a hint of animosity. Perhaps the associate librarian was worried he was somehow out to disparage Jefferson's reputation. Matt hoped that wouldn't turn out to be the case.

He directed Matt through a door and into an area labeled "Documents Room." They made their way to a small cubby along the windowless back wall. He gave Matt a cursory tutorial on how to use the library's proprietary software to search the large database of Jefferson correspondence. Then he disappeared as abruptly as he had arrived.

"Nice talking to you," Matt whispered under his breath sarcastically.

There was only one other person in the room. But he was so absorbed in whatever he was researching he'd barely acknowledged Matt's presence. There was something about libraries that always made Matt feel uncomfortable and out of place. Maybe it was because they were so stuffy and deathly quiet. Matt was just the opposite—perpetual motion and boundless energy. That's why, even though he had graduated summa cum laude from Brown University, he had rarely set foot inside the campus library.

But today was different. He had to find something—anything—that might provide a clue as to what Oliver and Landon Spate were keeping under wraps on the Blackfeet Reservation. And so, he would start at the beginning—with Jedediah Spate's agreement with Thomas Jefferson. The agreement that made the patriarch of the Spate family rich and provided the seed capital that ultimately helped make his descendants one of the wealthiest families in twenty-first-century America.

Matt soon discovered there were thousands of Jefferson letters cataloged in the library's computer database. But luckily they had all been digitized. All he had to do was search for terms he thought might lead to a relevant correspondence. That in turn would hopefully reveal a clue. The searchable database was divided into subcategories with titles like Political Correspondence, General Correspondence, Personal Correspondence, and so on.

Matt decided to start with Political Correspondence. On a whim, he entered the term *black tribe,* but it came back with no entries found. Evidently, this wasn't going to be that easy. Next he entered *conquistador,* but again there was nothing. He tried a series of terms he felt had potential. Very few hits came up. And even if a letter did get flagged, it turned out to be unrelated to anything of interest to Matt.

As he continued searching, he couldn't help but be fascinated as he read through the personal correspondence of the country's third president, albeit in digitized form. In many of the dispatches, Jefferson argued passionately against a strong central government. He came out adamantly against Alexander Hamilton's ambitious plan to establish a government-run central bank. Over and over again, Jefferson wrote eloquently in support of states' rights, pushing back against the strong nationalist desires of the Federalists. As Matt read on, it suddenly occurred to him how consistent Jefferson's highly constrained view of federal power was with the Spate family's antigovernment ideology.

Matt knew some historians believed Jefferson's anti-Federalist views were born out of fear that a strong central government might threaten slavery. Jefferson, after all was a Virginia aristocrat and slave owner. And a political base of Southern plantation owners had helped get him elected president in 1800. These same historians believed Jefferson had no intention of letting a strong, northern-dominated federal government destroy the economic engine of the South, which was so dependent on the institution of slavery. It would have been both personal and political suicide.

Matt continued his search and moved on to Jefferson's personal correspondence. But again, he came up empty. Frustrated, he rubbed his eyes and arched his back until a couple of vertebrae cracked loudly. He fought a yawn and decided to get up and walk around a bit. The room had acquired a third occupant, a bookish-looking woman. She stole quick glances at Matt from behind an ominously large stack of research materials. But the minute Matt looked her way she ducked back behind her books, like a prairie dog retreating into its burrow.

He had the urge to go outside and suck some fresh air into his lungs, but decided against it. Based on the chilly response he had received upon arriving, he feared the associate librarian might lock the door behind him and not let him back in. Instead, he returned to his seat in front of the computer to continue his tedious search.

He decided to move on to the General Correspondence subcategory. He tried every term he could think of, but to no avail. He didn't find a single reference anywhere that even remotely related to a black tribe of Indians, a conquistador helmet, or a fur trade agreement. And he hadn't come across any letters to or from Jedediah Spate.

He was about to give up when one last subheading at the bottom of the index caught his eye. It read simply, "Subject Unknown." Cataloged under this heading were letters in which either the addressee was unknown or the condition of the letter was such that its subject could not be determined. *What the hell.* He typed in the name Jedediah Spate.

Remarkably, he was rewarded. A single letter popped up on the screen. Matt wanted to jump out of his seat, thrust a fist in the air and scream "yes." But he knew his timorous roommates would rat him out. He'd be kicked out for sure. So he returned to the screen and began scrolling through the letter. That's when his excitement evaporated like a mirage in the desert.

The letter was dated October 1807. It was addressed to Thomas Jefferson and was signed by Jedediah Spate. But in between the salutation and the signature, the letter contained nothing but line after line of nonsensical gibberish.

Matt couldn't believe it. "What the hell is this?" he said out loud. To which he received a stern "shush" from the prairie dog across the room.

He reread the letter but still couldn't make any sense of it. He thought for a minute that it might have been written in Latin. But he soon concluded it wasn't. He'd taken the dead language in high school and he knew the words on the page bore little resemblance. He was beyond frustrated.

He had come all this way to find a letter that might give him a helpful clue, only to have it make absolutely no sense at all. But he was determined not to leave empty-handed. So before leaving, he pressed the Print button and snatched a copy of the letter off the printer. He was glad to be free of the stuffy confines of the library. But he was completely baffled by the letter stuffed inside the front pocket of his backpack. He hoped Buzz or Director Fox might have an idea what it all meant.

If they didn't, then it was back to square one—yet again.

25

Present Day
Washington, D.C.

The Society of the Cincinnati was an organization almost as old as the country itself. It had been formed, shortly after the conclusion of the American Revolution, by officers of the Continental Army who had helped secure America's independence from the British. Notable members included Nathanael Green, Henry Knox, Marquis de Lafayette, Alexander Hamilton, and, of course, George Washington, the organization's very first president. Its present-day headquarters were located on Embassy Row in the Dupont Circle neighborhood of Washington, D.C. That's where Matt was headed.

Buzz, the society's president, James Fox, its executive director, and Matt gathered inside Buzz's wood-paneled office. Unlike their previous search for Washington's surrender letter, the three men didn't know exactly what they were looking for this time.

"The last time we did this, we knew we were looking for a surrender letter from Washington. This time it's like we're flying without a compass," Buzz grumbled, as the three men sat around a square conference table.

"I know. Every time I feel like we've uncovered a solid lead, it turns out to be just another dead end," Matt remarked.

"So let's see this letter you found," Director Fox interjected, anxious to lay eyes on the document.

Matt handed the letter across to Fox. He studied it for a minute or two in silence, rubbing his chin. Then he handed it over to Buzz.

"I had a feeling that's what it was," Fox spoke up suddenly, "but I'd never actually seen an example of one before, so I wasn't sure. It's quite remarkable."

"You mind telling us what the hell you're talking about?" Matt prodded.

"Sorry, it's just so fascinating," he replied with a look of wonder. Sensing Matt's impatience, he finally relented and said, "This letter appears to have been written in code."

"In code?" Matt and Buzz said in unison.

Fox nodded in the affirmative.

"They had that back then?" Matt asked skeptically.

Fox answered, "They did indeed. As a matter of fact, Thomas Jefferson was somewhat obsessed with secret codes. He even made sure Meriwether Lewis was well versed in deciphering coded messages before he embarked on his journey to discover the Northwest Passage."

Matt looked at Buzz in disbelief and asked him, "Did you know about this?"

"Hell no, I just run the place," he said with a twinkle in his eye. "James is the expert." He turned to his scholarly subordinate, "Educate us, James."

Fox reached inside his briefcase. "When Matt called and told us about the letter written in gibberish, it occurred to me it might have been written in code. So I did a little research," he said. "Here, I brought a book with me that details Jefferson's early experimentation with secret codes." Fox handed it across the table to Matt.

"How about giving us the crib notes version," Matt prompted.

"Of course," Fox said. "Jefferson first became interested in securing his official communications while serving as George Washington's secretary of state in the early 1790s. With war threatening between England and France, and ongoing negotiations with Spain over American trade, Jefferson knew communiqués to his overseas representatives could easily be intercepted and read by the wrong people. That's when he began experimenting with different methods for coding messages."

"What kind of methods?" Buzz asked.

"Pretty ingenious ones considering we're talking about the end of the eighteenth century," Fox noted. "What he did was devise a system of twenty-six paper strips that could be arranged and rearranged to form a sort of flexible cipher system. And on each strip was written a scrambled version of the alphabet."

"So how did the guy on the receiving end unscramble the letters?" Matt asked, trying to follow along.

"The critical piece to making the whole thing work was the creation of a key word—or words—for which only the sender and receiver knew the identity. Without the key word you couldn't decode the letter."

"Son of a bitch," Matt blurted out with a sudden realization. "So what you're saying is without knowing the key word, we'll never be able to decode the letter I found."

"Actually," Fox admitted, "it's worse than that."

"The hits just keep on coming," Matt muttered.

"Go on, James," Buzz prompted.

"Well, it turns out these strips of paper, which amounted to twenty-six moving parts, weren't exactly practical for use in the field. They were cumbersome and could blow away in the wind. So, along with a man named Robert Patterson, a noted mathematician and fellow member of the American Philosophical Society, Jefferson invented what he called a wheel cipher," he explained. "He took his original design of alphabetized pieces of paper and had them punched into wooden disks. He then had these twenty-six wooden disks mounted on an iron spindle so the user could spin the disks to scramble or unscramble words."

Fox paused to reach into his briefcase one more time. He pulled out a sheet of paper and passed it over to Matt.

"Here's a picture of a reproduction of one of Jefferson's wheel ciphers. This one is housed in the National Museum of American History here in Washington."

"Perfect, so why don't we just use this," Matt pointed optimistically to the picture, "to decipher the letter I found?"

"Unfortunately, it's not that easy, Matt. You see, each wooden cylinder was numbered one through twenty-six. And the sequence in which they were threaded onto the spindle mattered. If just one of the numbered cylinders was out of sequence, then the message would never be able to be decoded."

"A more secure system," Buzz said. "The key word was no longer necessary. Instead, you had to know the order of the disks."

"Exactly," Fox replied.

"What the hell were Spate and Jefferson up to that they needed such a secure system?" Matt asked, more to himself than to anyone else.

"Unfortunately, that's a question we may never be able to answer," Buzz replied.

Matt ignored Buzz's pessimism. He turned back to Fox and said, "So what you're telling us is if we ever hope to decipher this gibberish," he held up a copy of the letter he had found at the APS, "we'll just have to get our hands on one of these original ciphers. Then somehow figure out the correct order of the numbered disks on the spindle."

"Hypothetically, that's true," Fox agreed, "but unfortunately,

Jefferson only had a handful of these made..."

"And let me guess," Matt said. "None of the originals remain."

"I'm afraid not."

"You got any good news in that briefcase of yours?" Matt said in growing frustration.

"I'm afraid not," Fox said, repeating himself.

26

Present Day
Savannah, GA

It took Matt more time than usual to get going that morning. He had caught the last flight out of D.C. and didn't get back home until well after midnight. His stiff neck was probably the by-product of falling asleep on the plane with his head wedged between the torturously rigid seatback and the hard plastic passenger window frame.

He usually followed his rigorous morning stretch with a run in Forsyth Park, but not today. He had overslept and was late for work. By the time he made it downstairs to his shop, Hawkins Antiques was already open for business. His spirits were lifted when he smelled the rich aroma of freshly brewed coffee. He conveyed a silent "thank you" to his mostly reliable and always irascible store manager.

Christina spotted Matt coming around the corner and voiced a typically blunt greeting, "You look like shit, boss."

"Not now, Christina, I'm not in the mood."

Not missing a beat, she replied, "That time of the month already?"

Matt brushed past her and headed directly for the steaming pot of coffee, which was beckoning him like a Greek siren. He poured himself a mug and held it reverently with two hands, as if it contained some magical elixir. He took a big sip and felt halfway human.

"I need my morning cup of coffee before I can handle my morning dose of Christina," he finally volleyed back. His first gulp of coffee seemed to rekindle his interest in engaging in the customary repartee with his store manager.

But Christina decided to let it slide. She knew Matt was tired. He'd gotten himself involved in yet another wild goose chase, and even though she would never admit it, she was worried about him.

"So how'd it go up in D.C.?" she asked.

"One step forward, two steps back," he said.

Matt had kept Christina apprised of the odyssey that had begun in Montana. She was aware he had been to both Philadelphia and Washington, D.C., in search of clues that might lead to some kind of resolution to the conquistador helmet mystery. She had stopped trying to get him to back off and drop the whole thing. She knew it wasn't his nature to abandon anything. And that included her.

Matt had given Christina more than a job when he had hired her a few years back; he had given her a sense of belonging. And that was not something a girl who had been abused by her father and who had run away from home at sixteen took for granted. She rarely let it show, but behind all her crass talk, she trusted Matt more than anyone else in her life. She loved him like a big brother and would be lost without him in her life.

"Anything I can do?" she said genuinely.

Matt peered skeptically over the lip of his mug. "What's the catch? Hey, wait a minute," he said, "if you're playing nice-nice to get another raise, you can forget it. I just gave you one six months ago."

"I'm not gunning for a raise. Jesus, Matt, there doesn't always have to be an angle you know," she said, honestly hurt. "The truth is you really do look like shit and I was...a little worried, that's all."

Matt backed off when he recognized her concern was genuine. "Hey, I appreciate the offer. But I'm not sure there's anything anyone can do at this point. For every door that opens, another one gets slammed in my face." He paused and took another big gulp of his coffee. "I don't know, maybe it's time to give this whole thing a rest for a while."

The bells above the front door jingled, signaling the arrival of the day's first customer. Both Matt and Christina turned, curious to see if the new arrival was a regular or one of Savannah's army of tourists. But the man who entered didn't appear to be either.

He was nattily dressed in a white linen suit and matching white shoes. And he sported a neatly trimmed white mustache and goatee. It looked to Matt like this guy had just stepped out of a Colonel Sanders look-alike competition. Matt hadn't seen one advertised in the local paper, but Savannah was known for sponsoring wackier events.

As he approached the front desk, Matt noticed his visitor had on a Hawaiian print shirt underneath his neatly pressed linen jacket. And the matching shoes weren't dress shoes at all: They were white Chuck Taylor high-top sneakers. Apparently the guy was something of an eccentric.

The man offered a toothy grin, "Are you the proprietor?"

Matt thought there was something vaguely familiar about him. Then he noticed the man's eyes. They were electric blue and flickered with playful mischievousness. Matt felt as though he had looked into those eyes before. But he knew that was impossible. There was no way he would have forgotten meeting this character.

"Proprietor?" Christina snickered sarcastically, under her breath. She stifled a laugh. Then she made a hasty retreat to the back room. Before leaving she remarked so only Matt could hear her, "This one's all yours, boss." He shot her a stern look in return.

Matt turned back around and introduced himself. But the man just stood there, sizing Matt up, as if debating his next move. All the while he had a crazy grin plastered on his face. A loopy kind of look you'd expect to see on a patient who'd missed his last round of meds. The image of a straightjacket and men in white coats popped into Matt's head.

Finally, Matt offered, "Are you looking for something in particular?"

The man began to chuckle. Then the chuckle gradually became a full-on laughing spasm. The sudden and unexpected outburst startled Matt. He took a reflexive half step back. *Maybe this guy did give an asylum the slip.*

Finally, the man composed himself and uttered through one last chuckle, "That, my friend, is the definition of irony."

If he was confused before, Matt was completely baffled now. The oddly dressed visitor appeared harmless and Matt didn't feel threatened. Apprehensive might be more accurate. He didn't quite know what to do with him. But after his sudden outburst, the man simply returned to staring at Matt with those impossibly blue eyes, as if he were an old acquaintance waiting to be recognized.

A bit exasperated, Matt finally gave in and asked, "Sorry, but have we met before?"

The man chuckled again. Then with an exaggerated bow and affected formal voice he exclaimed, "Harry Spate...at your service."

It took a moment for Matt to register the name. Then another moment for him to recover from the shock of having the infamously exiled youngest Spate brother standing inside his shop.

That's why he had looked so familiar, Matt suddenly realized. He had seen his picture in the newspaper clipping Becker had found. Then another thought struck him. He had stared into those eyes before—only they had belonged to Samantha.

He said, "Well, Mr. Spate, you're the last person I expected to walk through that door today."

"Call me Harry," he said with a dismissive wave of his hand. He did an about-face and looked around as if just noticing his surroundings. "What a fabulous place," he said enthusiastically. He immediately set out toward the back of the store. Matt came around from behind the counter and hurried to catch up with the intrepid intruder.

Harry wandered happily from room to room, inspecting Matt's eclectic collection of antiques and oddities. Suddenly, he stopped short, threw his hands into the air and shouted like an excited child, "Look at all this stuff."

He turned back around to face Matt, who still appeared a bit shell-shocked. He leaned in and whispered conspiratorially, "You know, I'm something of a collector myself."

Matt knew Harry hadn't come to buy antiques, but he decided to play along. He'd let him get to the real purpose of his visit in his own time. So he gave him the nickel tour of his shop.

After touring the place, Harry suggested they get some fresh air. They crossed over West Gordon Street and found a bench in the relative privacy of Monterey Square. Outside in the open, however, Harry became noticeably more guarded.

"Samantha says you can be trusted," he began abruptly, the conviviality completely disappearing from his voice. He glanced over his shoulder to ensure nobody was eavesdropping. "And there's nobody I trust more in this world than my daughter," he continued. "You need to know that if she hadn't told me to trust you, I wouldn't be here right now."

"Well, I appreciate that, Harry," Matt replied, "but I've got to be honest with you, I'm not sure the feeling is mutual. You Spates aren't exactly up there with the Boy Scouts on my trustworthiness meter."

Harry threw his head back and laughed approvingly. Then he said, "I can see why she likes you, Matt. You don't pull any punches."

Matt was pleased by the thought of Samantha's approval. And this surprised him. Then he recalled their meeting at the Crystal. How he had taken her hands in his after she had broken down and cried. There had been an emotional connection in that moment he hadn't admitted until now. Just as suddenly, another image flashed through his head—of Ally standing naked in front of a dying fire. He forced himself to push these distracting thoughts from his mind.

"Thanks for the compliment, Harry," he said to the man whose emotions unnervingly ping-ponged between jolly and paranoid in an instant. "But like I said, I'm not feeling very trusting at the moment."

"Would it make a difference if I told you that 'A. Friend' was Samantha's idea?" Harry offered up. He watched Matt's face closely for his reaction. It had the intended effect.

"You mean..." Matt began to say, surprised by this revelation.

Harry nodded. "Samantha insisted we set up some way to communicate with you, to warn you if necessary. Frankly, I thought it was too risky, but it turned out she was right."

Matt sat quietly, mulling over the implications of what he had just learned. There was no doubt Samantha's warning had saved his ass out on Ghost Ridge. But at the same time, she and her father had been using him. He wanted to trust her, but he couldn't shake the feeling he was somehow still being played. And that pissed him off.

"You act as if we were working together," Matt said angrily, "that we had some sort of partnership. But the truth is, you two were just manipulating me to serve your own cause. And I almost got shot because of it."

"Guilty as charged," Harry readily acknowledged. "I'm not going to deny we thought we could use your nosing around the reservation to our advantage." He paused looking for the right words, knowing he had to explain himself carefully if he hoped to enlist Matt's help going forward. He switched gears and explained, "But you've got to understand we've been at this a very long time. My daughter has put herself at great risk. And believe me, as a father, that's not easy to live with."

Matt, still simmering at how his life had been put at risk, shot back without thinking, "You seem to be doing OK with it." He immediately regretted his blunt remark when he saw the look on Harry Spate's face.

"That's not fair, son," Harry replied quietly. "My daughter is the most important person in my life." His voice cracked as he continued, "She's the only family I've got left."

Matt's tone softened. "So why did you ask her to do all of this?"

"That's the crazy thing," he said slowly, "I didn't. This whole undercover thing was her idea. She volunteered."

A couple of teenagers skateboarded past. Harry waited for them to exit the park before continuing, "A couple of years into her job at Spate Industries she discovered the extent of my brothers' unlawful activities, and she was disgusted. She decided something had to be done...and she wasn't going to quit until they were brought to justice." He paused. "She's stubborn that way," he added, with a touch of fatherly pride.

Matt couldn't help but be impressed with Samantha's courage, and he could certainly relate to her stubbornness. But he was still a bit miffed for being lied to and manipulated. He decided it was time to find out what Harry really wanted.

"Why did you come here today, Harry?"

Harry cocked his head slightly to one side as if he were perplexed by Matt's question. "Isn't it obvious, Matt? We'd like you to join us. Help us expose my brothers' activities to the world before it's too late."

Matt's instincts were setting off alarm bells in his head. "Look, Harry, I'm sorry for how they treated you, and I don't need any further convincing your brothers are a couple of bad guys. But I'm really not interested in getting in the middle of a pissing match over your family's fortune."

Harry looked at Matt with disappointment. "Is that what you think this is all about—money?" Agitated, he ran a hand through his goatee. "Haven't you heard what Samantha and I have been trying to tell you?"

"Come on, Harry, let's be real here. You haven't told me half of what you know," Matt said, his voice rising in anger. "I get it. Your brothers are a couple of sleazebags with lots of skeletons in their walk-in closets. And Spate Industries isn't going to take home the prize for being a model corporate citizen. But shit, Harry, there's a long line of companies out there thumbing their noses at environmental laws and lobbying Congress to protect their profits." Matt inched closer and said, "So why don't you tell me what this is *really* all about."

Harry looked away for a moment. When he looked up again, Matt's intense gaze hadn't abated. He knew the time had come to give Matt more. So he took a deep breath and declared, "You're right, Matt. It's time you understood what's really going on."

He wiped a bead of sweat from his brow before continuing, "What if I told you my brothers are...attempting to overthrow the United States government." He paused a moment to let the admittedly dubious accusation sink in. Then he asked, "Would that change your mind about joining us?"

"Wait a minute, are you saying you think your brothers are terrorists?"

"In a manner of speaking, yes."

Matt looked dumbstruck. His mind was spinning, trying to reconcile Harry's accusation with what he knew about Oliver and

Landon Spate. He had no problem believing they were greedy, crooked bastards who had probably been dumping toxic waste into the environment—but terrorists? It just didn't add up. They were billionaires for Chrissakes. Why the hell would they want to undermine the very democratic system that helped give them opportunity to accumulate all their wealth in the first place?

Then an odd smile appeared at the corners of his mouth. A more likely explanation had just occurred to him. He suddenly saw Harry Spate in a new light, and it wasn't a flattering one. The dual personalities, the Hawaiian shirt, the sneakers, with the white linen suit—it all made sense now. This guy wasn't eccentric, he was just plain nuts.

Matt placed both hands firmly on the bench seat and pushed himself up. "It's been nice talking to you, Harry." He turned and started to walk back toward his shop.

"Matt, wait," Harry called after him, "I know it sounds far-fetched, but at least hear me out..."

"Good-bye, Harry. This is my stop. You'll have to ride on to crazy town without me," he shouted over his shoulder without turning around.

Harry had no choice but to play his final card.

He shouted after Matt, "Aren't you curious to know where that conquistador helmet ended up?"

27

Present Day
Savannah, GA

Matt stopped, but his back was still turned to Harry Spate. He spun around, "Look, you crazy son of a bitch," he said, his voice a near shout, "I'm tired of being jerked around." He took two quick strides forward so that he was quite close to Harry. "Tell me everything you know about that goddamned helmet," he demanded.

Harry was frozen in place. "Of...course," he stammered, shaken by Matt's sudden outburst. "I was going to tell you, but you got up and left so quickly that I...I didn't have the chance."

"I'm here now, Harry," Matt replied angrily.

"Please," Harry insisted, "come sit back down. I'm willing to tell you everything, Matt. I *want* to tell you everything...because the truth is I think you're the best chance we've got to expose my brothers for who they are and what they're trying to do. But it's a long story, so please," he pleaded, motioning for Matt to come back to the bench.

Matt ran his hands through his thick sandy-blond hair. He forced himself to breath to help release some the anger pulsing through his body. After a long pause, he reluctantly returned to his seat.

Harry sat down tentatively, careful to leave a sizable gap between himself and Matt. "I always knew there was something strange about that helmet," he began. "I first saw it in my parent's home right after I graduated from college, back in the summer of '73. I asked my father where it had come from, but all he told me was that one of his drill teams had dug it up on a job site. But he never said where."

Matt snapped to attention. "Oh my God, the old guy in the fancy Cadillac that bought the helmet from Big Tom. That was your father?" he said wide-eyed.

Harry nodded. He continued, "My father didn't like to talk about it. It was almost as if he were afraid of it—like it was cursed or something. It was the same fear Samantha noticed on my brothers' faces when you showed up asking questions about it almost forty years later. That's when we knew this helmet was not some arbitrary relic found on a job site. It represented something much more important," he said.

"And *that's* when you decided to use my investigation to serve your own ends," Matt inserted.

Harry looked across at Matt and said sheepishly, "Yes, I'm afraid that's true."

More people had made their way into the park square. The new arrivals sat sipping their coffee, chatting on their cell phones, or simply enjoying the relative morning coolness. They knew Savannah's oppressive afternoon summer heat and humidity were not far away. Harry looked each one of them over suspiciously.

At least one mystery had been solved for Matt. Harry Spate's father was the man who had bought the helmet from Big Tom. But he still wasn't any closer to determining what the significance of the Blackfeet Reservation was to the Spate family.

"So how does Ghost Ridge factor in to all this?" Matt asked, still seeking clarity.

"That's what we were hoping *you* might figure out," Harry countered. "Samantha and I had no idea the helmet was tied to Big Tom or Ghost Ridge. We had never seen the newspaper article you found with Big Tom's picture holding the helmet."

"Seriously?" Matt asked.

"Why would we?" he answered defensively. "That happened a very long time ago, and the helmet had long since been forgotten. But we did know," he held his index finger up in the air like a prosecutor emphasizing a point, "that my family *was* hiding something out on Ghost Ridge. That's the only explanation for continually renewing the drilling rights but never putting any holes in the ground."

"So what the hell are they hiding?" Matt blurted out in frustration. He feared he was about to fall back into his maddening pattern of fitful progress—one step forward, two steps back.

"I truly don't know, Matt," Harry answered, looking around nervously. "But I'm absolutely convinced the helmet *and* the skull you found are tied to something big. It has to be something big, because it has put the fear of God into my brothers."

Matt shook his head skeptically but remained silent.

Harry filled the void. "Something's out there, Matt," he insisted, "and it just might be the thing that can help us expose the subversive plans of my brothers *and* their unscrupulous company."

"Don't start in on all that terrorist talk again, Harry," Matt warned.

Afraid Matt might bolt again Harry held up both hands and said, "All I ask is that you hear me out. Just listen to what Samantha and I have compiled on my brothers' activities over the past few years. If after I'm finished you choose to walk away...then I'll never bother you again. I promise." He looked expectantly at Matt, waiting for his response.

Matt figured he'd come this far. And Harry had solved the helmet mystery for him, so he said, "Alright, Harry, I'll listen to what you have to say. But if I think for one second you're bullshitting me, or if I feel like you're playing me again, then I'm out of here. OK?"

"Deal," Harry said quickly.

Harry collected his thoughts for a moment longer. Then he began, "Spate Industries had revenues of well over a hundred billion dollars last year, making them the largest privately held company in the country. And because they are private and debt-free, they don't have to pay dividends to shareholders or interest on any bank loans. The majority of the company's profits go directly into my brothers' pockets. I can't tell you exactly how much that was last year, because Spate Industries doesn't share their financial statements with the public. But I can say with confidence my brothers are the two richest men in America."

"Bill Gates and Warren Buffett are always number one and two on the lists I see," Matt countered.

"That's only because my brothers run a privately held entity, so nobody knows exactly how much money they take home in a year. And that's just how they like it. They are *very* secretive people."

"OK, I won't argue the point with you. I'm sure they have a shitload of cash sitting in their bank accounts."

"That's just it," Harry interrupted. "Their money is not sitting idly by in some bank account. It's funding the biggest threat to democracy our country has ever known."

Matt had promised to listen, so he remained quiet. But he couldn't hide the look of skepticism that had returned to his face.

Undeterred, Harry continued, "Do you remember learning in school about the Gilded Age that took place in America in the second half of the nineteenth century? It was during the time when the Industrial Revolution and advances in science helped the U.S. economy grow at the fastest rate in its history. And it was when industrialists and financiers like Rockefeller, Morgan, Carnegie, and Vanderbilt built their fortunes. But it was also an age of big political machines, payoffs, and patronage. Political corruption was rampant. Business leaders spent gobs of money to ensure government didn't regulate the activities of big business. Corruption reached into the halls of Congress and even into Ulysses S. Grant's White House.

"Unequal distribution of wealth skyrocketed, and working and living conditions deteriorated for the average American," he continued. "It got so bad there were eventually widespread calls for reform. Over time, new laws were passed and the big political machines were finally dismantled. But for a long while our democratic nation was literally in the hands of a small number of very wealthy individuals."

Matt nodded. "I've read a little bit about that period, but frankly I'd forgotten about it."

"Most people have. And most people, including you, would never dream it could happen again." He paused. "And that's exactly what my brothers are counting on."

"So what are you telling me—that they're building a political machine, like Tammany Hall in New York City?" Matt asked.

Harry laughed. "With the resources at my brothers' disposal, they make Boss Tweed look like an amateur." He pivoted in his seat to face Matt. "You need to understand my brothers *already have* in place the most comprehensive network of influence this country has ever seen."

Matt recalled his conversation with David Becker. "I have a friend who's an investigative reporter at the *New York Times*," he said. "He told me it's only recently come to light that your brothers are the secret money behind a vast network of grassroots political organizations."

Harry smiled. "Who do you think leaked that information to the press?" he said.

With a newfound respect, Matt smiled at Harry Spate for the first time. He said, "OK, Harry, you've got my attention. So how exactly does all this lead to the takeover of our democracy?"

"Make no mistake, Matt, the takeover has already begun—in fact it's almost complete," Harry replied ominously. "My brothers are following a familiar script from the industrialists of the Gilded Age, albeit with a twenty-first-century spin."

He explained, "First, limit the vote from the poorest segment of the population, through voting restrictions, voter ID laws, and immigration policies. Second, rewrite campaign finance laws so that wealthy corporate entities can provide unlimited funding to candidates who back their agenda. Third, control elections through creative redistricting to ensure your preferred politicians are never in danger of being voted out of office. And lastly, control the public dialog and public opinion through misinformation disseminated by quasi-legitimate think tanks, academia, or through outright owner-ship of media channels."

Harry lowered his voice to a whisper, "The script has been writ-ten, Matt. Most of the actors are already in place. They are *this* close," he held his thumb and index finger together, "to making a sham of our representative democracy."

Matt couldn't believe what he was hearing. Could something like this be possible in twenty-first-century America? He comment-ed, "I hate to say it, but as scary a picture as you've painted, it doesn't seem as though your brothers have broken any laws."

"Oh, they've broken laws, believe me. For starters, they've got politicians and judges on their payroll and they've dumped more cancer-causing toxic waste into the environment than any other company in America," he answered hotly. "And the last time I checked, it's a crime to conspire to bring down the United States government."

Harry realized he had become animated again, so he leaned back on the bench and admitted, "But you're right in the respect they will be hard to stop. They've been flying so far under the radar they're underground, for God's sake. You've got to realize they've been at this for close to forty years. And in that time of operating in complete anonymity, they've built an incredibly comprehensive and effective cover organization." Then he looked at Matt with a glimmer of hope. "*But*," he said with emphasis, "they are becoming impatient and they're starting to take more risks. And this just might be our chance to expose them."

"I'm not sure I'm following. How are they taking more risks?"

"Even with all their progress, it hasn't moved fast enough for them. They've realized they're not getting any younger. They'd like to finish what they started before they're too old to enjoy the fruits of their efforts." He paused and took a deep breath. "So they've begun to speed up their timeline."

"What does that mean?" Matt got up from the bench. Nervous energy had begun to course through his body, as if someone had thrown a switch.

"It means *murder*, Matt," Harry stated flatly.

Matt's face registered a mixture of shock and confusion.

Harry continued, "We believe they've begun to eliminate people who are standing in their way." He paused and then added solemnly, "Including the chief justice of the Supreme Court."

"Come on," Matt nearly shouted in disbelief. "You mean old Bob Saunders?" he said, referring to the recently deceased octogenarian Supreme Court justice. He'd been on the court since the Carter administration. "I read that he died of a heart attack."

"That's what the papers wrote, but we've talked to his doctor. According to his last physical, his heart was perfect. He was more fit then men twenty years his junior," Harry replied. "But that's not what really convinced us."

"Go on."

"A couple of years ago, Samantha uncovered an internal document that specifically called out the judge. Evidently, he had ruled against a number of immigration and redistricting cases that the Spate network had spent a lot of money supporting. To put it mildly, he had become a thorn in my brothers' sides—and an outspoken one at that. This document Samantha found said, and I quote, 'he is a problem that needs to be dealt with.' We really didn't think much of it at the time. But we changed our minds when the judge...and others...started dying."

"Others?" Matt said incredulously. "You mean the judge wasn't the only one you think they've murdered?"

"Matt, there were a total of ten names listed in this document—cleverly titled 'Enemies of the Spate.'" He paused and shook his head in disgust. "Anyway, in addition to Justice Saunders, over the past two years, two senators and two congressmen named on the list are dead. Two reportedly passed away from heart attacks and the other two died in what were termed 'tragic accidents,'" Harry said while making exaggerated quotation marks with both hands.

"Five out of the ten people on the list are dead, Matt. A little too coincidental, wouldn't you agree?"

Before Matt could respond, Harry added one final piece of evidence as proof of a widespread conspiracy orchestrated by his brothers and Spate Industries. "By the way," he said, "all of them held key positions of influence on key congressional committees. And here's the kicker, every one of the deceased has been replaced with someone friendly to Spate—including the newest member of our Supreme Court."

"Holy shit," Matt muttered. He sat back down heavily on the bench, weighed down by the gravity of Harry's words. "And all this is to limit the reach of the federal government?"

"Not *limit* the reach of the federal government, Matt," Harry scoffed. "They want to gut it."

"What do they have in mind?"

"You've heard of the term *hostile takeover*? When an unwanted bidder takes over a company that is unwilling to merge with them?" Harry asked.

Matt nodded. He had spent enough time on Wall Street to know exactly what the term meant.

"Well, that's what my brothers are doing. Only they're doing it covertly. And their target isn't another company—*it's the government of the United States.*"

"And if they succeed, then what will they do?" Matt asked, feeling slightly sick to his stomach.

"Once the government is neutered, corporate America will move in and fill the void," Harry replied grimly. "The first thing they'll do is repeal all forms of government taxation. This will open the door for the private sector to step in and institute a "fee for use" system. So if you want to drive on the highway, you'll have to pay a fee. If you want clean drinking water, you'll have to pay a fee. If you want your kids to go to good schools, you'll have to pay for it."

He paused to take a breath. "In the beginning people will cheer the fact they no longer have to pay taxes. But eventually they will come to realize that privatization doesn't come cheap. And that they'll be paying more in private fees than they ever did in taxes. But it will be too late. The wealthiest in society will be able to afford the better services, the better amenities, the better schools, and so on—but the average Joe won't."

He continued, "Next they'll eliminate any and all government oversight agencies—starting with the Securities and Exchange Commission, the Environmental Protection Agency, and the Occupational Safety and Health Administration. So that industry will be free to do as they please without fear of accountability or reprisal of any kind."

Matt remained silent; head down. Harry paused to catch his breath as well as to let Matt grasp the enormity of just how extreme his brothers' plan really was.

"Sounds just like the Gilded Age you described," Matt said in a voice barely above a whisper.

"Yes, with a little bit of the Wild West sprinkled in," Harry replied ominously.

Harry could see Matt had begun to grasp the grim reality of the picture he had painted. Now it was time to offer him a glimmer of hope. "There's still time to stop them, Matt. But Samantha and I need your help. So will you join us?" he asked, his blue eyes burning with renewed intensity.

Matt was shaken but undaunted. "What can I do?" he asked resolutely.

Harry replied simply, "Finish what you started. Find out what my brothers are so afraid of out on Ghost Ridge."

28

Present Day
Washington, D.C.

The Liberty Bell Americans headquarters was located just a few blocks south of perhaps the most recognizable symbol of democracy in the free world, the U.S. Capitol Building. The wedding-cake–style structure was actually comprised of two domes, one nestled inside the other, like Russian nesting dolls. The outer dome was simply a facade of cast iron painted bright white to match the stone edifice that supported it. Unfortunately, over its one-hundred-fifty-year existence, the cast iron dome had become brittle, slowly rusting away from water seeping through hundreds of tiny cracks. The government had finally set aside $60 million to finance the multi-year restoration project, which is why the building was presently encircled in enough scaffolding pipe to stretch more than fifty-two miles if laid end-to-end.

Landon Spate cast a disparaging glance at the ongoing construction. He could see it clearly from the LBA building's rooftop garden. *More money that our bankrupt government doesn't have to spend, but is spending anyway.*

The LBA was the largest of the twenty-seven organizations

Landon Spate and his brother Oliver secretly financed. The financial structure of the maze of groups was intentionally and painstakingly cloaked from the outside world by its organizational complexity. The sophisticated network involved over a dozen limited liability companies that would dissolve one day only to reappear two months later under a different moniker. The entire system was designed to shield Spate Industries' involvement from government auditors—as well as from the prying eyes of watchdog groups. And it had worked. Nobody on the outside had any idea where the money was coming from or whom it was funneled back out to. Only the primary underwriters of this sprawling array of advocacy groups—the Spate brothers—knew exactly how every dollar was being spent.

In the last election cycle alone, this interconnected group of think tanks, front groups, nonprofit foundations, and lobbyists spent over a billion dollars to finance subversive activities across the country. But this represented only a portion of the billions spent over a decades-long investment. And it was all aimed at achieving their ultimate goal—dismantling the U.S. government from the inside out. To achieve this desired change, the Spates not only had to infiltrate the halls of Congress, but they also had to win the battle for public opinion.

That's why they had just made a bid to acquire a large media conglomerate. The company had been targeted because it owned dozens of local television and radio outlets, as well as eight major newspapers—including the *Chicago Tribune* and the *LA Times*. If the acquisition were to go through, it would give Landon and Oliver Spate a more efficient way to win the battle for public opinion, by providing them direct access to an audience of tens of millions of readers, listeners, and viewers.

All these coordinated efforts had finally begun to pay off. Over the last decade, public sentiment had turned dramatically against the federal government. But the converts who fervently rallied around the Spates' carefully crafted patriotic rhetoric had no idea how far the puppet masters' plans were really designed to go. They had no idea the Spates would not stop until a small cadre of wealthy individuals—led by Oliver and Landon themselves—dictated the laws of the land. And if the Spates had their way, the general public would not know until it would be too late to turn back.

"So Mel, bring me up to speed on your latest round of candidate recruiting," Landon Spate addressed Mel Pratt, the brothers' main political lieutenant. Pratt held many titles within the organization because he was a brilliant strategist. He was also one of the few nonfamily members Landon and Oliver Spate entrusted with their most sensitive information.

"We've got another ten congressional candidates in the pipe-line—in districts we've targeted as having vulnerable incumbents. Primarily Democratic incumbents, but we're going after a couple Republican seats as well," Pratt replied.

One of the companies Pratt ran for the brothers was a consult-ing firm created to identify, recruit, and groom free-market–minded candidates for elected office. The firm had been charged with hand-picking local, state, and federal candidates who shared the Spates' free-market, limited-government agenda—and then grooming them to win elections.

"Democrat or Republican, it doesn't matter to me. If they're not in lockstep with our ideology then they've got to go," Spate replied coldly, before asking, "How about the Senate?"

"I'm comfortable we can get another five, maybe six candidates elected in the next cycle," Pratt replied. "But we're going to need more money. Attack ads aren't getting any cheaper. And neither are the candidates, if you know what I mean." He stared at his boss through eyes set a little too close together. These, combined with a prominent beak-shaped nose, made the Spates' man in charge look like a hawk constantly on the alert for prey.

"Money isn't an issue. We have plenty of passionate conservative donors who will gladly up their contributions," Spate replied assuredly. "So how many will that make in total?"

"We've got thirty-eight members already in place, so we should be at forty-three or forty-four Senators in our back pocket by the end of the mid-term election. And at least ten to fifteen more who will vote with us if push comes to shove."

"Push always comes to shove, Mel," Landon said with a sneer. "But that is good news, we'll finally have a majority voting bloc in the Senate," he looked silently toward the heavens as if to give thanks to a higher power. But Landon Spate was not a religious man. The closest thing to an altar he worshipped was located at 11 Wall Street in lower Manhattan—the venerable New York Stock Exchange.

"And let's not forget about the Supreme Court," Pratt offered, hoping to keep the good news flowing. "With that liberal old son-of-a-bitch Saunders out of the way, we have a five-to-four majority there as well."

But the celebratory mood was short-lived when Spate turned abruptly and asked, "What about the House?"

Pratt hesitated because he knew the picture wasn't nearly as rosy in the House of Representatives. "We're not quite as far along there," he admitted tentatively, wary of his boss's wrath, "but the latest grassroots media blitz definitely made an impact."

He looked across at Spate, hoping to move on. But his boss hadn't blinked. "If I had to put a number on it," Pratt continued reluctantly, "I'd say we'll have close to two hundred members on our team by end of the midterm elections. But," he added soberly, "it will take at least a couple more election cycles to achieve the same majority voting bloc in the House we're going to enjoy in the Senate."

"Two more election cycles?" Spate boomed. "That's not acceptable. We need to move faster."

"Yes...I know, sir, but Mr. Spate..." Pratt replied nervously. He could feel his starched oxford shirt sticking to his back. Pratt never called Landon or his older brother, Oliver, by their first names. He never felt comfortable using the more informal means of address—and the brothers never offered.

"We can't keep waiting for the electorate to vote our people into office," Spate interrupted. "It's time to accelerate our game plan." He looked hard at Pratt. "If we can't have the majority we need to push our legislation through, then we'll have to find a different way..." he chose his next words carefully, "to remove the obstacles standing in our way."

Pratt knew exactly what Spate was alluding to so he replied like a good soldier, "We have contingency plans drawn up already, sir, accidents and deaths that can never be traced back to us." He added in a more hushed tone, "Just like the tragic boating incident that killed the uncooperative senator from Michigan earlier this year." He paused. "All you have to do is say the word and we'll take care of the remaining five people on the list...using similar discretion, of course," Pratt said confidently.

The two men sat sipping their sweet tea, discussing murder as if they were swapping gardening tips. Each of the five members of Congress Pratt was referring to held powerful committee chair positions and each had been holding up key legislation the Spates' needed fast-tracked.

Spate leaned forward in his chair and said simply, "Do it." His cold stare was so unsettling an involuntary shudder crawled up Pratt's spine.

Just then Spate's phone rang. It was his contact in Montana. His mood darkened instantly. As if on cue, a large cloud blotted out the sun. He ignored the call for now, but it did remind him there was one thing that could upset everything. He turned to Pratt.

"Do you remember when I shared with you our suspicions that we have a mole in our organization?"

"Of course, you were convinced it was the only way to explain how the press got all that information on our organizational structure. Are you any closer to discovering who it is?"

"No, not yet. Any ideas?"

Pratt looked away nervously.

Spate could sense he was avoiding something. "What is it, Mel? What are you not telling me?"

Pratt hesitated a few seconds longer before replying, "After you first told me about it...I got to thinking...and, uh, you're not going to like this but..."

"Come on, Mel. Just say what's on your mind for God's sake," Spate chastised his lieutenant.

Pratt looked tentatively at his boss and said, "Your niece."

"Samantha?" Spate said, in surprise.

"She's the logical choice, sir. Her father hates you and she's got access to some very sensitive information..."

Spate held up his hands and said, "Stop. First of all, she doesn't have as much access as you think. Secondly, you don't think we already thought of her? Believe me, we did, and we've had her checked out many times. We've pulled her phone records, travel records, credit card information—we even had a private investigator follow her around for six months. There's no way she's had any contact with my dear brother in the eight years she's been working for us. If she's a mole, then she's also one hell of a magician." Then he said, "Got any other ideas?"

"No, sir, but I'll think about it some more," he promised.

"You do that."

Even so, Landon Spate made a mental note to check up on Samantha one more time, just to be sure.

29

Present Day
Savannah, GA

Another shell shot out of the launch tube and rocketed into the air. It slithered higher and higher into the night sky leaving a barely discernible trail of black powder in its wake. As it reached the apex of its trajectory, the time-delay fuse ignited and the shell exploded with a loud boom. Its payload was sent scattering in a multicolored star pattern that illuminated the Savannah River far below.

From his third floor apartment about a mile away, Matt couldn't see the annual Fourth of July fireworks display. But he could hear the loud booms as the shells exploded one after the other. It was just as well. River Street was one of the more touristy sections of Savannah and he usually avoided its cobblestoned streets at all costs. He wouldn't have been able to attend anyway as he had a living room full of guests.

Matt turned away from the window and addressed the gathering. "I want to thank everyone for coming. I know it was short notice and you'd probably all rather be somewhere else tonight. But

I hope you agree that, based on the circumstances, this meeting couldn't be avoided."

Seated to his left in his living room were Buzz Penberthy, James Fox, and Hank Gordon. Harry and Samantha Spate were to his right. Matt had briefed them all on his disturbing conversation with Harry the day before. And they had all subsequently rearranged their schedules to be with him that evening. Matt was grateful to each of them.

"Nonsense," Hank was the first to speak, "I wouldn't be anywhere else this evening. Thank you for including me. And thank you for the Madeira." Hank held his wine glass aloft in a silent toast. Matt had come to appreciate the fortified Portuguese wine, a favorite of both George Washington's and Hank Gordon's. As head of the local Madeira wine club, Hank had introduced Matt to the variety and he had quickly become a fan.

"I could think of a few other places I could be tonight," Buzz said with a wink, "but what the hell." He held up his bottle of Budweiser, following Hank's lead. "At least the beer's cold."

Director James Fox had listened carefully to Matt's explanation of the Spates' far-reaching draconian plan. He turned to Harry Spate and asked, "So what happens to the average American when your brothers and their cronies have control over Congress and the rest of the federal government?"

Harry pondered the question for a moment and then offered, "The Greek historian Plutarch once said when there is no brake on the power of great wealth to subvert the electorate the republic will be subjected to the rule of emperors."

"A plutocracy," Fox commented.

"Yes," Harry replied, "then a police state...followed inevitably by revolution."

"Revolution?" Fox gasped.

Matt's home shook from another loud boom sounding in the

distance. Some inebriated revelers whooped loudly on the street below.

"You show me a society with glaring inequalities and I'll guarantee you a rebellion. We only need to look at history for examples of societies that could not sustain the kind of rising inequality that occurs when a privileged donor class is in control of the government and the court system. The Roman Empire is one example, or more recently, eighteenth-century France—*before* the revolution."

"And then the peasants will rise up," Buzz interjected somberly.

Harry smiled wanly. "Yes, Buzz, there will come a tipping point when the average American will no longer tolerate the glaring inequalities. The American dream will be dead and buried. And like the farmers of France, the citizens will revolt and attempt to overthrow their oppressors—a revolution from within. It's not a matter of if, but when."

"Do you really think your brothers will take it that far?" Hank interrupted, his face was ashen.

"Without a doubt," Harry responded. "My brothers are fervent believers in their cause. They've spent billions to spread misinformation through their political network to help turn their private antigovernment agenda into a mass movement. Suddenly *all* government is bad. Any government oversight is considered anti-American. Or a term they like to throw around—socialistic."

Then he added with a touch of irony, "Hey look, I love capitalism, too. And believe me, I'm no fan of big government. But the reality is our free market system wouldn't exist as we know it without the presence of a government that created and maintained the rules and conditions that allowed it to operate efficiently and fairly. It's the only way a truly democratic society can survive. The sad truth is we *need* oversight and we *need* regulations. At the end of the day, we humans are a greedy, self-centered bunch. History has proven that time and time again."

The room fell silent.

Harry turned to Matt and said, "Unfortunately, by the time Main Street America wakes up and realizes they've given the keys of the kingdom to my brothers, it will be too late to reverse the process. The government will be controlled by the private sector. Our 'by the people, for the people' representative government will be a thing of the past. In its place will be a state of inequity never before seen in this country. And Oliver and Landon will sit atop it all—as kings of a dystopian future."

Samantha stood up purposefully. "Enough depressing talk," she said with strained optimism. Attempting to shift the conversation from problem to solution, she went on, "I'd like to hear more about this letter you mentioned to me on the phone, Matt. The one you found at the American Philosophical Society." Matt had briefly described the letter to Samantha the day before. "You said it was written to Thomas Jefferson by my five times great-grandfather Jedediah Spate?"

"There's not much else to tell, Samantha," Matt said dejectedly. "It's written in gibberish that turns out is actually some kind of code."

"So there's no way to figure out what it says?" Harry asked.

"Not without the right equipment," Fox replied.

"What do you mean the right equipment?" Samantha asked.

Hank, ever the teacher, assumed the floor. "Thomas Jefferson was a bit paranoid when it came to his more sensitive communiqués," he explained. "So he experimented with secret codes. He started with simple strips of paper but eventually created a device so sophisticated that its design was still in use right up until World War II."

"You're kidding," Samantha said, amazed.

"No, I'm not. Jefferson's original description for how to build and use his cipher device was among his papers stored in the Library of Congress. But they weren't discovered for more than a hundred years after they were first written." Hank continued, as if he were back in front of his AP history class, "For some reason they had fallen into obscurity and didn't resurface until the early part of the twentieth century. But after they were discovered, the U.S. Army was so stunned by the sophistication of Jefferson's design, they adopted his device. And it was used to code tactical field communications for close to two decades."

"So, wait a minute, are you saying the only way to decode the letter from Jedediah Spate is with one of these cipher devices?" Harry asked, getting back to the problem at hand.

"I'm afraid so," Fox jumped in.

"Don't any of these things still exist?" Samantha asked.

"Only replicas," Buzz offered. "The National Museum of American History in D.C. has one, as a matter of fact."

Samantha's face brightened. But Buzz held up his hand before she could speak. He anticipated where she was headed. "Even if we had a replica, it wouldn't matter."

"Why not?" she said, looking crestfallen.

"Because you need to know the sequence of the twenty-six disks on the spindle," Matt said. "If the disks aren't in exactly the right sequence, then the letters won't line up correctly and the message can't be decoded."

He stood up and walked to an oversized window that looked down over Monterey Square. The night sky was illuminated with an eerie glow from the distant fireworks. In one of the brighter flashes, Matt spotted the bench across the street where he and Harry had met the day before. He still couldn't believe all this was happening. Samantha came over and joined him by the window. She picked up an old metal baseball bat leaning up against the plaster wall.

"What's this for?" she asked.

"Security system," he said with a crooked smile.

"How'd it get this dent?" She smiled back at him, pointing to a large indentation in the barrel.

Matt's mind flashed back to his run-in with the hired thugs who had kidnapped Sarah Gordon. It had happened toward the end of their search for Washington's surrender letter. And it was a painful memory in more ways than one. He glanced over at Hank who seemed to know exactly what Matt was thinking. Hank gave him a reassuring smile.

Samantha witnessed the unspoken exchange. She was surprised to see the boyish vulnerability on Matt's ruggedly handsome face. It seemed incongruous with his assured nature. She suddenly had the urge to comfort him as he had done for her back at the Crystal. But she knew this was neither the time nor place.

The truth was she hadn't had the inclination for a relationship since she had gone undercover at Spate Industries. She was living a lie spying on her uncles, and she had always felt it would be unfair to draw another person into her clandestine and mostly paranoid existence. But Matt was different. He knew her secret now. And she couldn't deny her attraction to him. Even so, she suppressed these feelings and changed the subject.

She turned back around to face Buzz. "What did you call this device?"

"A cipher," he replied.

"A wheel cipher to be exact," Fox noted. "Here, I brought a picture with me." He got up from the couch and handed it to Samantha.

As Samantha scanned the picture of the replica of Jefferson's wheel cipher, Matt looked across the room at Harry Spate. His brow was ruffled and he was obviously deep in thought.

"What's up, Harry? You look like you're on to something," Matt said.

Harry shot out of his seat and frantically made his way to where his daughter was standing. He snatched the photocopy from her hands.

"Hey, Dad, what's the matter with you?" she said, annoyed at his more-than-usual erratic behavior.

"Oh my God," he blurted out. "I knew it, the minute you said wheel cipher...it just clicked."

"What clicked, Harry?" Matt asked in confusion.

"I knew it, I knew it, I knew it," he sang out and danced a little jig in the middle of Matt's living room.

Everyone stared at Harry Spate, mouths agape, waiting for him to finish his private celebration. They looked to Samantha to explain her father's odd behavior. But she just held her hands up in helplessness and said, "He gets like this when he's excited."

Finally, she grabbed her father's elbow and said sharply, "Dad." This seemed to get his attention so she asked, "Are you going to share what you're so giddy about?"

"Of course, of course," he said slightly baffled when he noticed everyone staring at him. "It's just that...there's one of these," he held the picture of the wheel cipher up so everyone could see, "in my brother Oliver's house in Oklahoma City."

There was stunned silence as everyone absorbed the implications of what Harry had just shared. Buzz was the first to respond. "You think it could have been Jedediah Spate's?" he asked tentatively.

"It has to be," he said excitedly. "It's been sitting in my brother's den for as long as I can remember. I know it was handed down to him by my father—being the oldest son—and it's been in my family for years. I always just assumed it was some kind of printing press or something. I had no idea it was a secret cipher."

"It makes sense he would have one," Hank posited. "Both the sender and receiver of the letter had to have matching ciphers with the same sequence of disks."

"Are you sure it's the same thing, Dad?" Samantha asked making sure her father hadn't lost his mind.

"Oh, I'm positive, dear," he assured his daughter. "It's in a glass case, like one of those cases you see in a museum. And it looks like it hasn't been touched in a hundred years."

Matt's mind was spinning already. But Harry's comment triggered a new thought. "What if it hasn't been touched in *two hundred years?*" he said. He was looking directly at Buzz with a cagey smile.

Buzz read Matt's mind. He answered without missing a beat, "Then the disks would be in the same position they were in when Jedediah Spate wrote that letter to Thomas Jefferson."

Fox smacked the palms of his hands together excitedly. "And if the disks are in the same position, then we can decode the letter."

"Exactly," Matt said with growing optimism.

"But first we'd have to get our hands on the wheel cipher," Hank said, offering up a sobering dose of reality.

"I think Matt's already thought about that little problem," Buzz offered.

"And what's the solution?" Hank asked.

"We steal it," Samantha and Matt answered in unison.

They both broke out laughing.

"Jesus Christ," Buzz leaned back heavily into his chair. "I'm surrounded by nut jobs."

30

Present Day
Savannah, GA

The energy inside the bar was electric. A popular rockabilly band had just taken the stage for their second set of the evening. There were actually three bars in the unpretentious local hangout—one on the ground floor, another in the basement, and a third on the outside patio. It catered to a crowd of mostly locals. But a few tourists looking for good live music occasionally wandered in. The place was a bit unpolished, but the staff was friendly and the atmosphere was great.

Matt and Samantha hadn't been inside more than five minutes when she grabbed hold of his hand and dragged him out onto the dance floor. He shuffled awkwardly to the beat of the music, trying not to make too much of an ass of himself. Matt wasn't much of a dancer and he knew it. But he didn't mind dancing with Samantha.

Most of the heads in the bar, male and female, turned when she had made her way onto the crowded dance floor. She had that effect on people. Her lengthy, perfectly shaped alabaster legs were hard not to notice—with all the right nips and curves from thighs to ankles. But it was her flowing, flaxen hair that had originally caught Matt's eye. Tonight, it cascaded down to the middle of her back in natural, soft ringlets that bounced in time to the music as she moved.

When the meeting at Matt's house had broken up, Samantha pulled him aside asked if he would take her out on the town. She was feeling edgy and needed a release for all the pent-up stress in her life. Matt said he knew just the place. He told her the music would be loud, the people-watching would be great, and the drinks would be cold. She thought that sounded perfect.

Matt's description had been right on the money. The crowd was an eclectic mixture of tattooed hipsters, punk rock college kids, and a smattering of tourists. Samantha had never heard of rockabilly before. Matt explained the name came from combining "rock and roll" with "hillbilly." The style was a unique blend of country and bluegrass with blues-infused classic rock and roll.

"Whatever it is," she said, dancing in place to the music, "it makes me happy." She turned to the bartender and shouted for two shots of tequila.

Matt had to smile. He had no idea Samantha had a wild side. But he had to admit, he liked it. They downed the shots. Matt was still sweating from all the dancing, so he took a long pull on a cold bottle of Bud to quench his thirst.

"It's nice to see you having fun," he said with a crooked grin. "I didn't know you could let your hair down like this." He gave her a playful shove with his shoulder.

She leaned in close to him and said seductively, "I have my moments." Matt could feel her warm breath against his cheek and smell her perfume. His pulse quickened.

She threw her head back and laughed. She felt more carefree than she had in a long time. "Bartender, two more beers," she hollered.

The band had taken a break. Now that they could talk without having to shout, Matt grabbed their beers and pointed to a table toward the back of the room. They were both feeling flushed and slightly buzzed from the alcohol, so it was good to sit down.

"This was a great idea, Samantha," Matt admitted. "I didn't realize how much *I* needed to get out and let loose."

She looked at Matt as if she were looking at him for the first time. He was very handsome—athletically built, with thick sandy-blond hair. And he had a smile that could stop a girl in her tracks. He was assured of himself, but not cocky. And he was smart and fearless. All in all, it was an appealing package.

"What are you looking at?" he said with a grin.

Her face turned momentarily serious. "I was just thinking it's been a long time since I've had this much fun. My life is not very... normal," she struggled to find the right word to describe her world. "I live in constant fear of being discovered by my uncles. I work all the time and, given the circumstances, when I'm not working I pretty much keep to myself." She exhaled deeply as if to exorcise the reality of her double life. Then she said genuinely, "Thanks for doing this, Matt. It really means a lot to me."

"Yeah, well, I decided to take one for the team tonight," he kidded. "I knew it would be tough duty. A night on the town with a beautiful woman and all, but I thought what the hell."

As usual, he had resorted to humor to keep the conversation light. But somehow that didn't seem right tonight. So he said, "Seriously, Samantha, I'm enjoying myself." He paused before adding, "I like spending time with you."

She reached across the table and put her hand over his, "Thanks," she said. But then she pulled it away, "Are you *surprised* you like being with me?"

He held her gaze for a moment. "The truth is I didn't want to like you at first; in fact, I wanted to hate you. Remember, I thought you were working for the evil empire," he smiled. "But when I found out all you've been through these last few years...well, it turns out you're a pretty remarkable woman."

She was smiling but her blue eyes were moist with emotion. She got up and grabbed Matt's hand. She led him around the corner toward an old-fashioned photo booth she had noticed on their way into the bar. She tugged back the curtain and closed it behind them. Her eyes conveyed both joy and sadness, but also desire.

Matt took her face in both of his hands and pulled her toward him. He kissed her deeply. There was a raw intensity to their embrace that surprised—¬even unsettled—him. But there was no denying he wanted her. And the feeling was mutual. She slipped her hands underneath his shirt. She needed to feel his body, feel the warmth of his skin. He hiked her sheer summer shift up over her waist, grabbed her backside firmly in his hands and lifted her off the ground. She wrapped her legs tightly around his waist.

They were reaching the point of no return, so she pulled back and said, "If we don't slow down, I might make love to you right here in this booth."

Matt took a quick look around at the cramped photo booth and deadpanned, "OK, just no pictures."

"Matt," she giggled, and climbed down off of him.

"Alright, alright, you can take a few if you want," he offered jokingly.

But she had already thrown open the curtain, "Come on, let's get out of here."

Matt awoke with a start. It was pitch black in the room and he was momentarily disoriented. He rubbed his two-day-old stubble and glanced at his bedside clock. The digital display registered that it was 4:30 in the morning. He looked to his left but Samantha wasn't there. He swung his legs off the bed to see where she had gone—but he had to pee first. He made a quick detour to the bathroom.

As he became more fully awake, the events of the evening began to slowly push their way into his consciousness. The first time they made love they had barely made it through the front door of his apartment. They had gotten as far as the chunky farmhouse table in his kitchen. Their lovemaking had been carnal, even rough. No inhibitions. *Thank goodness for sturdy early-twentieth-century construction.* Matt thought back on it with a smile.

The second time had been less harried but no less impassioned. By then, they had made it into Matt's bedroom. Instead of being a race to the finish, they took their time. And they reached a depth of feeling, a closeness, that hadn't been there the first time around. They explored each other's bodies more completely and their lovemaking became more synchronous. But that was the last thing Matt could recall—holding Samantha tightly as she fell asleep with her head on his chest.

He returned to the bedroom and noticed the French doors that led out to the balcony were ajar. He walked over and quietly pulled back one of the doors. She was standing with her back to him, looking out over the rooftops of his historic Savannah neighborhood. The top sheet from his bed was wrapped loosely around her body and her tousled blond hair was gathered in bunches below her shoulders. She was a vision in white against a pitch-black background. She could have easily been mistaken for one of the innumerable apparitions so famously believed to haunt the old port city.

"Hey," he whispered quietly, stepping onto the porch. Coming up behind her, he wrapped his arms around her waist. It was cool outside and he was naked. As he pressed his chest up against her back, he could feel the warmth of her body radiating from beneath the sheet. It felt good against his bare skin.

She leaned her head back against his shoulder. "It's so peaceful out here," she said softly. "You picked such a beautiful place to live, Matt."

"Actually, Savannah picked me," he said, remembering how he felt the first time he visited his adopted hometown more than a decade earlier. "She has a way of doing that to people. And once you're smitten, you can never leave."

She turned around and looked straight into his eyes. "I think I know that feeling. But I'm not sure Savannah's to blame."

He leaned in and kissed her gently on the lips.

She smiled. "I don't want this night to be over."

"Good," he said, pulling her closer, "'cause I'm not ready to let you go yet."

She lifted her head and kissed him again. Then she took a step back and let the bed sheet slip from her shoulders. It floated silently to the ground. She stood naked before him, full round breasts, narrow waist, and sloping hips—a statue of a Greek goddess, carved out of cream-colored marble by a master sculptor.

Matt could feel himself getting hard. She took a step toward him and gently guided him down into a chair by the French doors. She straddled him. He was inside her once more. They clung to one another and made love slowly—for the third and final time that evening. The first time on the kitchen table had been full of passion. The second was a more intimate encounter.

But with uncertainty over what the next few weeks held for them, their final union was tinged with desperation.

31

Present Day

Savannah, Georgia

Samantha departed on a flight out of Savannah that morning. Alone for the first time all week, Matt took the opportunity to go for a run in Forsyth Park.

At mile five his legs began to stiffen, but running helped clear his mind so he pressed on. He was still struggling to process the events of the last few days—events that had begun with Harry Spate's unexpected arrival in Savannah. Matt's initial skepticism of Harry's story had been replaced by fear, then anger, and finally by a fierce determination to stop the Spates' plans to overthrow the U.S. government. He shook off his fatigue and ran one more loop around the lush public park grounds.

He finally came to a stop at the south end of the park when his legs would go no more. Even though he was exhausted and dripping with sweat, he smiled inwardly as the image of Samantha on his bedroom balcony took shape in his mind. Just as quickly, however, it was unexpectedly replaced by the image of another woman, Sarah Gordon.

He and Sarah had shared an equally torrid romance during their search for Washington's surrender letter. Matt was still confused by how their passionate relationship had ended so abruptly. It occurred to him that he still had unresolved feelings for her even now that Samantha had entered his life. As usual, when it came to women, nothing was neat and tidy with him. Maybe someday he'd find clarity, it just wouldn't be today. He looked up and realized he was only a couple of blocks from Sarah's father's house. Perhaps that's the reason she had forced her way into his head. He was tired, thirsty, and a long way from home, so he made a spur-of-the-moment decision to pay Hank Gordon a visit.

After turning onto Hank's block in Savannah's Victorian District and making his way up the front stairs of his stately home, he knocked on the thick oak front door. After a few moments without a response he moved to the front window and cupped his hands around his eyes to peer inside. As usual, the circa 1870s home Hank had painstakingly restored was immaculate. Even though he couldn't see him, he could faintly hear Hank's voice coming from somewhere inside. *Maybe he's on the phone.*

He tested the knob on the front door. It wasn't locked. "Hello," he called, making his way into the foyer. No answer.

There was still no sign of him but hear could hear Hank a little clearer now. It wasn't until Matt entered the kitchen that the riddle was solved. Through a large picture window, he spotted Sarah's father standing in the courtyard garden behind his home. Hank hadn't been on the phone at all. There was another unseen person in the garden with him and they were apparently engaged in a heated argument.

His curiosity piqued, Matt walked further into the kitchen. A second person came into view through the window. The mystery man was Buzz Penberthy. Matt's eyebrows rose in mild surprise. It wasn't that the two men standing outside were unfamiliar to one another. In fact, they had both been at Matt's home the night before.

It was just that, to Matt's knowledge, Buzz and Hank did not socialize. And there was something else that gave him pause. He couldn't shake the feeling that the two men arguing in the garden had shared a lifetime of events together, not just the recent past.

Acting purely on instinct, Matt decided not to reveal himself. He stepped quietly toward the back door, keeping his body hidden from view. He wasn't sure why he chose to do this. Perhaps it was the conspiratorial manner in which the two men were attempting to keep their heated exchange from rising above a hushed decibel level.

He reached discreetly over and inched open the back door.

"Don't go getting all holier-than-thou on me, Hank," Buzz said hotly. "You're the one who suggested we recruit Matt in the first place."

Matt's brow furrowed in confusion. *Recruit?*

"Yes, but this time he could be in real danger," Hank fired back.

This time? Matt was suddenly finding it hard to catch his breath. And it had nothing to do with the run in the park.

"There's always danger, Hank, you of all people should know that."

"We need to tell him, Buzz. It isn't fair using him like this," he pleaded. "I'm telling you, I can't do it anymore. I won't."

"We use people all the time for the good of the cause. You need to calm down and stay the course," Buzz said, slipping easily back into the commanding tone that had served him well as a colonel in the U.S. Navy.

The two men stared stubbornly at each other, neither willing to back down.

Finally, Buzz held up his hands. "Look Hank," he said attempting to ease the tension, "we've been after the Spates for years. You can't get cold feet now, especially when we're so close to nailing those sons of bitches." He continued, "I understand your concerns, but this is bigger than Matt. Hell, it's bigger than us."

Hank opened his mouth to object but Buzz cut him off. "Now is not the time to forget the oath you took. Remember the reason we dedicated our lives to this organization."

Hank countered quickly, "I haven't forgotten." His voice caught in his throat and he looked away. "It's just that lately it seems our actions are causing more harm than good, especially to the people most important to me."

Buzz let a beat pass before responding. He knew he was wading into sensitive territory, so he said in a slightly more conciliatory tone, "If you're referring to Sarah, she's a grown woman. She made up her own mind."

"You and I both know she didn't have a choice," Hank replied tersely. "She was in love with him for Christ's sake. She couldn't go on lying." He added, "And I can't either."

Matt leaned against the wall to steady himself. The two men he trusted most in the world had betrayed him. They were clearly not who they claimed to be. Worse, they had apparently been using him as a pawn in some larger scheme. Matt's head was spinning with a thousand questions. *Who the hell were they working for? What cause had they both dedicated their lives to? How was Sarah involved in all this?* The pit in his stomach that formed after hearing the initial exchange had turned acidic. Bile rose in his throat.

"You can and you will," Buzz responded. He reached out and grasped Hank firmly by the shoulder. "At least for the time being, OK?"

After an elongated pause, Hank acquiesced with a terse nod of the head.

Seeing Buzz turn to leave, Matt scrambled out of the house. He bounded down the front steps two at a time. He had just enough time to make it down the street and around the corner before the front door opened.

Matt's eyes were moist with tears as he sprinted back toward the park. He felt equal parts hurt and angry. But more than anything else, he was scared; more scared than he had ever been in his life. As he ran, one thought kept repeating in his head: *Trust no one.*

Out of the corner of his eye, he spotted a large metal garbage can. He ran directly to it, leaned over the rim, and threw up his breakfast.

32

Present Day
Aspen, Colorado

It had the atmosphere of a high school pep rally. But instead of a marching band, the entertainment was headlined by a platinum-album rock band, albeit twenty years past their prime. And in lieu of a student section, the audience was comprised of hundreds of the wealthiest men and women in America and their spouses. The occasion was the biannual "retreat" hosted and funded by Oliver and Landon Spate. To gain an invitation to the exclusive three-day event, one had to possess two things: a serious free market conviction and an equally serious checkbook.

It was a typically crisp, gorgeous midsummer evening eight thousand feet up in the Rocky Mountains. A circus-size white tent had been constructed on the lawn of the five-star hotel just outside the resort town of Aspen. The tent had been custom-made for the event and held over a thousand people. Dessert had just been cleared from the white-cloth banquet tables, signaling the end of dinner. The complimentary bar, however, would remain open for hours. The guest speaker that had been arranged for the final evening of the three-day event was the charismatic governor of Arizona. A longtime friend of "the cause," he had just been welcomed to the stage by Oliver Spate.

The crowd went wild as he proceeded to deliver a rousing speech rife with patriotic rhetoric—and enough one-liners to buoy the half-in-the-bag-attendees' already boisterous mood. It didn't matter that it was a canned speech he had delivered many times before. The giddy congregation hung on his every word, interrupting him for applause more times than a partisan Congress at a State of the Union address.

It's no wonder their spirits had reached a fever pitch. They had just spent three meticulously orchestrated days attending rousing propaganda-filled workshops, lectures, and panels. Like pastors at a revival meeting, Spates' organizers had masterfully fanned the ideological flames of the attendees by offering seminars with titles like, "Government's Threat to Free Enterprise" and "Time to Take Back Our Country." All aimed at fostering an almost pious commitment to the Spates' deregulation and free market philosophies. If there were still any non-converts to the antigovernment cause prior to the conference, they were all believers by the time the last multimedia presentation was over.

All these frivolous trappings, however, were just the sleight-of-hand part of Oliver and Landon Spates' accomplished magic act. The Spates went to great lengths to perpetuate the illusion among the unsuspecting donor pool that they were all in this together. The brothers knew their crusade was an expensive one and they couldn't subsidize it on their own. They had to keep the donations flowing—so each of the attendees would be hit up for a minimum donation of one million dollars. And since unfettered capitalism didn't come cheap, they would be strongly encouraged to donate even more. Most would stroke their checks without hesitation. They believed the return on their money would far exceed their investment. The reality was the Spates had no intention of sharing the spoils of war equally when they had finally achieved their victory.

But they also knew they could not pull off a feat as audacious as the covert takeover of the U.S. government one million-dollar check at a time. They needed some big elephants. They needed strategic partners. So one by one, over the past thirty years, they had methodically recruited an ultra exclusive cartel of bankers, financiers, and industrialists from key strategic sectors of the U.S. economy.

The real action that evening took place far away from the over-the-top circus tent, the A-list entertainment, and the patriotic speeches. Ten men sat around a large conference table in a high-security, private guesthouse. It was located on a remote section of the resort property. With the exception of Landon and Oliver Spate, this meeting was not on any of the men's official calendars. And their presence was completely hidden from the other attendees.

Self-dubbed the Billionaires' Caucus, these were the richest, most powerful businessmen in the country. Their companies' combined market capitalization was larger than the gross GDPs of all but only a handful of countries in the developed world. They had the means, they had the will, and they had the same antigovernment beliefs—a philosophy that not so coincidentally lined up very neatly with their business interests.

Oliver Spate had the floor. "Gentlemen," he said, "at long last we have reached the home stretch. Total control over Congress and the complete takeover of our federal government is no longer a pipe dream. It will soon be a reality."

The men around the table nodded their heads in approval.

"And our campaign to change public opinion has also succeeded," he continued. "We are winning at the polls. And in those rare cases where we haven't won, we are taking the necessary measures to remove any...*impediments* to our progress." He was referring to the remaining names on the Enemies of the Spate list. And every person in the room knew it, because they had all previously approved of the action.

Oliver continued to brief the men on various initiatives and on specific details of the progress of their key objectives. His presentation was focused and professional, complete with bar charts, bullet points, and balance sheets. The scene was similar to one that played out every day in hundreds of corporate boardrooms across the country. The only difference was this board of directors was planning a covert but no less hostile takeover of the government of the United States.

After a discussion about the remaining financial commitments expected of each attendee, it was time to call the meeting to a close. But before he did, Oliver opened up the floor for questions. There was only one. It came from the CEO of the largest hedge fund in the country.

"It sounds like everything's going according to plan. But we all know every hostile takeover has its poison pill," he said. He was referring to a specific defensive tactic used by a corporation's board of directors against an unwanted takeover. "Do we have any blind spots we haven't considered?"

Oliver Spate's eyes shifted momentarily and imperceptibly in the direction of his brother. Landon Spate shook his head just once. The brothers knew there was one thing that could bring a heap of unwanted attention to them—and it was buried on an Indian reservation in northwest Montana. They also knew the last thing they needed at this critical juncture was the white-hot glare of national media derailing their life's work.

But it was a threat they had every intention of eliminating in short order. So Oliver stared back at his questioner with eyes as cold and lifeless as those belonging to the massive stuffed elk head on the wall behind him, and replied confidently, "Not a single one."

33

Present Day

Oklahoma City, OK

They were only a few minutes away from the leafy suburban enclave where Oliver Spate resided. Matt was amped up. The last and only time he had been involved in a burglary had been more than a year earlier. His thievery had been justified then because he was merely taking back what someone had stolen from him. This time around, his actions were motivated by what someone planned to take away from him and every other American—the democracy on which their country had been founded.

The eldest Spate brother lived alone with his wife on a secluded six-and-a-half acre property fifteen miles northwest of downtown Oklahoma City. The Frank Lloyd Wright prairie-style masterpiece had been built thirty years earlier. It sat on a private peninsula that jutted out into a deepwater lake. Considering Spate's net worth, the house was relatively modest at only four thousand square feet and four bedrooms. But it did have a private pool, temperature-controlled wine cellar, squash court, and gourmet Italian kitchen designed by Pininfarina—the same family of designers responsible for some of Ferrari's best-selling car models. But the home's signature feature was a wall of windows that overlooked the pool and lake. The glass expanse covered the entire first floor of the residence.

The exposed glass was only one of the things that worried Matt as he and Samantha drove north out of Oklahoma City. A more troubling concern was the guardhouse that sat at the head of the quarter-mile driveway. And the armed security guard inside. But Samantha had assured him her credentials if not her face would be familiar to the man on patrol. All these thoughts were racing through Matt's mind as he lay curled up in the trunk of the rental car.

A few minutes earlier, Samantha had pulled over to the side of the road. Matt had squeezed his large frame into what would have to be his hiding place for the final leg of their journey. As she had slammed the trunk shut sealing him inside, he couldn't help but conjure up images of mafia hit men. It was uncomfortably warm inside the cramped, dark space but Matt would have to deal with it. It was all part of a plan they had formulated in Savannah the week before.

The plan had come together rapidly, primarily due to the opportune timing of Spates' biannual donor retreat. Samantha had told them Oliver's Oklahoma City home would be deserted because he, his wife, and his personal assistant would all be attending the event in Aspen. It hadn't taken long for Buzz, Fox, and Harry to agree this was the perfect opportunity to steal the wheel cipher.

The plan called for Harry to get on the phone with the guard and pose as his brother Oliver. Evidently their voices were nearly identical. He would explain to the guard he had left behind a critical file and had sent Samantha back to retrieve it. It was decided Matt's presence was just too much to explain, so he would hide in the trunk. Only when they had made it down the long drive to the house and completely out of sight of the guard shack would it be safe for Matt to come out. Of course, they wouldn't have a house key, so Matt would have to pick the lock on the front door. After nearly a week of practice using a method taught to him by a locksmith friend in Savannah, Matt felt pretty confident he could get it done. Once inside, they would have to quickly make their way to the study. There they would remove the two-hundred-year-old wheel cipher and replace it with an exact replica.

This final piece of the plan had been made possible by Director Fox. He had called in a favor from a connection at the National Museum. The contact agreed to let them borrow their replica of Jefferson's wheel cipher, although he was not told the reason they needed it on such short order. The Society of the Cincinnati had then hired a master woodworker to craft an exact replica from the replica. The man had worked fifteen-hour days over the course of the weekend. It was critical he constructed the replica so it appeared to be two centuries old. When it was completed, it wasn't perfect, but they hoped that once inside the glass case it would be good enough to fool the casual observer. Oliver Spate would no doubt be able to tell the difference upon close inspection. But given the amount of time Jefferson's cipher had been sitting in his office undisturbed, they believed it was highly unlikely he'd ever look that hard—at least that's what they hoped.

As Matt lay curled up in the darkened trunk, he thought back to his chance encounter with Buzz and Hank in Savannah. He had been devastated after discovering he was being played by people he thought were his friends.

At first he wanted to confront Buzz. Then he thought better of it. He made the decision to go on playing along as if nothing had changed. He still wanted desperately to stop the Spates' insidious endgame. But now he had a second objective. Expose the organization that had surreptitiously recruited him and manipulated him for its own ends. What those ends were was still unclear. But he vowed to uncover the truth behind the lies that Buzz and Hank—

and even Sarah—had fed him. *Trust no one.*

Samantha pulled up in front of the guardhouse. She said a silent prayer as she rolled down the driver's side window.

"Yeah," the young guard said, annoyed he had been pulled away from the ball game being broadcast on the radio. He looked to be in his mid-twenties.

"Hi," Samantha replied cheerily. "I think we've met once before. I'm Samantha Christie," she said pleasantly.

"Oh yes, ma'am," the guard said with a glimmer of recognition. Hers was not a face you easily forgot. "What can I do for you?"

"Oh," she sounded surprised, "didn't Mr. Spate call to tell you I was coming?" She looked convincingly confused.

"Uh, well...no, he didn't," he responded.

"He asked me to retrieve a very important folder he left behind. He told me he'd call to let you know I was coming," she sounded distraught. "I flew all the way here from Aspen to get it." She put on her best pouty face.

"Jeez, Miss Christie, I'm sorry but," he glanced down at his clipboard to see if the night-shift guard had left any notes for him, "there's nothing here that says he called, and I'm not allowed to let anyone past the gate without Mr. Spate's permission." He glanced back at Samantha who looked like she was about to cry. Then he offered, "There is a number I could call...but it's only supposed to be for emergencies." He looked a bit nervous now.

That was her opening. Samantha said, "Oh no, I wouldn't want to get you in trouble. I'll just call him on my cell phone." She took out her phone and dialed. "Oliver, yes, it's Samantha. I'm here at your house but the guard didn't know I was coming so...what...yes, OK...I'll put him on." She handed the phone to the anxious-looking guard and said, "He'd like to speak with you."

The guard put the phone to his ear and retreated into the guard shack to speak privately with his employer. Evidently, Harry gave a convincing enough performance as his brother because thirty seconds later the gates began to open. But just as Samantha was about to drive on through, the guard came back outside and said, "I'm gonna need to go with you. Unaccompanied visitors aren't allowed." He walked around to the passenger side and got in the car before she could object.

As they drove down the long driveway, Samantha spoke loudly hoping Matt would overhear her and understand their situation had changed. They had company.

She parked and walked up to the front door. The guard followed behind. She hoped he'd make a move for his keys to open the door. But he didn't. Clearly Matt would not be able to pick the lock with the guard right there. She would have to improvise. She stalled to give herself a moment to think. She made a show of fishing around inside her purse looking for a key that wasn't there. Then with feigned exasperation, she said, "It's been a long day and I can't seem to find the damn key. I could look around in my other bag in the car but I'm kind of in a hurry. Can you let me in?" She smiled and tossed her blond hair flirtatiously over her shoulder.

The guard seemed to consider what he should do for a moment. "No problem, Miss Christie," he said. I've got a key." He opened the door and let them in. Just before she closed the door behind them, Samantha inconspicuously hit the trunk release button on her electronic key fob. She hoped it worked.

Matt had heard every word. When the latch on the trunk disengaged, he slowly pushed the lid open and crawled out. He wiped his brow with the back of his sleeve and breathed in deeply. He wasn't a big fan of small spaces. And the warm summer day made his confinement that much more unbearable. Samantha and her father had drawn a schematic of the house so Matt knew the exact location of the study. As he peered through the sidelight window next to the front door, he could see Samantha heading in the opposite direction. "Good girl," he said to himself. He knew she was leading the guard away from the study so Matt could get in and make the switch.

He raced back to the car and pulled the replica of the eighteen-by-nine-inch cipher from the trunk. He could still smell faint traces of the brown wood stain that had been applied in an attempt to give the facsimile an aged patina. He returned to the front door and slowly cracked it open. Less than a minute later he was in the lion's den—Oliver Spate's study. Sitting atop a credenza behind an enormous mahogany desk he spotted the genuine wheel cipher. Matt found himself in awe as he stared at Jefferson's remarkable invention. He had had a similar feeling of awe when he had first laid hands on Washington's surrender letter. But he knew this wasn't the time for gawking.

He attempted to remove the glass cover from its wooden base to get to the cipher inside. But it wouldn't budge. Matt had a feeling it wasn't going to be that easy. He looked around the edges of the case and noticed a Phillips head screw held each of the four corners firmly in place. Buzz had made sure Matt packed a compact set of screwdrivers for exactly this scenario. He would have to work fast.

Sarah had already scoured the kitchen keeping up the charade of searching for the fictitious forgotten file. "He said he left it on the kitchen counter, but maybe it's in the living room," she said, stalling to give Matt more time. She began searching through the contents on the large coffee table, "maybe it got mixed up with the magazines," she said. Although it was obvious there was nothing that even remotely looked like a file full of papers.

"What about Mr. Spate's study?" the guard reasoned. "Seems like a place for a file to be, don't you think?"

"Maybe," she said, "let me just take a quick look in the downstairs bathroom. You know how you men like to read in there," she said with a sardonic smile.

The guard smiled back but then glanced at his watch. He was starting to run out of patience. "Hey," he said, "I need to get back to my post. Maybe it's just not here."

She knew she had pressed her luck as far as it would go. She hoped she had given Matt enough time to make the swap and get back out to the car with the real cipher. She'd know soon enough. "You're right," she said, "I've taken enough of your time already. If it's not in the study then I'll just let Mr. Spate know we looked everywhere and couldn't find it." She walked slowly toward the other end of the house.

As they made their way around the corner, Samantha spotted Matt racing through an open doorway directly across from the study. He had a wheel cipher in his hands. She prayed it was the original—and that Matt was on the way out, not in. Eyes wide, she came to an abrupt stop in the middle of the hallway. The security guard was about to round the corner behind her. Thinking quickly she turned and sneezed loudly. Her head jerked forward and then back again and her blond hair went flying. The guard reflexively turned away so as not to be caught in the line of fire. The diversion worked. By the time she turned around again, Matt was nowhere to be seen.

Luckily, there had been a stack of files sitting on Oliver Spate's desk. Samantha spent a few minutes sifting through the files, again stalling for time. She hoped Matt had reinserted himself into the car trunk by now. Finally she grabbed an innocuous-looking folder and exclaimed, "Oh, thank God, here it is."

As they turned to leave, she glanced back behind her. She was relieved to see there was a cipher inside the glass case—but she had no idea if it was the original or the fake.

After the guardhouse disappeared from her rearview mirror, Samantha decided she had driven far enough away. She rounded one more bend and pulled off to the side of the road. The car came to a skidding stop on some loose gravel. She was panicked because she had no idea if Matt had even made it back inside the car, let alone if he had successfully made the switch. Before clambering out of the driver's seat she reached down and pressed the trunk release button on the door panel. Heart pounding, she raced to the back of the car and threw open the trunk.

Matt squinted up at her with his trademark crooked smile, and mimicking like a little kid on a long trip whined, "Are we there yet?" He pushed himself up to a seated position.

Samantha threw her arms around him in relief.

"Hey, hey, be careful," he teased, "you wouldn't want to damage Mr. Jefferson's toy would you?" Across his chest he held the real cipher, complete with twenty-six wooden disks threaded onto an iron spindle.

Samantha's blue eyes twinkled with delight. "You got it," she said with excitement.

"We got it," he answered. They shared a long kiss on the side of the road.

It was a strange place to share a kiss, but it had been a very strange day.

34

Present Day
Connecticut

The two-term senator from Connecticut was a rising star in the Democratic Party. As a result of his electrifying keynote address at the last Democratic National Convention, Senator Mark Waterford had quickly risen to national prominence. At only thirty-eight years old he was still very young, but many assumed he would run for the presidency sometime in the next eight years.

The press had taken to calling him the Democratic Party's best hope for a return to Camelot—a reference to John F. Kennedy's 1960s White House years. Not only did Senator Waterford look like JFK, he had his charisma, intelligence, and military background. As a U.S. Marine he had served with distinction in the Iraq War in 2003, receiving a purple heart for being shot during a firefight in Baghdad. He had married his high school sweetheart and together they had a five-year-old young son and two-year-old daughter. The family had become a favorite of the press corps, because of their photogenic good looks and seemingly perfect life.

Congress had just adjourned for a two-week summer holiday and Senator Waterford was driving home to Hartford from his Washington, D.C., apartment. It would be a welcome break for the senator, as it had been a long and trying month on Capitol Hill. The bickering and divisiveness between the two political parties had reached an all-time high.

Eight years earlier, he had run for the Senate on a moderate platform vowing to find the middle ground between Republicans and Democrats. He knew it would be perceived by many as idealistic and risky—mainly because the middle ground in America had eroded to a very small piece of turf defended by a shrinking minority of people. He had been counseled by political veterans to abandon his moderate beliefs and his campaign platform based on "finding compromise." Conventional wisdom said moderates were unelectable in America's current extreme left and right culture. But he did it anyway and, remarkably, he won. Six years later he was reelected.

During his eight years in the Senate, he had done his best to remain true to his promise to respect both sides of the aisle. He worked hard to change the prevailing culture of personal attacks with intelligent debate. He fervently believed resolution to differences on issues would require level heads and compromise: both sides considering the other's position and hammering out an agreement. That, he had often repeated, was statesmanship at its best. That's what great leaders throughout American history had always done. Because they understood democracy worked only through finding compromise—or an acceptable middle ground.

To his credit he had worked with both Democrats and Republicans on a number of bills over the years. He had good friends and was well respected by members of both parties. But there were some issues on which he simply would not give in—and campaign finance reform was one of them.

He came from modest means and had been voted into office without the aid of big money. And he felt that was the way it should be. There was no question in his mind that allowing corporate money to flood the political marketplace had corrupted America's democracy. As a result, he had recently spearheaded a push to advance a constitutional amendment to restore the ability of Congress to establish campaign fund-raising and spending rules that would prevent billionaires and corporations from buying elections. But party lines had been clearly drawn on the issue and compromise had proven extremely difficult.

Still he had vowed both publicly and privately not to give up until big money's influence over the election process was effectively thwarted. He knew this would make him some enemies along the way, and perhaps even cost him some friends on the Hill. But it was a risk he was willing to take because he believed it was the right thing to do to preserve America's democratic principles.

It was close to eleven o'clock in the evening by the time he crossed the border from New York to Connecticut. He was less than two hours from home. He smiled at the thought of kissing his kids good night as they slept soundly in their beds. He was also looking forward to two weeks of family time at a friend's lake house in New Hampshire.

The good news was the traffic had thinned considerably. He had decided to use the less-traveled and more scenic Merritt Parkway instead of the always-congested Interstate 95. It seemed like a good idea at the time, but it had started to rain and visibility on the dimly lit old parkway had diminished considerably.

He glanced into his rearview mirror and saw the glare of a truck's halogen lights coming up quickly behind him. It couldn't have been a very large truck as the overpasses on the historic parkway that had opened to the public in 1938 were too low for semitrailers. The roads had become slick and Waterford cursed at the idiot driver for going too fast and for having his headlights on their high-beam setting. His anger turned to dread, however, as he realized the fast-approaching truck was making no attempt to pass him.

Waterford yelled out in panic as the truck rammed directly into his back bumper at sixty-five miles an hour. His Chrysler sedan immediately began to hydroplane. Remarkably, the senator was able to regain control of his car before it fishtailed into an all-out spin. But just as he did, the truck slammed hard once again into the left corner of his rear bumper. The sedan's tires lost contact with the asphalt for just a brief second—but that was all it took.

The car was sent airborne.

It rolled five times before leaving the road and tumbling down into a rocky ravine, coming to rest on its roof between a large boulder and a massive oak tree.

Waterford was in an upside-down position still strapped into his seat by his shoulder harness. He could feel blood oozing from his head and chest. He was conscious but his breathing was shallow and raspy. He knew from his combat experience what that meant—his lungs were filling with blood and he was probably dying. But the excruciating physical pain was nothing compared to the overwhelming sadness he felt as his thoughts turned to his wife and children. He knew he would never see them again. Tears began streaming down his face.

A tree branch snapped loudly in the woods behind him. A man approached slowly and knelt down beside the blown-out driver's side window. He didn't look particularly menacing; in fact, his eyes registered no emotion at all.

Waterford struggled to speak. He only had the strength to utter a single word. "Why?" he gurgled through his own blood.

But the man did not answer. He simply stared at Senator Mark Waterford until he was positive the would-be-Camelot president had taken his final breath.

35

Present Day
Washington, D.C.

It had been barely a month since Matt and Buzz departed for Montana. They had made the trip with the hope of solving the mystery of a conquistador helmet and the black tribe described by Meriwether Lewis. Matt never anticipated where that innocent search was going to lead them. He rattled off the list of improbable events in his head. *They had discovered a 200-year-old African skull. He and Ally had been shot at on Ghost Ridge. Samantha Christie was actually the daughter of Harry Spate. Oliver and Landon Spate were close to completing a covert takeover of the U.S. government—and they had killed at least four elected officials as well as a Supreme Court judge along the way. And he had been deceived and manipulated by a shadow organization with its own secret agenda.*

And Big Tom was dead.

The only way to make Big Tom's death count for something now would be to derail the Spates' seditious plans. Intellectually, Matt understood there were more important reasons for signing on to help Harry and Samantha. Starting with saving the lives of the five people whose names still remained on the Enemies of the Spate list. And if that weren't reason enough, he also knew if the Spates controlled the government, then the lives of every American would be forever changed. But in his heart what really drove him to nail the Spates' was his guilt over Big Tom's death.

In some ways Matt felt they hadn't made any progress at all since leaving Montana. But he hoped today would change all that. They had the letter from Jedediah Spate, the patriarch of the Spate clan. And now they had Jefferson's wheel cipher. The four men had assembled in Buzz's office. They were seated around the large conference table where Matt had first shared the coded letter he had found in the library of the American Philosophical Society.

"Are you ready?" Buzz asked.

"Let's do it," Matt replied resolutely.

This was the first time Matt had been face-to-face with Buzz since he learned of his friend's deception. It took all of his self-control not to reveal what he knew. But for now he would act his part. He was confident that if he played his cards right he would learn the truth. In the meantime, his focus had to remain on stopping the Spates from fulfilling their terroristic plans.

Buzz nodded at Director James Fox. Fox removed the printed copy of Jedediah Spate's letter from his briefcase.

"You know if this doesn't work we're back to square one," Matt forewarned. The wheel cipher sat directly in front of him. He gazed down at it wondering if Jefferson's imaginative innovation would reveal any secrets that day.

"It'll work. Those disks look like they've been frozen in place for years," Harry Spate commented optimistically. They all understood that if the order of the disks had been tampered with in any way, they would never be able to decipher the message.

"There's only one way to find out," Buzz interjected. He looked at Fox, "Read the first twenty-six letters of the correspondence, James."

The letters of the alphabet were inscribed in a random order on the edges of the twenty-six wooden disks. The men had read enough about the wheel cipher to know exactly how it worked. They knew the sender of the cipher message, in this case Jedediah Spate, would have arranged his disks in the same agreed upon order with Thomas Jefferson. To encode his message, Jedediah would simply have spun each of the disks to spell out the first twenty-six letters of his message from left to right in a row across the twenty-six disks. Then he would have looked to any other row, either above or below the real line of text, and pick one to use as his cipher. So if the real message was "a most excellent man," then the chosen line of cipher text above it or below it might have read "qytiombypjnreyvmz," or complete gibberish to prying eyes. No numbers, punctuation, or spaces were used.

As the receiver of the message, Jefferson would have arranged the disks on his matching wheel cipher in the same prearranged order. He would then enter the enciphered or garbled message by spinning each disk until all twenty-six letters were visible across one horizontal line. Then he'd slowly turn the iron spindle and look for the one line of legible text above or below the line of gibberish. The line with the real message would clearly stand out from the rest. Jefferson would have then transcribed this first part of the message onto a blank sheet of paper. This procedure would be repeated for the next twenty-six letters of the message, and so on, until the entire message was deciphered.

Fox began reciting the first letters of Jedediah Spate's ciphered correspondence aloud. Matt dutifully spun the first disk like a combination lock until he found the first letter. He continued on to the second disk, and so on, until all twenty-six letters had been spelled out in a row across the disks on the iron spindle. Very slowly he turned the spindle and began searching through the other rows of text for recognizable words.

At first he didn't see anything intelligible. He began to lose hope. Then suddenly he stopped. His hand froze in place on the spindle.

"What is it, Matt?" Harry asked nervously. "Do you see something?"

Matt remained motionless for a moment longer and then a huge grin spread across his face. "It works," he shouted out. "It really works."

"What does it say?" Fox leaned in to get a closer look.

"It says, '*I wish to inform you of our great,*'" Matt read the first twenty-six letters of the deciphered message. Then he said excitedly, "Come on, James, give me the next set of letters." When the first sentence was completely transcribed, Matt read it aloud, "'*I wish to inform you of our great success in our undertaking against the Negro tribe.*'"

They looked at one another in disbelief.

Twenty minutes later they had deciphered the entire letter. When it was complete, Matt read it in its entirety. When he finished, the men sat in stunned silence.

"Oh my God," Harry exclaimed, horrified at what his ancestor had helped perpetrate.

Buzz was next to speak. "Apparently murder runs in the Spate family," he said, somewhat callously. Harry cringed and hung his head in shame.

"Except this wasn't just murder," Fox replied, still dumbfounded, "this was genocide."

"And it was carried out with the assistance of the U.S. Army. With the complete knowledge of President Thomas Jefferson," Matt interjected soberly.

"Not just his knowledge, this mission was *ordered* by the president," said the ex-navy colonel. "Read that second paragraph again."

Matt looked at his transcribed notes. "'*As per your orders,*

General Wilkinson and his troops went to great lengths to ensure the eradication of the Negro tribe was complete. Their village was completely destroyed and not a living soul was left to tell of the misfortune bestowed upon them. Their bodies were disposed of quite cleverly so as never to be found. There is nothing now that shall prevent us from taking up the proposed fur trade commerce plan on a large scale."

Fox leaned over Matt's shoulder and said, "And evidently Meriwether Lewis was kept in the dark about all of this. This line here toward the very end states, '*The troops have been sworn to silence and are to return directly east. These steps were taken to prevent the chance of any news from our endeavor from ever reaching St. Louis. You can be assured our actions here will not become known to Mr. Lewis.*'"

"Jesus Christ," Buzz shook his head in disgust. "They wiped out a colony of people who had lived on that land for more than two hundred years."

"But why?" Matt asked puzzled.

"Clearly, Jefferson was afraid the black tribe presented a threat to the fur trade. And for whatever reason, he didn't entrust Lewis to take care of the problem for him," Buzz replied.

"Who's General Wilkinson?" Matt then asked, turning to Fox.

"General James Wilkinson was something of a scoundrel," Fox explained. "He served in the Continental Army during the Revolutionary War. But he was forced to resign because of his involvement in a number of scandals and controversies. He was eventually reinstated and even became commanding general of the United States Army at one point. Later on he was appointed to be the first governor of the Louisiana Territory. It was there he developed some close ties to the Spanish. But it wasn't until after his death that it was discovered he had actually been a paid agent of the Spanish Crown."

"Sounds like Jefferson chose the perfect man for the job," Buzz said cynically.

Harry suddenly brightened, "This is a horrible discovery, but it's exactly the break we've been looking for." He rubbed his goatee as he said, "If we can prove my ancestors were involved in an atrocity of this proportion; that they essentially built their fortune on the deaths of an entire people, it will deal a severe blow to the Spate public image."

Matt responded, "Maybe, but it happened over two hundred years ago. Do you think anyone will hold it against your brothers?"

"I know my brothers weren't directly involved in the initial act. But if we can prove they've been covering it up for the last forty years, then they'll be seen as culpable."

"And don't forget about Big Tom," Buzz interjected. "If we can bring enough heat on your brothers, then maybe someone will talk and reveal what really happened to him."

"As much as the death of Big Tom is a tragedy," Harry said delicately, "my hope is that we can use this two-hundred-year-old atrocity as a means of exposing their current conspiracy to infiltrate and take over our government."

"How's that?" Matt asked.

Harry explained, "Once the spotlight from the genocide conspiracy is shining brightly, we go to the press with the evidence Samantha and I have been building on my brothers' subversive plans. All the lawyers, lobbying firms, and money in the world won't be able to halt the momentum against them when *that* news breaks. The Justice Department will have enough to establish probable cause. And just as importantly, they'll have the public's support to open up a full investigation."

"The genie will be out of the bottle," Buzz quipped.

"Exactly," Harry said.

They turned to Matt who still had a look of concern on his face. "You're forgetting one thing," he said. "In order to prove a massacre took place out there, we're going to need more than a coded letter as evidence."

He locked eyes with Buzz. "We're going to need to get back onto Ghost Ridge. There's a mass grave out there somewhere and we need to find it."

36

April, 1807

Charlottesville, Virginia

Winter had barely begun to release its grasp on the Blue Ridge Mountains of Virginia. The light rain that had been falling for hours had mercifully abated. The horse-drawn carriage had only one passenger that evening, not including the driver. It had been a slow and uncomfortable journey. They should have arrived hours ago but the muddy, rutted roads had made the going quite perilous. It was nearly dark as the carriage wound its way up the side of the mountain, atop which President Jefferson's home rested.

Jedediah Spate was damp and chilled to the bone by the time he arrived at Monticello. One of the more than one hundred African slaves working on the plantation ushered Spate through Monticello's East Portico entrance. Jefferson mumbled an apology for the miserable weather as the house slave dutifully helped Spate out of his overcoat. The two men entered the two-story Great Hall. As they passed through the hall, Spate marveled at the variety of Indian artifacts that filled the expansive room. There were bows, arrows, poisoned lances, peace pipes, wampum belts, buffalo hides, and even cooking utensils. There were so many Indian artifacts, Jefferson joked, visitors to Monticello had taken *to calling it Indian Hall.*

*Jefferson's lifelong fascination with American Indians had start-
ed in his youth. He had always romanticized their courage, stoicism,
and dignity. He equated these traits to Roman virtues he so admired
and studied as part of his classical education growing up. He ideal-
ized Indians to such an extent he even told friends later in life that
part of his family was descended from the legendary Indian princess
Pocahontas. While he believed Indians to be savages, he thought they
were noble men who had the potential to become civilized. This was in
stark contrast to how he felt about African slaves whom he thought to
be genetically inferior. He rejected the possibility that a free black man
could ever be civilized, let alone live peaceably with whites.*

*The men turned left out of the Main Hall and into Jefferson's
private library. Jedediah Spate went and stood by the warmth of the
fire that burned brightly in the small fireplace.*

*"I've heard a good many things about you, Mr. Spate. I under-
stand your import-export business is thriving," Jefferson began.*

*Spate had arrived in America twenty-five years earlier from
Germany. Shortly after he arrived, he had begun buying furs from
trappers and Indians and eventually established a fur goods shop in
New York. Over time, Spate had purchased a dozen ships and had
built a prosperous import-export business, but a recent embargo threatened to destroy his burgeoning fur business.*

*"Actually, sir, the Embargo Act you signed into law has dealt my
commercial endeavor a severe blow," Spate replied evenly, doing his
best to mask his anger. "Since my ships no longer have clearance to
undertake voyages to overseas ports, my business faces potential ruin."*

*The Embargo Act had been in response to violations of U.S.
neutrality during the Napoleonic Wars. American merchantmen and
their cargo were being seized as contraband of war by the European
navies.*

Jefferson was well aware of the difficult times that had befallen

Mr. Spate. "Unfortunately, it was a necessary step to protect our sovereign interests. It will no doubt work itself out in time." He poured two glasses of Madeira wine and handed one to his guest. *"But I've requested your presence this evening to discuss another matter—one which I believe will replace your recent losses by a factor of ten or more,"* *Jefferson said tantalizingly.*

His cheeks flushed by the warm fire and the Madeira, Spate replied, "I can assure you, sir, you have my fullest attention."

The two men sat in matching wingback chairs in front of the fireplace. Jefferson proceeded to fill Spate in on Meriwether Lewis's breathtaking fur trade proposal—the one Lewis had begun to outline while leading the famous western exploration that had concluded just eighteen months earlier. The crux of the plan centered on utilizing the waterways he had discovered and the Indian relations he had fostered. He wanted to redirect the fur trade from the Mississippi to the mouth of the Columbia River—essentially opening up a direct route to the Far East and cutting the British out of the equation altogether.

"Sounds ideal," Spate remarked evenly, wondering how he figured into all this.

"There is one problem," Jefferson replied.

Just three months earlier Jefferson had met with Lewis, right after his triumphant return from the expedition. Ironically, the president was sitting with Spate in the same room where he and Lewis had gotten down on their hands and knees to study the remarkable map drawn by Captain William Clark. Since that day, Jefferson had ample time to ponder Lewis's remarkable revelation regarding the black tribe. He had discreetly discussed Lewis's claims with trusted colleagues at the American Philosophical Society. And after much debate, Jefferson finally concluded this "tribe" was most likely comprised of descendants of escaped slaves from one of the early Spanish explorations of the Americas.

Jefferson shared Lewis's sighting of the conquistador helmet shrine and the tribe's European-sounding language with Spate. Then he shared his escaped slave hypothesis.

Spate paused a moment before responding. It was a lot to take in. Finally, he said, "If what Lewis claims he saw and heard is accurate, then I think your conclusion is entirely plausible, sir." Then he said hesitantly, "But I'm still perplexed as to how any of this pertains to me."

Jefferson took another sip of Madeira, peering over the rim of his crystal glass at Spate. The time had come to make his proposition. He got up and stoked the fire with an iron poker.

"Yes, I'm coming to that. But first, there's one more thing Lewis said to me about this so-called black tribe. He claims they were quite aggressive. And because they control a piece of territory critical to the fur trade strategy, he fears they will present a real obstacle to our success."

Spate remained silent. He knew the president had more to say.

"I think you'll agree we cannot let a hostile tribe put our entire fur plan at risk. Besides," he added, "if news got out that there was a tribe of escaped slaves living freely it would..." he searched for delicate phrasing, "set a bad precedent."

The Great Dismal Swamp was one thing, but a group of escaped black slaves living in essentially a free colony in the United States, well that was a whole other matter altogether. He simply could not let news of a free tribe of black men become public, primarily out of fear it would embolden East Coast slaves to initiate a massive slave uprising of their own. It would be catastrophic for Jefferson and all southern plantation owners, and he would do everything in his power to prevent it from happening.

Jefferson went on to present Jedediah Spate his plan to eradicate the "Negro tribe," as he had taken to calling the black-skinned people described by Lewis. The plan would be carried out by Spate with the help of General James Wilkinson. Once the tribe had been dispensed with, Spate and his New York–based company would be granted the spoils of war—exclusive rights to the fur trade west of the Mississippi and the millions of dollars in expected profits that came along with it.

Jefferson had chosen General Wilkinson precisely because he was known to be a man of very few scruples. His checkered past had included participation in various questionable activities, including the so-called "Conway Cabal," a conspiracy intended to overthrow George Washington and name Horatio Gates as commander-in-chief of the Continental Army during the Revolutionary War. He had also been accused of treason for allegedly passing U.S. and French secrets to Spain before and after the Louisiana Purchase. Somehow Wilkinson had survived all of this and more with his military standing relatively intact. The final reason for Jefferson choosing him was he had been Governor of the Louisiana Territory prior to Meriwether Lewis's appointment to the role the prior month. So he was very familiar with the geography and could leverage his nefarious local relationships to assemble the right team to ensure the mission's success—and its absolute secrecy.

Jedediah Spate had a similarly unprincipled reputation, which is why Jefferson had chosen to award the fur trade business to his company and not his young protégé Meriwether Lewis. Lewis was far too right-minded to ever agree to such a radical and venal plan. Spate on the other hand, was known for being a shrewd and unscrupulous businessman. He had built his import-export business on the backs of immigrant dock laborers and political connections. And most importantly, he had done it outside the law when it was required. So he would certainly not let a tribe of Negroes get in the way of a potential fortune in fur profits.

An evil grin escaped from the corners of Spate's mouth. He said, "Mr. President, I would be honored to serve you in this matter."

Jefferson did not smile back. He considered himself a civilized man and was not happy to be doing business with the likes of Jedediah Spate. But he knew in this particular case he had no choice. That didn't mean he wouldn't do his damndest to ensure his partnership with Spate remained a secret.

"You must act very quickly," he ordered, "Wilkinson will remain acting Governor in St. Louis for some time still. Mr. Lewis has many matters to attend to here and it will more than likely be the end of the year before he assumes his official duties. It is imperative this mission be completed before then. Lewis cannot find out about this, do you understand?"

"Of course," Spate said.

Jefferson continued, "I will authorize Wilkinson to use whatever military resources he needs. You should make arrangements to leave for St. Louis immediately."

"There is one more thing," Jefferson got up from his chair and walked to the other side of the room. He returned with an odd-looking wooden device Spate had never seen before. It appeared to be a series of wooden disks threaded onto an iron spindle, and on each disk were placed tiny randomized letters.

"When the mission is completed successfully, I wish for you to notify me via courier. But the letter must be written in code using this wheel cipher," Jefferson ordered.

He spent the next ninety minutes teaching Spate how to use his cleverly designed invention. At the end of the tutorial he excused himself to go to bed.

Jedediah Spate left the following morning. The president was not present to bid him farewell.

37

Present Day
Great Falls, Montana

Buzz had just radioed the control tower in Great Falls to tell them they were fifty miles out. Matt sat beside him in the copilot's seat. He studied Buzz's face as the ex-navy pilot expertly adjusted one of the seemingly infinite controls on his private plane's instrument panel.

He knew the reason he had admired Buzz was because he reminded him so much of his father. Matt had spent his entire life trying to prove himself worthy of his father's respect and admiration. It had driven him. And by most measuring sticks he had achieved success—an Ivy League academic scholarship, numerous athletic accomplishments, a moneyed Wall Street career, and so on. But in his own mind he had fallen short. He left Wall Street, his marriage ended in divorce, and most damning of all, he never served his country in the military. He knew that his now-famous search for Washington's surrender letter was as much driven by his desire to unearth the truth as it was to prove his worthiness to his long-since deceased father.

His thoughts returned to the present and his current quest

to bring down the Spates. Matt knew these were bad men doing bad things. He understood they threatened the very freedom and democracy his father had risked his life to preserve. These were reasons enough to want to bring them to justice. But this is not what motivated him. Ultimately, he knew this was his chance to serve his country. This was his war. It had become his endgame in more ways than one.

Matt glanced again across the cramped cockpit. He felt foolish for it, but a part of him still yearned to trust the man behind those steel-blue eyes. He wished he could turn back the clock to a time when he still believed Buzz to be the tough but fair man who lived his life honorably, both on and off the battlefield. The man who once told him how he tried to live his life according to the three hallowed words spoken by famous World War II general Douglas MacArthur—duty, honor, country. The sad truth was, that man was gone forever. And as with the death of any close friend, a void had been left behind by his departure—a void not marked by sadness but rather by anger.

"What are you thinking about?" Buzz's voice came through Matt's headset. He smiled and said, "You look like you're about ready to clock somebody."

Matt hadn't realized that his fists were balled up and his jaw was clenched. He forced himself to relax. "I guess I'm just ready to go to battle."

"Be careful what you ask for," Buzz cracked. The plane pitched slightly as he banked to starboard and assumed a new bearing toward Great Falls.

Another voice crackled through the headset, saying, "Are we almost there?" It was Dr. Lane, sitting directly behind them. The African American history professor from the University of South Carolina had joined the expedition at Matt's request. He figured they could use the professor's expertise and credibility should they discover evidence of a mass grave.

Buzz announced over the communication system they'd be in Great Falls in less than thirty minutes' time.

Matt asked, "Are you prepared for what we might find out there, Professor?"

"I imagine that one is never prepared to uncover evidence of genocide, especially one perpetrated against people of his own race," he replied. "But unfortunately, it wouldn't be the only slaughter of a tribe carried out by our government. One of the worst took place just one state over from Montana—at Wounded Knee Creek in South Dakota. More than one-hundred-fifty members of the Lakota Indian tribe were massacred, including forty-seven women and children."

Buzz piped in, "Not one of the U.S. Army's finest moments for sure. I believe that was one of the first battles where the famous Hotchkiss revolving cannon was used. It had five 37-mm barrels and was capable of firing 68 rounds per minute. Those poor people never had a chance."

Dr. Lane turned to the man sitting next to him and asked with a measure of disdain, "Is it true your family has been covering up this incident for more than two hundred years?"

Harry Spate squirmed slightly in his seat. Even though he shared the same last name, he felt little kinship to either the modern-day Spate clan or its patriarch, Jedediah Spate. He answered somewhat apologetically, "I'm afraid it is. Although for the majority of that time there was really no need for a cover-up per se, primarily due to the fact nobody outside of a relatively small group of men ever knew the atrocity occurred. It was only when the conquistador helmet was found that my father intervened."

"And bought up the lease rights to the land surrounding Ghost Ridge," Matt added.

Harry nodded. "Yes," he said.

"Why didn't he just blow the site up so nobody would ever find it?" Matt asked.

"That's a good question, and I'm not sure I have the answer. One possible explanation is he died shortly after he found the helmet. And when my brothers took over, I think they just felt the situation had been contained. They probably didn't think much about it until..."

"Until we showed up asking questions about that damn helmet," Matt finished Harry's sentence, still feeling responsible for what had happened to Big Tom.

Harry nodded. "My guess is it won't take them long to come up with a plan to permanently dispose of all the evidence of the massacre," he offered. "Maybe they already have."

"That's assuming they know exactly where that evidence is." Dr. Lane interjected.

"You think it's possible they don't know?" Matt asked incredulously.

"Like Harry just said," Dr. Lane hypothesized, "it was essentially forgotten for more than two hundred years. They probably don't even know where the original village was, let alone where the bodies are buried."

"He's right," Buzz said. "We may be closer to knowing the exact location than they are. My guess is they haven't done the thermal imaging we have to narrow down the location of the original village. They never had a reason to, at least up until the last month."

"Are we sure the remains are even still out there? Wouldn't they have turned to dust by now?" Matt asked.

"Bones last a very long time, Matt," Dr. Lane answered, "especially in the right conditions. Of course, it depends on the moisture content of the ground, temperature, depth, bacteria concentrations, calcium levels in bones, and a host of other conditions. But don't forget," he noted, "that skull you found was over two hundred years old."

"Good point," Matt said.

After landing in Great Falls, the men made their way over to the Lewis and Clark Interpretive Center to meet up with Ron Patterson. Ally was there with him. Matt had called the day before and asked her to join them there to discuss a plan for finding the mass grave on the reservation. He asked her to bring along her grandfather, Crooked Nose, so he could help pinpoint on a map exactly where he used to hike while searching for gold out near Ghost Ridge. They needed to narrow their search even further if they hoped to quickly find evidence of a mass grave.

Along the way they stopped at a local deli to grab some take-out sandwiches. Matt happened to glance at a rack of newspapers by the door on the way in. The headline of the *Great Falls Tribune* stopped him in his tracks. It read: "*Connecticut Senator Killed in Car Crash.*" Matt snatched the newspaper off the rack and started reading. Mark Waterford, a Democratic U.S. Senator had been killed while driving from Washington, D.C., to his home in Hartford, Connecticut. Details were scarce, but police indicate darkness and wet roads may have contributed to the senator losing control of his car. It was apparently a single-car accident.

The article went on to say that Waterford was a rising star in the Democratic Party and was believed to have had presidential aspirations. Most recently, he had been championing efforts aimed at campaign finance reform, but he faced stiff opposition from conservative lawmakers.

"This is bullshit," Matt shouted.

"What's wrong?" Buzz asked, and turned to see what had made him so upset.

Matt held up the headline so Buzz could read it.

"Damn," Buzz said, "I actually met him at a veterans function in D.C. He was a real charismatic guy—full of passion to change the ways of Washington. What a waste," he shook his head sadly. "I'm assuming by your reaction, you must have known him, too?"

"No, I didn't know him, Buzz," Matt said with a look of anger mixed with fear. "Senator Waterford was the next name on the Enemies of the Spate hit list."

Ally sprang from her chair when Matt entered the room. They hadn't seen each other since their harrowing experience out on Ghost Ridge. She leaned in to give Matt a kiss on the lips, but he turned his head ever so slightly so that it ended up being an awkward peck on the cheek. Ally seemed confused by Matt's aloofness, but she let it go. She figured he had more important things on his mind.

"Where's Crooked Nose?" Matt asked, looking around.

"Oh, he wasn't feeling well enough to make the drive down," Ally said.

"That's too bad," he said, disappointed at Crooked Nose's absence.

After seeing the look of discouragement on Matt's face, she added, "But don't worry, he showed me on a map where he used to hike."

"Oh, well that's good," he said, still sounding mildly annoyed.

"Are you OK?" She asked. "You seem...distracted."

"No, I'm fine, just a little jet-lagged I guess." He turned and introduced Ally to Dr. Lane and then to Harry Spate.

Ally appeared shocked after being introduced to the brother of Oliver and Landon Spate. Matt noticed her trepidation. He smiled. "Don't worry," he said, "he's on our team."

Ally forced a smile. "Of course, it's just unexpected, that's all," she said, although her face betrayed her concern.

"Shall we get down to business?" Ron Patterson began, motion-ing toward the back of the room. Thermal maps from their original helicopter reconnaissance as well as topographical maps of Ghost Ridge were spread out on a large conference table.

"Absolutely," Matt said.

They gathered around the table. Matt picked up a bright red marker.

"Right here is where Ally and I found the skull. As you can see, it's a little to the northeast of where the original fort was built." He pointed to the rectangle shape Patterson had drawn on the same map weeks earlier. "My guess is the skull was carried here from somewhere upstream. The question is where."

Everyone inched closer to the table. They began scanning the thermal imaging printouts for red areas to the northeast of where the original fort once stood. But it was futile. There was nothing that stood out as an area of interest large enough to contain the bodies of potentially hundreds of people.

Matt switched gears. He grabbed hold of the topographical map and pulled it toward him. "Ally, can you show us where your grandfather used to hike, back when he was looking for gold?"

"Sure."

She studied the map for a minute. She traced her finger along a ridgeline that ran north to south, parallel to Ghost Ridge. "Accord-ing to Crooked Nose, right along here is where he felt the presence of the spirits of the lost black tribe," she said. "He couldn't recall exactly where, but he's sure it was along this route."

Matt grabbed a different color marker and drew a dotted line along the trajectory Ally had just traced with her finger. "OK," he said. "The good news is that a section of this ridgeline is northeast of the fort, which means the skull could have washed downstream from there."

"The bad news," Buzz spoke up, pointing back to the thermal maps, "is that there are no concentrated areas of red color anywhere near where Crooked Nose was panning for his golden fortune."

They kicked around a few more ideas over the next hour but made little progress. Frustrations were starting to grow. They knew they needed to narrow down their search to one or two high potential areas because that's all they would have time to explore, assuming they were able to sneak back onto the reservation undetected at all.

"If there are hundreds of bodies buried somewhere out there," Dr. Lane spoke up, "we should be able to see them on these maps, right?"

Something had been eating at Matt but he couldn't quite put his finger on it. Dr. Lane's question gave him an idea. "Not necessarily, Doc," Matt replied excitedly.

He raced across the room and grabbed his backpack. He quickly found what he was looking for—a copy of the decoded letter from Jedediah Spate to Thomas Jefferson.

"What's up, Matt? You're obviously on to something," Buzz said.

"Dr. Lane just reminded me of something Jedediah Spate wrote." He began reading out loud from the deciphered letter, "*General Wilkinson and his troops went to great lengths to ensure the eradication of the Negro tribe was complete. Their village was completely destroyed and not a living soul was left to tell of the misfortune bestowed upon them.*" He paused. "Here it is," he continued, reading more slowly now, "*Their bodies were disposed of quite cleverly so as never to be found.*"

"Quite cleverly so as never to be found," Matt repeated. "Maybe if they were so cleverly disposed of, they were put in a place that wouldn't register on a thermal image."

The room went silent for a moment. Then Patterson spoke up.

"I remember reading about thermal imaging cameras sometimes being blocked by dense stone."

"As in granite?" Matt asked.

"That would do it."

"Well, I can tell you from firsthand experience there is a hell of a lot of granite out in those hills. Ally and I hid behind one particularly large chunk of it while being shot at by the Spates' men." Ally involuntarily rubbed the spot where the bullet had grazed her temple.

Matt walked back over to the set of maps spread across the table. "It makes sense." He scanned the maps again. "It's an elegant solution, in fact," he said.

"What do you mean?" Buzz asked.

"They didn't have time to bury hundreds of bodies, but they still needed to dispose of the evidence of their crime. So they looked around and found the perfect answer to their problem," Matt replied. He looked up triumphantly but nobody had caught on to his line of thinking.

"A cave," he finally shared.

"My God," Harry Spate said excitedly, "that has to be it."

Heads nodded in agreement.

"So instead of looking for a large patch of red color on the *thermal* maps," Patterson said, "we should be looking for a large outcropping of rock on the *topographical* maps. A spot along the ridgeline that looks like it could have once been a cave. Because if you're premise is correct, Matt, the cave is no longer there. They most likely would have dynamited it shut, sealing the bodies inside."

With this new theory about what had happened in mind, they returned to the photos and topographical maps. It didn't take them long to pinpoint the perfect outcropping. It was located just a quarter mile northeast of where Ally and Matt had conducted their original search. And it was right in the middle of the ridgeline where

Crooked Nose once hiked.

"Can your son get us out there?" Matt asked Ron Patterson.

"He's standing by. I just need to give him enough notice to fuel up the chopper and he'll be ready."

"Good, then I suggest we leave first thing in the morning." Matt looked around expectantly at the rest of the team. There were no dissenters.

"There's just one thing," Patterson spoke up tentatively. "If the cave was dynamited shut, how are we going to get in there?"

Dr. Lane had clearly been thinking the same thing, because he answered quickly, "Based on the evidence, my guess is that after two hundred some odd years, a gap or two has developed in the sealed entrance. It's the only way to explain the skull Matt found."

After the meeting broke up, Ally pulled Matt aside and asked how he expected to sneak back onto Ghost Ridge without the Spates' men knowing about it.

Matt answered, "Samantha has a plan for diverting Spate's guys away from the area for the day."

"Samantha Christie?" Ally said, dumbfounded. "You mean the woman who works for Spate Industries?"

Matt shared the real identity of Samantha Christie. He revealed she was really Harry Spate's daughter, and that she had secretly been working as a mole inside her uncles' company for years in an attempt to compile enough damning evidence to bring Spate Industries to justice.

Ally's face registered her shock, but she recovered enough to ask, "Are you sure you trust her?"

"Ally, she's the one who sent me that text message when we were out on Ghost Ridge. She's 'A. Friend.' So, yes, I trust her, and so should you. She saved our lives."

Ally shook her head slowly from side to side, still trying to absorb the unexpected turn of events. "So what's her plan for diverting Spates' guys?" she said, still skeptical.

"She's back on the Blackfeet Reservation arranging the diversion as we speak—a surprise training exercise of some kind. She somehow convinced the police chief the exercise came at the request of Oliver Spate. Once I call and tell her we're on for tomorrow, she'll set the wheels in motion."

Ally finally relented. "OK Matt, "if you trust her, then I guess that's good enough for me." She looked down at her watch and exclaimed, "Oh shit, I was supposed to check in on my grandfather. I need to step out and give him a call. I'll be right back."

38

Present Day

Ghost Ridge

Blackfeet Reservation, Montana

There was very little chop in the air that morning. And for that, Matt was grateful. The less-than-one-hour helicopter flight up to the Blackfeet Reservation from Great Falls had been relatively smooth. They had just passed over Browning and were only a few minutes from landing near Ghost Ridge. It was warm and very tense inside the cramped cabin.

Ron Patterson sat in the copilot's seat alongside his son. Stu had once again been enlisted to airlift Matt and his friends out to Ghost Ridge. Matt was surprised Ron wanted to accompany them, given his age and balky heart. But there had been no talking the Lewis and Clark expert out of participating in an excursion that held the potential for such historical significance. Harry Spate, who sat staring out the starboard window, wasn't about to miss the trip either. But he had very different reasons. Not the least of which was to exorcise some family demons—both past and present. Buzz, Dr. Lane, and Ally sat in seats directly across the cabin, facing Matt and Harry.

"Don't worry, Matt. We'll find it," Buzz said reassuringly. He had noticed the look of concern on his young friend's face.

Matt nodded but his brow remained furrowed. His eyes landed on Ally's exotic face. As if she could feel the weight of his gaze upon her, she looked up from cinching her backpack. She smiled confidently and gave him a flirtatious wink. He gave her a weak smile and then turned to stare out the window, lost once again in his own thoughts.

The chopper landed in a clearing within sight of the outcropping they had identified on the maps the day before. Stu stayed behind with the chopper in case they needed to make a hasty exit. The rest of the incursion team hiked the short distance into the site. Matt took a moment to look around at his companions. He knew they were all wondering the same thing. Was there a cave hidden behind the imposing wall of granite in the distance or was this just another tantalizing dead end?

Ten minutes later, the team arrived at the site. At Buzz's direction, they immediately spread out and began searching for an opening concealed among the forty-foot-high facade of stacked boulders. Matt noticed that the ridgeline followed the bends of the stream northward. He could see Chief Mountain standing defiantly in the distance. As his eyes returned to the more immediate surroundings, it occurred to him the outcropping they stood in front of didn't look any different from the rest of the terrain. His spirits sagged. It didn't look promising.

Meanwhile, Buzz had heaved himself up onto a Volkswagen Beetle–sized boulder. It offered him a better line of sight. Matt never ceased to marvel at how a man already past the retirement age hadn't lost a single step.

"You see anything?" Matt yelled, hopefully.

"Nothing," Buzz grunted back. The sweat glistened off his close-cropped hair like morning dew on newly cut grass. "Why don't you two," he said to Matt and Ally, "start to climb up that side.

If there's an opening, it's probably going to be up here, not down there where the rocks have settled."

He pointed at Harry, Ron, and Dr. Lane, "But just in case, you guys explore the base of the wall." Buzz knew the overweight Patterson, the bespectacled Lane, and the skittish Harry Spate were probably not capable of traversing a thirty-foot vertical wall of stone. But like a good military commander, he made sure everyone had a role to play in the mission.

Matt gave him a thumbs-up signal and picked a path for his ascent. Ally did the same twenty feet further down the wall. The three amateur climbers inched their way up the rocky fortification toward the overhanging ridge above their heads. They stopped every so often to shine their flashlights into cracks and crevices between boulders that looked promising. The summer sun had begun its own climb skyward. It foretold a hot day was in store. About thirty minutes later they were halfway up the face when Ron Patterson called out from below.

"I think I might have found something," he yelled out.

They could hear his voice but couldn't see him. "Where the hell are you, Ron?" Matt shouted back, still unable to spot him.

A hand appeared from in between two boulders, waving frantically. "Over here," a slightly muffled voice could be heard saying. He was at the southern end of the outcropping, where the rock pile merged with the side of the ridge. One by one, Matt, Buzz, and Ally descended from their respective perches. Dr. Lane and Harry hurried over to join them.

The irrepressible historian stuck his head out from between two rather impressive-looking pieces of granite. "I'm afraid I'm too fat to squeeze in there, but I think I've found a tunnel through the stone."

"Are you sure?" Buzz asked skeptically.

"Come see for yourself," Patterson offered. He slid his girth gingerly down off the three-foot-high boulder that partially obscured the sliver of an entrance.

Back on solid ground and panting heavily, Patterson said excitedly, "When I shined my light in there, it went right on into the blackness. I couldn't see where it ended."

Before Buzz could respond, Matt leaped up onto the boulder and disappeared into the gap.

About ten minutes later he reappeared. He hopped down off the rock. His clothes were covered in dirt but he was wearing a familiar crooked grin. "Ladies and gentlemen," he exclaimed, "if you'll follow me, the eleven a.m. cave tour is about to begin."

"Son of a gun," Harry exclaimed.

"Seriously?" Buzz chimed in.

"It's a tight squeeze. But if you're not opposed to crawling on all fours, then I think everyone should be able to make it." He turned to Ron knowing he wouldn't be physically able to join them. "We need someone out here to warn us in case anyone arrives unexpectedly. Can you do that?"

"Of course. But wait," Ron said. He reached down and grabbed hold of some Petzl® headlamps from the pile of gear on the ground and handed them out. "You'll need these. It's going to be dark as night in there."

Matt led the way, followed by Ally, Dr. Lane, and Harry Spate. Buzz brought up the rear. They had to crawl for about fifteen yards, veering to their left around a large rock, and then another ten yards, at which point they could stand up in a hunched-over position. They had to shuffle another ten feet until they could stand up completely straight.

They had arrived in what appeared to be some sort of antechamber. Ally was right behind him. Eyes wide, she tugged on his arm and pointed to the wall beside them. In the dim light they could see crude but beautiful hand drawings of birds, buffalo, and what appeared to be the sun, moon, and stars. They breathlessly waited for the rest of the party to join them. Buzz was the last to arrive.

"OK," Matt said. "This is as far as I got the first time. There's a narrow passageway behind me that leads further inside. Everyone turn on their headlamps." They did as instructed. The place lit up like somebody just flipped on halogen headlights in a two-car garage—which was about the size of the space they were standing in.

The solid rock ceiling above their heads was about eight feet high. "This was probably the original opening to the outside," Dr. Lane guessed. "The passageway ahead probably leads to a larger chamber."

"Do you think they lived in here?" Harry asked.

"No, most likely the cave was used more for ceremonial purposes," Professor Lane explained.

Buzz caught Matt's eye. They were both thinking the same thing. *Is this where Meriwether Lewis saw the religious shrine made out of stone with the conquistador helmet on top?* Matt nodded at Buzz. Adrenaline began to course through his body.

"You ready?" he asked.

"You bet your ass I'm ready. Let's roll," Buzz said. His blue eyes shined brightly in the reflection of the headlamps.

Matt turned and led the party deeper into the ancient cave. It had been carved into the side of the ridge over the centuries by the relentless forces of nature. Twenty paces later the roof of the cave began to slope upward. The walls around them became less constrictive. Matt stopped when he reached the middle of a wider opening. It appeared to be the size of a large basement—about forty-feet long by twenty-feet wide by fifteen-feet high.

"Well, I'll be damned," Buzz exclaimed. "There it is."

"What—there what is?" Harry turned around quickly to follow Buzz's gaze.

Buzz headed across the room to a large stone standing in the back of the room. It had been expertly chiseled into a perfect rectangular shape. It stood about four feet high and sat on a square pedestal approximately three feet wide.

Matt filled the rest of the team in. "Meriwether Lewis described seeing a shrine made out of granite with a conquistador helmet sitting on top. We think it was the same helmet that Big Tom found."

Dr. Lane approached the shrine reverently. He bent over and rubbed his hand along the structure's smooth surface. "Something's been carved into the side," he said excitedly. "It appears to be letters of some kind."

"Can you make out what it says?" Matt asked expectantly.

Lane studied the carvings more closely. "Oh my God," he gasped and turned to face the group. His face was marked by a mixture of shock and awe.

"What is it, man?" Harry pleaded.

"They're letters but they don't spell out words," he remarked.

"Sweet Jesus, don't tell me these guys wrote in code, too?" Buzz lamented.

"Roman numerals," Dr. Lane answered. "The letters are MDCX."

He looked up and translated, "The year 1610."

"My God," Harry exclaimed.

"It looks like you were right, Dr. Lane," Matt marveled.

"What do you mean?" Ally asked, confused.

Lane explained, "Matt is referring to my hypothesis that the ancestors of this black tribe were most likely escaped slaves from one of the last expeditions of the Spanish conquistadors. The expeditions ceased just after the turn of the seventeenth century. So this date fits."

"There's just one problem," Buzz spoke up from the other side of the room. He had performed a quick recon of the room while the others had been gathered around the shrine. The place was empty. "No bodies."

"But there's got to be," Harry said desperately.

"Come on, everyone," Matt said, taking charge, "start searching. They've got to be in here somewhere."

They spread out and began combing the room. Matt held his lantern high in the air in hopes of uncovering a potential crawl space above them. He even rubbed his hands along the wall's cool, rough surface in a desperate attempt to find a hidden door that would cleverly swing open like in the movies. But there was nothing like that. Frustrated and deflated, they gathered back in the center of the room.

"Sorry, guys, it looks like my theory about them using the cave to dispose of the bodies was a bust," Matt grumbled.

"The cave was here," Dr. Lane said, trying to stay positive, "and we did make a remarkable find that further corroborates Lewis's claims. So I wouldn't call it was a total bust."

"No," Harry replied with a resigned sigh, "but without proof of a massacre, we don't have the evidence we need to tip the scales of justice *and* public opinion against my brothers."

39

Present Day

Ghost Ridge

Blackfeet Reservation, Montana

"Let's regroup back outside," Buzz suggested. "We need to clear our heads and think through our next move."

"Good idea," Matt said. He began to lead the way out.

Single file, they left the chamber that held the shrine and started down the hallway toward the entry chamber. Walking with her head down, Ally failed to notice Matt had abruptly stopped in the middle of the passageway. She slammed into his back.

"Jesus, Matt," she said. "Why'd you stop?"

Matt stood frozen in the middle of the cramped hallway.

"Hang on a second," he said. He directed his headlamp to the right. "There's another hallway over here. We didn't see it on the way in because the walls overlap. The opening is only visible if you're on the way out," he shouted with excitement.

"Lead the way," Buzz said with renewed hope.

The passageway started toward the front of the cave but then doubled back to the rear. They now traversed a long tunnel that angled downward at a thirty-degree angle. The hallway began to widen so four people could walk shoulder-to-shoulder.

Buzz sidled up next to Matt and Ally. "This must lead to a lower chamber of some kind," he said.

"Yeah and to a much bigger room, by the looks of this tunnel," Matt answered with anticipation.

As they angled deeper into the earth, the air became stale and slightly noxious. They rounded the last bend. And that's when they saw it—a large cavern ten times the size of the ceremonial room above them. But this room wasn't empty.

Spread out in a fan-shaped pattern covering every inch of the coarse, sandy floor in front of them were bones. Very few complete skeletons were visible. Instead, a mass of disjointed appendages stuck out at every conceivable angle like a gruesome, jumbled jigsaw puzzle. Hundreds of remains were piled one on top of the other, two feet deep. Upon closer examination, it became clear many of the bodies had been dismembered. Arm and leg bones bore butchering marks where bone had been cut through and broken at the joints. These poor people weren't just murdered, they were slaughtered. The cave had finally revealed its horrible secret.

Each of them reacted to the horrific scene in their own way. Harry Spate fell to his knees and began to sob, repeating, "What have you done?" over and over. Ally stared ahead stoically, apparently in shock. Matt and Buzz shook their heads in disgust. Anger flashed in Dr. Lane's eyes.

"Bastards," Buzz finally uttered. "They didn't even spare the children." Noticeable among the remains were the skeletons of children, even some infants.

Matt knelt down and put his arm around Harry. "This has nothing to do with you, Harry. This doesn't define you or represent who you are," he said firmly.

Harry composed himself and looked gravely at Matt. "We need to tell the world about this. Someone needs to be made accountable."

"We will, Harry. I promise you, we will."

Ally suddenly bolted out of the room and ran back up the hallway.

Matt turned around to follow her but Buzz reached out and grabbed his arm. "Let her go, son," he said. "She needs to deal with this in her own way. We all do."

The men stood there, silently staring at the carnage trying to imagine what it must have been like. Buzz moved carefully toward the tangled web of bones. Something caught his eye. He knelt down and picked it up.

"What is it?' Matt asked.

"A brass button."

He handed it over to Matt.

The brass had oxidized but the U.S. eagle insignia was clearly visible. The eagle's wings were spread wide and a letter was stamped across its breast. "What does the capital *R* mean?" Matt asked.

"It stands for rifleman," Buzz explained. "This button came off a U.S. Army rifleman's coat."

Matt turned the button over in the palm of his hands. He tried to envision the rifleman as he and his fellow soldiers shot, reloaded, and shot again—over and over until everyone was dead. It was probably during one of these reloads that the gun snagged and tore the button off his coat. Matt wondered, *Were these men simply following orders? Did they feel any remorse?*

"Come take a look at this," Dr. Lane said.

Matt pocketed the button and walked to where the professor was squatting down. He pointed down at the ground. The top half of a fixed bayonet lay inside the rib cage of one of the larger skeletons. The muscle, tissue, and skin had long since decomposed, leaving only twelve pairs of ribs behind.

Matt looked over at Buzz, who had a puzzled expression. "What's wrong?" he asked.

"Something about these bodies makes me think not everyone was killed here inside the cave," he said. He motioned with his lantern. "The bodies toward the front are piled one on top of the other. And they're almost all male skeletons."

"So what does that mean?" Matt said.

"If I had to guess, I'd say the warriors of the black tribe battled the army regiment outside. Then their bodies were dragged in here afterward. And the fact that man over there died at the end of a bayonet tells me there was hand-to-hand combat. I think these men put up a fierce fight," he said with growing respect.

"I have to agree with Buzz," Dr. Lane said. "The bodies of the women and children are all back there." He pointed toward the rear of the cave. "That means they were most likely rounded up after the fighting was over. Then they were herded in here and butchered like cattle. The warriors' bodies were dragged in last and stacked up front."

"And then they dynamited the mouth of the cave shut," Harry Spate said, completing the reconstruction of events from two hundred years earlier.

Buzz glanced down at his watch. They had been inside for over an hour. It had been thirty minutes since Ally had run distraught from the cave. He didn't like being separated from the rest of his squad. It wasn't good military protocol.

"We should go topside and join the others," he said.

They emerged one by one from the narrow tunnel. It took them a few seconds to adjust to the harsh light of day. As their eyes adjusted, they realized they were not alone. There were a dozen well-armed men dressed in military fatigues surrounding the mouth of the cave.

Matt thought about darting back inside, but a mercenary he hadn't noticed jumped down from a boulder above him, blocking his path. He pushed Matt roughly with the butt of his automatic rifle. Matt stumbled forward and almost knocked over Harry Spate. He glared back at his assailant but remained silent.

In the distance they could see a second helicopter next to the one in which they had arrived. There were two more men standing over a kneeling Stu Patterson. Their pilot looked unharmed, but without the use of the helicopter they weren't going anywhere anytime soon. Matt turned to find Ron Patterson. He knew he must be worried sick about his son. Ron was standing beside Ally and he looked more than worried; he looked petrified. But it was not for the reason Matt expected. There was an automatic pistol stuck in his ribs.

And Ally was holding it.

"Ally, what the hell are you doing?" Matt shouted out.

A large, well-built man who had been talking into a wireless earpiece approached. He was clearly the man in charge. Before Matt knew what had happened, the man slammed his fist into his midsection. Matt doubled over in pain and fell to one knee.

As he struggled to take a full breath, another helicopter swooped in and landed—but this one wasn't unmarked. It was labeled *Spate Industries* in bold blue letters. After the propellers wound down and the whine of the jet engine subsided, two men emerged from the cabin. They walked slowly toward the awaiting assemblage at the mouth of the ancient cave.

40

Present Day

Ghost Ridge

Blackfeet Reservation, Montana

As the two men approached, Matt immediately noticed the resemblance.

Landon Spate was the first to speak. "Hello, little brother," he said to Harry with a sneer. The two older brothers were dressed in khakis and button-down oxford shirts. It was as if their country club lunch had just been interrupted.

Harry didn't respond.

Oliver took a long stride forward to get a closer look at his youngest brother. At well over six feet tall, the eldest Spate towered over Harry. The last time the two men had been together was at Spate Industries' corporate offices in Oklahoma City. And that meeting had taken place more than a decade earlier—right after the board of directors had authorized the buyout of Harry's shares in the company.

"You look older, Harry. A lot of stress in your life these days?" Oliver smiled condescendingly, his eyes purposely falling on the automatic weapons aimed in his brother's direction.

There was still no response from Harry. He only glared at his brothers, trying his best to hide his crushing disappointment at being discovered.

Oliver continued, "Imagine our surprise when Ally called us and revealed your little plan to unearth the family's long-buried secret." He noticed Matt turn at the mention of Ally's name. "Ah, Mr. Hawkins, you must be so disappointed in your *paramour*." He was clearly enjoying himself. Oliver's hand reached over and gently caressed Ally's arm. She gave him a coquettish smile in return.

Matt knew in an instant she was Oliver's lover. He felt sick to his stomach, but he wasn't about to let Oliver Spate get under his skin. "I've never been a very good judge of women," he said coolly.

"Ha ha, bravo, Matt..." He forced a laugh. "May I call you Matt? You didn't really think we'd let you expose...this," he said, turning toward the entrance to the cave. "Did you?"

Matt tried to remain calm. "Why did you even let us get this far?" Matt asked, wiping a bead of sweat from his brow. "You could have stopped us a long time ago."

"Oh, we were going to, believe me. But Ally convinced us otherwise." He winked at his undercover operative. She gave a mock curtsey in return.

Matt glared at Ally with undisguised animosity.

"She talked us into letting you continue your search, for two reasons. The first had to do with your famous reputation; she said you wouldn't give up until you found the bodies. And second, because she had a hunch your search would lead the mole in our organization to reveal himself—or in this case, *herself*," he gloated. His eyes shifted again to Harry.

Harry flinched at the thinly veiled reference to his daughter.

Oliver turned fully in his estranged brother's direction. "Yes, dear brother, we now know that our lovely niece Samantha has been spying on us on your behalf," he said, anger flashing in his eyes. "It's a pity she's not here now. But no matter, she will be dealt with soon enough."

"If you touch her, I swear I'll kill you," Harry shouted. It was the first time he had opened his mouth since his brothers had arrived. He lunged forward, but one of the commandos intercepted him easily, clamping him in a chokehold in seconds. The commando's beefy arm began to cut off Harry's oxygen supply.

Oliver shook his head contemptuously and waved his man back. He released Harry from his viselike grip but remained in close proximity.

"So let me get this straight," Matt said after the commotion had subsided, "you knew about the massacre but you didn't know where the bodies had been stowed?"

Oliver nodded.

"Our father proudly shared the story of the Negro Tribe with us, as his father had shared it with him. Of course, he never told Harry about it because he never trusted him—thought he was *soft* like his mother." Oliver looked disdainfully at Harry before adding, "He knew Landon and I would see Jedediah Spate as a visionary. And that we would understand he did what was necessary to secure his family's future—and the future of his descendants."

"He murdered an entire people, you monster," Harry shouted. "The Spate family fortune is nothing more than blood money." Spittle flew from his mouth and landed on Oliver's cheek.

"See what I mean, Harry" Oliver calmly pulled a handkerchief from his pocket and wiped away the spit. "You're too soft."

"Anyway, where was I?" he continued. "Oh yes. Alas, Jedediah never left behind instructions as to the exact location of the...burial site."

"Call it what it really is...a mass grave," Dr. Lane seethed.

Oliver continued as if Dr. Lane wasn't there. "Jedediah figured since no one knew about the tribe of escaped slaves, then nobody would come looking for them. And he was right. The only thing we knew, from family lore, was that the tribe had been disposed of in an old cave. But as you can see," he motioned with his arm at the vast landscape around them, "there are thousands of square miles out here. It would have been like trying to find the proverbial needle in the haystack."

Landon Spate took over from his brother, "Everything was forgotten for almost two hundred years," he began. "But then that damned Indian had to go and find the helmet. When my father read about Big Tom's discovery all those years ago, he immediately knew its significance. You see, Jedediah told his son about seeing the shrine and the conquistador helmet. And the story was passed down through the generations. That's why my father knew he had to go buy that helmet...to protect the family name."

"Then he bought the lease rights to the land surrounding Ghost Ridge where Big Tom found the helmet," Matt surmised.

"That's right. And for the past forty years the situation was completely under control, just as it had been for the preceding two centuries—until you came along and stirred the pot."

He approached Matt, "I must admit, we were worried when you first showed up asking all those questions. But like my brother said, Ally convinced us we could use your search to our own ends."

"So you decided to let us find the mass grave for you," Buzz spoke up.

"Right again," Landon confirmed.

"And now you intend to rebury it, only this time for good," Buzz jumped in.

"Ashes to ashes, dust to dust," Oliver interjected with a spiteful smile. He motioned to the lead commando. The commando in turn signaled to two of his men. They quickly ducked inside the entryway to the cave. They had large backpacks slung over their shoulders.

"Can you tell me what's inside those packs, Colonel?" Oliver quizzed Buzz.

Buzz answered flatly, "My guess would be an incendiary device of some kind, probably containing thermite or white phosphorus." Then he turned and explained to Matt, "It's a nasty little chemical cocktail that adheres to surfaces. Once ignited, it will burn through solid steel. Unfortunately, by the time it burns itself out, they'll be nothing left in there but charred earth."

"Indeed," Oliver crowed triumphantly, "the legendary black tribe will return to its official status *as a legend.*"

Disgusted and angry, Matt took a step toward Ally. "Why?" he asked.

She considered his question for a moment. Then she shrugged her shoulders and replied simply, "Because growing up poor sucks."

"So everything you told me was a lie?" Matt was still pissed off at himself for being so easily duped.

Given the current circumstances, Ally figured she had nothing to lose by telling Matt the truth, so she said, "Not everything. My parents really were killed in a car accident when I was a teenager. And I really did shoot my husband in the nuts with a shotgun," she smiled coyly. "In fact, it was after that incident the Spates approached me to work for them—to keep an eye on their interests on the reservation. They bailed me out of jail, paid for my lawyer, and got the charges reduced to self-defense. I've been working for them ever since."

Matt retraced the steps of their "chance" meeting in his mind. "The dead crow in my car outside the diner the day we first met. You arranged that, didn't you?"

"Oh, you should have seen your face," she said, chuckling. "I had read about you and I knew trying to scare you off would only make you dig in your heels. This, of course, is exactly what we wanted. And here we are," she said.

Her words cut right through him. As painful as it was, he

needed to know everything, so he asked, "One thing I can't figure out is the shooting out on Ghost Ridge." He was still trying to put together all the pieces of Ally's intricate charade. "How did you fake getting shot in the head?"

She reached into her pocket and pulled out a pocketknife. "Sliced my temple and pretended like I was knocked out. I knew with all the chaos and blood that you'd never guess the wound was self-inflicted."

"Just another way to cement our partnership, huh?" Matt scoffed.

"Well, I thought it had been cemented in the sleeping bag the night before." Ally batted her eyes exaggeratedly. "But I wasn't taking any chances. I needed you to trust me completely," she said, before adding with an arrogant smile, "and you did."

Matt had no reply. He felt embarrassed and used, but most of all, he felt like a fool.

She concluded, "In Great Falls yesterday when you told me about Samantha being the mole, I knew I'd earned your trust. Of course, I immediately left to call my bosses."

"And when Ally told me that my brother Harry was planning on sneaking onto the reservation with all of you to find the cave," Oliver jumped in, "well that was just too good to pass up. Landon and I immediately cleared our schedules so we could be here to... welcome you."

"That's why you ran out of the cave earlier," Buzz realized. "It wasn't because you were shocked or upset at finding the remains of hundreds of innocent people. It was to tell your bosses we'd found what they were looking for and the coast was clear for their arrival."

Ally shrugged again. There was nothing left to say.

"If you think we're *not* going to tell the world about this, you're severely mistaken," Harry said defiantly.

Buzz and Matt exchanged knowing glances. They both understood there was no chance of that happening.

Landon Spate's eyes narrowed. "No, brother, you were never one to keep your goddamned mouth shut, were you. That's why we're going to take care of that for you."

"The same way you silenced Big Tom?" Matt seethed.

"Yeah, as a matter of fact," Landon remarkably admitted. "Once again we have Ally to thank. She found a clever way to rid us of that problem; a carefully placed sedative to dull the big Indian's senses. Then a shove at just the right moment into the grill of an oncoming eighteen wheeler—isn't that about right, Ally?"

Ally didn't look happy to have her role in the murder of Big Tom revealed in front of so many people. Her eyes flashed with anger for a moment, but then she turned to Matt and said, "If it makes you feel any better, he was so out of it he probably never felt a thing."

Harry's face turned ashen. "You think you can kill us and get away with it?"

Dr. Lane felt suddenly faint. He sat down on a nearby rock. The thought of his two children growing up without a father was more than he could bear.

"People know we're out here," Ron Patterson offered weakly.

"I doubt that," Landon countered. "But even if they do, it won't matter. The helicopter accident will be investigated and determined to be just that—a tragic accident that needlessly snuffed out the lives of six sightseeing tourists."

"Just like the boating accident that killed the senator from Michigan?" Matt said. "Tell me, Landon, how does it feel to have all that blood on your hands?"

"My brother and I sleep very well at night, Mr. Hawkins. This is a war. And the senator you referred to was eliminated because he chose to fight for the wrong side."

"War?" Matt replied in disbelief. "You're murdering innocent civilians."

"We prefer to view them as enemy combatants," he said with a sneer.

"But you had them killed just the same."

"They were occupying territory that we wanted," Landon said, his voice rising. "So yes, Mr. Hawkins, we had them eliminated. In war there are casualties."

"You can use all the military analogies you want. But at the end of the day, you're nothing more than a couple of mafia Dons putting contracts out on people who make it onto your Enemies of the Spate list," Matt chided.

Landon shared an alarmed glance with his brother Oliver.

"That's right, we know about the list, you sick bastards," Matt seethed. "And we know Senator Waterford from Connecticut was the next name on it. He had a wife and two little kids, for God's sake."

"You're damned right we killed that son of a bitch," Landon roared. "And we'll add more names to the list if that's what it takes." He took a step forward and slapped Matt hard across the face.

Matt stood his ground defiantly, but he didn't dare make a move to retaliate. As much as he wanted to, he knew he'd be stopped by the mercenaries before he had the chance. Instead, he smiled through gritted teeth and said, "Is that all you've got?"

Landon looked ready to explode.

"That's enough," Oliver said firmly, placing a steadying hand on his brother's shoulder.

As usual, the older brother exhibited a calm, almost clinical coolness. "No, that's not all we've got, Mr. Hawkins." He glared at Matt. Then he turned and addressed his man in charge, "Has the chopper been properly rigged?"

"Yes, sir, the charge is set to go off when the aircraft reaches three thousand feet. It will ignite the fuel line and then...catastrophic failure."

Buzz said, "What makes you think I'm getting on that heli-copter willingly? You'll have to shoot me first. And when they do an autopsy on my body they'll discover I have a bullet in my head. That'll shoot your tourist accident story straight to hell."

Oliver replied evenly, "You have five grandchildren, I believe, isn't that right, Colonel? You want them to live nice long lives, don't you?" The conspicuous threat hit home. Buzz's stare turned icy.

"And you," Oliver turned to Ron Patterson, "have a lovely wife of more than forty years." Patterson looked down in defeat. The warnings were enough to silence any further thoughts of insurrection. Oliver smiled victoriously.

"You'll all get on that helicopter and you'll die like men," Landon jumped back in. He was speaking to the group but his eyes never left Matt's.

"Let's go," Oliver ordered, before his brother lost his cool again.

The military detachment began marching the five men toward the booby-trapped helicopter.

41

Present Day

Ghost Ridge

Blackfeet Reservation, Montana

Buzz kept waiting for Matt to look his way. Matt was marching five paces in front of him and hadn't turned around. They needed to try something, because there was no goddamn way he was going to board that chopper under his own power. He wanted to make his move, but he'd need Matt's help if they were going to stand half a chance of succeeding. To have any hope at all, they'd have to wrestle a weapon away from one of the mercenaries. But they were running out of time.

The valley floor was a flat, dusty expanse sandwiched between two ridgelines spaced no more than a quarter mile apart. They had covered enough distance that the ancient cave was about two football fields behind them now. The helicopter sat just ahead. Still Matt hadn't turned around. Buzz finally decided he couldn't wait any longer. He pretended to stumble over a stone and fell clumsily to the ground. Matt swung around to see what had happened.

The two men locked eyes. Finally, Buzz had his opportunity to convey his unspoken signal to spring into action. But to his surprise, Matt shook his head firmly from side to side. Buzz shot him a questioning look. But he had learned to trust his younger friend, so he grudgingly got to his feet and brushed himself off. They continued along their death march.

Nobody spoke. The only sounds were of scuffling boots against dirt and rock. Matt could see Stu Patterson up ahead. He was bleeding from a cut on his cheek. Evidently, the former army chopper pilot hadn't surrendered without a fight.

Suddenly, a shrill cry broke the relative silence. Everyone turned in unison.

The commandos raised their guns to their chests instinctively. The noise came once again, but this time it sounded more like a grief-stricken wail or howl. They still they couldn't spot its source. Finally, the lead commando grunted, "Up there." He pointed to an outcropping above the ancient cave.

A single horse had just crested the ridgeline. Its rider wore an impressive Indian headdress with bright white feathers sticking straight up from the crown of his head before cascading down across his shoulders. Brightly colored felt side drops ran vertically down either side of his face to the top of his chest. He whooped again and shook a spear horizontally above his head. The handle of the spear was decorated with colorful paints and embellished with feathers and fur.

Matt wondered if everyone was thinking the same absurd thought—was the spirit of the black tribe returning to exact its revenge? *Maybe Crooked Nose isn't so crazy after all.* Then the horse pivoted and he caught a glimpse of the Indian in profile—and one very recognizable and very pronounced beak. That's when Matt realized Crooked Nose really was nuts, because he was the rider of that horse.

"OK, shows over," Landon Spate scoffed. "Let's get this over with. I've got an engagement this evening."

Before anyone had a chance to move, more riders summited the ridge alongside Crooked Nose. But these men were riding horses of an iron variety—trail bikes, dirt bikes, and even some ATVs. They were a ragtag group of men from the res, dressed in jeans, T-shirts, and baseball caps. But they were still a beautiful sight to behold. Harry shouted out with joy. Ron Patterson gave Dr. Lane an enthusiastic slap on the back. There was hope after all.

Matt watched in amazement. They didn't exactly look like fierce warriors. *Hell, they don't even look like weekend warriors.* All told, there were probably forty men up on the ridge. Matt glanced around him at the dozen or so military mercenaries loaded down with automatic weaponry. Then he looked back at the ridge. The war party's weaponry consisted of old hunting rifles, some crossbows, and a few handguns. He had a sinking feeling. This battle was going to be over before it even started.

Is this the best you could do, Samantha? Where the hell is the FBI?

42

Two Days Earlier
Savannah, GA

Matt had been waiting for Dr. Lane to arrive in Savannah. Buzz was going to be landing at a private airfield south of town in less than two hours. Harry Spate would be with him. The plan was for the four men to fly to Great Falls on Buzz's private plane. Once there, they would review the thermal maps once again with Ron Patterson—in hopes of narrowing their search around Ghost Ridge.

Matt's phone began to ring. He thought it would be Dr. Lane checking in on his drive down to Savannah from Columbia, South Carolina. But when he answered he was surprised to hear the voice of Big Tom's nephew, Bobby, the Chief Mountain Hot Shot fire-fighter.

"Sorry to bother you, Matt, but you told me to call anytime, so..." Bobby said.

"No problem, Bobby," Matt said, recovering quickly from his initial surprise at the unexpected call. "What's up?"

"Well...it's about the helmet," he said.

That got Matt's attention. "What about it?"

"I've been talking to my aunt," he said, "trying to see if she remembered anything about the day Uncle Tommy found it. At first she was too upset to remember anything. But she came to me out of the blue this morning and said she did recall Tommy saying something."

"Really?"

"It's not much, but I figured you'd want to know." He paused, and then said, "She said he thought the helmet must have been carried to where he found it by the spring runoff, from somewhere upstream."

Matt could hear the hope and the pain in Bobby's voice. The thought occurred to him that perhaps the reason Bobby was sharing this piece of information was for his own closure. To somehow help Matt finish what his uncle had started.

"That's very helpful, Bobby," Matt replied gently, even though he knew "upstream" covered thousands of acres of land and wouldn't help narrow the search dramatically. "I really appreciate it."

"Yeah, sure," Bobby said.

Matt brushed a sandy-blond lock of hair back from his eyes and looked down at his watch. He really didn't have time for a long chat. But he also didn't have the heart to cut the call short. So he asked, "How's your aunt doing, Bobby? The last time I saw her she was pretty upset."

"She's a little better each day," he answered. "You know," he added apologetically, "she didn't really mean those things she said to you that morning."

"I think she probably did, and maybe I deserved them. But thanks for saying so anyway, Bobby. Besides, I know it had already been a long day for your aunt by the time we showed up," he said. "Ally told me she'd been with her since very early that morning."

"Ally? Who's Ally?" he asked.

"Excuse me?"

"Nobody was at my aunt's house that morning except me."

"Wait a minute. You didn't call Ally to come and help you console your aunt?" Now it was Matt's turn to be puzzled.

"No, Matt, I didn't call anybody named Ally," he said. "I don't even know anybody named Ally."

"Bobby, you must be mistaken. Ally is Crooked Nose's granddaughter. She said she's been a friend of your aunt's for years," Matt explained, panic rising in his voice.

"That's impossible. Old Charlie doesn't have any grandkids. He and his wife weren't able to have any kids of their own," Bobby insisted. "Someone's lying to you."

Matt was stunned into silence.

"Matt, are you still there?"

"Uh, yeah, I'm still here," Matt sputtered. "Thanks for the call, Bobby. You've been more helpful than you'll ever know."

"OK," he said somewhat dumbfounded. Then he added, "Hey, will you call me if you find out anything more about the helmet? I know it sounds stupid, but I'd kind of like to know, for Uncle Tommy's sake."

"Sure, Bobby, and thanks again."

After ending the call, Matt's mind was spinning. As shocking as it was, there was only one possible explanation for Ally's lies.

She was working for the Spates.

Matt was in full panic mode now. He forced himself to take a few deep breaths to calm down. How much had he told Ally? He had already called her and asked her to meet him the next day in Great Falls. She was going to join them on their search for the mass grave out on Ghost Ridge. That meant Oliver and Landon Spate knew of their plans to find evidence of their family's role in the massacre.

He began to pace back and forth across his living room. This was disastrous. He picked up his metal baseball bat and began smacking it against his palm loudly as he thought through his options. *Think, Matt.* He kept pacing. The noise from the street traffic below gradually faded from his consciousness as he forced himself to focus. Then he stopped abruptly in the middle of the room.

He realized he did have one big advantage: They didn't know that he knew about Ally. He let this thought bounce around inside his brain for a few minutes until a plan began to slowly take shape. It was time to turn Ally's deceit against her.

The first call he made was to David Becker. He shared with him the shocking news about Ally and asked if he had any connections in the FBI. As usual, Becker offered his help without a second thought. After hanging up with the *New York Times* investigative reporter, he dialed Samantha's number. He briefed her on Ally's double-cross and outlined his idea for how to use this knowledge to their advantage. They spent the better part of an hour hashing out the details. Matt gave her Becker's number and told her he was expecting her call. After speaking with Becker, Samantha caught the next flight out of Oklahoma City.

She would be in Browning on the Blackfeet Reservation before nightfall—ready to play her part in turning the tables on Ally and the Spates.

43

Present Day

Ghost Ridge

Blackfeet Reservation, Montana

Oliver Spate's authoritative voice snapped everyone back to reality. "If they try to interfere," he said, pointing to the Indians assembled up on the ridge, "kill them." He was speaking to the lead commando. "Make it look like a drug deal gone bad."

He and Landon then took one last look at their sibling. "Poor Harry, always choosing the wrong team," Landon said patronizingly.

Oliver started to say something but then simply turned and walked away. The jet engines on the corporate helicopter had already begun to wind up. The two mercenary soldiers inside the cave should have been close to destroying the evidence by now. It was time for the Spates to make their exit. As usual, they would leave the messy work to someone else.

The head commando began barking out instructions to his troops. He ordered the bulk of his soldiers to use their superior firepower to push the Indian war party down the other side of the ridge. He and two other men would escort Matt and his five companions to their helicopter. They would stay with them until it was airborne. Then the entire unit would regroup and board the last helicopter.

They would follow Stu Patterson's aircraft at a safe distance until it detonated. Only then would their mission be accomplished.

Before Ally walked away to join Oliver and Landon Spate on their corporate helicopter, she nonchalantly turned and blew a smug kiss toward Matt. He gave her the middle finger in return. He knew it was childish, but it made him feel better just the same.

A minute later, they all watched as the helicopter bearing the Spate Industries insignia took off. Just as it disappeared over the western foothills that led into Glacier Park, the first shots were fired on the ridge behind them. Evidently, the Blackfeet Nation had decided to make a stand. They had dismounted from their vehicles and were using them as shields against the soldiers. They were using the higher ground to their advantage.

Matt looked at Buzz with an expression that said, *now it's our turn.*

Buzz nodded in acknowledgment. If they were going to die today, it wasn't going to be in a booby-trapped helicopter three thousand feet in the air.

A second later, Buzz lashed out with his foot, catching the left knee of the soldier closest to him. There was a loud pop and the man crumpled to the ground grabbing at his leg in pain. Buzz was on top of him in seconds. Matt took advantage of the distraction and threw a vicious right elbow into the jaw of the guard closest to him. The man fell to one knee, but didn't go all the way down.

Seeing his friends spring into action emboldened Dr. Lane. He jumped onto the back of the burly lead commando. That was all the opening Matt needed. The steel toe of his work boot caught the kneeling combatant square in the ribs. The automatic pistol flew from the soldier's hands and clattered along the loose gravel on the hot valley floor.

Buzz seemed to have his man subdued. And for a moment, Matt thought they might just have the advantage. But when he

turned around to check on Dr. Lane, he found himself staring down
the barrel of an M16 semi burst rifle. The lead commando apparently had no trouble dispensing with the professor, who was lying
prone on the ground, bleeding from a blow to the head.

They had put up a valiant effort, but it had failed.

Just then, two helicopter gunships came roaring over the top
of Ghost Ridge. One swooped in and immediately engaged the
soldiers who were exchanging fire with the Blackfeet. The second
gunship banked low and came to a midair stop, hovering no more
than two hundred feet from where Matt and Buzz were being held
at gunpoint. The letters *FBI* were clearly visible on the side of the
chopper. A commanding voice came over the microphone. "Drop
your weapon, now."

The commando's face registered indecision for the first time
that morning. As if reading his mind, Buzz said, "It's over, soldier.
Put the gun down and live to fight another day."

The muscles in the mercenary's face began to twitch. He was
clearly torn by what to do.

"You were a marine once, right?" Buzz asked, attempting to
establish some sort of rapport.

"Oorah," was the former marine's cynical reply.

"I'm sure they'll take that into consideration...when the time
comes," Buzz said, trying to sound hopeful.

"No, Colonel, they won't," he said.

Matt was sure they were about to be killed, but Buzz could see
in the former marine's eyes he had no intention of shooting them.
But he wasn't about to face a lifetime in prison either.

"Don't do it soldier," Buzz urged. But it was too late. He jerked
his rifle to his shoulder as if to shoot the two men standing in front

of him. Two quick bursts came from the open door of the helicopter. The commando was dead before he hit the ground.

After landing, agents wearing signature blue FBI windbreakers over their bulletproof vests swarmed out of the chopper. They came running toward Matt and his drained, bruised, and battered companions. Everyone seemed to be fine, but Matt was worried about Ron Patterson. During the skirmish, he had seen him clutching at his chest when he tried to come to the aid of Dr. Lane.

Matt brushed aside the FBI agents, assuring them he was OK. He quickly made his way to the usually affable Lewis and Clark expert who was being attended to by his son, Stu.

"Is it your pacemaker?" Matt asked. Patterson was having trouble breathing but he had enough strength to nod. "We need some help over here," Matt shouted to be heard over the rhythmic beating of the helicopter's propellers.

An agent with a medic kit raced over to help. Matt left Patterson's side. He moved to his left and kneeled down to check on Dr. Lane. It looked like the professor might have suffered a concussion but he seemed to be coming around. Matt could hear the firefight raging behind him on Ghost Ridge. He glanced over his shoulder. The FBI agents in the first helicopter had landed and had forced the mercenaries to flank left and take cover in a small stand of scrub pines. Matt's eyes scanned back to his right. That's when he noticed the opening to the cave.

"Oh shit," he said. He scrambled to his feet.

He had forgotten about the two soldiers with the backpacks full of explosives. They were still inside. He spotted an automatic pistol on the ground to his left. It was the one he had kicked out of the hands of one of the soldiers. He picked it up and turned to Buzz.

"There are still two commandos inside the cave," he said. "We can't let them destroy that evidence."

"What about the FBI?" Buzz shouted. "Shouldn't we let them handle..."

"No time," Matt said, and he was gone.

"Son of a bitch," Buzz grunted in resignation, "I'm getting too old for this shit." He grabbed the M16 rifle off the lead commando's lifeless body. The two men sprinted to the right, angling well away from the gunfight raging to their left. They made it to the mouth of the tunnel two minutes later.

Matt scrounged two flashlights from the gear they had been forced to leave behind after their capture. He was about to enter the tunnel when Buzz grabbed his arm.

"Wait," Buzz said, panting heavily from their sprint across the valley, "leave the flashlights off...it's too dangerous. We'll have to feel our way through the tunnel—from memory."

Matt nodded. He squeezed through the opening in the rocks and crawled on his hands and knees down the long, dark passageway. Buzz was right on his heels.

The two men slowly groped their way along, hugging the sidewall until they were standing in the antechamber where they had first assembled. That seemed like a lifetime ago. It was amazing how insulated the cave was. They could barely hear the gun battle raging outside. That meant the two men down in the lower chamber of the cave had no idea of the events taking place in the daylight above them.

Buzz switched on his flashlight carefully, covering the lens with his hand. Only an amber glow escaped through his fingers—but it was enough to allow them to gain their bearings. They still saw no sign of the two commandos. Buzz took the lead using his shielded flashlight to guide their way.

"Hang on a minute," Matt said suddenly.

Buzz pivoted around. "What's up?"

When he turned, his eyes went wide with surprise. The muzzle of Matt's automatic pistol was leveled at the middle of his forehead.

Buzz was a man who had flown scores of combat missions during his tours in Vietnam and the first Gulf War, so he quickly regained his composure. He spoke calmly and said, "You want to tell me why you're pointing your weapon at me?"

The two men were no more than three feet apart in the cramped confines of the cave. "You want to tell me who you're really working for?" Matt replied bitterly.

"I know this has been a hell of a day for you, but . . ."

"Don't," Matt cut him off mid-sentence. "I was in the kitchen at Hank Gordon's house. I overheard your conversation in the garden."

Buzz's confident facade slipped, if only for a second. He said, "Look, I don't know exactly what you heard but it's not what you think."

"No shit," Matt said incredulously. "Apparently there are a lot of things that aren't what I thought. And a lot of people who aren't who they said they were. Now cut the bullshit, Buzz. Tell me the name of the organization who recruited me without my knowledge—the same organization you evidently dedicated your life to."

Buzz looked long and hard at Matt. Finally he held up his hands in resignation and said, "OK. I planned on having this conversation someday soon anyway." He looked around and shrugged. "I guess this is as good a place as any. I took an oath a very long time ago to serve the Society of the Cincinnati."

"Come on, Buzz, I'm not screwing around."

"Not the society that you, or the general public, or most of the membership, is familiar with," he continued. "There's another faction hidden deep within the society and we operate in total secrecy."

The tunnel suddenly went completely dark.

Matt's wrist was bent back at an odd angle causing the gun to fall harmlessly from his hands. His legs were kicked out from under him and he was flat on his back on the hard surface of the subterranean floor seconds later. That's when he realized his mistake. Buzz had been holding the only source of light. It was a point of leverage he had used to his advantage.

When Buzz turned the flashlight back on, Matt saw the roles had been reversed. Now it was Buzz's weapon pointed directly at him.

"I'm sorry I had to do that," Buzz said. "Believe me, that's not how I wanted this to happen."

"You son of a bitch," Matt seethed.

"I know how you must feel about me, especially after what you overheard that day. But I hope you'll change your mind when I have the chance to explain myself," Buzz replied, still breathing heavily from his sudden exertion of energy.

"Don't count on it," Matt grunted. He massaged his wrist, testing to make sure it wasn't broken.

"I promise we'll have this conversation, Matt, but right now we've got bigger fish to fry."

"Sorry if I'm not going to put my faith in any promises from you."

"I know I'm the last guy on Earth you should trust right now. But you have to believe me when I tell you we're the good guys. The bad guys," he jerked his head over his shoulder, "are down there. And if we don't act fast, they're going to blow up the evidence we need to nail Landon and Oliver Spate once and for all."

Matt got to his feet. He knew Buzz was right about one thing, they had to stop the two mercenaries from blowing up the cave. "It's funny. I've been obsessed with finding out who you really are and who you really work for, but you know what? It just occurred to me, as I was lying there on my ass in the dirt, that I don't really care anymore. The Buzz I thought I knew is already dead to me."

Matt could tell the comment had stung his onetime surrogate father. But he didn't care. "After we finish this I don't ever want to see or hear from you again, understood?"

Buzz needed Matt's help at the moment, so he nodded reluctantly.

"Now hand me my gun," Matt demanded, "and let's do this."

They quickly found the hidden hallway that led to the lower level and began their descent. Within minutes, they heard the sound of muffled voices. They slowed their pace.

Buzz was puzzled. They should have seen lights by now. *How were they setting their incendiary devices in the pitch dark?* Then it hit him. They must be wearing night-vision goggles equipped with infrared illuminators—it's the only way they could see this deep in the cave without a natural light source.

Buzz pulled Matt close and whispered in his ear. He had a new plan of attack in mind. They'd have to improvise, because they couldn't shoot at what they couldn't see. They stayed pressed tightly against the cool wall of the natural corridor. Quietly they advanced, until they could go no further without increasing the risk of being discovered. They stopped just around the corner from the cavernous room that held the mass grave—and their enemy.

Just as Buzz had instructed, Matt picked up a loose stone and tossed it into the darkness. It clattered against the tunnel wall. The voices inside came to an abrupt halt. Matt waited until he heard the two men approach cautiously. They were just around the bend in the corridor. Then they stopped and it was completely silent.

Finally, he heard a voice not more than ten paces away. "You heard that, right?" the first one said.

"Let's finish this and get out of here. This place is freaking me out," the second one replied.

Matt made his move.

Staying crouched low, he swung around the corner and into

the open hallway. The soldiers could see him clearly through their night-vision goggles—but only for a moment. Before they had time to react, Matt switched both flashlights on and shined them in the direction of where he guessed the men were standing. Buzz had assured him that because of the way night-vision goggles amplified light, the two mercenaries would be blinded by the sudden illumination.

Sure enough, the two men yelled out in pain, reflexively lowering their weapons to shield their eyes. The bright light felt like a thousand needles entering their corneas. One of the men, however, had instinctively squeezed the trigger on his semiautomatic rifle. Bullets were sent thumping into the earthen ground and ricocheting off the stone sidewalls at 1,700 miles per hour. The sound was deafening in the confined subterranean space.

Buzz timed his move perfectly. The beams from Matt's flashlights gave him just enough illumination to line up his targets. Without hesitating, he fired off a series of bursts from his M16 as he moved left to right. The two mercenaries hit the floor of the cave with simultaneous thuds. They had both been hit.

Matt tossed Buzz one of the flashlights and he shined it in the direction of the fallen commandos. Buzz approached them slowly and carefully. One looked to be dead, shot through the throat. The other was breathing in short raspy breaths. Buzz felt awful about taking the life of another man, but in this situation, he had no choice.

He turned back toward Matt. But all he saw was a flash flying through the air.

Matt had launched himself from his squatting position and pounced on the chest of the injured combatant. He grabbed hold of the man's arm and pinned it beneath his knee. Two quick punches later and the man had been rendered unconscious.

Buzz looked both startled and confused.

"When you turned toward me, he reached for something in this pocket," Matt said between heavy breaths. He reached into the left breast pocket of the soldier's uniform. He pulled out a small electronic device and held it up to the light. It was a detonating trigger. Buzz said grimly, "That son of a bitch was about to blow this place to kingdom come—and all of us along with it." The two men's eyes met. They shared the unspoken realization they had come close to losing everything.

But now they had their proof.

The gruesome photos of the massacred tribe would no doubt hit the front pages of newspapers and be splashed across television news shows across the country. It would deal a severe blow to Oliver and Landon Spates' carefully guarded public image. Especially when it was revealed they had been covering up the atrocity for decades.

They now had exactly what Harry Spate needed—the means to bring a lot of unwanted attention to Oliver and Landon Spate. Matt's only hope now, as he and Buzz began to make their way out of the cave, was that Harry and Samantha had compiled enough evidence to warrant the government's opening up a full investigation on Spate Industries' seditious antigovernment activities.

44

Present Day

Ghost Ridge

Blackfeet Reservation, Montana

The firefight outside was over. Three mercenaries were dead and two more lay on the ground wounded. The rest were cuffed and being led to one of the helicopters. It took a minute or two for Matt's eyes to adjust to the bright sunlight after emerging from the cave. Buzz set out in search of the FBI person in charge. He needed to let him know there were two additional bad guys inside—one dead and the other incapacitated. He would also alert him to the incendiary device that would need to be carefully disassembled.

The valley floor was crawling with people. More agents from the FBI had arrived to help secure the area. They were joined by agents from the Bureau of Indian Affairs. Most of the Blackfeet had made their way down from the ridge on their trail bikes and ATVs. Through the swirling dust storm kicked up by the helicopters, dirt bikes, and swarms of people, Matt spotted Big Tom's nephew, Bobby, headed in his direction. The two men embraced.

"I don't know what we would have done if you guys hadn't shown up," Matt said gratefully.

"I'm not sure we would have been able to hold those guys off much longer with our hunting rifles and crossbows," Bobby admitted. "It's a good thing the FBI came when they did."

"How did you know we were out here anyway?" Matt asked, confused.

"Your friend Samantha called me in a panic. She said the FBI was running late. She was worried you'd need help before they could get here. I guess she was right," he said with a smile.

"The FBI was running late?" Matt said flabbergasted.

"You can't make this stuff up, right?" Bobby smiled. Then he explained, "Apparently there was a pissing match between the FBI and the BIA over who should have jurisdiction over the operation."

Matt shook his head in disbelief.

"Anyway," Bobby continued, "once Samantha told me these were the people that killed Big Tom it didn't take me long to round up some guys." He pointed over his shoulder at his Blackfeet brethren behind him. "My uncle had a lot of friends on the res."

"I bet he did," Matt said.

Bobby nodded toward the cave entrance. "Is that where the helmet came from?"

"It is, along with the skeletal remains of hundreds of innocent people," Matt said grimly.

"You mean the legend of the Dark Tribe is real?" Bobby said, amazed.

"Turns out it wasn't a legend after all," Matt replied. "Hey, where is that crazy son of a bitch Crooked Nose anyway?"

Bobby pointed up to the ridge above them.

Old Charlie had dismounted from his horse. He was performing some sort of ritual dance. He was too far away for Matt to hear him, but he looked to be chanting.

"What's he doing up there?"

"Honoring the dead, I guess old Crooked Nose wasn't as nuts as everyone thought."

"No, I guess not. Hey, thanks again, Bobby," Matt said. He

reached out and shook Bobby's hand.

"Take care, Matt," Bobby responded. "Don't be a stranger, OK?"

Matt nodded appreciatively. As he turned around, he thought he spotted a shock of blond hair amid the sea of blue FBI jackets. He put a hand up to shade his eyes from the sun. And that's when he saw her. She was standing next to her father.

By the way Harry was gesticulating, Matt guessed he was filling the agents in on the harrowing events from that morning. Samantha's blond hair was tousled by the wind, and the stress of the day had put an edge to her normally soft features. But even amid the chaos, she still looked beautiful.

Matt waited for her to turn his way. As if reading his mind, she brushed the hair from her face and looked over. Matt smiled. Samantha excused herself and hurried over to where he was standing. She came to a stop directly in front of him. Her eyes were moist as she reached out and caressed his cheek. He pulled her toward him and they shared a passionate kiss, oblivious to the maelstrom around them.

He released her. "A hell of a rescue party you organized," he said.

"Desperate times call for desperate measures, right?" she said with a smile.

He chuckled. "Bobby told me what happened. You should've seen the looks on those commandos' faces when old Crooked Nose came over the top of that ridge. It was priceless."

She laughed, leaned in, and kissed him again.

"You know," Matt said, raising his eyebrows in exaggerated flirtatiousness, "there's a private, dark cave behind me...if you're interested."

"Stop." She smacked his chest playfully. "Besides, it's not that private from what I've heard." She turned serious and asked, "Is it

really true? They slaughtered the children, too?" Her expression
was horrified.

Matt answered somberly, "It's true. No one was spared. Jedediah Spate was not going to leave one living soul behind to tell what
happened."

"Bastards," she said in disgust.

"I can't argue with that," he said, "but their deaths won't be in
vain—at least not anymore. By the time Dr. Lane and the team of
forensic experts he's arranged for are done documenting everything,
the whole world is going to know exactly what happened here."

A silver-haired FBI man approached quickly. Matt and Samantha were still locked in an embrace. He cleared his throat. "Ah,
sorry to interrupt, but you must be Matt Hawkins. I'm Agent
Hanrahan," the man announced, extending his hand in an awkward
greeting, "from the Salt Lake City office."

Matt disengaged from Samantha. "You guys cut it pretty close,"
he said, shaking the agent's hand.

"Yeah, there was a little bit of a snafu. But, uh...anyway," he said
clumsily, quickly changing the subject, "were you able to get it all?"

Matt slowly unbuttoned his shirt to reveal a miniature recording device strapped to his chest. "I got every word Oliver and
Landon Spate spoke. There should be enough on here to implicate
them in multiple murders, along with a host of other crimes." He
handed the device over to the FBI man.

"So how did you know the Spate brothers would show up
today?" Agent Hanrahan asked, pocketing the recording device
Matt handed him.

"To be honest, we didn't," Matt admitted. "Once we found out
Ally was working for them, we decided to set our own trap. We
knew she would tell Oliver and Landon that their brother, Harry,
would be here today. We were hoping that would be enough incen-
tive for them to make an appearance. Lucky for us, we were right—

they just couldn't resist the opportunity to be here in person to stick it to their brother one last time."

"I've got to give you credit, Mr. Hawkins, you've got balls," Hanrahan said.

"Sometimes more balls than brains, I've been told," Matt replied truthfully.

"Well, thanks for all your help." The agent nodded stiffly in appreciation. "We'll be in touch soon. And Ms. Spate, we're ready to leave whenever you are." He walked away leaving Matt and Samantha alone to say their good-byes.

She explained, "The FBI wants me and my father to accompany them to Oklahoma City. Evidently the authorities were waiting there for my uncles when they landed. They've got them in custody and have already raided their corporate headquarters. They need our help navigating through the mountains of files." She looked deflated to be separating from Matt yet again.

"Go on, Samantha, do what you need to do," Matt said. "You've been waiting a long time for this day to come."

She turned to leave, then paused and turned back around. "Matt, I...I want this to work," she said. "Between you and me, I mean. I just don't want all of this," she motioned at the tumultuous scene around them, "to get in the way of *us*." She felt suddenly embarrassed and looked down at the ground.

Matt put his thumb and index finger under her chin. He tilted her head up and looked into her eyes. "I want this to work, too. Besides," he said, "all of this is what brought us together."

They embraced one final time and then she was gone.

45

Present Day
New York, NY

Shredders were operating in overdrive throughout the Spate-funded coalition of think tanks, lobbying firms, and political action groups. Ever since the Feds raided the company's corporate offices in Oklahoma City, word had gone out quickly through the organization to destroy any and all sensitive files.

The FBI had scooped up Oliver and Landon the minute they landed back in Oklahoma City. In an unprecedented move, within hours after the events on Ghost Ridge, they had seized control of Spate Industries—freezing all of its assets. Without funding, the extensive and elaborate network of covert operating companies and affiliated political organizations ground to an immediate halt. On the direct orders of the president of the United States, a federal grand jury was scheduled to be convened immediately. Formal charges would soon be brought against Oliver Spate, Landon Spate, and the rest of the members of the Billionaires' Caucus by the attorney general of the United States himself.

Matt had flown to New York to meet with David Becker and brief him on the events of the past week. Becker was to be given an exclusive on the story. The *New York Times* had already agreed to run a five-part investigative series that would detail the Spate brothers' Machiavellian plan to usurp the authority of the U.S. government. The American public would be shocked at just how much they had been fooled by the Spates' carefully orchestrated campaign to promote their free market agenda—which was really just a cover for their radical plan to tear America's democracy out at the root.

It had been a long day of meetings, and Matt was exhausted. He decided to have a beer at the hotel bar in midtown Manhattan where he had been staying for the past two nights. He couldn't wait until all this madness was over and he could return to his home in Savannah. It was late in the afternoon and the bar was fairly empty, which suited Matt just fine. He had been talking most of the day, sharing his story with Becker and his associates at the *Times*.

He sat by himself at a small round table toward the rear of the dimly lit establishment. He glanced up at the television. CNN was continuing its all-day coverage of Spate Gate, as it had been dubbed. Matt rubbed his face with his hands, trying to release the tension that had built up during the day. When he removed them from his eyes, he was startled to see a very large and very bald man standing directly in front of him. The man was obscuring his view of the television, and most of the rest of the bar, for that matter.

Noticing Matt's surprise, he said in a deep but congenial voice, "Do you mind if I join you?"

It took Matt a moment to react. He recognized the man's face, but couldn't put a name to it. Then it hit him. The person asking to join him was the most powerful lawman in the country—Stan Krueger, the no-nonsense director of the FBI.

"Of course, Mr. Director," Matt finally stammered, getting up out of his chair.

"Please, call me Stan," he said. "I hear that Mr. Director bullshit so much that sometimes I forget my own name." He offered a tired smile.

Matt took an immediate liking to him. "You want a beer?" he asked.

"That sounds great."

Matt pointed to his empty mug of beer and held up two fingers. The waitress brought another round over a minute later.

"You've been a busy guy these past few weeks," the director said, more as a statement of fact than a question.

"Yes, sir, busier than I wanted to be," Matt said, exhaling slowly.

"I bet," the director said. He picked up his pint glass and downed half of it in one swig.

"Long day for you too, eh?" Matt said with a smile, nodding toward the half-empty glass.

"Long days are part of the job description, unfortunately," he grumbled.

The director of the agency that served as both a federal criminal investigative organization and an internal intelligence agency looked exhausted. His suit was rumpled, he had dark circles under his eyes, and it looked as though he hadn't shaved in three days. Matt thought it had probably been that long since the poor guy had slept. He was sure Director Krueger had been through his share of high-level meetings and had taken a grilling about how something as big as Spate Gate had happened on his watch.

Krueger took another swig of beer. He seemed to appreciate the anonymity provided by the darkened bar. It was probably his first moment of peace all day. Matt hated to ruin the moment, but his curiosity was piqued. Finally, he spoke up, "So what did you have on your mind, sir? I mean, I'm all for a cold beer...but I'm sure you've got more important places to be." He paused before adding, "Is there something I can do for you?"

"Hell, son, you've already done more for your country than you'll ever know," Krueger's gravelly voice rumbled like thunder fading into the distance. "I just wanted to come and personally thank you for handing us Oliver and Landon Spate on a silver platter." He crumpled up a cocktail napkin in his hands and tossed it back down onto the table. "You probably won't believe me when I tell you this, because it's going to sound like I'm trying to cover my ass. But the Spate boys and their merry band of billionaire friends have been on our radar for some time now. We just couldn't ever piece the whole thing together." He smiled wanly and said, "Evidently, we needed an antiques store owner to do that for us."

"All I did was investigate an old conquistador helmet," Matt said. "You should really be thanking Samantha Spate. She's the one who spent the last five years of her life spying on her uncles. Without her, you wouldn't have a case."

"I know, that's why I flew out to Oklahoma City yesterday and thanked her in person," the director smiled slyly. "She's the one who told me where I might find you."

"In Manhattan or at the hotel bar?" Matt asked jokingly.

"Both," the director laughed.

"You really think they could have done it?" Matt asked, referring to the brothers' plan to overthrow the government from within.

Krueger's face darkened, and he responded grimly, "If you had asked me that a week ago, I would have said not a chance. But now we're starting to realize they were a hell of a lot further along than any of us ever knew."

"How close?" Matt asked, eyeing the director in stunned disbelief.

"Close enough to see the finish line," Krueger said. "Of course, that's just between you and me. Officially, we had everything under control."

Turning more serious, Matt asked, "So what's going to happen to them? I'm sure they've got the best lawyers money can buy."

"They do, but I've got something that trumps that—the National Defense Authorization Act."

"The what?" Matt asked.

"It's a bill recently signed into law by the president that allows me to treat the Spates as terror suspects. Essentially, it means they're enemy combatants—so I can detain them indefinitely without trial," the director commented confidently. "All the lawyers in the world aren't going to be able to free these guys until we're done with them."

"Good," Matt said, "and also ironic."

"Why's that?" the director asked.

"Just something Landon Spate said to me out on Ghost Ridge," Matt remembered. "He claimed they were fighting a war against enemy combatants, and that in a war there were always casualties."

"He's about to find out just how true his words were," Krueger said with a severe look.

Matt was glad he wasn't in Landon and Oliver Spates' shoes at the moment. The standard rules of due process were clearly not going to apply in their case. Justice would no doubt be meted out, and it would be thorough. Director Krueger would personally see to that.

Matt changed the subject. "What about Ally; what's going to happen to her?"

"She's cooperating fully, although it won't really matter," Krueger admitted. "She'll spend the rest of her life in a federal penitentiary."

"Did she admit to killing Big Tom?"

"She didn't just admit to it, Matt, she bragged about how easy it was," he said with a look of disgust. "Our psychologists tell me she's got some type of personality disorder—the woman feels absolutely no remorse. They're continuing to run tests on her as we speak."

"Jesus," Matt remarked, still feeling ashamed for falling for her act.

"She would have also killed Old Crooked Nose if it hadn't been for an undercover agent working on the res," Krueger revealed.

"You had an agent working on the res?" Matt asked in shock.

"Technically, no, the FBI didn't. The Bureau of Indian Affairs did. They're part of the Department of the Interior," he explained.

That probably accounted for the pissing match that had caused the delay in the FBI arriving on the scene that day on Ghost Ridge.

"Anyway," the director continued, "they had their own investigation under way on Spate Industries—related to their oil activities, or lack thereof, on the Blackfeet Reservation. Evidently, they had placed a guy there a while back. He's the police chief, goes by the name of Chief Hall."

"What?" Matt nearly shouted. "The guy with the big white cowboy hat and who's built like a bowling ball?"

Krueger chuckled. "I heard you two had a little run-in."

"I can't believe it," Matt said, still shocked. "So he stopped Ally from killing old Charlie?"

"I'm told he put him in protective custody right after Big Tom was killed. He was afraid his knowledge of Ghost Ridge might make him the next target," the director explained.

The more Matt thought about it, the more it made sense. He said, "The night Big Tom didn't show up at the bar, Chief Hall all but forced Crooked Nose out the back door. We thought he was trying to stop him from talking to us, but he was really just trying to protect him. Ally would have killed him too."

Director Krueger sensed Matt's anger at Ally. "Don't beat yourself up over her," he said knowingly. "There are lots of evil people out there; more than you could ever imagine. Unfortunately, I come across them every day in this job. You weren't the first one to be fooled by a highly functioning psychotic. And you won't be the last. These people are very believable because to them their behavior is normal, not abhorrent. That's why the neighbor of the serial killer always says, 'but he seemed like such a nice guy,' even after the discovery of a dozen women buried in his basement."

"Thanks, Stan, but it still stings," Matt admitted.

"I understand," he said. He leaned down and reached into a leather briefcase sitting by his feet. He pulled out a large envelope and handed it across the table. "Maybe this will make you feel better." Matt could feel something inside—about the size of a small book.

The large man heaved himself up somewhat reluctantly from the table. He had to get back to Washington. "Consider this a small token of our appreciation for everything you've done for your country."

"I didn't know the FBI was in the business of handing out gifts," Matt said with a wry smile.

"Who said anything about the FBI?" The imposing G-man replied. He gave a quick wink and walked away.

Ten seconds later, Krueger disappeared out an inconspicuous back door. Two men whom Matt hadn't noticed before got up from the bar. They followed their boss into a narrow alleyway outside. A large SUV with tinted windows was waiting for them.

46

Present Day
New York, NY

Matt was still trying to make sense of Krueger's parting comment, when another man entered the side door through which the director had just departed. This time, however, it was a man Matt knew very well. Or at least there was a time when he thought he had.

Buzz Penberthy sat down in the same chair Krueger had vacated moments earlier.

A look of shocked disbelief crossed Matt's face. "Jesus, the director of the FBI is in bed with you? Who the hell are you people?"

Buzz answered without hesitation, "We're patriots trying to protect our country from those who wish to cause it harm."

"No. Wait. Stop," Matt said, holding up his hands. "I don't want to know. I meant what I said back at Ghost Ridge. I don't care what games your little secret society is playing. I don't want any part of it."

"Unfortunately, there is nothing *little* about what we do, Matt. Life, liberty, and the pursuit of happiness is serious business."

"Oh please, don't quote the Declaration of Independence to

justify your actions," Matt replied disdainfully. Then a thought occurred to him. "But while we're on the subject, let's talk about those unalienable rights the Founding Fathers wrote so eloquently about. Let's talk about my rights." A few heads in the bar turned as Matt's voice rose in anger. "Don't I have the right to know when I'm being recruited? Don't I have the right to consent to putting myself in harm's way? Don't I have the right to know the truth?"

Buzz sat stoically, staring down at his folded hands resting on the table. "You have the right to all those things," he said quietly. "And I'm truly sorry I couldn't be truthful with you. It's a part of this job that I truly detest, but unfortunately, discretion is how we've maintained our effectiveness for more than two centuries."

"Two centuries?" Matt said in amazement.

Buzz nodded. "You've got to remember, the future of this country was anything but assured in the early years following the revolution," he explained. "So, shortly after the Society of Cincinnati was created by officers from the Continental Army, another more secretive organization was created. In the beginning, only a handful of people were involved. In fact, George Washington himself handpicked the original inner circle of patriots—a cross section of military men, financiers, academics, and others. The group called themselves the Ring and their charter was simple: to prevent usurpations of power in our newly formed government."

"I thought the checks and balances built into the Constitution were supposed to take care of that," Matt said cynically.

"You're right. Checks and balances were designed for exactly that purpose. But Washington had devoted his life to securing our country's freedom. He wasn't about to leave anything to chance."

Matt scoffed at the notion. "So he created a secret organization, one that operated outside the margins of the same government he helped create. Don't you see the irony in that?"

"I can assure you, the irony was not lost on Washington. But in the end, he determined that total secrecy was the only way to effectively watch over the three branches of government, the newly formed central bank, and other institutions critical to building and maintaining America's democracy—unencumbered."

"Ah, there it is," Matt said, jabbing his index finger in the air. "The key word—unencumbered." He smiled cynically. "So tell me, Buzz, who are the checks and balances against you guys?"

"We are."

"A little bit of a conflict of interest in that arrangement, wouldn't you say?"

"It's not perfect, I'll grant you that. But the Ring has been pretty effective these last two centuries. Believe me, this country would be a very different place if not for the work we've done and continue to do."

"Spare me the conspiracy theory of the world bullshit, Buzz," Matt scoffed and looked away.

"Come on, Matt, you know me better than that. I'm not talking about some Area 51 alien nonsense or that the lunar landing was a hoax. What I am telling you with absolute certainty, however, is that the American history books you and I were taught from in school are incomplete at best." He paused and waited for Matt to look him in the eye. "I know this because we've been there— from the Civil War, to the assassination of JFK, to the recent stock market crash. The Ring has operated behind the scenes to protect the interests of the United States of America."

Matt shook his head, feeling both disbelief and disgust simultaneously. "Forgive me if I have a hard time accepting your word as gospel."

"Damn it, Matt. You don't have to believe me. You just lived it. Do you think Landon and Oliver Spate are the first to threaten our democracy? Come on, you're smarter than that. Throughout our country's history there have been men like the Spates. And, unfortunately, there will be more in the future. All of them hell-bent on exploiting the liberties we enjoy to their own benefit. It's our job to stop them."

"You keep talking about the work you did. The fact is, you wouldn't have stopped the Spates if I hadn't connected the dots for you," Matt said hotly.

"You'll get no argument from me," Buzz answered honestly. "And you should be damned proud of what you accomplished." He paused before adding, "But who do you think put you onto their scent to begin with?"

A waitress approached their table but Matt waved her off.

He stared at Buzz, unsure of what to believe anymore. Running an agitated hand through his unruly hair, he said quietly, "So you were using me all along?"

Buzz took a deep breath before exhaling slowly. "Yes we were. But the truth is, you weren't the first and you won't be the last. It's one of the keys to our success."

"Why don't you guys do your own dirty work? Why do you need people like me?"

Buzz smiled and said, "We're not the CIA, Matt. It's true we've accumulated a healthy endowment over the years, courtesy of some of our wealthier members, to help fund our endeavors. But our resources are not unlimited. Make no mistake, we need the help of ordinary citizens to bring down the bad guys. Besides, it's much more authentic and effective when ordinary people are involved." He paused before adding, "It's also how we've managed to fly under the radar all these years."

"So you just keep on manipulating unsuspecting people like me year after year? How do you live with yourself?"

"Unsuspecting, yes—most of our citizen recruits don't know our people are behind the scenes pulling strings and feeding them information to ensure their progress toward the ultimate objective.

But unwilling, no. Like you, most people we choose don't need a lot of coaxing. And we don't just pick anyone, Matt. We go through an exhaustive process and select only people with a specific skill set, knowledge base, or connections we need to execute the mission. But most importantly, we look for people with character who are motivated to do the right thing."

Matt's eyes narrowed as a disconcerting thought occurred to him. "So what breadcrumbs did you lay down for me to follow, Buzz?"

"I can't tell you that."

Matt got up to leave. "Then I'm done here."

He had taken only a single step away from the table when Buzz gave in. "Wait," he said.

Matt turned around slowly.

"Alright, I owe you that much." He motioned to the empty chair. "Please."

After Matt sat back down, Buzz began, "We had identified the Spates as a threat a number of years ago. We suspected their endgame was to infiltrate the government and use it to further their own warped agenda. At the time, we had no idea how far they intended to go. The problem was we could never get close enough to them to gather enough proof. They were very careful and very secretive. And to make matters worse, they had done a masterful job of building antigovernment sentiment among the American people—which was critical to greasing the skids for their planned takeover."

"Go on."

"We had built an extensive dossier on them, their family history, the political propaganda machine they had financed, and all their current and past business dealings. Everything they owned or invested in had a purpose—all except one."

Matt responded instantly. "Ghost Ridge," he said.

"Exactly. They bought the lease rights to all that land out there and they never did a damn thing with it. Our big break was when Meriwether Lewis's field notes turned up. When he referenced the Blackfeet incident, we thought there might be a connection. We knew the Spates had to be hiding something out there—maybe it was something big enough to hurt them. So we brought the field notes to you."

"The first breadcrumb."

Buzz nodded. "There were others—like James Fox arranging your meeting with your Lewis and Clark expert, Ron Patterson. There was Hank's recommendation to bring in Dr. Lane to help with the skull you unearthed. Leads we knew you would follow until you unraveled the mystery behind their land holdings out on the Blackfeet Reservation."

Matt's jaw went slack. How easily he had been manipulated. "All those people are on your team?"

"No, Ron Patterson and Dr. Lane were simply resources we put in your path to help—more breadcrumbs to use your words. They have no connection to us. We are purposefully a very small operation, but the people we do have are smart, and in some cases, very well connected," Buzz said, nodding at the door Krueger had exited.

Matt's eyes glazed over. He was spent.

"We used you, Matt," Buzz admitted. "I used you. But now I'm being honest."

Matt said nothing, so Buzz pressed on. "We live in a cynical world—probably more cynical than at any other time in our nation's history. People have lost faith in our government, our financial institutions, our law enforcement, and the people running them. And that is a recipe for disaster. The Spate brothers understood this and came very close to exploiting this cynicism to uproot our democratic way of life."

He pointed at Matt with a renewed intensity. "But you wouldn't

let them. And do you want to know why? Because you have principles; you believe in the ideals of the Founding Fathers just like we
do. When I first met you, I knew right away you were different.
Hank had told me as much and he was right." Matt flinched at the
name of another man who had betrayed his trust. "You're an ideal-
ist, Matt, and you don't know how much I respect that. It's one of
the many reasons I grew close to you. Men with ideals are a rare
breed these days."

"Why are you telling me all of this?"

"Because I want you to join us."

Matt couldn't believe what he was hearing. "You claim you're
an organization that defends our democracy, yet you operate
outside its laws," he answered cynically. "You say you admire people
with principles and ideals, yet you manipulate them without their
knowledge. And you want me to join you?" He glared at Buzz
incredulously.

Buzz leaned forward and said in a hushed voice, "You may not
realize it now, but being asked to join our organization is an honor.
Ninety-nine percent of our citizen recruits never even know we
exist, let alone are asked to join us. There are very few men—three
to be exact—I have ever personally recruited to join us. Actually,
one was a woman."

"Sarah?" Matt interjected without hesitation.

Buzz could see the pain in Matt's eyes. His tone softened as he
said, "No, Hank brought her into the fold. And please don't ask
me for names. I've already told you more than I should have." He
abruptly pushed his chair away from the table. "It's up to you now. I
know you may not agree with our methods and you may think us a
bunch of hypocrites for hiding behind a veil of secrecy in the name
of freedom. But I hope in time you'll come to the same conclusion
we all have. The preservation of our great nation and the liberties
our democracy affords us comes at a cost."

He stood up.

"It's your decision, Matt. If your answer is no, I'll honor the request you made of me out on Ghost Ridge. You'll never see me again." Before leaving he added, "Either way, that package is yours. You've earned it."

He turned and walked out of the bar using the front door this time.

Matt watched him leave. Bewildered and exhausted, his eyes returned to the package resting on the table next to his unfinished beer.

47

Present Day

New York, NY

He sat there staring at it. A minute went by, then five. After all he had been through, Matt was a little spooked by the over-sized manila envelope. It looked innocent enough, but he knew better than that—especially considering who gave it to him. At last he leaned forward and tentatively reached for the package.

It was unmarked and very light. He turned it over and undid the clasp on the back. He peered inside and saw that a note was enclosed. He carefully pulled it out. It was from Harry Spate.

Dear Matt,

I hope this letter finds you well. I cannot begin to thank you for all you did to help us bring my brothers to justice. I had dreamed of this day and the satisfaction it would bring for many years. But now that it has come to pass, the only emotion I have is overwhelming sadness for the innocent lives that have been lost, both past and present; for the despicable actions of my brothers; and most of all for the pain and loss inflicted upon my daughter all these years. I can only hope that time will heal.

The enclosed was found during the FBI's search of Oliver's resi-

*dence. It was locked away securely in his private safe. Evidently, it
had been secretly handed down to eldest Spate sons for the past two
hundred years. I fear there can only be one explanation for how this
ended up in my family's possession. It's yours now. Do with it what you
like. It certainly doesn't belong to my family.*

I am forever in your debt.

Cordially,

Harry Spate

Matt placed the letter down on the table. He picked up the
envelope once again and reached inside. Very carefully, he removed
the contents. It was a small book of the type commonly used by
surveyors in fieldwork. It was approximately four by six inches in
size and bound in red morocco leather. And it was very old.

Matt knew in an instant what it was. His hands began to tremble.

He knew he was holding the long-rumored but largely dismissed
missing journal from Lewis and Clark's expedition to discover the
Northwest Passage. He glanced nervously around the bar. But
nobody was paying him any attention. He placed the book carefully down on the table in front of him and turned to the first page.

It was dated *July, 1806.*

For the next thirty minutes, he read Meriwether Lewis's handwritten journal. Remarkably, the book contained Lewis's official
written account of his chance encounter with the "Black Tribe"
while on the Marias leg of the expedition. But this accounting was
in much greater detail than the field notes that had been found in
the rolltop desk bequeathed to the Society of the Cincinnati. The
black tribe was described in great detail, including observations on
their clothing, mannerisms, artifacts, and housing. Matt guessed
that Lewis wrote his field notes immediately after his encounter. He
then must have transcribed those hastily scribbled notes into this
more formal red leather-bound journal at a later date—after meet-

ing back up with Captain Clark and the rest of the men.

Lewis seemed to have been impressed by his captors. He used terms like *powerfully built*, *proud*, and *well-ordered*, to describe the people and their village. Matt was astounded to read Lewis's description of the "ceremonial cave" and of seeing what appeared to be a "large carved altar" with an "odd metal helmet" sitting on top. The drawing of the helmet in the journal had much more detail than the sketch they had found in the lost field notes. And there was no mistaking it: it was the same helmet Big Tom had stumbled upon almost two centuries later.

Matt found himself becoming emotional as he tried to reconcile the once proud people with the pile of broken bones they had found in the cave where Lewis had once been held captive. His sadness quickly turned to anger. He was angry at Jefferson for authorizing the massacre; angry at Jedediah Spate for overseeing it; and angry at Oliver and Landon Spate for covering up the atrocity.

He picked up the letter from Harry Spate once again. Something had been nagging at him. Harry had said, "*I fear there can only be one explanation for how this ended up in my family's possession.*" Matt had a feeling he knew what Harry meant by that.

The only way Jedediah Spate could have gotten hold of the journal was by taking it from Meriwether Lewis. And the most logical time to have taken it was on Lewis's fateful return trip from St. Louis to Washington, D.C., in October of 1809. That would have been three years after he had returned from the expedition and two years after the massacre of the black conquistador tribe. Along the way, he spent the night at an inn just south of present-day Nashville, Tennessee, on the Natchez Trace. He had all the journals with him in a large travel trunk. It would be the last night of his life.

Priscilla Grinder, the wife of the owner of the inn, claimed to have heard men arguing and several gunshots on the night of Lewis's death. And so began the questions surrounding Lewis's apparent suicide. For the next two hundred years, conspiracy theorists held that someone had murdered Meriwether Lewis that night and stolen one or more of his journals. But they could never come up with a plausible explanation as to why, so their claims of a murder conspiracy had been dismissed by most historians.

Until now.

48

October 10, 1809

Grinder's Inn

Natchez Trace, Tennessee

It had taken Meriwether Lewis and his traveling companions three days to traverse more than a hundred miles. They were traveling along a route called the Natchez Trace. Originally little more than a narrow trail used by Indians in the region, it was now the main overland route from New Orleans to Nashville. Notoriously dangerous and known for its robbers and thieves, it had acquired the nickname the Devil's Backbone. Lewis, nonetheless, chose this route as he considered it safer than a sailboat trip to Washington. He could not risk his journals falling into the hands of the British and their warships patrolling the eastern seaboard of the United States.

Lewis had departed St. Louis almost six weeks earlier. He was headed back east to meet with former president Thomas Jefferson at his Monticello home. His mission was twofold: to seek the former president's assistance in clearing significant debts he believed had been wrongly attributed to him by the U.S. War Department, and, more importantly, to confront him regarding the shocking atrocity that had come to his attention two months earlier.

While drinking at a local St. Louis tavern, Lewis, who was now the governor of the Louisiana Territory, had been confronted by a former U.S. Army private. At first, Lewis passed him off as nothing more than a drunken ruffian. That is, until the man shared details about a place he shouldn't have known about.

Upon seeing Lewis drinking alone at the end of the bar, the man approached and asked if he was the famous Meriwether Lewis. Lewis had never felt comfortable with the notoriety the expedition had brought him. He wasn't famous necessarily, but upon occasion people would seek him out. He politely replied that he was indeed the man in question and then quietly returned to his tankard of beer. Rather than leave him be, the man sat heavily down on the wooden stool next to him.

"Just thought you should know," he said in a low conspiratorial voice, "we put them runaway niggers in their place." His words were slurred and his breath stunk of beer and onions.

Lewis turned to face the filthy man. He told him he had no idea what he was talking about.

The man burped loudly and wiped spittle from his chin with a dirty shirtsleeve. He cocked his head to the side and looked at Lewis questioningly through unfocused eyes. Then he burst out laughing and smacked the governor on the back. "Oh right, we're supposed to keep it hush-hush and all." He took a raspy breath and leaned in closer. "But I thought you deserved to know that we done killed 'em all. You know, them black Injuns you found...or escaped slaves, or whatever the hell they were. And we right good and buried 'em where ain't nobody ever gonna find 'em," he slurred. His pupils were dilated and he was sweating profusely.

He cackled again before picking up his tankard and taking a big swig. Beer sloshed over the rim as he set it back down clumsily on the bar top.

Lewis's eyes narrowed and his face turned crimson. He stood up and grabbed the smaller man gruffly by his shirt collar and pushed him up against the wall. "Tell me everything. Leave nothing out or so help me I'll have you executed," he warned. For the next thirty minutes, the squirrely little man told Lewis every last detail about the savage massacre of the Negro tribe.

Two months later, Governor Lewis still struggled to make sense of what had happened. He felt sick to his stomach whenever he thought about it. But on a more personal level, he felt betrayed by the man he had considered a father figure all these years—Thomas Jefferson. The drunken ex-soldier at the bar never mentioned Jefferson's name. He claimed General James Wilkinson was the man in charge of the mission. But Lewis knew Jefferson was the man ultimately responsible for the atrocity that had occurred.

Besides William Clark, Jefferson was the only other person Lewis had told about his encounter with the black tribe. As he thought back on the day he told Jefferson, he remembered the president's strange reaction when he had shared the story with him. But he had never again broached the subject with him and could not fathom why Jefferson had ordered the slaughter. He had so many questions. And he was determined to get answers directly from the mouth of the former president.

That morning on the Natchez Trace, the small party awoke to discover two of their horses had wandered off. After a short discussion on how to proceed, the decision was made for Lewis to ride on alone while his traveling companions stayed behind to find the missing horses. They would rendezvous at the first hospitable inn that Lewis chanced upon.

It wasn't until early that evening that Lewis came upon a pair of roughly hewn cabins in the woods. The woman of the house was home alone with her children. She explained that her husband was away hunting. Lewis requested and was granted accommodations for the night. After stowing his saddle and the trunks containing his journals in his room, he joined the woman and her children for supper. He talked very little and didn't linger after eating. He stayed only long enough to enjoy a whiskey and a smoke of his pipe on the front porch. Then he retired to his bedroom in the adjoining cabin.

Later that evening, his sleep was fitful. For the past two months he had been having the same recurring nightmare. The dream never altered. He was alone in a dark cave lying at the foot of a stone pedestal—the pedestal with the strange helmet he had seen at the camp of the black tribe. As he lay there, soldiers piled body after dead body of women and children on top of him. When he attempted to scream, his voice was mute. And when he tried to get up and run, he found his body was strangely paralyzed. He lay there helpless as the dead bodies kept coming—until they covered him completely. A river of blood washed over him.

The nightmare always ended at the same spot. Just as he was about to take his last breath before being buried alive, he would awake in a panicked sweat. This time, however, the real nightmare had just begun.

"Don't move," the man said.

Lewis opened his eyes to find a pistol aimed at the middle of his forehead.

With his free hand, the man struck a match and lit a candle on the table beside the bed. Only then did he step back so that his face was no longer in shadow.

"Who are you?" Lewis uttered in sleepy confusion. He had met many men in his life, but he didn't recognize the face at the other end of the pistol.

The man took a careful step back and sat down on a spindly wooden chair by the door, the whole time keeping the pistol leveled at Lewis.

"My name is Jedediah Spate."

"Have we met?"

"Not until tonight. It's a shame, really, that we couldn't have met under different circumstances. But unfortunately, a certain young private couldn't keep his mouth shut."

Lewis couldn't hide his surprise. He knew then this was no ordinary thief; this man had come to kill him.

"You're one of Wilkinson's men," he guessed.

"Hardly," the man scoffed. "More like...an associate."

Lewis propped himself up on his elbows to get a better look at his assaulter.

"Easy does it," Spate warned.

"What do you want with me?" Lewis demanded angrily. Truthfully, he was angrier at himself for not hearing the man enter the room. That wouldn't have happened a couple years ago, but he knew his faculties had been dulled by disease and drink.

"Unfortunately for you, that idiot private got drunk again and mouthed off about his chance encounter with you. As fate would have it, one of Wilkinson's men overheard him. Evidently, the little prick couldn't keep his mouth shut to save his life. Which, of course, ended up costing him his life," Spate said matter-of-factly. His cold grin appeared ghoulish in the shadows cast by the flickering candle. "And I'm afraid it's going to cost you yours."

"Why are you doing this?" Lewis asked, partly out of curiosity but mostly in an attempt to stall.

Spate laughed and replied, "For the same reason I do everything. I've been promised lots of money. And I can assure you, I intend to cash in on that promise." He paused before adding ominously, "so I can't allow you to go back east and make a fuss about all this."

"Jefferson will not let you get away with murdering me," Lewis shouted as he sat up and swung his legs off the side of the bed.

"Of course he won't." Spate got up and in two strides stood directly in front of Lewis. "That's why this must appear as a suicide."

In a single motion, he cocked the gun and fired.

Lewis adroitly jerked to his left as the pistol exploded causing the discharged lead ball to only narrowly graze his skull. He sprang from his bed and charged through the smoky haze. Spate was taken off guard by the speed and strength of the wounded Lewis. He only had time to step to one side just as he was tackled. It was enough so he didn't take the full force of Lewis's weight upon him. Still, the two men hit the floor hard. They locked arms, each man clutching and clawing to gain the advantage.

The wound to his head was beginning to take its toll on Lewis, however. He was dizzy and losing strength and the blood running down his face obscured his vision. By the time he saw the second pistol, it was too late. During the struggle, Spate freed one hand and reached down into the waist of his pants. His fingers grasped the handle firmly. It was already loaded. All he had to do was aim and fire. This time he hit his mark.

The ball entered Lewis's right breast and passed downward through his body, exiting out his back. The famous explorer knew in an instant it was a fatal blow. He slumped over to one side, his strength spent. Blood flowed freely from his chest. He knew with absolute certainty it was only a matter of time before he would be dead.

Perspiring mightily, his chest heaving up and down from the unanticipated struggle, Spate clambered to his feet. He made his way across the tiny room and quickly searched the trunks containing the journals. It didn't take him long to find the journal he was looking for—the one dated July 1806. He held it up to the candlelight and grinned demonically. Terrified screams from Mrs. Grinder next door snapped him from his reverie. His task completed, he decided it was time to go. Before leaving, however, he bent down and placed the two spent pistols on the floor beside Meriwether Lewis.

He needed to make sure that the world, and especially Thomas Jefferson, believed that the famous but also terribly troubled Meriwether Lewis had lost the battle with his inner demons.

49

Present Day
New York, NY

The story broke in the *New York Times* the next day.

David Becker's front-page investigative piece set off a firestorm that would rage across the media landscape for months. As anticipated, the sensational news of a discovery of a two-hundred-year-old massacre grabbed hold of the American public's fascination. And once Becker had America's attention, he skillfully connected the past to the present—revealing not only Jedediah Spate's personal involvement in the massacre but also Oliver and Landon Spates' involvement in its subsequent cover-up.

The Spate family fortune was exposed to be blood money built on the back of genocide. But this represented only the first step in tearing down the false edifice of respectability the family had carefully constructed over the decades. Revealing the family's true seditious intentions would come next. And this revelation would, like the snap of a hypnotist's fingers, awaken the American public to just how close they had come to losing their democracy.

Day after day, Becker's stories appeared on the front page of the venerable newspaper. Relying heavily on the evidence compiled by

Samantha over the last five years, he methodically and relentlessly laid out the Spates' plans to take over the U.S. government. He began at the beginning with the radical views of George Spate, and how the father had passed along his extreme philosophy to his two oldest sons. He then divulged the epiphany that struck Oliver and Landon after their father had passed away. How they realized if their dream of an American plutocracy were ever to be achieved, they would need to camouflage their radical ideology in rhetoric more acceptable to the mainstream public.

Becker then turned his attention to the vast machinery that powered the Spates' engine of deceit. He named names—all of them. He splayed open the network of Spate advocacy groups, think tanks, and lobbying firms for the world to see. He reported on the Spates' sophisticated but nonetheless shady shell game of shuffling funds from holding company to holding company, so that government auditors could never tie the wide-ranging network's source of funding back to them. But the secret was now out as Becker revealed which shells the money was hiding under. And more importantly *whom* that money bankrolled.

The public relations spin machine was on full cycle. Senators, governors, state representatives, and federal judges all scrambled to distance themselves from any affiliation with Spate-backed organizations. But for most of them it would prove to be too little and too late. The majority would either be indicted for crimes against the government of the Unites States or be voted out of office in the next election cycle.

There were some fringe elements that continued to defend the Spates, claiming the entire story had been fabricated. But their charges of a government conspiracy rang increasingly hollow as the evidence continued to mount. The final nail in the coffin came when Becker divulged the alleged murders authorized by Oliver and Landon. A copy of the Enemies of the Spate internal document was "leaked" to the *New York Times* and published in its entirety. It was subsequently revealed that the government would soon charge the brothers with the murders of six public officials—including the chief justice of the U.S. Supreme Court and Senator Mark Waterford from Connecticut. Evidently, in return for a reduced sentence, the Spates' top lieutenant, a man named Mel Pratt, had been fully cooperating. But the secret recordings Matt had made out on Ghost Ridge would provide the most damning evidence.

Nobody had seen or heard from either Spate brother since the FBI had taken them into custody on the airport tarmac in Oklahoma City. Rumors to their whereabouts had been debated on news programs for weeks and ranged from the severe to the ridiculous.

Guesses as to where the government had stowed them included Guantanamo Bay military detention camp, the basement of the FBI building, a bunker in the desert, and even Alcatraz. Amid the gallows humor, however, it was not lost on the American public just how close the country had come to handing their country over to a couple of rich ideological zealots. And the mood turned deadly serious when it became clear that the rising power of money in politics was making a joke of America's democracy. A groundswell of support for campaign finance reform had already begun to build.

As a result of the ongoing investigation, many of the top executives and most of the board members of Spate Industries had been forced to resign. At the strong urging of the government, the remaining board of directors had asked Harry Spate to return as interim CEO until a permanent management team could be found. One of the first things Harry did was to initiate an internal investigation of the plethora of legal allegations against the company— from toxic waste spills to oil skimming to wrongful death suits. He promised swift and thorough action aimed at righting past wrongs, as well as sweeping reforms to guard against a repeat of such transgressions in the future.

Samantha agreed to stay on at Spate Industries as part of the transition team. She had also begun talks with the Bureau of Indian Affairs and the Blackfeet Nation to nominate the site of the original fort and ancient cave for designation as a National Historic Landmark. Spate Industries would underwrite the cost of a state-of-the-art museum to be housed on the parkland.

The museum's mission would be to document the history of black conquistadors and their role in the Spanish explorations of the Americas during the 1500s. But the primary purpose of the historic landmark would be to honor and remember the West African slaves who traveled more than a thousand miles to live freely in northwest Montana, and the remarkable sacrifice they made to establish a colony of their own, ironically around the same time as Plymouth Colony was being established in Massachusetts.

Professor Horace Lane had been tapped to run the museum. He would lean heavily on the guidance of Ron Patterson and his years of experience running the Lewis and Clark Interpretive Center. Patterson had made a full recovery from his minor heart attack out on Ghost Ridge, and his brand-new pacemaker had him feeling ten years younger. He had made a solemn promise to his doctors to lose some weight, but his wife's pies had thus far kept him from keeping it.

Epilogue
2 Months Later

It wasn't much to look at. According to a peeling painted sign hanging from the collapsed main gate, Big Lake cemetery had been around since the late 1800s. It wasn't very big—maybe ten acres in size. Most of the crooked rows of headstones either sagged to one side or were split in half like jagged teeth in a jack-o'-lantern. Weeds sprouted out of crevices and cracks everywhere like unwanted hairs from an old man's ears. The place even smelled bad. Perhaps that had something to do with the EPA sign posted by the front gate. It warned that surrounding wetlands might have been contaminated by embalming formaldehyde fluids leaching into the groundwater.

It was a damp, gray morning made worse by a stiffening north wind that tore down out of the Canadian Rockies and raced across the flat plains of northwest Montana. It looked like it could rain at any moment. Matt pulled the collar of his jacket up snugly beneath his chin. He leaned forward into the elements and stepped through the front gate.

As he made his way through the sad, forgotten cemetery, he

replayed the conversation with Buzz Penberthy in the Manhattan bar. He still had trouble believing Buzz and the clandestine organization known as the Ring had gone undetected for more than two centuries. But then he remembered how easily he himself had been manipulated.

Buzz had told him the country would look very different had it not been for the work his secretive organization had done over the years. As much as Matt was still angry at Buzz, he couldn't help but be intrigued by the opportunity to find out exactly how they had changed the trajectory of the nation. Even so, a large part of him still wrestled with the hypocrisy of it all. So much so that he had yet to give Buzz an answer.

He kept walking until he came upon some freshly turned earth, the byproduct of a recently dug grave. It had to be the one he was looking for. God knows it looked like there hadn't been anybody else buried in this place in years. He approached slowly until he was close enough to read the headstone. The inscription told him he had arrived at the final resting place of Thomas Running Crane, or Big Tom as his friends had called him.

Matt knelt down next to a prickly weed that had popped up beside the grave. Nature had already begun her relentless reclamation of the cemetery's most recent burial site. He pulled it up and tossed it aside, as if to say "not yet." That's when he noticed the Hot Shot firefighting medal resting atop the granite headstone. Another was lying on the ground nearby. Matt knew it must have been Bobby's way of honoring his uncle. He picked up the fallen medal from the damp ground and brushed it clean. The he gently returned it to the top of the headstone.

Now it was his turn. He reached into his pocket and pulled out a crisp one-hundred-dollar bill. He placed it in on the ground in front of the grave marker, pinning it in place with a loose stone. The bill represented the other half of the two hundred dollars Matt had promised Big Tom for taking him out to Ghost Ridge. Matt smiled sadly as he recalled Tom's huge hand resting on the backseat of the car and the way he had winked at him after demanding his money.

"A deal's a deal, right big guy?" Matt whispered as his eyes welled up.

He sensed someone approaching. He turned around and saw Samantha walking toward him. She smiled and his heart jumped.

They had spent the last three days together—just the two of them in a secluded cabin that Samantha had rented bordering Glacier National Park. It had been more than a month since they had seen each other. During that time, both of their lives had been consumed by the Spate Gate scandal. The media, the FBI, and, in Samantha's case, Spate Industries had all required their undivided attention. The American public's furor over the scandal had reached a crescendo but had finally abated. That's when Matt and Samantha had seized their opportunity to get away.

They spent their nights eating like kings, drinking too much wine, and making love with carefree abandon. They spent their days taking long walks and catching up on events from the prior month.

Even though the initial shock had worn off, they still had a hard time grasping just how close their beloved country had come to returning to a bygone age of corruption, greed, and hedonism. They were not naive enough to think America's current democratic system was perfect. But even with all its flaws, they knew it was better than any other system on Earth. And they were proud of the roles they had played in saving it.

Matt never once mentioned his conversation with Buzz to Samantha. He reasoned he wouldn't know where to begin to explain something he didn't even comprehend. Either way, it dawned on him he was now the one keeping secrets. *Have I already made my decision?*

Samantha reached out and caressed Matt's face. There were

tears in her eyes, too—tears of sadness but also of joy, because she felt freer and happier than she had been in years, and because she was in love.

Matt knew he was falling for her as well. And, as usual, this scared him. He was well aware his relationship track record was spotty at best, so he made a silent vow to give this one the attention it deserved. He leaned down and kissed Samantha gently on the lips, as if to seal the promise he had just made to himself.

"Are you sure you're ready?" she asked.

At first Matt thought she had read his mind and was talking about the answer he owed Buzz. But then he realized she was simply checking to make sure he was set to leave.

"I'm ready," he said with a crooked smile, "for whatever comes next."

She smiled wide and took his hands in hers. Fingers intertwined, they turned and walked out of the cemetery. The strong north wind was now at their backs.

####

Author's Note

While the story of the black conquistador tribe and their massacre on the orders of Thomas Jefferson is entirely fictional, many of the historical places, dates, and events in this book are factual.

❖ Black conquistadors were real. They were on every major Spanish-led expedition into the United States from the early 1500s through the early 1600s. Most were of Iberian or West African descent. Although they never made it into Montana, they did make it as far north as Colorado and Kansas.

❖ Field notes from the Lewis and Clark Expedition were, in fact, discovered in an attic in St. Paul, Minnesota, in early 1953—almost one hundred fifty years after they were first written. The notes had been tightly wrapped in newspaper and stuffed into a drawer of a rolltop desk. The desk had once belonged to Captain Clark when he was acting as superintendent of Indian Affairs in the 1830s.

❖ There have been countless conspiracy theories regarding the alleged missing journals of Lewis and Clark—too many to account for here. Suffice it to say, there are many people who continue to believe Meriwether Lewis was murdered. But most historians, along with Thomas Jefferson and William Clark, believe he took his own life. As recently as 2009, however, the descendants of Meriwether Lewis petitioned the National Park Service to exhume his remains (which are buried on national parkland in Tennessee) to put the matter to rest once and for all. They were refused.

❖ There is an unexplainable gap in Meriwether Lewis's journal writing during the month of July 1806. At the time, he was within twenty miles of present-day Glacier National Park. It was not uncommon for Lewis to strike out on solo hikes while on the expedition—sometimes for more than twenty miles at a time.

❖ Thomas Jefferson, along with Robert Patterson, a professor of mathematics, chemistry, and natural philosophy and a member of the American Philosophical Society, developed the first wheel cipher. It was so far ahead of its time that after Jefferson's cipher disappeared, it took U.S. Army cryptographers more than one hundred years to develop essentially the same device. This device served the army well from WWI into WWII. There is a replica of Jefferson's wheel cipher in the National Museum in Washington, D.C.

❖ The American Philosophical Society was started by Benjamin Franklin in 1731 and is still in operation today. It is located within Independence National Historical Park in Philadelphia, PA. It is the current home of the original Lewis and Clark journals along with many other fascinating historical artifacts.

❖ Among the many things that Meriwether Lewis took west with him on his expedition to find the Northwest Passage was a special cipher for encoding messages designed by President Thomas Jefferson. The cipher consisted of a table of twenty-six rows and twenty-six columns of sequentially arranged letters, plus a key word. It is not known if it was ever used.

❖ Chief Iron Jacket was real. Born around 1790 (the exact date is unknown), Iron Jacket was a Comanche chieftain and medicine man. The Comanche believed he had the power to blow bullets aside with his breath. Legend had it he could not be killed. His magical powers, however, turned out to be a coat of iron mail left over from Spanish conquistador forays into Arizona more than a century earlier. The jacket failed to protect him in the end, however, as he was killed by Texas Rangers in the Battle of Little Robe Creek in 1858.

* The Lewis and Clark Expedition spent more time and traveled more miles in Montana than in any other state. The Lewis and Clark Interpretive Center sits on the eastern bank of the Missouri River, in Great Falls, Montana. It is a must-see for any Lewis and Clark enthusiast.

* Thomas Jefferson had an agreement with the American Fur Company to open up the Northwest to the fur trade. The American Fur Company was owned by John Jacob Astor. The Astors would go on to become one of the richest families in America.

* Fear of slave rebellions was never too far beneath the surface of Jefferson's thinking. When slave revolts occurred in the French-controlled island of Saint-Domingue (now Haiti), Jefferson aligned himself with Napoleon in wanting to see the slave rebellion crushed.

* In his lifetime, Jefferson owned hundreds of slaves. For decades, historians have debated his conflicting views on slavery. One point cannot be debated, however. Unlike George Washington, who granted freedom to all his slaves in his final will, Thomas Jefferson did not free the more than one hundred thirty slaves working at Monticello at the time of his death. Instead, they were sold posthumously to pay down the family debt.

* The Spates are entirely fictional, but it is true there is more "dark" money flowing into elections through Super PACs and corporate giving than ever before in American history.

* Including capital gains, the share of national income going to the richest one percent of Americans has doubled since 1980, from ten percent to twenty percent, roughly where it was during the Gilded Age at the turn of the twentieth century.

MATT HAWKINS RETURNS
IN TED RICHARDSON'S
NEXT NOVEL.

NATION OF HUCKSTERS

While attending the funeral of a former Wall Street colleague, Matt Hawkins is confronted by the sister of the deceased. Kate is adamant that her brother did not commit suicide, as the police report claims—he was murdered. She believes he had stumbled upon a subversive plot intended to collapse the world financial markets and cripple the United States' economy in the process. But before he could blow the whistle, he was pushed in front of a New York City subway train.

Matt and Kate's search for the truth leads them back in time to a series of seemingly unrelated historical events—from a vast gold deposit allegedly first discovered by Indian warrior Geronimo; to a puzzling cover-up by President Theodore Roosevelt in 1905; to a secret society with its roots in one of America's oldest universities. As they connect the dots from past to present, they are determined to get to the bottom of the conspiracy. But to succeed, they must contend with a powerful alliance of adversaries intent on finishing the financial war they started.

AN EXCERPT FROM THE
FORTHCOMING

Nation of Hucksters

By Ted Richardson

Prologue
Early 1880s
Mogollon Mountains in
Southwestern New Mexico

The small band of Chiricahua Apaches had evaded the U.S. Cavalry yet again. Their warrior leader, Geronimo, had driven what was left of his ragtag collection of followers, half of whom were women and children, relentlessly. He had little choice. He had to gain separation from the more than four thousand pursuing U.S. troops. Two days earlier they had crossed the border from Mexico back into the newly designated territory of New Mexico in the United States. After their third successive all-night march, they were finally in range of their homeland.

After years of press exposure, Geronimo's name had become synonymous with lawlessness and savagery in the minds of the American public. East Coast newspapers branded him a butcher and sensationalized the many raids he and his Apache warriors had conducted throughout the Southwest. But for Geronimo and his followers, the raiding and plundering of ranchers, prospectors, and anyone else with food, supplies, or horses to steal was simply a matter of survival.

Geronimo finally relented and let his small party of sixty people pause to rest. They had reached the Gila River valley at the base of the Mogollon Mountains. Geronimo knew that only the rugged mountains of his homeland would provide his people with the secure refuge they so *desperately needed. During the brief respite, Geronimo and a handful of his warriors rode on ahead to scout the best route up into the towering peaks that rose imposingly in front of them. With a large Bowie knife strapped to his side and rifle slung across his shoulder, he cut an imposing figure. The sun glinted off the silver-washed barrel on his Winchester Model 1876 lever-action rifle as he led his men forward. Although he was not tall, he was powerfully built and possessed a grim determination that both intimidated and impressed his followers. He was also believed to possess shaman-like powers that only added to his mystique.*

This land was familiar territory for Geronimo. He had been born nearly sixty years earlier not far from the valley they had just entered. With green peaks that reached ten thousand feet high, steep canyons, and rocky ravines, it could be an unforgiving place—but not for Geronimo. He knew this place better than most men; perhaps better than anyone else alive. In his youth he had hunted elk, buffalo, and deer here. And he fished and trapped along the Gila River that flowed in a looping southwesterly direction toward the neighboring territory of Arizona.

This is the place where he had learned how to fight and been initiated into manhood. At the age of seventeen, after successfully participating in a number of raiding parties, he had been formally accepted as a full-fledged warrior. Since then, he had led more raids and killed more men than he could count. He knew he was nearing the end of the line—that the army of soldiers chasing him would not give up until his head was at the end of a pike. But he forced these thoughts from his mind and set his sights on the terrain in front of him. He had an uncanny knack for reading the land, so it didn't take him long to locate the best route around the cavernous ravine that lay just ahead.

A few hours later, Geronimo and his followers had snaked halfway up the first peak, leaving the prickly cactus that clung to the lower slopes of the Mogollon Mountains behind them. Still not satisfied, he pressed his people forward. It wasn't until he noticed that Douglas fir and aspen had replaced cactus and oak as the predominant vegetation that he eased his pace. He only relented because the changing terrain signaled to him they had reached an elevation at which they would be safe. He dismounted from his horse and signaled to his people this was where they would make camp for the evening. They had arrived not a moment too soon. Flashes of lightning from a fast-approaching late summer storm lit up the dusky sky and large drops of rain began splattering noisily on the rocky ground.

The next morning, Geronimo arose at dawn. He needed to visit a special place from his youth—and he needed to do it in secret. He slipped quietly out of camp, moving as if his feet never touched the ground. Geronimo was a master at not only reading the land but also at traveling without leaving a trail. If he didn't want to be tracked, then no man alive could follow him.

On foot, he moved swiftly through the thick forest, following natural landmarks that only had meaning for him. Five miles later, he came upon a confluence of two rivers. He paused and breathed in deeply. He knew he was close. His mind raced back to a time before all the raids, the killings, and the running. He couldn't have been more than ten or eleven years old when his mother had brought him here. The memory of his mother, who was murdered by Mexican soldiers during a raid thirty years earlier, brought back anger as raw for him as the day she had died. But that anger was quickly replaced by sadness—at her death and the deaths of so many of his people over the last half century. What was once a thriving and proud tribe of more than three thousand now numbered in the hundreds.

Before entering the mouth of the hidden cave, he reached into a bundle strapped to his belt. He carefully removed a still smoldering ember he had wrapped in damp tree bark back at camp. He proceeded to assemble a makeshift torch by wrapping a resin-soaked cloth around a large stick he found on the ground nearby. He blew on the smoldering ember until it sparked and touched it to the cloth. The cloth erupted in flame. With torch in hand, Geronimo entered the sacred place.

He followed a route from memory that took him more than four hundred feet deep into the subterranean cave. The rough, naturally carved sidewalls dripped with moisture as he made his way further into the abyss. His heart pounded in anticipation as he remembered the spot he had seen only once before, a lifetime ago. Suddenly, the tunnel angled sharply to the right and widened into a vault-like chamber. Geronimo knew he had reached his destination.

The only sound he could hear was the moisture dripping from the walls of the cave—and his own breathing. He extended the torch out in front of him. As if by magic, the room was instantly bathed in a golden yellow glow. A smile crept slowly across his normally grim face. He took one step closer so he could see the source of the reflection more clearly. There were veins of gold as big as pack mules embedded throughout the quartz-filled walls of the chamber. In awed reverence he reached out and touched the golden treasure with the tips of his fingers. He felt a familiar energy surge through his veins.

Somehow this golden cave had escaped discovery by both the Spanish conquistadors in the 1500s as well as those who sought their fortunes in the centuries since. In the late 1850s and early 1860s, prospectors from the East Coast began arriving in the hundreds to the new town of Pinos Altos just south of Chiricahua country in the new territory of New Mexico. Their arrival was precipitated by a large gold strike just north of an old Spanish copper mine. For a time, the prospectors respected Apache territory. But eventually the lure of riches drew them further upstream. Their infringement upon Apache land led to inevitable confrontation and eventually an all-out war that lasted close to a decade. Ultimately, the flow of prospectors subsided—partly because of *the threat of Indian raids but mostly because the initial gold strike near Pinos Altos was never replicated.*

As Geronimo exited the cave and began walking back to camp, the words of his mother reverberated in his mind. This sacred golden place, she had told him, would endow Geronimo with great Power. To receive the Power, his mother had said, all he needed to do was reach out and touch the golden wall. The Apache Indians believed in the concept of Power—and that a chosen few were endowed with more Power than others. The source of this Power could come from the natural or supernatural world. He had listened to his mother that day years before and placed his hands on the largest vein of gold embedded in the wall. Afterward, she made him swear to never tell another living soul about their special place. If he did and the golden chamber was unearthed, Geronimo's Powers would be destroyed forever.

His mother had spoken the truth that day. He touched the golden walls and they had helped him become a great warrior and fearless leader of men. His followers revered what they believed to be his supernatural Powers. They believed he could make it rain; that no bullet could ever kill him; and that he could heal the sick. The Power had worked. And Geronimo had never revealed its source.

This latest journey home had been long and arduous. But Geronimo had come for a reason. He was desperate. He needed to visit the golden chamber one more time, because he needed the Power of invincibility now perhaps more than at any other time in his life.

1

Present Day

New York, NY

The fluorescent lights in the drop ceiling above his desk hummed like a nest of angry wasps. The air-conditioning in the forty-two-story Wall Street office building had automatically switched over to its warmer overnight setting more than two hours ago. It wasn't particularly hot, but the back of his blue button-down oxford was wet with perspiration. He leaned back in his chair and loosened his tie a notch further.

A door slammed at the end of the darkened corridor. He glanced down at his Rolex—it was almost eleven o'clock. He got up nervously from his desk to have a look. But it was only the night janitor emptying wastepaper baskets from under the desks of his coworkers on the trading floor. The wheels beneath the fifty-gallon garbage can squeaked noisily. Headphones planted firmly in the janitor's ears made him oblivious to the noise. The man continued on down the hall, head bobbing up and down to the music.

"Pull yourself together, man," Adam whispered to himself. He took a deep breath to calm his nerves before returning to his desk.

Adam Hampton was the thirty-nine year old director of the

Commodities Trading Group at Morton Sinclair, one of the largest investment banks on Wall Street. The firm actively traded in most of the major commodity markets, but their primary focus was in the oil and gold sectors.

Adam had been recruited heavily by Morton Sinclair because he was confident, aggressive, and brilliant. He had worked for two other blue-chip investment banks prior to landing at Morton Sinclair a decade earlier. Since then, he had made countless millions in profits for the firm. His efforts had been rewarded with a promotion to the head of the commodities desk. He was very good at what he did and he loved his job—at least until recently.

When he stumbled upon some irregularities in a series of commodity trades a few months earlier, he had thought nothing of it. But then those same irregularities popped up a few weeks later. After some digging, he noticed a distinct pattern to the timing of trades that dated back more than two years. But his curiosity turned to outright suspicion when he got stonewalled trying to determine the name of the client for whom the trade orders had been executed. The account in question was known as a "shadow account" because the identity of the client was hidden behind a series of ambiguous shell companies.

Undeterred, he dug deeper and began to uncover a financial conspiracy so massive that at first he didn't believe it. From what he could determine, not just his firm but at least five other major U.S. investment banks were complicit in the scheme. But much of what he had uncovered was circumstantial evidence. He knew he couldn't blow the whistle unless he had ironclad proof.

After some internal debate, he made the decision to enlist the help of a computer hacker. He needed to gain access to the commodities trading history of the five investment banks he suspected of participating in the conspiracy. He paid the hacker to surreptitiously breach the computer database systems of the firms involved so he could prove their wrongdoing. With this decision, he had reached the point of no return.

He knew what he was doing was illegal, but he had no choice. The men behind the scheme were corrupt and he couldn't just look the other way and let them get away with it. He was raised on the principles of fair play. There was a right way to live your life and a wrong way. If someone was cheating the system, it was your obligation to call them out. In the three weeks since he hired the hacker, he had secured enough evidence to make his case. But he also received something he hadn't counted on.

For the last two hours, he had been sitting at his desk reading and rereading the latest set of encrypted files. They had been sent to him earlier in the evening from his determined but less-than-principled hacker friend. He ran a nervous hand through his hair because he still couldn't believe what he was reading. *This was a game changer.*

He knew right from the start he had stumbled upon a widespread financial conspiracy. But with this latest information, it had become clear the endgame was much more insidious than simple fraud.

This revelation not only scared the shit out of him, it also made him realize he was in way over his head. He needed help. The question he had been wrestling with for the last hour was what to do about it. Finally, he picked up the phone and dialed the number of a man in whom he had recently confided—a man he believed he could trust.

Adam finished his call quickly and rode the elevator down to the lobby. He exited the building. It was approaching midnight and the streets of downtown Manhattan, comprised mostly of office buildings, were deserted. He walked two blocks west to the Wall

Street subway station to catch the Uptown 4 train to the Upper East Side.

He found himself walking faster than usual and looking over his shoulder at the slightest sound. He knew he was probably being paranoid, but he couldn't help himself. A lot of people were involved in the conspiracy he had uncovered. And, as he had startlingly discovered that evening, some of those people were very powerful. He would be glad when this whole thing was over. Maybe he'd finally get a good night's sleep again.

He made his way down the steps beneath the streets of lower Manhattan. The oppressively humid updraft from the depths below hit him like a summer gale. Far from fresh however, this breeze was a stale-smelling mélange of urine, dirt, steel, and the sweat from tens of thousands of straphangers that rode the trains every day. He remembered when he first arrived in Manhattan. He couldn't imagine how anyone could stomach the smells and the claustrophobic confines of the New York City subways. Seventeen years later he knew he couldn't survive a day without them. In fact, the subterranean sights and smells barely registered with him anymore. He had become a true New Yorker.

He swiped his disposable subway card through the electronic reader and hurried through the turnstile. The loudspeaker announced the train below was preparing to leave. He ran down the last set of concrete stairs, two steps at a time. But by the time he made it to the lower platform the train had already started to pull away from the station.

"Damn it," he cursed his bad luck. He looked up and down the length of the platform and discovered he was the only person in the station.

He spotted a wooden bench nearby and sat down to wait for the next train. He realized his heart was racing again. He visited his doctor the month before because he hadn't been sleeping and had lost ten pounds. The doctor told him these were classic symptoms of work-related stress. *If only he knew.* He prescribed some anti-anxiety medicine and told Adam to take some time off.

Unfortunately, the patient had done just the opposite. He spent the ensuing days running the frenetic commodities trading desk and nights trying to discreetly unwind a financial conspiracy of growing proportions. As a result, he hadn't gotten more than three hours of sleep any night since his initial discovery of the trading anomalies.

He reached into his jacket pocket, pulled out a bottle of pills, and popped one in his mouth. He hoped it would settle his racing heart and jangly nerves. He found it hard to sit still so he got up and began to pace. He walked to the edge of the platform and craned his neck to peer down the tracks. There was still no train in sight.

He heard a noise coming from the far end of the platform. He could see the tops of a pair of men's black dress shoes slowly descending the concrete stairs.

Five minutes later, the shattered body of Adam Hampton lay lifeless on the tracks.

After more than twenty-five years as a business professional, Ted Richardson parlayed his fascination with American history and love of a good mystery into writing his own works of fiction. His independently published first novel, *Imposters of Patriotism* was released in June 2014 to enthusiastic reviews. *Abolition of Evil* is the sequel that follows Matt Hawkins on his next historical adventure. The third installment in the series, *Nation of Hucksters* is currently in development. Richardson lives in the Atlanta area with his wife and two daughters.

Visit him on Facebook at
www.facebook.com/AuthorTedRichardson